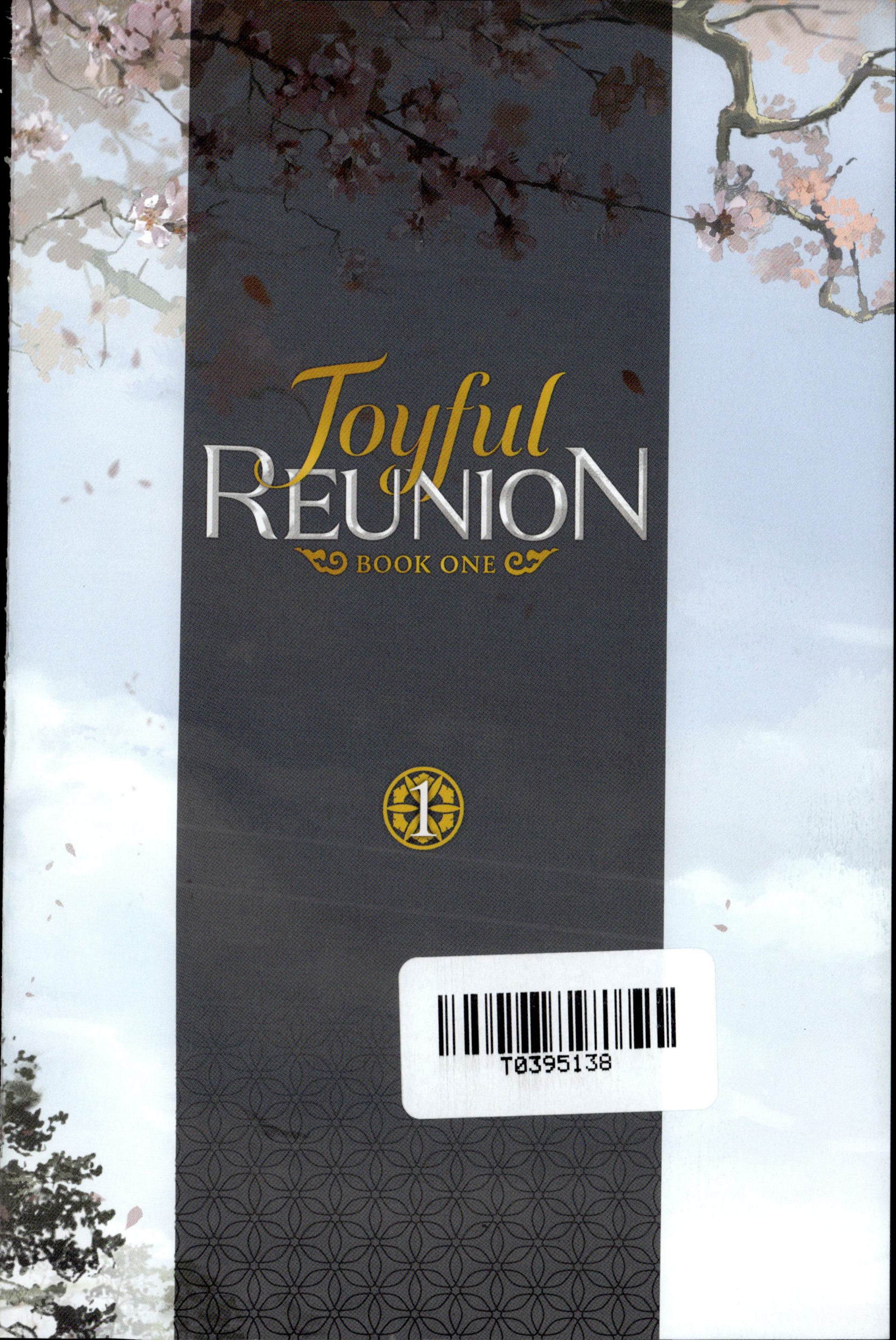
Joyful
Reunion
BOOK ONE
1

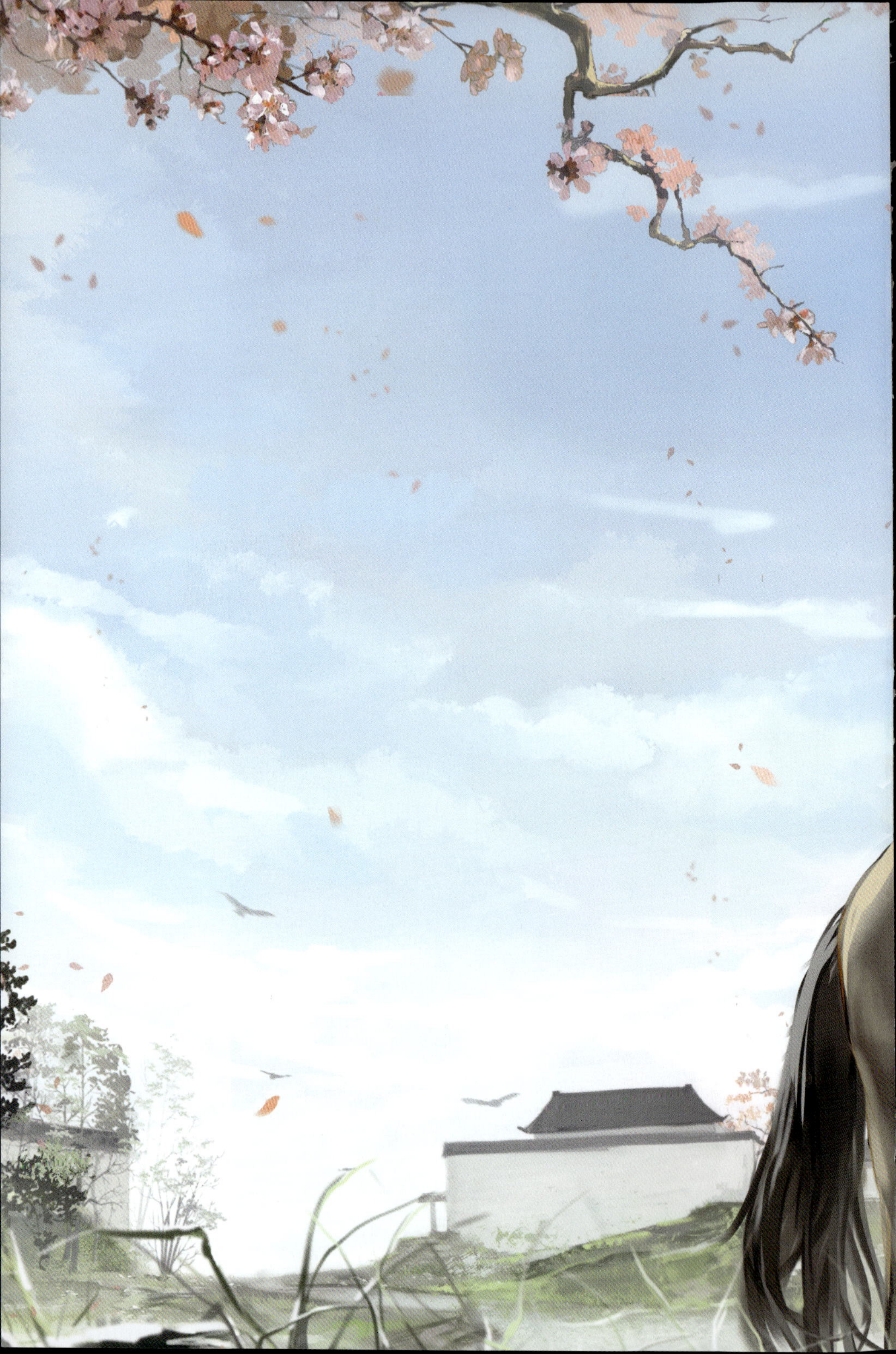

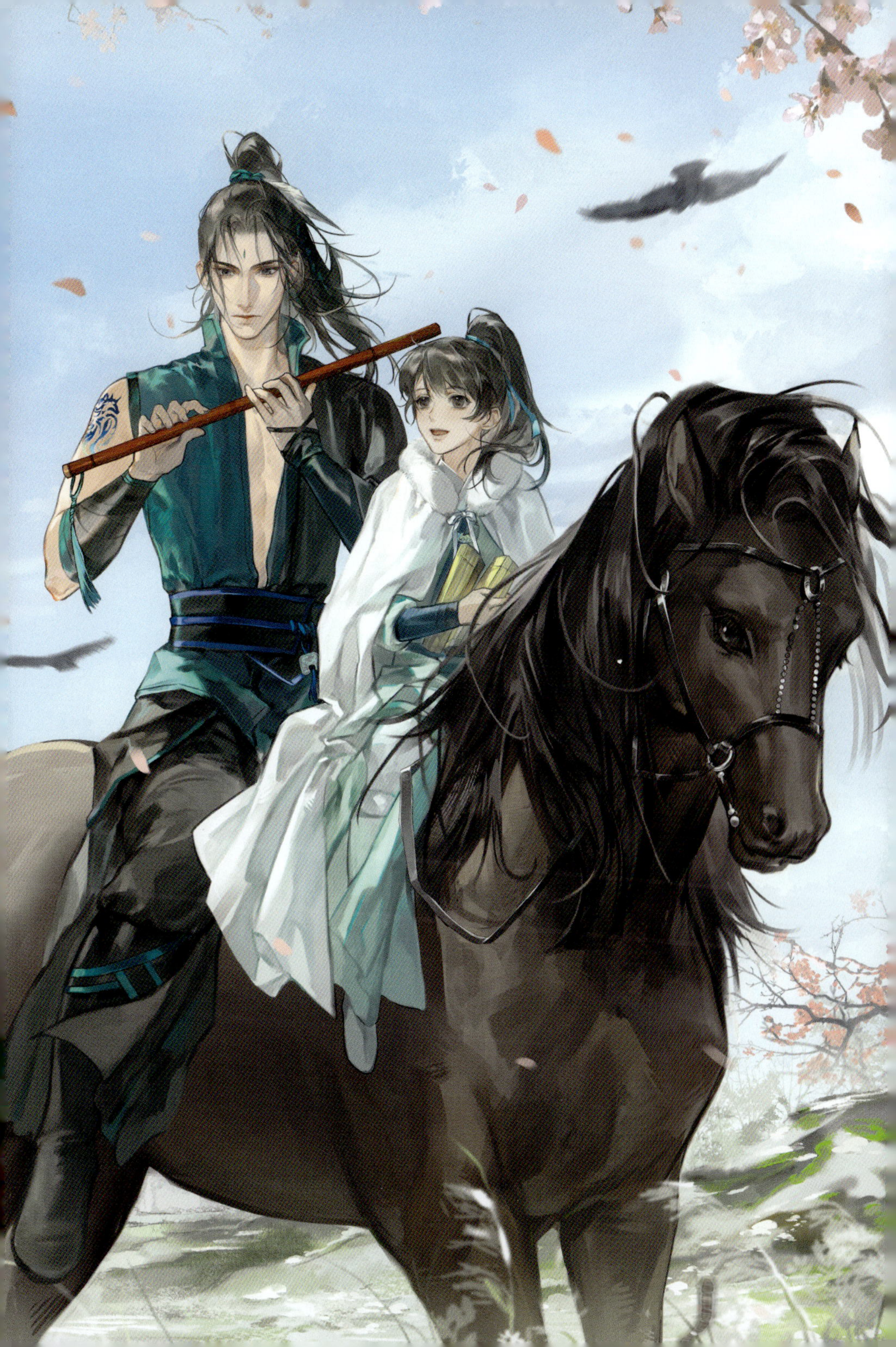

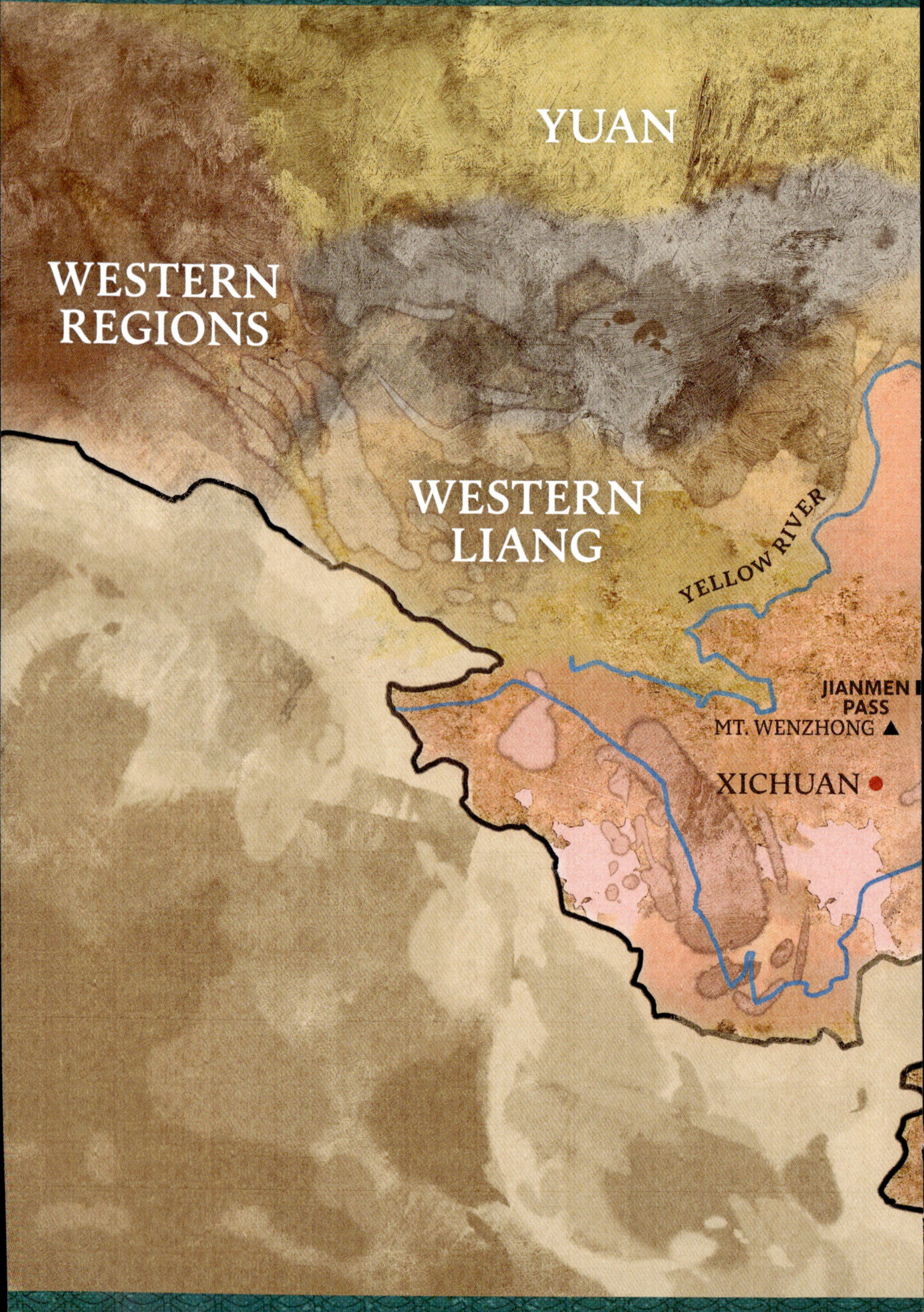
YUAN
WESTERN REGIONS
WESTERN LIANG
YELLOW RIVER
JIANMEN PASS
MT. WENZHONG
XICHUAN

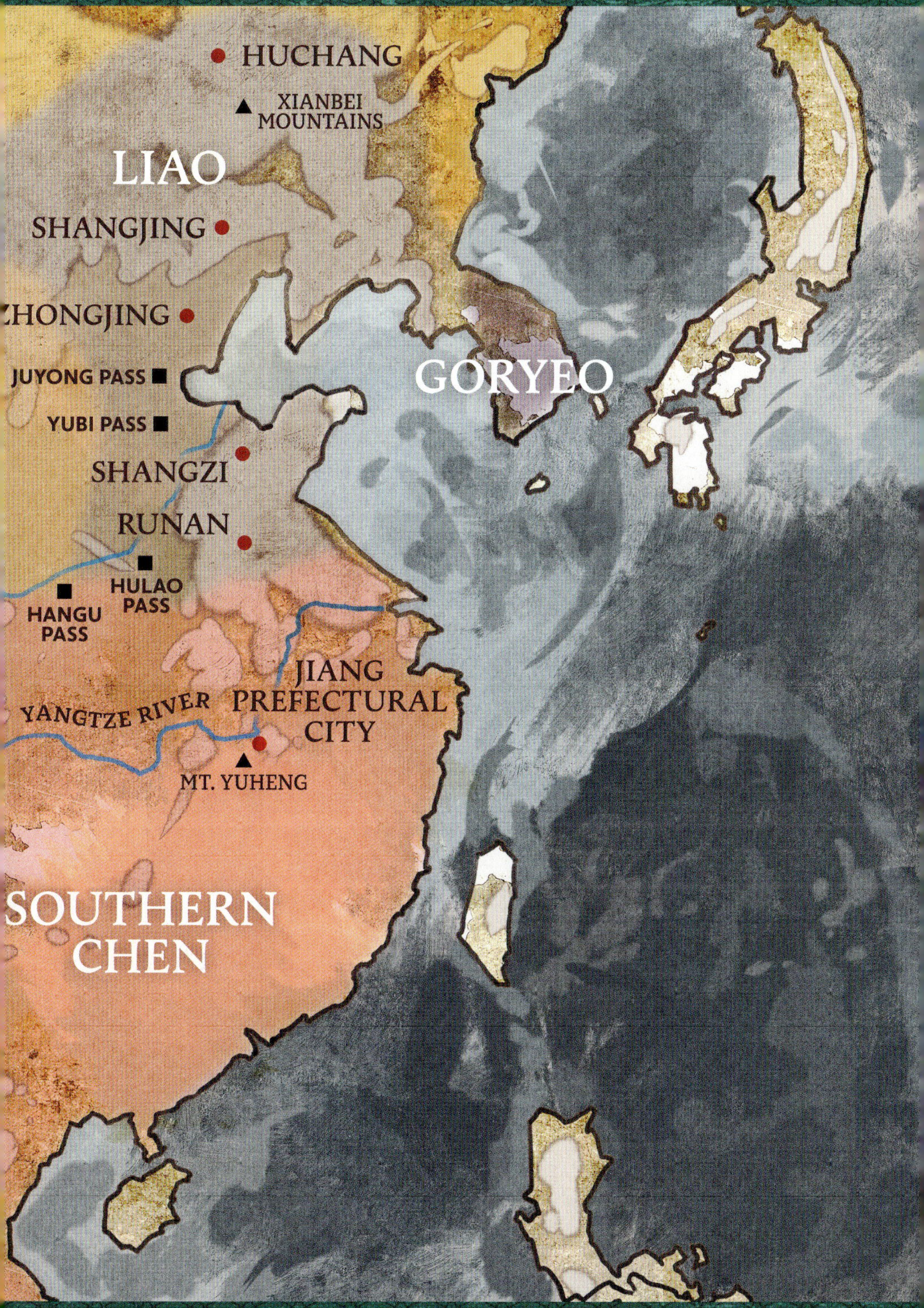

HUCHANG
XIANBEI MOUNTAINS
LIAO
SHANGJING
ZHONGJING
JUYONG PASS
YUBI PASS
SHANGZI
RUNAN
HULAO PASS
HANGU PASS
GORYEO
JIANG PREFECTURAL CITY
YANGTZE RIVER
MT. YUHENG
SOUTHERN CHEN

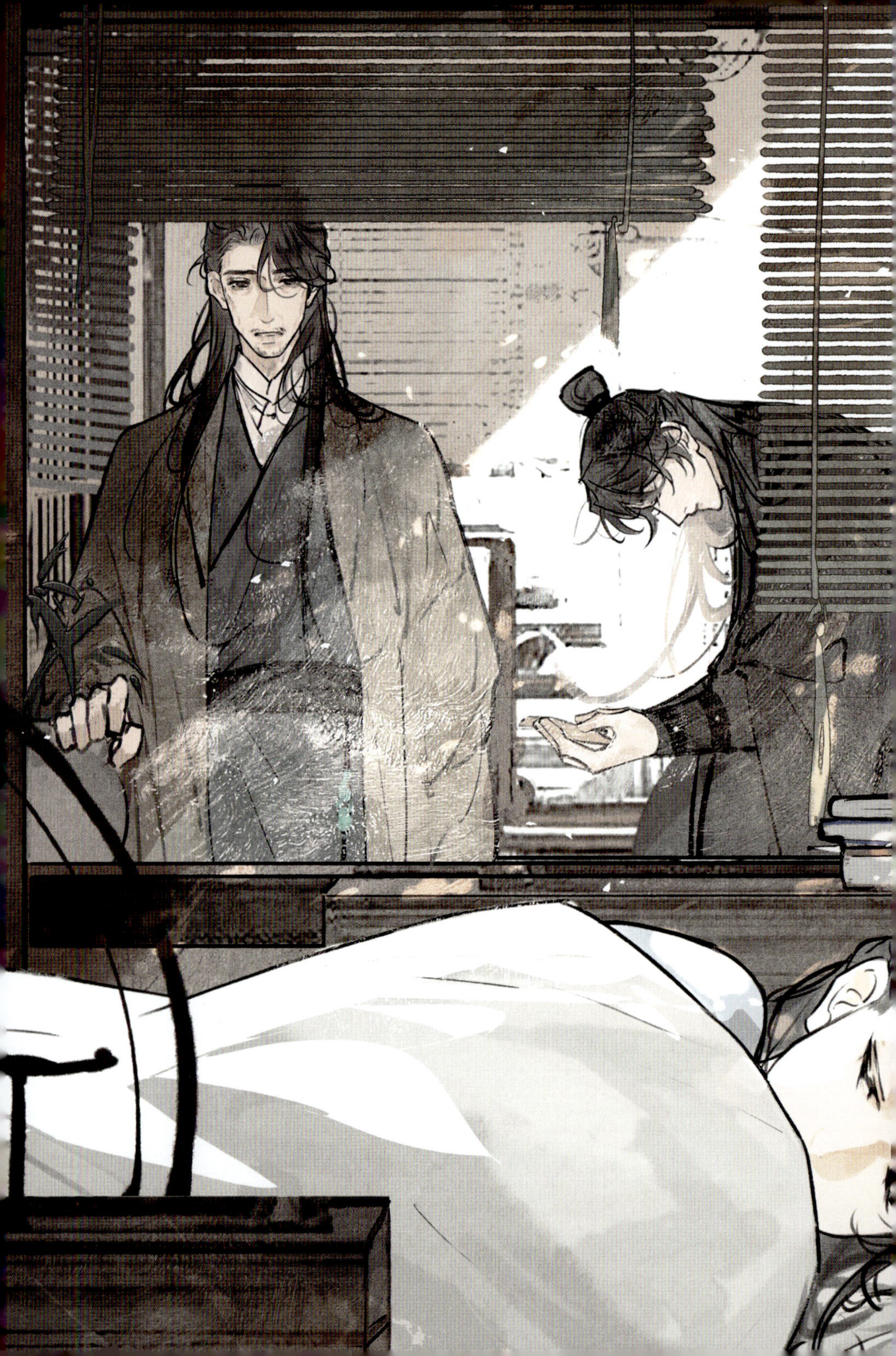

BOOK ONE
相見歡

WRITTEN BY

非天夜翔
FEI TIAN YE XIANG
(ARISE ZHANG)

ILLUSTRATED BY

PORRIDGE
QIANGTOU (墙头)

TRANSLATED BY

MIMI, SUIKA, AND YUNYUN

Seven Seas Entertainment

JOYFUL REUNION VOL. 1

Published originally under the title of 《相見歡》 by 非天夜翔 Fei Tian Ye Xiang
Author© 2025 非天夜翔 (Fei Tian Ye Xiang)
This edition arranged with JS Agency
English Translation copyright ©2025 by Seven Seas Entertainment Inc.
All rights reserved.

Cover illustration by Porridge
Interior illustrations by Qiangtou (墙头)
Bookmark (double-sided) by Ruthie (kkcoocool)
Paper folding screen characters by Zolaida
Paper folding screen back by Qiangtou (墙头)
Sticker sheet by Bakuten
Shikishi by Midori

No portion of this book may be reproduced or transmitted in any form without written permission from the copyright holders. This is a work of fiction. Names, characters, places, and incidents are the products of the author's imagination or are used fictitiously. Any resemblance to actual events, locales, or persons, living or dead, is entirely coincidental. Any information or opinions expressed by the creators of this book belong to those individual creators and do not necessarily reflect the views of Seven Seas Entertainment or its employees.

Seven Seas press and purchase enquiries can be sent
to Marketing Manager Lauren Hill at press@gomanga.com.
Information regarding the distribution and purchase of digital editions is available
from Digital Operations Manager CK Russell at digital@gomanga.com.

Seven Seas and the Seven Seas logo are trademarks of
Seven Seas Entertainment. All rights reserved.

Follow Seven Seas Entertainment online at
sevenseasentertainment.com.

TRANSLATION: Mimi, Suika, yunyun
ADAPTATION: Lee Mandelo
INTERIOR, LOGO & COVER DESIGN: M. A. Lewife
COPY EDITOR: Jehanne Bell
PROOFREADER: Ami Leh, Hnä, Foxghost
EDITOR: Kelly Quinn Chiu
PREPRESS TECHNICIAN: Salvador Chan Jr., April Malig, Jules Valera
MANAGING EDITOR: Alyssa Scavetta
PRODUCTION MANAGER: Clay Gardner
EDITOR-IN-CHIEF: Julie Davis
PUBLISHER: Lianne Sentar
VICE PRESIDENT: Adam Arnold
PRESIDENT: Jason DeAngelis

Standard Edition ISBN: 979-8-89373-392-1
Special Edition ISBN: 979-8-89561-092-3
Printed in Canada
First Printing: June 2025
10 9 8 7 6 5 4 3 2 1

Joyful Reunion

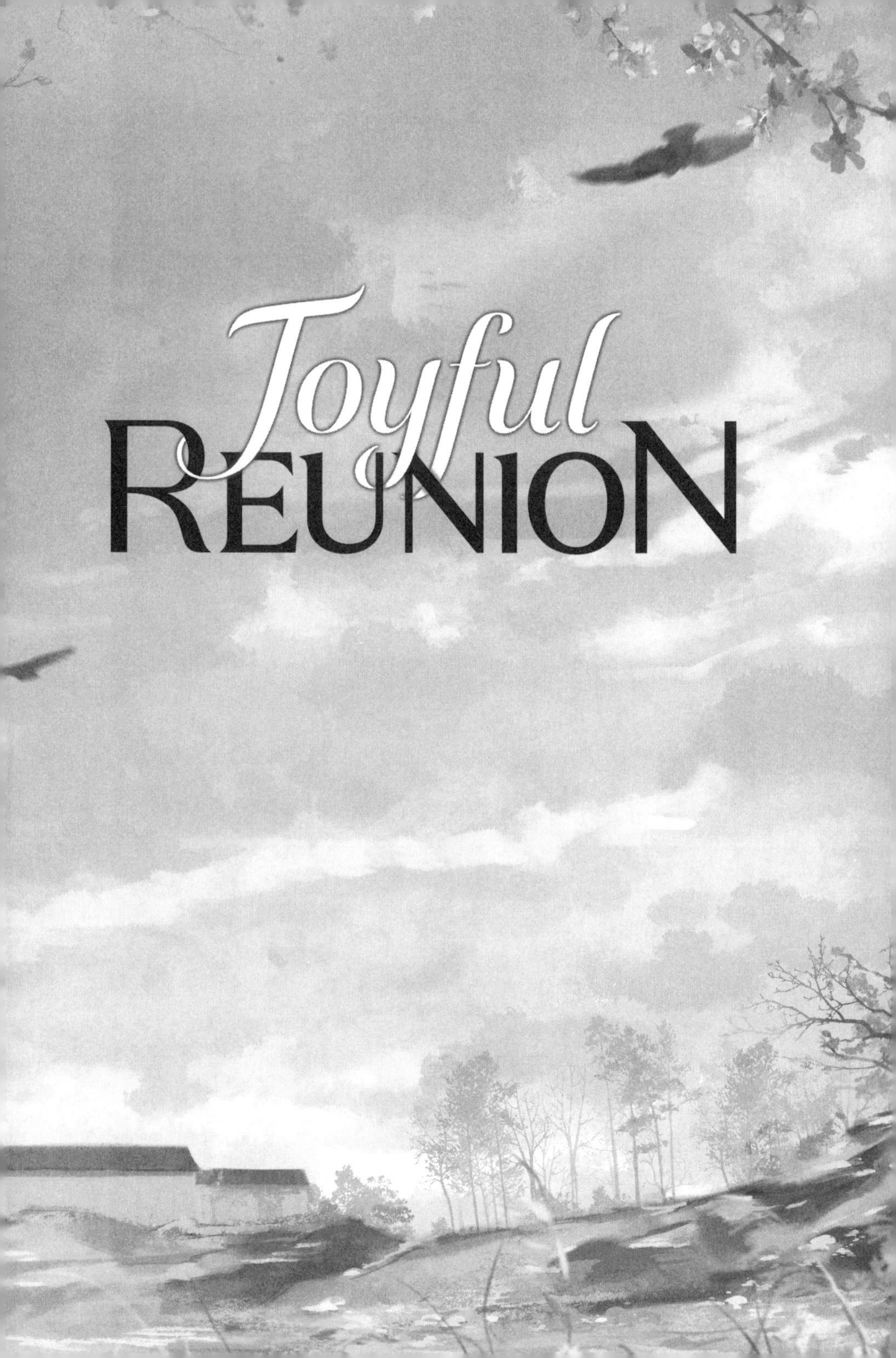

Preface

ASSASSINATION is an important subject in literary works, and contract killing is one of the oldest professions in history. It is often said that when a country falls into disorder, when a sovereign loses the ability to govern, or when a war comes to a standstill, assassins are relied on to restore the status quo. When I first began writing *Joyful Reunion*, I pictured it as an assassin story. I wanted to tell, using a fictional historical setting, a tale of warriors across the land in this age of cold weapons.

All warriors bear their own beliefs and have their own missions in life. In antiquity, when blades and poison still had a role to play, a powerful assassin could determine the governance of an entire empire and the fate of its people. But if this assassin were to take off his stealthy disguise and come out of the dark, would he be cold and ruthless, a mere tool for killing—or would he also feel the full emotional spectrum of an ordinary person?

Thus, in this story, I came up with Four Great Assassins, all of different ages, who are retained by sovereigns and protect them with utmost devotion, and as a result must answer complex questions that test the nature of humanity. As a prince lost to the world of commoners, Duan Ling finds his fate entwined with theirs as he slowly makes his way back to his court with hopes of taking his rightful place. The other protagonist, Wu Du, faces myriad challenges as Duan Ling's guardian. Even so, they protect each other and stand by each other's side, and, with their own modest power, fight against imperial authority, the civil officialdom, and countless other hardships, finally completing their life's mission.

Among my works, this story is written in a more classical style—many of the beliefs and attachments of these ancient assassins exist no longer, yet the sparks of humanity still flicker across time between the pages of the history books. I'm thrilled this story can be translated and published in English, and I hope this will be a brand-new experience for my readers.

FEI TIAN YE XIANG (ARISE ZHANG)

ARC 1
Flight Across the Silver River

The woodland flowers shed spring colors before their time, Helplessly battered by the chilling rain and gales.

—Lines from "Joyful Reunion" by Li Yu, an end-of-dynasty Tang sovereign during the Five Dynasties and Ten Kingdoms period.

1

THE BLIZZARD RAGED, and within the endless expanse of snow, an army coiled like a serpent. Thousands of cavalrymen surged after a lone warrior clad in black armor, the steed beneath him galloping so hard and fast that blood foamed from its nostrils. A storm of arrows rained down upon him, darkening the snowy fields.

"Foolish! Arrogant!" The pursuing general shouted over the distance, "If you know what's good for you, you'll surrender and return to Dongdu with me to stand trial!"

"Even you betray me!" the warrior roared back furiously.

"Jianhong!" Another formation of a thousand swarmed in from his flank. In that moment, enemy forces blanketed the snow as far as the eye could see. A deep, resounding voice rang out from the reinforcements. "Your Highness, you have no one left. You cannot do this alone—why drag this out? Continue to resist, and you will only ensure more soldiers lose their lives. Do your former brothers-in-arms mean nothing to you?"

"Brothers-in-arms?" the warrior sneered, sheathing his sword. "The oaths of the past have turned to lies. Who remembers what promises we made back then?! Must you overthrow me at all costs, even if you sacrifice the lives of every soldier here today?"

"There is little difference between life and death—but though the living world is vast, it no longer holds a place for you!"

War drums pounded amid the swirling snow.

Boom! Boom! Boom!

The beat was like the footsteps of a colossal god walking into the world from the infinite bounds of the horizon, every step stirring up a squall that veiled the sky and blotted out the sun.

"Give up, Your Highness. You have nowhere to run."

Upon the hill, a third formation of cavalry loomed into view within the blizzard, and a young, handsome general took off his helmet and tossed it into the snow. The freezing winds carried the young man's voice to his ears. "How about you hand over the Guardian, enjoy a cup of wine, and I'll send you on your way to the afterlife? Everyone must someday die." His voice was mellow over the storm. "So why must you be so stubborn?"

"You're right." Li Jianhong's robe fluttered beneath his armor. He sat up in the saddle amid the wind and snow and spurred his horse onward, calling out, "Everyone must die, but it is not yet my time. The one to lose their life today…will not be me!"

Far away from Yubi Pass, where they fought, there rose the lonely melody of a Qiang flute, mingling with the powdery snow to scatter on the ground. The cavalry raised their spears to the drumbeat; when it stopped, the three formations would merge and launch their thousands of spears at the Prince of Beiliang, Li Jianhong.

"Enough talk," Li Jianhong said, his voice cold. "Who wants to die first?"

"If you wish to fight to the death here and abandon your former glory, you may," the young general roared. "A thousand gold and the title of marquis to whoever takes Li Jianhong's head today!"

CHAPTER ONE

The drumming ceased, the cavalry shouted in unison, and with a roar that echoed between heaven and earth, Li Jianhong wheeled around and spurred his horse at a reckless gallop toward the army streaming down the snowy slope. The troops yelled as they charged downhill.

Tens of thousands surrounded one man, soldiers cutting toward the formation's center. Li Jianhong dropped the reins and pressed his knees to his horse's flanks. Left hand hefting a longspear and right hand unsheathing his blade, he charged against the tide of onrushing cavalrymen. The snowpack collapsed with a rumble, submerging the pursuing soldiers and their horses in wild, powdery snow.

Blood misted the air as Li Jianhong sliced through a charging cavalryman's glaive with one hand, speared the galloping horse, and heaved it back toward the enemy. Limbs parted from bodies under his sword. Its sharp blade cut through iron like mud as it cleaved through the incoming hordes. It was ten thousand to one, but Li Jianhong slashed through the formation like a tiger among a flock of sheep.

His steed approached a cliff towering thousands of feet above the darkness below. The lip collapsed under its hooves with a thunderous crash, and, unable to escape, countless men and horses tumbled in with the debris. At the edge of the abyss, Li Jianhong spurred his warhorse into a jump.

For a moment, all that could be heard on the snowy hill was a long whinny, the slowing of footsteps in the snow, and the din of the avalanche. The sky darkened, as if a cloud had rolled over the north. The commander of the pursuing troops stopped his horse at the edge of the cliff, a scattering of fine snow dusted over his copper armor. "General, we couldn't find the traitor."

"No matter. Withdraw for now."

2

Springtime grass grows upon the fallen kingdom, its palace buried beneath ancient hills.[1]

After the emperor of Liao marched south and conquered the city of Shangzi, formerly held by the Chen Empire, the Han people retreated south through Yubi Pass. Capitalizing on their victory, the Liao army swept onward and claimed another three hundred li[2] of land south of the pass, including Hebei Prefecture. Runan, a city in the prefecture, had been a thriving trade and distribution center linking the Central Plains and the lands north of the Great Wall—but when it fell to the Liao Empire, the Han people fled west and south. Once the largest city in Hebei, it was now filled with broken tiles and dilapidated houses. Not even thirty thousand families remained.

One of these remaining families was the Duan clan.

The Duan clan was neither too large nor too small. They owned an oil mill as well as a pawn shop, and they dabbled in reselling items to passing merchants. The head of the household had died of consumption before he reached thirty-five, and it was left to his widow to keep things running smoothly for the whole family.

---

1   A verse from the second poem in a set of three poems by Tang dynasty poet Li Bai, entitled "Jinling." It reminisces about the glory of the Tang dynasty as well as its decline.
2   A traditional measure of length. One li is approximately five hundred meters.

On the eighth day of the twelfth month, the day of the Laba Festival, Runan was bathing in the burnished glow of the setting sun, its bluestone-paved alleys alight as if tiled in gold—when a blood-curdling scream erupted from the Duan clan's courtyard.

"You stole from the madam?!"

Blows rained down on a muddy child dressed in rags, the housekeeper's stick thudding against his body. Bruises splotched his face, and one of his eyes was swollen; bloody scratches ran down his arms.

"Say something, you little bastard! You beast!"

The child tried to run, darting behind the nearest building to hide, but collided instead with a servant girl. The impact knocked her wooden tray from her hands, and the housekeeper screamed at him once more.

With nowhere left to flee, the child turned and desperately tackled the scolding woman to the ground, then punched her in the face. When she moved to hit him again, he opened his mouth and bit her.

"Help!" the housekeeper shrieked.

Her cry alerted the stableman, who rushed across the courtyard with hayfork in hand. Unhesitating, he struck the child over the head. The blow knocked him senseless, and he fainted—but the beating continued. The stableman thrashed him bloody, carrying on until the pain itself roused him again, then grabbed him by his dirty collar and threw him into the woodshed. The door slammed and the lock clanked.

The child lay dazed and wounded on the woodshed floor.

"Wontons! Get your wontons!" called an old man's voice outside. Every evening, the wonton seller Lao-Wang strolled the streets with his goods in baskets tied to a pole across his shoulders.

"Duan Ling!" A child's voice shouted from beyond the courtyard. "Duan Ling!"

The sound of his name dragged him back to consciousness. Duan Ling's shoulder had been gouged by the hayfork, and a rivet had punched a bloody hole into his palm. He swayed, nearly staggering as he stood.

"Are you okay?" the child outside yelled.

Duan Ling gasped for breath, his face scrunched in agony. After making an attempt to stand, he slumped back against the wall and forced out an "Uh-huh." The child outside, reassured, hurried away.

He slid slowly down the wall and collapsed onto his side, where he lay curled up in the damp, dark woodshed. Gray sky was all he could see through the shed's high window. Fine snow drifted through the air, and among the clouds there seemed to be a sparkle of starlight right at the center of the sky.

A frosty silence rolled in as the evening darkened to night. Thousands of families across Runan lit warm, homely lamps and fires while the snow softly blanketed their roofs. Only Duan Ling was left trembling in a cold woodshed, too hungry to think. Hazy, disorganized scenes crossed his mind's eye. Sometimes he saw his deceased mother's hands. At others, he saw Madam Duan's beautifully embroidered robe, or the housekeeper's ferocious, scowling face.

"Wontons!" Lao-Wang cried again.

I didn't steal anything, Duan Ling thought. He squeezed the two copper coins in his good hand a little tighter, his vision darkening. His consciousness was blurred, patchy. *Will I die?*

Death had always seemed so distant. Just three days before, he'd seen a crowd surrounding a beggar who'd frozen to death under the Bluestone Bridge. In the end, his body had been hauled onto a cart, transported to the city outskirts, and tossed into a mass grave.

Duan Ling himself had joined the fun and followed the corpse cart with a few other children. He saw the beggar's body wrapped in a straw mat and buried in one of the pit's open graves, next to another that was yet empty. Perhaps, after his death, he'd be buried next to that unnamed beggar.

As the night wore on, cold seeped into Duan Ling's stiffening body. His shallow breaths became a pale white mist, drifting into the air and mingling with snowflakes. For a confused moment, he thought the snow had stopped and the sun had appeared before him, like a summer morning's dawn.

The imaginary sun resolved into the light of a lamp shining on his face as the woodshed door creaked open.

"Come out!" barked the stableman.

Another man—whose voice he did not recognize—asked, "This boy is Duan Ling?"

Duan Ling was lying on his side, facing the door. With much difficulty, his muscles spasming, he managed to sit upright. A stranger brushed past the stableman and knelt before him, examining his bruised face.

"Are you sick?" the man asked.

Duan Ling's mind was hazy with shadows and hallucinations. The stranger produced a pill from his robes and pushed it past Duan Ling's lips, then scooped him up from the cold ground. Through his disorientation, Duan Ling caught a whiff of the man's scent. With each swaying step away from the woodshed, he grew warmer—first from being held in the stranger's arms, and then as the air lost its chill.

A hole had torn in Duan Ling's worn old coat during the beating, and the reed flowers sewn inside for insulation spilled onto the stranger as he walked.

CHAPTER TWO

Dim lights flickered against the dark, lonely night, and the dried reed flowers scattered behind them down the long corridor. From either side came the unrestrained laughter of maidens, underlaid with the rustle of falling snow outside warm rooms. The world continued to warm and grow brighter; Duan Ling seemed to travel from freezing winter to balmy spring, from the dark of night to the light of day.

The world is an inn for all beings, days mere passersby in the face of eternity.[3]

Duan Ling's breathing deepened as, slowly, he regained consciousness.

The stranger had carried him to the main hall, which was brightly lit and comfortably heated. Madam Duan lounged on a divan with a piece of scenery-embroidered satin resting loosely in her hands.

"Madam," the man said.

Madam Duan's words held a smile as she asked, "Do you know this child?"

"I don't," said the stranger—but he continued holding Duan Ling in his arms.

The medicine the man fed him had dissolved on Duan Ling's tongue. His frozen-stiff core finally seemed warm again, his strength returning. Though the stranger held him against his chest, both of them facing Madam Duan, Duan Ling dared not lift his gaze. He saw only a small portion of the splendid brocade covering the divan.

"Here is his birth certificate," Madam Duan said.

Her housekeeper stepped forward and offered it to the stranger.

Duan Ling was short, sickly-looking, and skinny. He struggled weakly in the man's arms in fear, and was put down again; once

---

3   Lines from "A Spring Evening Banquet in a Peach Garden" by Tang dynasty poet Li Bai.

settled back on his unsteady feet, he leaned against the man for support. He noticed the stranger was wearing black robes, damp martial boots, and had a jade pendant in the shape of an arc fastened to his waist.

"Name your price, Madam," said the man.

"Honestly, the Duan clan should never have accepted this boy in the first place," Madam Duan said with a smile. "But when his mother came back with child, it was the middle of winter and she had nowhere else to go. As the saying goes, heaven cherishes life. I took her in. But once she settled down here, there was no end to it."

The man said nothing, only gazing with steady intent at Madam Duan as she paused. After a long moment, she sighed. "I'll put it this way: He was entrusted to me by his mother, Duan Xiaowan. She even gave me a letter. Would you like to see it, my lord?"

The housekeeper brought him the letter as well, which he tucked away without so much as a glance.

"I don't even know your name," Madam Duan continued. "If I just hand you the letter and the child without asking any questions, how will I explain myself to Duan Xiaowan when we meet in the afterlife?"

The man, once again, remained silent.

Madam Duan spread her sleeves and said in a more flirtatious tone, "Duan Xiaowan's pregnancy was mysterious to begin with. I assumed the past could be left well enough alone after she was gone, but if you take this child away tonight...what if his father sends someone looking for him in the future? I wouldn't be able to tell them anything. Isn't that right?"

Still, the stranger said nothing.

Madam Duan smiled at him once more, conciliatory, then turned her gaze on Duan Ling. She beckoned him over, but Duan Ling shrank back instinctively and hid behind the man, clutching tightly at his robes.

"Ah." Madam Duan scoffed lightly. "Still, my lord, you should offer me some explanation."

Finally, he spoke: "I don't have one. I only have money. Name your price."

Madam Duan was speechless.

As the man fell into stern silence again, Madam Duan realized he would provide her nothing aside from payment for raising Duan Ling. He would not tell her who he was, regardless of any trouble it might cause for the Duan clan. The pair watched one another quietly for a short while, and then the man reached into his robes and withdrew several colorful banknotes.

"Four hundred taels," she said, finally naming her price.

The man passed over the appropriate banknote.

Duan Ling watched the housekeeper accept the payment, and his breathing stuttered to a halt. He had no idea what this man wanted to do with him. He'd heard the maids say before that on bitter-cold winter nights, there were people who would come down the mountain and buy children to bring back as offerings to be eaten by monsters. A terrible fright rose within him.

"I'm not going!" he yelled. "No! No!"

Duan Ling turned to run, but only made it a single step before the maid grabbed him painfully by the ear and dragged him back.

"Let go of him," the man said in his deep voice. He laid a hand on Duan Ling's shoulder, and that hand felt like it weighed more than a thousand pounds. Duan Ling couldn't move even when the housekeeper released him.

The housekeeper carried the banknote to Madam Duan, who frowned slightly when she accepted it.

"Keep the change," the stranger told her. To Duan Ling, he said, "Let's go."

"I won't! I won't go!" Duan Ling cried.

Madam Duan still hadn't lost her smile. "Where are you going in the dark? Why don't you stay the night here and set off in the morning?"

Duan Ling wailed at the top of his lungs as the man looked down at him with a furrowed brow. "What's wrong with you?" he asked.

"I don't want to be fed to monsters! Don't sell me! Don't—" Duan Ling wriggled free and tried to dive under the table, but the man was much faster. He grabbed the boy and flicked several acupoints with his slender fingers, sealing Duan Ling's voice; Duan Ling promptly collapsed. The man picked him up again, and under Madam Duan's suspicious gaze, carried him outside.

"You don't have to be afraid," the man said quietly, holding Duan Ling under his arm. "I won't feed you to any monsters."

Outside the residence, the knife-cold wind blew snow flurries into their faces. Duan Ling's throat seemed obstructed by an odd barrier of air—he opened his mouth but couldn't make a sound.

"My name is Lang Junxia," the man said. "Remember it: Lang Junxia."

"Won—tons!" Lao-Wang called into the night from the stall to which he'd returned.

The wonton stall's yellow lamp shone through the falling snow; Duan Ling's empty stomach clenched as he gazed at it desperately. The man—Lang Junxia—came to a stop, paused, then set Duan Ling down and tossed a couple of copper coins into the bamboo tube at the front of the stall with a jingle.

Somehow, this simple action calmed Duan Ling. Who was this man, and why had he taken him from the Duan residence? Lang Junxia pressed on Duan Ling's back to unseal some acupoints;

his throat was suddenly free of obstruction. He was about to scream again when Lang Junxia shushed him. Duan Ling watched as the old man brought them a steaming bowl filled to the brim with meaty wontons, sesame seeds and crushed peanuts sprinkled on top. A small piece of fat was dissolved in the soup, giving off a tantalizing fragrance, and potherb mustard garnished the bowl.

"Eat," Lang Junxia said.

Duan Ling immediately forgot everything else and grabbed the bowl, scarfing down the wontons despite how they scorched his tongue and throat. His hunger overcame his fear, and he kept his head lowered to wolf the whole meal down as quickly as he could. As he slurped a mouthful of soup, a fox-fur coat fell across his back.

When he had drunk every last drop from the bowl, he put down his chopsticks and sighed before turning around to look at Lang Junxia. The man's complexion was tan, like a person in a painting, and his nose was tall, his eyes deeply set. The lights in the alley and the flying snow reflected in his pupils. The fall of his clothes hinted at an upright, strong figure, and his black outer robe was embroidered with ferocious monsters baring fangs and flashing claws. His fingers were long and beautiful, and he carried a shining sword at his waist like a hero in an opera.

Duan Ling had seen people return from the capital in splendor, riding high on their horses through the streets of Runan. From his hiding spot in the crowd, he'd watched the commotion, observing the young men dressed in silk and satin, flushed with their own success.

None of them had been as good-looking as this man—yet Duan Ling couldn't have put into words what made him so handsome.

Suddenly he was incredibly frightened once more. Perhaps Lang Junxia was a monster turned man, who would soon bare his

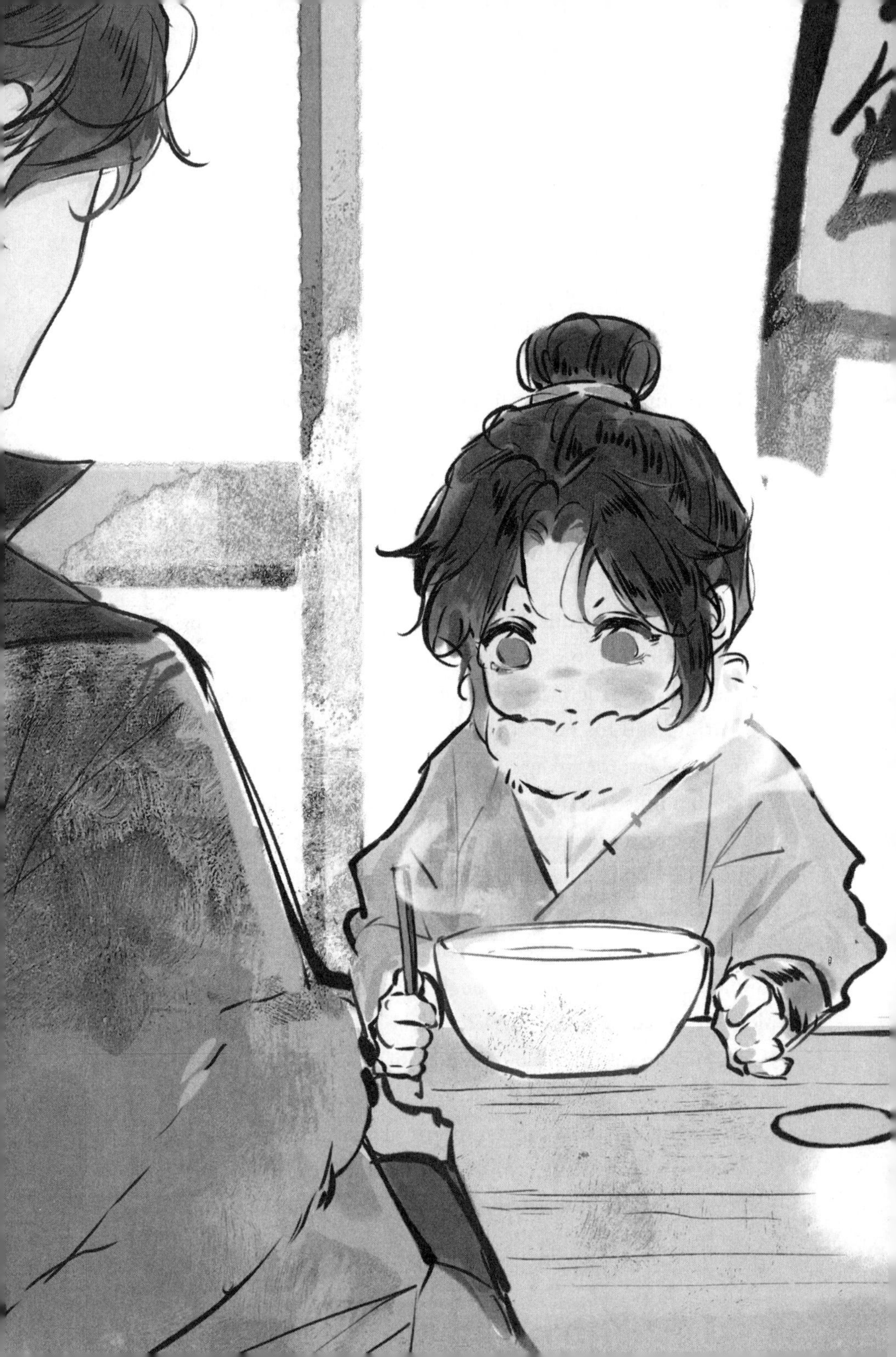

fangs and eat him alive. Lang Junxia, on the other hand, merely stared at him intently.

"Are you full?" he asked. "Do you want anything else to eat?"

Duan Ling didn't dare answer. He was already planning his escape.

"If you're full, let's go."

Lang Junxia reached his hand out to Duan Ling, but Duan Ling shied away fearfully. He looked over at Lao-Wang for help, but the old man wasn't paying them any mind. Lang Junxia flipped his hand over and caught Duan Ling's instead. Duan Ling didn't dare struggle any further and obediently went along with him.

Back at the Duan clan household, a servant came forward to report: "Madam, the man brought the bastard to eat wontons in the alley."

Madam Duan gathered her coat around her and blinked, unsettled. She called for the housekeeper. "Have someone follow them. Find out where he's taking the child."

Thousands of families had lit up their homes for the night in Runan. Duan Ling's face had gone red from the cold, and his feet stung from walking barefoot in the slush as Lang Junxia led him through the streets. Only after they arrived at Diancui Pavilion in the center of the city did Lang Junxia finally notice that Duan Ling had no shoes. He frowned and picked him up, then whistled toward the building. A horse trotted out at his signal.

Lang Junxia settled Duan Ling atop the horse and wrapped his coat tighter around him. "Wait for me here. There's something I need to attend to."

Duan Ling looked down at him. Lang Junxia's face was handsome, as if carved from jade, with gleaming, sharp eyes. Stray reed flowers still clung to his hair. Lang Junxia motioned for the boy to wait, then turned and disappeared into the night with a flare of his robes, like a falcon spreading its wings.

Thoughts ran wild in Duan Ling's mind. Who was Lang Junxia really—and should he run now? But the horse was very tall, and he didn't dare jump down for fear of breaking his legs or the horse kicking him. He debated whether he should leave his fate to this strange man or create it himself. In any case, where would he even run to? Right as he made up his mind to take the leap, however, a figure flashed around the corner of the alley.

Lang Junxia stepped into the stirrup and swung easily astride the horse. "Hup!" he cued the horse forward.

His mount's hooves rang against the bluestone path as the horse pranced out from the alley and down the streets—ready to leave Runan behind on this dark and lonely night.

Duan Ling sat in front of Lang Junxia, smelling the damp odor rising from his own clothes. Surprisingly, Lang Junxia's robes were dry, as if he'd sat before a fire, and smelled pleasantly of shaobing flatbread. There was a tiny burnt spot on the sleeve cuff of the hand holding the reins.

The spot hadn't been burnt before. Where had Lang Junxia gone, and what had he done?

Duan Ling recalled another story. Legend had it that, during the last dynasty, some rogues were killed in a dispute and buried in the dark ravine outside the city. They'd rotted there for hundreds of years, waiting for children to pass by so they could take over their fresh, young bodies. Their shades would first take the form of humans, each undeniably handsome and skilled in martial arts—and then, after they'd found a victim, they would lure the child back to their grave, unmask their rotten face, suck away the child's vital essence, and inhabit their body. The unlucky child, their body stolen, would thus lie in the grave for all eternity, while the corpse monster shifted into their skin and strutted back into the mortal world to live a good life.

Duan Ling couldn't stop trembling. He desperately wanted to leap off the horse and run away, but the horse was simply too tall; he would probably break his legs if he jumped down.

Was Lang Junxia a corpse monster? Duan Ling's head was spinning as he sat in the saddle, stiff with terror. If the corpse monster wanted to absorb his essence, should he lead the monster to someone else? *No,* he thought—he couldn't harm others.

A man at the city gate opened it for Lang Junxia, and their horse cantered south along the official road through the snow. Realizing that they weren't headed toward either the mass graves or the dark ravine, Duan Ling began to relax. The rhythmic, steady pace of the horse's stride made him feel settled and sleepy, and gradually he dozed off, engulfed in Lang Junxia's dry, refreshing scent. Two long ravines stretched across the landscape of his dreams, like a shadow play sweeping across a curtain.

The heavy snow was like a white sheet, the green peaks of the mountains like ink. The horse galloped across the wintry expanse like the stroke of a brush over paper.

3

"Two bowls of Laba rice porridge, please."

Warmly glowing lights accompanied Lang Junxia's voice. Duan Ling was so sleepy he couldn't open his eyes; he rolled over dazedly as Lang Junxia patted him awake.

In the guest room of the inn they had stopped at, a server brought over two bowls, the porridge within thick with beans, dried fruit, and nuts. Lang Junxia handed one to Duan Ling, who scarfed his meal down again as his darting eyes stole glances at Lang Junxia.

"Still hungry?" Lang Junxia asked.

Duan Ling gave him a suspicious look. When Lang Junxia sat on the bed beside him, Duan Ling shrank nervously backward.

Lang Junxia had never cared for a child before, and seemed confused by Duan Ling. Lacking any candy to coax the boy with, after a moment's consideration, he untied the jade pendant from around his waist and held it out to him. "You can have it."

The jade arc was slightly translucent, like a piece of sugar brittle; Duan Ling didn't dare reach for it. His gaze shifted from the jade pendant to Lang Junxia's face.

"If you want it, take it," Lang Junxia said.

The words were warm, but his voice held no emotion. With the jade held between his fingers, he stuck his hand out toward the boy.

Duan Ling nervously accepted the pendant, poring over it intently, until finally his eyes lifted to Lang Junxia's face again.

"Who are you?" Duan Ling asked—then, as if it had just occurred to him, he continued, "A-are you my father?"

Lang Junxia didn't answer right away. Duan Ling had heard countless rumors about his father: Some said his father was a monster in the mountains; some said he was a beggar. Others said his father would come back for him one day—that Duan Ling was destined for wealth and nobility.

"No," Lang Junxia said. "My apologies for disappointing you, but I am not."

Duan Ling hadn't really believed it himself, so this answer wasn't particularly disappointing. Lang Junxia seemed to be mulling something over, but when he shook off his abstraction, he said nothing more except to bid Duan Ling to lie down. Lang Junxia pulled the blanket over him. "Go to sleep."

The whistle of wind and snow echoed in Duan Ling's ears. They had already traveled forty li from Runan, and Duan Ling was still covered in healing wounds; the instant he fell asleep, nightmares of being beaten started all over again. Sometimes his body twitched uncontrollably, or he whimpered and screamed, trembling the whole time.

At first Lang Junxia had lain down on a mat on the floor—but when he realized Duan Ling's nightmares were never-ending, he slept beside him instead. Whenever Duan Ling reached his hand out, Lang Junxia covered it with his own, large and warm. Eventually, Duan Ling's dreams seemed to settle, and he fell into restful sleep.

The following day, Lang Junxia requested hot water and gave Duan Ling a bath, washing his whole body clean. Duan Ling was so skinny his ribs showed through his skin, and old scars were scattered across his arms and legs. His older wounds hadn't healed before new ones were laid over them, and the hot bathwater stung all his collected hurts. But Duan Ling paid the pain no mind; he was focused on playing with the jade arc in his hands.

"Did my father send you?" Duan Ling asked.

"Shh." Lang Junxia held a finger to his lips. "Don't ask me anything. I'll tell you little by little. For now, if anyone asks, tell them that your surname is Duan and your father is named Duan Sheng. You and I are from the Duan family of Shangzi, and your father travels between the cities of Shangjing and Xichuan for business, so he entrusted you to your uncle's household. Now that you're older, your father sent me to bring you to Shangjing to study. Got it?"

Lang Junxia applied medicine to Duan Ling's wounds, dressed him in an underrobe, and wrapped him in a slightly oversized coat lined with silky mink fur. He led him outside, sat him on the horse, and looked directly into his eyes. Although still unsure, Duan Ling returned Lang Junxia's gaze for a long moment, then nodded.

"Repeat it back to me."

"My father is Duan Sheng."

Their steed galloped all the way to the riverbank, where Lang Junxia dismounted. At the crossing, he led the horse and carried Duan Ling across the frozen river.

"I came from the Duan family of Shangzi..." Duan Ling repeated.

"...to study in Shangjing."

Lang Junxia lifted him into the saddle again, and Duan Ling swayed on the horse, drowsy.

Thousands of miles away, below Yubi Pass, Li Jianhong limped onward. He staggered more than he walked, his body a lurching collection of wounds and fractures. The only things he carried with him were the sword on his back and the red cord around his neck.

From that red cord hung a pendant of flawlessly clear white jade.

A gust of wind scoured away the dusting of snow on the jade, which seemed to glow warmly in the darkness. In a distant corner of the world, from another jade pendant, a powerful force called. Between them stood the Xianbei Mountains that the northern goshawks could not cross, and the frozen winter streams through which fish could not swim. But the force that called from the other side of those waters was binding—it was fate. The power drawing him forward despite his agonies was rooted in his very soul, flowing in his veins.

Through the howling blizzard, he heard something approaching. Was it a pack of wolves in the wilderness, or a whirlwind set to destroy the world?

"Skychaser!" Li Jianhong roared.

A pitch-black steed galloped toward him, its pure-white hooves frothing up clouds of snow. The warhorse's whinny pierced the sky. Li Jianhong grabbed the reins and used all his remaining strength to swing himself onto the horse's back.

"Go!" Li Jianhong shouted as he rode Skychaser into the blizzard.

Crossing river after river, Lang Junxia and Duan Ling headed north; as the temperature dropped, the number of people they encountered rose. Lang Junxia repeatedly warned Duan Ling to keep his past a secret. Once he had finally memorized the backstory Lang Junxia taught him, Lang Junxia entertained him with stories of Shangzi, amusing Duan Ling such that, little by little, he forgot his hurts and worries.

Like the wounds on his body, Duan Ling's nightmares also healed slowly but steadily. The wounds on his back scabbed, and the scabs fell off. Only a few pale, soft scars remained by the time their long journey ended at the most opulent city Duan Ling had seen in his life.

Shangjing's tall buildings reflected light like the sea, and the people's luminous clothes and carriages flowed by, shining like river waves. The setting sun cast a ruddy light from the western side of the Xianbei Mountains, glowing warm over the surrounding wild expanse; the shining band of the river coursed around the city like a shimmering, ice-crusted belt.

The city towered in the twilight.

"We're here," Lang Junxia said.

Duan Ling was bundled tightly within his oversized coat; the journey had been much too cold. Held in Lang Junxia's arms, seated on his horse, Duan Ling gazed at the distant rooftops of Shangjing. He squinted slightly, feeling warm inside despite the winter chill.

Nightfall arrived alongside them at the gates of Shangjing. The city was heavily guarded, and as Lang Junxia handed over his official documents, the guards eyed Duan Ling.

"Where are you from?" a guard asked.

Duan Ling stared at him, and the guard stared back.

"My father is Duan Sheng." Duan Ling had his story well-memorized. "I'm from the Duan family in—"

The guard interrupted him to ask, "What's the relationship between you two?"

Duan Ling looked at Lang Junxia. "His father and I are friends," Lang Junxia replied.

The guard read the documents over and over again, then finally—reluctantly—let them through. The streets were brightly lit and piled with snow on either side; it was the end of the year, a season of festivities when drunk men clung to the lampposts and enjoyed their wine on the side of the road, when women entertainers played their instruments and sang for passersby in front of the railings. Even more people sat or lay down outside the boisterous pubs. Courtesans' bold calls spilled into the night, and martial artists with swords belted at their waists stopped for a look. Filthy rich merchants, drunk beyond reckoning with pretty women in their arms, staggered down the street. One nearly upended a noodle stall. Carriages clanked as they sped down the icy roads, and at a carrier's cry, another luxurious sedan was lifted high off the ground by its men, as if houses moved freely through the streets of Shangjing.

Galloping was banned on the main road, so Duan Ling sat alone on the horse's back while Lang Junxia led it by the reins. The boy drank in the city sights with intense curiosity through the sliver of visibility allowed by his fur hat. Once they turned into an alley, Lang Junxia mounted the horse again and spurred it back up to speed, its hooves throwing snow into the air as they galloped down the narrow lane.

The music faded, left behind on the main streets, but the lights remained bright. Red lanterns hung on either side of the quiet alley, and the only sound was the crisp clacking of hooves on icy paving stones. The further down the side street they traveled, the more numerous and secluded the two-story houses flanking them became, with countless strings of lanterns layered and stacked overhead. Even the falling snow was consumed by their constant, warm light.

Upon their arrival at the alley's back gate, Lang Junxia told Duan Ling, "Get down."

A beggar sat beside the gate. Without so much as looking at him, Lang Junxia flicked several silver coins into his bowl, which clinked against one another at the bottom. Duan Ling turned his head to better see the beggar, curious, but Lang Junxia turned his head forward again, then patted the snow from his body and led him inside. Lang Junxia was clearly familiar with the place; they passed without assistance through an open-air pergola covered in snow and the central courtyard, accompanied by the distant thrumming of a zither, before turning toward a side wing.

After leading them into a room, Lang Junxia seemed to relax a little. "Sit. Are you hungry?"

Duan Ling shook his head. Lang Junxia settled him on the low table in front of the stove, then dropped to one knee. He removed Duan Ling's fur-lined coat and the cap with its muffling ear flaps, dusted the snow from his boots, and sat down cross-legged before him. He looked up at Duan Ling with a hint of gentleness in his eyes, hidden so deeply it was there and gone again in a flash.

"Is this your home?" Duan Ling asked.

"This place is called Qionghua House," Lang Junxia explained. "We'll stay here for a few days before I take you to your new home."

Duan Ling had taken Lang Junxia's earlier *Don't ask me anything* to heart, and rarely questioned the man during their journey. He kept his doubts hidden, like an alert, uneasy rabbit that appeared calm from the outside. Yet even without questions, Lang Junxia often explained things to him at his own pace.

"Are you cold?" Lang Junxia asked. He took Duan Ling's chilled feet into his large, warm hands and rubbed them briefly before frowning. "Your body's too weak."

From behind Lang Junxia, a girl's crisp voice called out, "I thought you were never coming back."

Duan Ling raised his head. A beautiful girl in an embroidered jacket stood at the door, two serving girls trailing behind her.

"I had business to attend to," Lang Junxia said without turning toward her. He untied Duan Ling's belt, then turned and opened his travel pack, retrieving a dry change of outer robes for the boy and helping him into them. Only once he was shaking out the damp robe did he finally glance over at the girl, who took it as an invitation, stepping into the room and peering down at Duan Ling.

Her intense regard made Duan Ling uncomfortable, and his brows drew together. Before he could speak, she asked, "And who is this?"

Duan Ling sat up straighter, and his practiced litany flashed through his mind: *My name is Duan Ling, and my father is Duan Sheng...*

But before the words left his mouth, Lang Junxia answered for him. "This is Duan Ling." He turned to Duan Ling and said, "This is Miss Ding."

Remembering the manners Lang Junxia had taught him, Duan Ling cupped his hands toward her and looked her up and down. The girl Ding Zhi—who was as lovely as the angelica flower of her namesake—smiled and bowed to Duan Ling. "Hello, Duan-gongzi."[4]

"Has the one from the Northern Court arrived yet?" Lang Junxia asked offhandedly.

"The military report from the border said the general hasn't returned in three months due to continued fighting below Jiangjun Ridge," Ding Zhi said as she took her seat beside them. She said over her shoulder to the serving girls, "Bring some snacks for Duan-gongzi."

---

4   A respectful way to address a young man.

Ding Zhi picked up the teapot, poured a cup, and handed it to Lang Junxia. He accepted the offering and took a sip, then said, "Ginger tea—it'll drive away the cold," before handing the cup to Duan Ling.

Throughout their journey, Lang Junxia would always taste any food or drink first to confirm it was good before giving it to Duan Ling; the boy had become used to it. But as he drank his tea, he caught a strange look in Ding Zhi's eyes, which had narrowed slightly as her stare intensified.

The maid returned with a selection of pastries Duan Ling had never seen—or even heard of—before. Lang Junxia seemed to anticipate his excitement and reminded him, "Eat slowly. There'll be dinner later."

Over the course of their journey, Lang Junxia had admonished Duan Ling repeatedly that no matter what he was eating, he shouldn't cram his meals down as fast as possible. This went against all Duan Ling's instincts, but he had to listen to Lang Junxia—and slowly, he realized that no one was going to snatch his food away anymore. He chose a pastry, held it gently in his hands, and nibbled without rushing. Ding Zhi sat quietly, as if nothing happening in the room had anything to do with her. This continued until the maids brought two food boxes and laid them on the low table. Lang Junxia urged Duan Ling to take a seat, indicating that he should eat, and only then did Ding Zhi kneel down beside Lang Junxia with the pot of warmed wine to pour for him.

Lang Junxia blocked the cup with his fingers. "Drinking will cause trouble."

"This is the Liangnan Daqu liquor sent as tribute last month," Ding Zhi said. "You don't want to try it? Madam set it aside just for you, whenever you came back."

Lang Junxia didn't reject the liquor a second time; Ding Zhi poured him a cup, and he drank. She poured another, and he drank again. She poured a third cup—after Lang Junxia finished that one, he turned the cup over and placed it rim-down on the table.

Duan Ling watched attentively the whole time.

Ding Zhi moved to pour a cup for him as well, but Lang Junxia reached two fingers out and caught her sleeve. "He's not allowed to drink," Lang Junxia said.

The girl gave him an apologetic smile.

Duan Ling *did* want to drink—but his desire to be obedient for Lang Junxia superseded his desire for alcohol. While he patiently ate his dinner, Duan Ling continued to wonder where he'd been brought and what the relationship was between Lang Junxia and the girl. He snuck peek after peek at them, his uncertainty flickering across his face. He wished they would talk a little more, just so he could listen.

Lang Junxia still hadn't told Duan Ling why he'd brought him here. Did Miss Ding know—was that why she didn't ask where he was from?

Miss Ding, too, stole glances at Duan Ling from time to time, as if doing calculations in her head. When Duan Ling set down his chopsticks, she finally spoke, and his heart jumped into his throat even though all she asked was, "Did those dishes suit your taste?"

"I've never had them before, but they were good," Duan Ling answered.

Ding Zhi laughed. As a servant girl cleared the food boxes away, she said, "I should take my leave."

"Go, then," Lang Junxia said.

"How long are you in Shangjing for this time?" Ding Zhi asked.

"I'll be staying permanently," he replied.

Ding Zhi's eyes seemed to brighten. With a slight smile, she said to the serving girl, "Accompany my lord and Duan-gongzi to the side courtyard."

The maid led the way with a lamp; Lang Junxia wrapped Duan Ling in his own fur-lined cloak, scooped him into his arms, and carried him through the corridors until they arrived at another courtyard—this one filled with rustling bamboo. Duan Ling heard a cup shatter across the courtyard in a different building, followed by a man's drunken tirade.

"Don't look around," Lang Junxia cautioned Duan Ling. He carried him into the room and glanced back at the maid who'd followed them inside. "There's no need to wait on us."

She bowed and left. The room held a gentle fragrance, and though there was no brazier, the air was warm. A furnace under the floors provided heat, and smoke billowed through the underground spaces.

Lang Junxia had Duan Ling rinse his mouth as he prepared for sleep. Lying on the bed in his underrobes, Duan Ling felt awfully drowsy. Lang Junxia settled on the bed beside him. "Tomorrow I'll take you to look around."

"Really?" Duan Ling exclaimed with a brief burst of energy.

"Yes," Lang Junxia said. "I'm going to sleep now. I'll be in the next room."

At this, Duan Ling grasped forlornly at his sleeve. Lang Junxia gave him a confused look, but with a moment of thought, he understood—Duan Ling wanted him to sleep here.

Since they'd left Runan, Duan Ling hadn't been separated from Lang Junxia for a moment. They ate together in the morning and they slept together at night. Now that Lang Junxia planned to leave him by himself, of course Duan Ling would be frightened.

"Then..." Lang Junxia hesitated. "Never mind. I'll stay with you."

Lang Junxia shrugged off his underrobe, baring his sturdy, muscular torso, and lay down beside Duan Ling, draping an arm over the boy. Duan Ling nestled his head in the crook of Lang Junxia's strong arm and chest; as soon as he did so, his eyelids grew heavier, and he fell easily into sleep. Lang Junxia's skin carried the pleasant scent of a man, and Duan Ling had already become accustomed to smelling it on his outer robe and his body. He felt he would no longer suffer any nightmares, so long as Lang Junxia held him.

But the day had been so full that his mind was overcrowded with new, complicated information; his dreams leapt and spun, too numerous for the span of a single night. During the second half of the night, the snow stopped falling and the world settled into an unusual silence. Duan Ling somehow found himself awake, disoriented from the countless dreams flooding over him, but when he turned over, he found only a still-warm cover.

Lang Junxia had disappeared, but his body temperature lingered. The absence made Duan Ling nervous. Unsure of what to do, he tiptoed out of bed and opened the door. Lights glowed from the next room over. Duan Ling padded barefoot down the corridor, then raised himself onto his toes to peek through the window.

The room was open and bright, with curtains draped across one side. Lang Junxia was in the midst of undressing, his back turned to the window.

His collar was fastened at the jut of his throat, and he undid it slowly before hanging his brocade robe on a nearby clothing rack. As his clothes slid down his body, a broad back, defined waistline, and well-formed buttocks were revealed, inch by inch. His naked male body was on full display, as lean and strong as a warhorse, and when he turned to the side, Duan Ling saw his virile erection.

Duan Ling's breath caught, his heart pounding wildly. He took an involuntary step backward and knocked over a flower stand.

"Who's there?" Lang Junxia called as he turned toward the door.

4

STARTLED, Duan Ling scurried away.

Lang Junxia hastily threw on his outer robe and left the room barefoot, emerging into the corridor just as the door to Duan Ling's room slid closed with a soft *thud*.

Lang Junxia followed him inside. Duan Ling had already burrowed back into his blankets and was pretending to sleep; Lang Junxia didn't know whether to laugh or cry. He went to the washbasin and wrung out the wet cloth, then dropped his outer robe to the ground and began to wipe down his once-again nude body. Duan Ling cracked his eyes open just enough to see him across the room. Lang Junxia turned slightly, and, as if to settle his restless emotions, pressed the cold, wet cloth over his erection, attempting to force himself soft.

A silhouette appeared at the window.

"I'm going to sleep; I won't be coming over," Lang Junxia said in a low voice.

Footsteps retreated down the corridor, and Duan Ling rolled over toward the wall. Moments later, Lang Junxia put on his underpants and slipped into bed, his chest pressed to Duan Ling's back. Duan Ling squirmed his way around, and Lang Junxia lifted his arm so he could once more rest his head on his shoulder. Comfortable again, Duan Ling fell quickly back to sleep.

Lang Junxia's firm muscles, warmth, and pleasant scent transported the dreaming Duan Ling to a southern winter, where he was embraced by a fiery sun.

The same night in Xichuan, it drizzled steadily, and the rain soaked everything.

Candlelight cast the shadows of latticed windows across the outdoor corridor. Two figures walked slowly through the shadows, followed closely by a pair of guards.

"He escaped, even though he was surrounded by twenty thousand soldiers," said one of the men.

The other replied, "Don't worry. I've set up an impenetrable encirclement, blocking Liang Prefecture and the northeast roads. Unless he grows wings, he won't be able to cross the Xianbei Mountains."

"I told you handing him over to those people wasn't a good idea. He fought beyond the Great Wall for many years; he's too familiar with the terrain. Once he enters the forest, we'll never see him again!"

"We've made our move. There's no turning back now. The emperor has grown old; he ignores government affairs. And with the fourth prince so sickly... Even if he were to return, we could still charge him with neglect of duty. Don't tell me you've lost your nerve, General Zhao?"

"You—!"

This General Zhao, as he was called, wore a military uniform; his name was Zhao Kui, and he was a cornerstone of Southern Chen's government as well as the commander in chief of their military. The man walking with him wore an official's purple robe. He was a senior minister of the first rank, a man of significant

CHAPTER FOUR

status. The candlelight threw their shadows onto the stone spirit screen outside the corridor; after the brief exchange, they both fell silent. Behind them, the two guards followed with arms folded, unspeaking.

The guard on the left sported a White Tiger tattoo on his neck and wore a bamboo hat pulled low to cover the upper half of his face. The curve of his mouth peeked out as if he was smiling.

The guard on the right was tall, at least six feet, and every part of his body was hidden save for his eyes. He wore gloves and a cloak, and his face was covered by a mask. Above it, his gaze, sharp and sinister, swept over his surroundings—an automatic awareness.

"We must send someone to intercept him immediately," Zhao Kui said, his voice clipped. "He's in hiding while we are out in the open. If we delay too long, something could change, and that will mean more trouble for us."

"We can't mobilize troops beyond Yubi Pass. All we can do now is wait for him to show himself," the official replied.

Zhao Kui sighed. "If he takes refuge in Liao and returns with troops behind him, I'm afraid it will complicate things."

"The emperor of Liao will not lend him troops," the official said. "We have already settled upon a plan with the Southern Court. He will not survive the journey to Shangjing."

"You think too little of him." Zhao Kui turned to face the dark, rain-soaked courtyard, the gray hair at his temples damp as he shifted toward the official and continued, "There's a mongrel working for Li Jianhong, a man of mixed Xianbei and Han descent. I don't know who he is or where he came from; I suspect he's the one you've been looking for all this time. That Xianbei mutt's movements are enigmatic, and nobody knows his name. He was the last pawn Li Jianhong had hidden."

"If he's as you describe, I imagine Wu Du and Changliu-jun here would like to meet him. After all, there aren't many in this world worthy of being their rival," the official said. He turned to the guards: "Have you ever heard of him?"

The masked guard, Changliu-jun, was first to reply. "I know of him, though I don't know his name. Some call him the Nameless Assassin. He has a history of misdeeds and a reputation for being difficult to control; I'd be surprised if he obeys Li Jianhong's orders."

"What misdeeds?" Zhao Kui asked.

"He betrayed his sect, killed his master and his father, and turned on his fellow disciples. He is ruthlessly cruel, devoid of humanity, and never spares anyone," Changliu-jun said. "If you've heard the phrase 'the Chilling Edge seals throats in one strike'—that's him."

"That doesn't seem out of the ordinary for an assassin," the official said.

"A fatal strike to the throat," Changliu-jun said in a deep voice. "That means he doesn't listen to anyone's explanations. An assassin's duty is to kill, but not without cause; even if he killed the wrong person, the Nameless Assassin wouldn't so much as blink."

"But if I remember correctly," the official said, "Li Jianhong still carries the Guardian of the Realm. As long as he holds this blade, this assassin must obey him."

"Even if Li Jianhong has the Guardian, he must be able to bear its weight to command others," Changliu-jun replied.

"Forget it," Zhao Kui replied. The silence stretched until he said at last, "Wu Du."

The guard in the bamboo hat murmured in acknowledgment.

"Set out tonight," Zhao Kui said. "Don't stop until you locate Li Jianhong. When you find him, wait to act—I will send someone to you. After this mission is complete, bring his sword and his head to me."

The corner of Wu Du's mouth lifted slightly. He cupped his hands, bowed, and was gone.

A short time later, a carriage rattled out of the alley beyond the back gate of the general's estate. The wet stone of the road reflected distant lights.

"Have you seen that man's blade, Chilling Edge, before?" the official asked from within the carriage.

"All those who have seen Chilling Edge are dead," Changliu-jun replied from the driver's seat. He seemed to consider saying more—then he cracked his whip and turned back toward the road.

"From what you've seen..." The official reclined on the carriage's brocade couch and asked, casually, "How does Wu Du compare to this Nameless Assassin?"

"Wu Du has concerns, but the Nameless Assassin has none," Changliu-jun replied. "Wu Du is too competitive, and he hates losing. The Nameless Assassin has nothing to lose."

"Nothing to lose?" the official repeated.

"Only those with no one and nothing to lose are worthy of being assassins," Changliu-jun said calmly. "If you intend to take a life, you must sacrifice your own first. But once love enters the picture, an assassin will begin to cherish his life—he'll be afraid to die, and then he will be defeated. It's said the Nameless Assassin has no family, and he doesn't kill for fame or reward. Perhaps killing is just a hobby for him. Compared to Wu Du, he would be at a slight advantage."

"And what about between you and Wu Du?" the official asked.

"I hope to exchange blows with him at least once."

"A pity you will never have the opportunity," the official said elegantly.

Changliu-jun did not reply.

"And what about between you and Li Jianhong?" the man asked, his tone still casual.

"Whoa!" Changliu-jun called to the horses. When the carriage came to a halt, he lifted the curtain to allow the official to step down. Hanging outside the estate where they'd stopped was a lantern with a surname printed on it: *Mu*.

They'd arrived at the residence of the prime minister of Southern Chen—Mu Kuangda.

"If I, Wu Du, the Nameless Assassin, and Zheng Yan were to band together," the masked man replied, returning to the prime minister's earlier question, "then we might be a match for His Highness the third prince."

Under the bright morning sun, snowy Shangjing looked like a gilded city—and Qionghua House, a paradise. A servant girl brought breakfast and said, "My lord, Madam is waiting to speak with you after your meal."

"Tell her not to wait," Lang Junxia replied. "I have business to attend to this morning; I'll be on my way after breakfast. Please send her my thanks."

When the servant had gone, Duan Ling asked, "Are we going out?"

Lang Junxia nodded. "Just don't speak too much while we're outside."

Duan Ling agreed that he wouldn't. He realized he had probably interrupted Lang Junxia the night before, but as he didn't know what his guardian had been doing in the other room, he didn't dare bring it up. Fortunately, Lang Junxia seemed to have

CHAPTER FOUR

forgotten all about it. After breakfast, he and Duan Ling left through the back alley once more.

A carriage waited outside. The curtains were lifted, revealing Ding Zhi's lovely face. "You've only stayed one night. Where are you going now? Didn't you say you wouldn't leave again? Come ride with me."

Lang Junxia held Duan Ling's hand, hesitating in the face of her invitation, but Duan Ling pulled at him—wanting just as much to be on their way.

"We have business elsewhere," Lang Junxia said. "I wouldn't want to intrude."

Ding Zhi gave up, unable to sway him, and Lang Junxia took Duan Ling to the city center. The sights he saw along the way were dizzying in their grandness. Shangjing was a hub of trade for the north; forty-one Hu tribes from three different cities beyond the Great Wall all traveled to Shangjing to buy and sell their wares. Adding to the bustle was a large party of diplomatic envoys from Southern Chen, come to congratulate the empress dowager of Liao on her upcoming birthday. A dazzling array of items filled the market stalls: sugar figurines, antique treasures, precious medicinal herbs, hairpins, cosmetics, and much more. Duan Ling wanted to eat everything he saw, but the donkey-meat rolls he'd previously coveted in Runan were what he most wished to taste.

Lang Junxia led Duan Ling to a clothier and ordered the boy two sets of new robes, then found a calligraphy stall and requested the four treasures of the study—inkstone, ink, brush, and paper.

"Do you know how to write?" Duan Ling asked him.

The shopkeeper brought out an inkstone from Duan Prefecture, an ink stick from Hui Prefecture, an ink brush from Hu Prefecture, and fine paper from Xuan Prefecture.

"These are for you," Lang Junxia said. "You have to learn how to read and write before it's too late."

"You have a good eye, Gongzi." The shopkeeper grinned. "These are quality items from the merchants up north who came through only two years ago. The paper hasn't fully arrived though; if you want twelve stacks, I'll need to go collect them from another store."

"We Khitan aren't so picky," Lang Junxia said with a casual air. "It's just for good luck. No need to go now; please just deliver it to Ming Academy before the sun sets tomorrow."

"This is too expensive," Duan Ling said, feeling a twinge at how much Lang Junxia had spent.

"Be diligent in your studies, and success and glory will follow," Lang Junxia replied. "The ability to read and write is a priceless treasure."

"Am I going to school?" Duan Ling asked.

When he had lived in Runan, he had been jealous of the children who attended school. He'd never thought he would be able to do so, and he was overwhelmed by gratitude. He stopped in place, gazing up at Lang Junxia.

"What's wrong?" Lang Junxia asked.

Duan Ling's emotions were hard to put into words. "How am I to repay you?"

Lang Junxia looked back at Duan Ling with both pity and kindness. After a moment, he forced a smile and answered seriously, "Going to school and studying are merely what you should be doing. You don't need to repay me. In the future, there will be no shortage of people you will repay instead."

After buying his supplies for school—and eating plenty of food in between—Duan Ling received a hand warmer and an embroidered cloth pouch from Lang Junxia. He placed Duan Ling's jade pendant inside the bag, then looped its red string over his neck and tucked the pouch into his robes next to his underclothes.

"Remember," Lang Junxia warned. "You can't ever lose this."

Lang Junxia led Duan Ling away from the bustling city center and turned onto a long, quiet street. An old building with white walls and a black roof, snow piled in the dips of the tiles, faced the street, simple yet elegant. Snowy pine and cypress trees stood in the courtyard, and the sound of children's voices carried into the street.

Duan Ling perked up when he heard it. Since he'd started traveling with Lang Junxia, he hadn't seen any kids around his age. Unlike when he used to run around in the mud in Runan, he'd been well-behaved the entire journey; he wondered what the children in Shangjing did for fun.

Lang Junxia entered the courtyard, and Duan Ling followed. It had been swept clean of snow, and three boys, each nearly a head taller than him, stood around ten steps away. The boys were throwing arrows into a nearby pot. When they heard newcomers approaching, they looked up and saw Duan Ling, who nervously edged closer to Lang Junxia.

Without pausing, Lang Junxia walked on to the inner hall, where an old man with a head of white hair and a white beard sat drinking tea.

"Wait here for a bit," Lang Junxia said.

Duan Ling, wearing one of his new robes—this one an indigo blue—stepped to the side of the corridor to wait while Lang Junxia entered the room on his own. He could hear low voices from inside. After a distracted moment, he spotted another young man emerging from behind a courtyard pillar; he stood in front of the school's large bronze bell to observe Duan Ling. Gradually, several more children around eight or nine years old gathered in the courtyard, all of them staring at Duan Ling and murmuring among themselves. One moved as if to come speak to him, but the tallest boy stopped him and stepped forward under the bell.

"Who are you?" the tall boy asked.

Inside his own head, Duan Ling answered, *My name is Duan Ling, and my father is Duan Sheng...* But he didn't say anything aloud. He had a feeling these boys were looking for trouble. Supposing that Duan Ling was shy, the other children laughed, and though he didn't know what exactly they were laughing at, it upset him nonetheless.

The tall boy came forward. He was holding an iron rod, and he tapped it against his opposite palm. "Where are you from?" he asked.

When Duan Ling tried to back away, the boy set a hand on his shoulder and yanked Duan Ling toward him. He pressed the iron rod beneath Duan Ling's chin, tipping his head back slightly, and teased, "How old are you, anyway?"

Duan Ling wished he could shake him off, but instead he stood frozen for a long beat. When he finally pushed the young man away, he didn't dare flee—Lang Junxia told him to stay put. The other boy was a full head taller than Duan Ling and dressed in the northern style, in a coat lined with wolf fur and a fox-tail hat. He had black eyes with a hint of star-blue, and his skin was a healthy brown. Standing before Duan Ling, he looked like a wolf cub on the cusp of gangly adolescence.

"Huh," the tall boy said, reaching for the red string around Duan Ling's neck. "What's this?"

Duan Ling dodged his hand.

"Come here." He had guessed by now that Duan Ling was holding back; it felt as if he was punching cotton, all soft give—and that was boring. He patted Duan Ling's face. "I asked you a question. Does your mouth work?"

Duan Ling gazed at the tall boy with fierce eyes, hands balling into fists. In the other boy's estimation, Duan Ling was a spoiled little dandy from a rich family; surely he'd be crying for mercy after a single blow. But before he hit him, he wanted to tease him just a little more.

"Seriously, what is it?" the tall boy repeated, grabbing the cord around Duan Ling's neck again. He leaned close to Duan Ling's ear, reaching to pull the cloth pouch free, and whispered, "Was the man who went in just now your father, or your brother? Or is he a little househusband your family raised for you to marry? Do you think he's bowing and begging the headmaster?"

The gathered children began to laugh again. Duan Ling, afraid the pouch holding his pendant would tear, trailed along as the boy yanked him, holding tightly to the red string.

"Hup!" the tall boy commanded, leading him by the neck. "Look, you're a donkey!"

The children laughed louder, and Duan Ling's face flushed hot. Before the boy could say another word, Duan Ling's fist flew into his field of vision, followed immediately by the blinding pain of a broken nose. The force of the blow knocked the boy right onto his back.

Chaos ensued. Nose bleeding freely, the tall boy rushed for Duan Ling as if to lift him. Duan Ling bent at the knees and tackled his opponent, arms around his waist. The impact threw them both from the corridor into the garden. The children cheered raucously and formed a loose circle to watch them wrestling in the snow.

Duan Ling took a punch to the face, followed by a solid kick to the chest that put him flat on his back, seeing stars. The tall boy jumped astride his chest and began beating him, the blood from his broken nose pouring down on Duan Ling's face and neck. Duan Ling's vision went dark beneath his fists. He gathered enough strength to grab the other boy's ankle and yanked, throwing him off to one side.

Like a mad dog, Duan Ling pounced and bit down hard on the boy's hand, shocking the circle of spectators. The boy screamed in pain, grabbed Duan Ling by the collar, and slammed his head against the bronze bell.

With a resonant *dong*, Duan Ling collapsed to the ground, his whole head buzzing.

5

"Stop it! Stop it, now!" a harried voice cried.

The noise had finally caught Lang Junxia's attention, and he rushed into the courtyard like a gale of wind. The headmaster was right behind him, bellowing, "Stop!"

The children immediately scattered, fleeing behind the wall. The tall boy tried to make a break for it too, but only took a few steps before the headmaster stormed over and grabbed him. Lang Junxia paled at the sight of Duan Ling sprawled on the ground; he hurriedly picked him up to check his injuries.

"Why didn't you call for someone?!" Lang Junxia was furious.

Duan Ling's stubbornness was astonishing. If he'd shouted, Lang Junxia would have realized something was wrong, yet he'd remained silent throughout. Lang Junxia had assumed the children were only being so noisy because they were playing with a ball.

Duan Ling's left eye had begun to swell. He looked pitiable, but gave Lang Junxia a small smile.

An hour later, Lang Junxia had cleaned the blood and dirt from Duan Ling's face, hands, and robes as best he could.

"Serve the headmaster some tea," Lang Junxia ordered. "Go."

Duan Ling had just been beaten up; his hands shook around the teacup, which clinked and rattled against the lid.

"If you intend to join my Ming Academy, you'll have to learn to control that temper of yours," the headmaster said evenly. "And if you can't relinquish this violence, I will show you a path. Head to the Northern Court, and you'll find your place there."

The headmaster gazed steadily at Duan Ling, but didn't take the tea he offered. Duan Ling held the cup for a while, unsure what he should say or do. At last, since the headmaster wouldn't accept it, he set the teacup on the table, accidentally splashing tea onto the headmaster's sleeves in the process.

The old man's expression darkened immediately; he barked, "How dare you!"

"Headmaster." Lang Junxia hastily dropped to one knee. "I failed to teach him properly; he doesn't understand the rules."

Duan Ling had suffered enough humiliation today already; the other boy's contemptuous words still rang in his ears. He pulled at Lang Junxia. "Get up."

But in a rare display of upset, Lang Junxia commanded Duan Ling, "Kneel! Kneel right now!"

Duan Ling had no choice; he knelt. The sight seemed to mollify the headmaster slightly. He said coolly, "If he doesn't understand the rules, then teach him properly before you bring him back. Whether an official's child or the prince of a nation, no student can say that they don't know and obey the rules here!"

Lang Junxia remained silent, and so did Duan Ling. The headmaster's mouth had gone dry from speaking, so he finally drank some of the tea Duan Ling had served him. "Every child who attends this school is treated equally. If you fight again, you will be expelled."

"Thank you, Headmaster," Lang Junxia said with relief.

He made Duan Ling bow three times, which Duan Ling did with some reluctance, before leading him away from the headmaster's rooms.

Passing through the front courtyard, they saw the tall boy kneeling in front of the wall, reflecting on his error. Duan Ling glanced over at him, and the young man turned his head and stared right back; both their eyes were filled with resentment.

The pair returned to Qionghua House, where Lang Junxia began applying medicine to Duan Ling's face. He frowned. "Why didn't you say anything, or call for help, instead of fighting?"

"He hit me first," Duan Ling said.

"I'm not blaming you," Lang Junxia replied as he dampened the towel. "But you couldn't have beaten him. Why didn't you run?"

"Oh," was all Duan Ling could think to say.

"If someone provokes you again, you need to think carefully before you act," Lang Junxia continued patiently. "If you can beat them, then fight. If you can't, run away, and I'll get even with them later. You can't risk your life in a fight. Understand?"

"Okay," Duan Ling said. For a moment, the room was quiet. Then Duan Ling asked, "Do you know how to fight? Teach me."

Lang Junxia put the towel down and silently gazed at Duan Ling. Finally, he said, "One day, there will be many who will mock you— and a great many more who will want to kill you. Even if you learn to fight, are you going to kill them each one by one?"

Duan Ling didn't really understand, and looked at Lang Junxia in confusion.

"You're to learn how to read, and you're to learn the ways of the world. With these, in the future, there will be millions of methods for killing. How long would it take using only your fists? If you want revenge, study hard."

Another brief silence fell between them.

"Do you understand?" Lang Junxia asked. Duan Ling didn't—not really—but he nodded anyway. Lang Junxia tapped the back of his hand. "Never repeat what you did today."

Once again, all Duan Ling said was, "Oh."

"You'll move into the academy tonight," Lang Junxia said. "I'll take you later this evening. You can buy or borrow whatever else you might need."

Duan Ling's heart lurched in his chest. Lang Junxia was all he had. Nobody had ever treated him so well in his life; it was as if he'd finally found his proper place—and now they had to separate?

"But what about you?" Duan Ling asked.

"I have other matters to attend to," Lang Junxia said. "I've already discussed the schedule with the headmaster: I'll pick you up from school on the first and fifteenth of the month, and you'll be given two days' holiday. I'll review your homework, and if you've done everything, I'll take you out to have fun."

"I won't go!" Duan Ling blurted out.

Lang Junxia stopped what he was doing. His eyes met Duan Ling's, a deeply serious expression on his face. Though he said nothing, his aura pressed on Duan Ling—an aura of absolute authority.

Duan Ling hung his head in defeat, holding back tears.

"You're a good boy, and you'll do great things in the future," Lang Junxia said, calm and steady. "After leaving Runan and Shangjing... there will be no more hardships for you. Even if some arise, they won't compare to the past. You're just going off to study; what's there to cry over?"

Lang Junxia watched Duan Ling's expression as he spoke, slightly confused, as if he couldn't understand the boy's fear and sadness.

Throughout their journey he'd learned and thought many things about Duan Ling, but still this child managed to surprise him. He might be naughty at times, but he was never unruly in front of Lang Junxia. Compared to spending years in a dark woodshed in Runan, Lang Junxia imagined that the world Duan Ling was now entering would be peaceful and comfortable. He was only going to school, so why did he look like he was being sent into the wolf's den? Duan Ling's disobedience seemed merely a child's whim to him— when nobody pampered the boy, he was like a half-withered grass, but once someone paid him attention, he became spoiled.

After much consideration, the only bit of wisdom Lang Junxia could think to impart to him was this: "Only those who endure hardship can become truly great."

In the evening, snow fell again. Duan Ling was no longer interested in attending school, but he didn't have a choice. He felt as if nobody had ever asked him what *he* wanted since the day he was born. Lang Junxia was kind on the outside, but his insides were steel-solid; he spoke sparingly, but once someone defied him, his aura shifted and he became like a wolf opening its eyes in the quiet, dark night.

The second Duan Ling even thought of disobeying, that powerful aura would rear up, smothering his soul under its weight until he gave in. Lang Junxia was unbudging on both the big and small matters of everyday life.

The next morning, Lang Junxia bought Duan Ling a few last daily necessities, then sealed and delivered the money for tuition to Ming Academy. He entered a school building on the fringes of the complex from the east.

"I asked Ding Zhi to have a friend look after you for a bit," Lang Junxia said. "High-ranking officials often drink at Qionghua House. She'll have someone warn that Mongol boy you fought with. I doubt he'll come looking for trouble again."

Servants had cleaned and lit a fire in the courtyard. The stove stood beside one of the walls, and though it wasn't quite as warm as Qionghua House, it was still comfortably toasty. Duan Ling was already familiar with the dining hall. Two meals were served per day, and students should gather for them at the toll of the bell. He took the bowl and chopsticks Lang Junxia had bought for him and followed along to his new room.

Duan Ling sat at the little table, and Lang Junxia bent over to make the bed for him.

"You must keep the jade pendant with you always," Lang Junxia reminded him for the umpteenth time. "Hide it under your pillow when you sleep, and wear it when you're awake. Don't lose it."

Duan Ling said nothing, but his eyes were red at the rims. Lang Junxia pretended not to see.

The four treasures of the study had also arrived, and the Ming Academy staff accepted them for him. After he finished making the bed, Lang Junxia settled down across from Duan Ling. He was the only one staying in this remote courtyard, and as the sky darkened, servants came by to light the lamps. Under their warm glow, Lang Junxia sat with the still, quiet beauty of a sculpture, while Duan Ling simply sat in a daze.

Only once the school bell had rung three times did Lang Junxia get to his feet. "Go, it's time for your meal. Don't forget your bowl and chopsticks."

Picking them up as instructed, Duan Ling wordlessly followed Lang Junxia back toward the dining hall. When they reached the footpath out front, Lang Junxia said, "I'm leaving now. I'll come and pick you up on the first of next month."

Duan Ling stood stock-still.

"Go on and eat," Lang Junxia urged him. "Remember what I told you. When the bell rings, you must get up—early and without delay. For the first few days, a servant will guide you."

Lang Junxia motioned Duan Ling up the path to the dining hall, but the boy didn't move. They stood facing one another in a painful silence. Duan Ling, his new bowl and chopsticks in hand, opened his mouth as if to finally speak, but nothing came out.

In the end, it was Lang Junxia who turned away first; as soon as he began walking down the path, Duan Ling followed.

Lang Junxia glanced back at him, then quickened his steps, not wanting to stay any longer. Duan Ling chased him all the way to the back gate of the school, still holding his bowl, where the guard stopped him. Duan Ling stood just inside the gate, tears welling in his eyes as he gazed after Lang Junxia.

The sight made Lang Junxia's head hurt. He turned again and said, "Go back! Or I'm not coming on the first of the month!"

Duan Ling stood, forlorn, on the other side of the gate. Lang Junxia felt for him, but knew he shouldn't stay longer. With a few quick strides, he disappeared from sight.

The old man guarding the gate said comfortingly, "Study hard and learn, so you can become an official in the future. Go back, now."

Duan Ling turned away, wiping his tears as he walked. The yellow lanterns of the school were lit against the evening darkness. After a few turns, he no longer recognized the way back and sat down, dejected, in the corridor.

Fortunately, the headmaster and a few of the teachers soon passed by where he was seated, crying, in the heavy snow.

"What are you doing there?!" The headmaster didn't recognize Duan Ling at first, and angrily continued, "Why are you so weak and sniveling? What kind of behavior is this?!"

Duan Ling jumped to his feet, afraid of upsetting the headmaster again and making Lang Junxia angry too.

"Which family is this child from?" a teacher asked.

The headmaster studied Duan Ling for a moment before he remembered. "Ah—the boy who started fighting the minute he arrived. You weren't so delicate when you were brawling, young man. Follow the teachers."

Duan Ling followed the group of teachers all the way to the dining hall. By the time he arrived, the other students had almost finished, and the table they shared was a mess of half-eaten dishes. The servants brought Duan Ling his meal, which he polished off in a flash before setting his bowl and chopsticks down. Another servant took them away to be washed; his name had been engraved on both so they wouldn't be lost.

Duan Ling returned to his room for the night, alone.

From somewhere nearby, he could hear the sound of a flute.

The instrument's melodic voice floated by, like a parting song from the dusky city of Runan. Everything felt dreamlike—in the month since Duan Ling had come to the north, he'd thought he'd forgotten all about the Duan clan. Lang Junxia, that steady presence by his side, was evidence of the start of his new life.

But now, alone in the quiet dimness of his school room, listening to the sound of crackling firewood beneath his window and the faraway flute, Duan Ling didn't dare close his eyes. He was afraid that when he opened them, he would be back in the dark woodshed, bruised and fearful. The nightmare seemed to wait in the shadows of the room, ready for him to fall asleep so it could whisk him back to Runan, thousands of li away, the moment he lost consciousness.

Yet strangely, the flute's song held the nightmare at bay, producing countless images in his mind's eye of floating peach blossoms to accompany him to sleep.

Lang Junxia stood under the eaves, his cloak blanketed in snow.

After waiting silently for a while, he fished out a letter from his robes—never delivered—and read it with a frown.

Xiaowan:

Greet this letter as if you greeted me. As proof of its authenticity, my messenger bears the token you did not accept that year.

Someone in Southern Chen has betrayed me, and the situation has become urgent. To prevent your being taken hostage by assassins sent by the court, please follow my messenger north. I will meet you in Shangjing before the third day of the first month.

Hong

Midnight arrived, and with it, the fourth day of the first month. There had been no sign of Li Jianhong.

Lang Junxia returned to his room in Qionghua House and packed his things. He changed into dark robes for stealthier night travel and threw on a black cloak.

"Where are you going now?" Ding Zhi asked from the doorway.

"I have business," Lang Junxia replied.

"I've already arranged for someone to watch over that child," Ding Zhi said. "The city guard captain's younger brother will take care of him."

"Buy me a house. No need to clean it." Lang Junxia placed an appropriate banknote under the paperweight.

"When will you be back?" Ding Zhi asked.

"The fifteenth."

Ding Zhi stepped into the room. She seemed to hesitate before asking, "The child you brought here. Who are his parents?"

Lang Junxia stood tall and upright near the door, cloaked all in black with a mask over his face, which he stared at Ding Zhi from within. His eyes were clear and bright. Lightly, he pressed his thumb forward against the hilt of his sword; the blade flashed cold in the lamplight.

"The news from the south is that the emperor of Chen has stripped Li Jianhong of his military power," Ding Zhi continued. "Wu Du set out north with eighteen assassins from the shadow squad overnight, most likely to track him down. I wondered, since you didn't follow Li Jianhong and instead sought out this child…"

Lang Junxia slowly raised his left hand, holding the sword, and Ding Zhi fell silent.

"Who else knows of this?" Lang Junxia asked, pressing the sheathed sword to her neck. A few inches of sharp blade peeked out near the hilt, gleaming against her throat.

"Just me." Ding Zhi raised her brows slightly, lifted her chin, and looked into Lang Junxia's eyes behind his mask. "If you kill me now, you can protect this secret forever."

Lang Junxia pondered this without moving, sword to her neck. Then he withdrew his hand, walking past Ding Zhi with a last sidelong glance.

"Watch out for Wu Du," Ding Zhi said softly.

Lang Junxia said nothing more. He strode into the back courtyard, swung onto his horse's back, and galloped away into the night.

When Duan Ling next opened his eyes, the sun had risen. The bell rang, each peal more urgent than the last. A servant outside his door said, "Duan-shaoye,[5] it's time for morning reading. Please come with me."

Duan Ling had neither suffered through nightmares nor awoken back in the woodshed in Runan. He tossed the previous day's worries aside. Per Lang Junxia's instructions, he brushed his teeth and washed his face in a hurry, then joined the children in their morning reading class.

---

5   An address used for the young master of an affluent household.

6

"IN THE BEGINNING, the heaven was black and the earth was yellow; the universe was chaos…"

"Gold is produced from the waters of Li River; jade is from the caves of Mount Kunlun…"

"Agriculture is the basis of governance, from spring sowing to fall harvest…"

Duan Ling sat in the last row in the back, nodding his head along with the other children and trying his best to follow their lip movements. Although he had no real idea what text he was reciting, as luck would have it, he'd heard these lines before while eavesdropping outside a private school in Runan, and the syllables rolled easily off his tongue. Before long, the words began to cohere in his memory, and he was able to follow the rhythm.

After morning recitation ended, the teacher handed out yellow primers with pictures and text for teaching reading. Because Duan Ling had started school late, the stack of materials on his desk was thicker than most. He had difficulty recognizing the characters, and after learning some of them, he found himself distracted, wondering if he'd see the boy he'd fought with yesterday.

Ming Academy had been built by the Han people who'd surrendered and remained in the north after Liao's southern expansion. The school was divided into three areas: the Hall of Enlightenment, the Hall of Ink, and the Chamber of Tomes. Children would first enter the Hall of Enlightenment, where they learned the basics of reading and writing; once they had conquered that and passed the examination, they would advance to the Hall of Ink, where they studied more complex texts. The final hall, the Chamber of Tomes, taught students the Khitan, Han, and Tangut languages, how to properly write essays, and the practice of the six arts: ceremony, music, archery, chariotry, calligraphy, and mathematics. Once there was nothing left to learn within the Chamber of Tomes, the student departed Ming Academy and entered Biyong Academy, under the Southern Court's Privy Council, to study the Five Classics and take the imperial examination to become an official of the empire.

As such, the collected residents of Ming Academy were of differing scholastic levels. The tall boy Duan Ling had encountered the previous day was currently a student of the Hall of Ink, and thus it wasn't until lunch that Duan Ling caught sight of him. The boy put one foot up on the bench and glared at Duan Ling as he ate from an iron bowl. Nobody dared sit next to him.

A Han boy scooted over to Duan Ling's side. "You're Duan Ling, right?"

Duan Ling looked at him carefully. He was only a little older than Duan Ling, but he seemed much more mature. His robes were luxurious, with a golden crow embroidered on his collar and a lapis lazuli brooch on his right lapel. His eyebrows were dark and thick as ink, his red lips and neat white teeth the picture of health. In short, he looked exactly like a noble young master.

"How...did you know?" Duan Ling asked.

"Someone asked my brother to have me look after you and make sure you're not being bullied," the boy whispered back.

"Who's your brother?" Duan Ling said.

The boy didn't answer, instead pointing over at the young man Duan Ling had fought with. "He's from the Borjigin clan, but his father still has to work like a dog for the Han clan. If he causes you any more trouble, go to that guy over there and report him."

As he spoke, he pointed to another, older boy across the room who was surrounded by other students. The young man was chubby, with a kindly face and a cheerful demeanor. He wasn't handsome by any means, but plenty of the other children were following him around.

"Just tell him, 'Han-gongzi, the kid from the Borjigin family keeps bothering me,'" the boy told Duan Ling, "and then ask him to help you."

Duan Ling didn't entirely understand, but he sensed the boy's good intentions. The boy asked, "So, is the official in your family from the Northern Administration or the Southern Administration?"

The only answer Duan Ling could give was, "I don't know."

The boy followed up with another question: "Han or Khitan?"

"Han. My father is Duan Sheng; he does business in Shangjing," Duan Ling replied.

The other boy nodded, understanding. "Ah, merchants. I'm from the Cai clan, and my name is Cai Yan. My brother is Cai Wen; he's the captain of the Shangjing city guard. I'm Han, and Han-gongzi over there is also Han. If you get bullied again, come find us."

Having said his piece, Cai Yan took his bowl and left without further explanation. He wasn't especially worried about Duan Ling; he was simply completing a task his elder brother had asked of him.

Duan Ling finished eating and went back to his room to nap until the school bell rang again in the afternoon. Winter days made the students languid. Afternoon classes were for learning writing, but the warm fire in the lesson room made everyone drowsy; a few students took their writing paper for a pillow and slumped over, drooling.

"Spread out the characters as you write them," the headmaster droned on. "Don't be stingy with paper—"

Now that the first day of school was underway, many of Duan Ling's worries flew to the back of his mind; he cherished the hard-earned opportunity he'd been given and concentrated on his writing practice.

When the headmaster passed by, he smacked the sleeping child next to him on the face with a ruler. The boy's cheek immediately began to swell, and he burst into tears as if a dam had opened. The headmaster snatched him up by the collar and made him stand in the corridor as punishment. Duan Ling shuddered and gazed after the crying boy, no longer daring to show the slightest hint of fatigue.

As the days went by, the things Duan Ling had worried would happen did not come to pass. The young man he'd fought with didn't try to get revenge; Cai Yan and the others didn't treat him any differently. Everything at Ming Academy was done by the rules, organized and straightforward. Nobody asked prying questions about his origins or why he'd enrolled at the academy; his presence seemed unremarkable, as if he was simply one of the pine trees in the courtyard—as if he had been there all along.

Every evening after classes finished, Duan Ling tossed and turned alone in his bed, remembering the flute music he'd heard on the first night. He'd never heard it again since. The melody had fluttered up and down across the wind like withered flowers blowing in from the south, carrying a touch of melancholic longing. Spring would have arrived in Runan by now, right? When Duan Ling recalled the flute's song, it reminded him of the verses he'd learned from the headmaster:

In the beginning, the heaven was black and the earth was yellow; the universe was chaos.

The sun and moon wax and wane, the stars are scattered.

Winter arrives and summer takes its leave; autumn harvests become winter stores.

Excess days the leap year forms, yin and yang tuned to the scale of twelve...

Over the course of the morning recitations, while many students' heads bobbed drowsily as they held the *Thousand Character Classic*, Duan Ling had learned to recognize most of the characters in only half a month. Today, the teacher pointed out a sentence with his ruler. Duan Ling recited it, and the teacher pointed to another phrase; Duan Ling recited that correctly as well, and the teacher moved his ruler again.

"What character is this?" the teacher asked.

Duan Ling kept his posture straight and answered, "*Jun*, as in ruler."

"And this one?" the teacher continued.

Finally, Duan Ling reached a character he didn't know; the teacher smacked his palm with the ruler. He dared not make a sound, even though the center of his palm burned sharply.

"The character is *bi*, as in jade," the teacher said, walking down the rows of students with his hands behind his back. "As in Master He's jade; the *bi* from Yubi Pass; a gentleman as dignified as jade. Next."

Duan Ling rubbed his hands together to soothe the sting, then pressed his left palm against the cool porcelain wall of the ink plate. The teacher tested them all, and punished a good number with the ruler. By the time the bell rang, the sky had gone dusky; the teacher said, "Class dismissed."

The students stood from their desks and began chattering right away. It was the first of the month: the day students returned home for a brief break. Carriages and whickering horses had gathered outside the Ming Academy gates, the crowd so dense that wading through it was difficult. The children looked around eagerly, as if waiting for a festival to begin. The first few days of school, Duan Ling had only looked forward to Lang Junxia picking him up, and the waiting had been torturous—but as the holiday approached, his excitement had subsided to a background thrum.

The porter called out names, one by one, and students were released to their guardians. Many children tried climbing onto the fence for a better view, but the teacher with his disciplinary ruler shooed them away.

Duan Ling stood on the steps. He raised himself onto tiptoe and peered outward, as far as he could see. With Lang Junxia's height, he normally stood out in a crowd, easy to spot—but Duan Ling didn't see him. Perhaps he'd been delayed by the alley traffic. Lang Junxia usually rode; naturally it would take longer for him to make his way in than those on foot.

"Yuan clan—Yuan-shaoye."

"Lin clan—"

The porter called names, and the children left, handing over their name plaques. As the crowd of students in the outer courtyard dwindled steadily, Duan Ling wondered again if Lang Junxia was stuck somewhere.

"Cai clan—Cai-shaoye."

Cai Yan emerged from the gathered students and nodded back to them. Duan Ling was still looking for Lang Junxia when Cai Yan caught his eye and waved. "Where's your father?"

"He'll be here soon." Duan Ling didn't bother explaining that the one picking him up wasn't his father. Cai Yan left through the front gates, where a young man riding a horse pulled him up and sat Cai Yan before him in the saddle. Duan Ling gazed enviously at the pair for a moment; the young man returned his look briefly before he turned and galloped away.

After half an hour, only a dozen or so students remained in the courtyard, and the carriages and horses left in the alley had thinned considerably. By the time the porter called out the last name, Duan Ling and the boy who'd rung his head against the courtyard bell were the only two left. Duan Ling sat down on the steps, tired of standing, while the other boy shifted from foot to foot, leaning against the gate so he could watch the street. Finally, the headmaster and teachers, now changed into casual clothes, passed Duan Ling and the other boy on their way out. Both parties bowed to each other with cupped hands, and the teachers opened their umbrellas and headed home for the break.

The sunset's orange glow shaded toward night's dark purple, casting the pine trees' shadows on the walls. The porter closed the front gates.

"Leave your name plaques here," he said. "If someone comes for you later, I'll send for you."

The other boy handed over his plaque, but he didn't leave immediately. He stepped to the side and lingered a final moment before turning to go. Duan Ling read the engraving on his plaque: *Borjigin Batu.*

"What do we do now?" Duan Ling asked the porter, anxious. He looked around for the boy named Batu, but he'd already disappeared.

"Go to the dining hall for your dinner," the porter replied. "Do whatever else you're supposed to do for the evening free time. If nobody comes to pick you up, take your bedding and sleep on the second floor of the library."

He had waited for nearly half a month, only for his hopes to be dashed. His disappointment was immeasurable. Deep down, though, he still believed Lang Junxia would come. After all, he'd never broken a promise to Duan Ling; he always delivered. Something must have delayed him.

Duan Ling returned to his room. He'd begun to sort out his things for the night when he heard the bell ringing in the front yard again. But there were no more classes today—he hurried to the courtyard and saw Batu's back from afar.

He understood, suddenly, that Batu wanted Duan Ling to come eat with him.

His childish grudge toward Batu had been largely forgotten; hatred came and went quickly for the young. Duan Ling no longer felt any hostility toward him, but rather some measure of sympathy.

For the two days of the break, five or six servants remained behind at Ming Academy. The kitchen staff prepared a large pot of stew, and several people—including the porter—lined up for food. Only two oil lamps burned in the dining hall, and only one table had been set. Duan Ling approached with his full bowl; seeing that there was no place for him to sit, Batu scooted aside to make room.

As Duan Ling hesitated, Batu finally spoke, impatient: "Sit down—I'm not going to hit you. Are you that scared?"

Duan Ling thought to himself, *Who's scared of you?* Perhaps he hadn't fully let go of their previous encounter—but it wasn't as if he could eat standing. He sat down next to Batu without another word.

What if Lang Junxia really didn't come for him—that night, or ever again? Duan Ling's anxiety increased with every minute. *Lang Junxia will definitely come,* he thought. Maybe Qionghua House had coaxed him to stay for dinner with their fine food and drink, so he couldn't leave on time.

Maybe he was drunk and would come for Duan Ling when he sobered up.

After dinner, Duan Ling returned to his room and his silent waiting. The stove fire had been extinguished to save charcoal during the break, and his room was as cold as ice. Duan Ling, unable to sit still, was pacing the room when he remembered that the porter said he was supposed to spend the night in the library. He realized there must be a fire there—he painstakingly rolled his quilt, shouldered it, and crossed the inner courtyard toward the library.

The servants had already arrived, settled and sleeping on the floor. There was a charcoal stove in the corner of the courtyard outside that was never extinguished, its pipe connected to the kitchen. Other pipes underground provided the heat required to prevent moisture from gathering in the library, which held the academy's collection of texts, and to keep the frost at bay, which would crack the bamboo slips and old scrolls, or shatter the ink sticks.

As soon as Duan Ling entered, a servant said to him, "Shaoye, you're a student; please go to the second floor."

Though the second floor was dark, it was very warm. The snow outside the window shone bright as day under the moonlight, and the scattered shadows of snowflakes dotted the translucent white window paper, creating a hazy glow. The tall bookshelves were wreathed in darkness, and a single lamp stood at the center of a wide wooden desk. By its light, Duan Ling could see that the shelves were stuffed with books, documents, and wooden slips. When the emperor of Liao had conquered the south, he'd plundered the Han capital—and because he greatly appreciated the written word, he'd transported their books and documents all the way to Shangjing, Zhongjing, and Xijing for storage.

In addition to these texts, there were original copies of works by the masters of previous dynasties. Before the Battle of Huai River, these books had been stored in the Imperial Academy of Southern Chen, where ordinary people couldn't access them. Now the dust of history had settled over the collection, dimly lit by the glow of a solitary lamp. How many holy souls of sages, from ancient times to the present, were scattered within this library's scrolls?

Batu had already spread his bedding beside the low desk. Duan Ling hesitated, unsure if he should too, but Batu didn't even glance his way—instead, he walked over to the nearest shelf and began flipping through the books. It seemed enemies truly were destined to meet on narrow roads. Although Duan Ling wasn't entirely comfortable around Batu, he didn't consider him an actual enemy. He imagined Batu felt the same. Both boys thought there was no real reason to be so cold to each other, but neither wished to be first to make peace.

Duan Ling spread his cotton-padded mattress on the other side of the wide desk with the lamp standing as a barrier between them. The desk provided a dividing line between their rival territories; they did not encroach upon one another. He, too, selected a book to pass the time while he waited for Lang Junxia. Because he was still learning to read, he found it laborious, and preferred books with illustrations. He ended up flipping through *Herbal Classics*, a record of medicines and insects with plenty of strange pictures. Duan Ling laughed a little as he read. When he looked up, he found Batu staring at him from across the desk.

Batu seemed even less interested in reading than Duan Ling. He fiddled with this, skimmed through that—several books were already piled up in front of him. He flipped through a few pages of every book before tossing it aside; he shifted his sitting position and scratched at his neck; finally, he shrugged off his top and tied his outer robe around his waist, leaving him shirtless. After another few minutes, he seemed to get cold and wrapped himself in his quilt. Head sticking out of the blanket, he looked like a scruffy street urchin.

After seeing all that, Duan Ling set aside his book as well. He yawned and lay his head down on the desk, drowsy. The sound of the night watchman's clapper echoed from a distant alley, audible over the wind and snow; it was hours past sunset, but Lang Junxia had not appeared.

Perhaps he wouldn't come tonight at all.

Duan Ling's chaotic thoughts raced, leapt, and turned on themselves. Lang Junxia had taken him from the Duan family more than a month ago. In his short time at the academy, Duan Ling had learned new things every day—but he still hadn't learned why Lang Junxia had come for him in the first place.

My name is Duan Ling, and my father is Duan Sheng. Duan Ling recited the words in his mind. Had Lang Junxia brought him to Shangjing because his father, Duan Sheng, asked him to? But if that was so, why hadn't his father come to see him? And the "business" Lang Junxia said he was attending to when he left—what business was that? *Perhaps to him, I'm not important—I'm no different from a cat or dog he had to place.* Maybe after Lang Junxia settled him down here, Duan Ling thought, he'd sent a letter to Duan Ling's father saying that he'd discharged his duty, and it didn't matter to him anymore whether Duan Ling was alive or dead.

Duan Ling tossed and turned in his bedding on the floor until his most despairing thought returned: What if Lang Junxia never came back?

Lang Junxia wasn't under any obligation to pick him up. They weren't related by blood, nor were they friends—all Duan Ling had was his word.

He reached into his robes and stroked the jade arc through its embroidered pouch. A strange bitterness surged in his heart, a fading light dragging him deeper into misery. Lang Junxia might have lied to him, like when the cook lied to him after his mother died, saying his father would come for him. After that, Duan Ling had waited for a long, long time—but his father never arrived. Maybe Lang Junxia was the same. He might have said those words just to comfort Duan Ling, but he wouldn't ever return.

His eyes burned, and he buried his face in the quilt.

When he heard the faint noises Duan Ling was making, Batu glanced over through the gap beneath the desk. Seeing Duan Ling trembling under his quilt, he climbed nimbly up onto the desk's surface and leaned over the other side.

"Hey," Batu murmured from above. "Are you crying? What's wrong?"

Duan Ling ignored him. Batu crouched with his knee on the desk and held onto its edge as he bent down and tried to tug Duan Ling's quilt away, but Duan Ling held on tightly. Batu reached his bare foot down and kicked at Duan Ling's quilt, then scrambled down and tugged the quilt free just enough to bare Duan Ling's face. He wasn't properly crying, but his brows were scrunched with the effort.

Batu sat down cross-legged beside him, staring. Duan Ling stared back. A tacit understanding seemed to pass between them, and Duan Ling ducked his head.

"Don't cry," Batu said. "Hold it in."

He sounded impatient, but his words held no trace of disgust, as if he spoke not from contempt, but experience. He reached out and laid his hand on Duan Ling's head, briefly stroking his hair, then patted his arm.

Suddenly, Duan Ling felt much better.

On that day, Batu was ten years old, while Duan Ling was eight and a half. Light and shadow flickered in the library. The tiny speck of a lamp shone amid the heavy snow, brightening Duan Ling's new memory. The night's snowfall seemed to cover his dark past as well, and in that moment, his world underwent a subtle shift. The dividing line—the desk, the lamp—between Batu and Duan Ling had separated them at first into different spheres. Yet strangely, as they sat together in the warm library, Duan Ling felt his past memories blur. The beatings and scoldings from the Duan family no longer tormented him, nor was he troubled by the hunger that had been his constant companion.

He said, "My name is Duan Ling. My father is Duan Sheng."

In one stroke, Lang Junxia had erased the stains and spots on the paper of Duan Ling's life. Or maybe the stains had been painted over by a darker ink. His worries were different now.

"He doesn't want you anymore," Batu said casually.

They sat against the table with their shoulders touching, hugging the quilt around their bodies as they stared at a painting hung on the opposite wall.

"He told me he would come," Duan Ling said, stubborn.

"My mother says no one in this world belongs to you." Batu gazed at the lush, golden painting of the Cang Prefecture landscape and lazily continued, "Wife, sons, daughters, parents, brothers, falcons in the sky, horses galloping on the plain, rewards from the Khan..." Batu paused and cracked his knuckles. "...none of this is promised to you either. Only you belong to yourself."

Duan Ling glanced sidelong at him. Batu had a natural scent, reminiscent of damp wool, which mingled with the musk of his fur coat that hadn't been washed in who knew how long, and the oily smell of his hair.

"Is the man you're waiting on your father?" Batu asked.

Duan Ling shook his head.

"A retainer?"

Duan Ling shook his head again. Batu tried a third time, confused. "Is he really a househusband? Where's your father, or your mother?"

Duan Ling continued shaking his head, and Batu stopped asking.

After a long silence passed: "I don't have a father," Duan Ling told Batu. "I'm an illegitimate child."

He'd guessed long ago that the name Lang Junxia taught him was only a story he made up. Otherwise, why had he never mentioned this Duan Sheng again?

"What about you?" Duan Ling asked.

Batu nodded. "My father abandoned me here. He told me he'd take me home once a month, but he hasn't come for three."

"He lied to you," Duan Ling said to Batu. "Don't believe him, and you won't get tricked."

Batu replied, more listless than before, "Ah, but I still believe him sometimes."

"Do you often get tricked?" Duan Ling asked.

"Not really." Batu lay on his side, looking directly at Duan Ling. "More in the past, but not as much now. If you know it's a lie, why do *you* still believe him?"

Duan Ling didn't respond. He wanted to believe Lang Junxia wouldn't lie to him; after all, he was so different from the others.

As the night deepened, only the snow outside made any sound. Duan Ling and Batu lay on the floor together, one on his front and one on his back. The bedding carried Batu's boyish scent. Duan Ling didn't know when they fell asleep, but he had stopped hoping for anything beforehand. He understood that Lang Junxia wouldn't come the next day, or even the day after—just as when the adults in the Duan family used to fool him with stories about his nonexistent father.

Bastard, your father's here to pick you up!—Duan Ling had heard this line countless times. He'd fallen for it again and again, until he became clever enough to stop believing it. But the adults grew more clever still, using different tricks on him. Sometimes they told him there was a guest, and that the madam had ordered him to greet them, so he would run over—full of hope and dirtying the main hall—only to be met with a beating. Sometimes they pretended to whisper in front of Duan Ling and accidentally reveal some information to him, but if he showed any reaction, they would laugh at him and leave. Everyone in that household had loved to see him cry.

Maybe he had been abandoned at Ming Academy, but at least school was much better than life with the Duan clan. In that regard, at least, he could be satisfied. One should be content with what one has—a bald monk had told him this once while begging for alms. Though the monk had died in Shangzi, in the end…

Duan Ling's dreams were boundless, a peaceful and harmonious slumber. Just as he dreamed of the river in Runan turning green at the end of spring, shimmering under the sun with golden waves, Batu shook him awake.

"Hey," Batu said. "Someone's here for you."

Duan Ling was groggy with sleep. He reached for Batu without opening his eyes, but the other boy blocked his hand. "Is this him?" Batu asked.

He heard Lang Junxia's low voice: "Duan Ling, I'm here to pick you up."

Duan Ling's eyes startled open. He looked disbelievingly at Lang Junxia, then at Batu.

Batu held the lamp up so the light shone on Lang Junxia's face, making Lang Junxia's brow crease in discomfort. Afraid Duan Ling might be kidnapped by a stranger, Batu asked again, "Is he the right one?"

"It's him," Duan Ling said. He reached out, wrapping his arms around Lang Junxia's neck to be picked up.

"Thank you for taking care of him," Lang Junxia said to Batu.

Batu set the lamp down, looking annoyed. Duan Ling was so sleepy he could hardly keep his eyes open; he wanted to say something to Batu before he left, but the other boy crawled under the low desk back to his bed and covered his face with his quilt.

Outside, Shangjing slumbered under a blanket of snow. The coldest time of the year had arrived. Lang Junxia wrapped Duan Ling in a quilt and galloped away from the school; as they traveled, the cold wind in his face roused Duan Ling. When he realized they weren't heading toward Qionghua House, he asked, "Where are we going?"

"A new home," Lang Junxia answered absently.

A new home! Duan Ling was suddenly wide awake. No wonder he came late, he thought—he was preparing the house. He looked up at Lang Junxia, who seemed a little pale.

"Are you tired too?" Duan Ling felt Lang Junxia's weight leaning heavier onto him, so he reached back and touched his cheek.

"No." Though Lang Junxia still seemed drowsy, the touch had woken him slightly.

"Have you eaten?" Duan Ling asked.

"Yes," Lang Junxia answered. He wrapped an arm around Duan Ling and hugged him. His broad hand felt cold, colder than usual.

"Where's our new home?"

Lang Junxia made no reply. The horse turned a corner into a secluded alley, passed through a shuttered market, and finally entered the outer courtyard of a small residence, where they dismounted in the darkness. Duan Ling was overjoyed, and without waiting for Lang Junxia to lead the horse in, ran toward the door with a cheer.

The main gate was locked. When he stepped inside, he could see that the whole place was in a state of disarray. It was a single courtyard residence, with six buildings arranged around a central outdoor space, ringed by an open corridor. The lanterns that should've been hung outside the entrance had been left discarded in the gatehouse.

"Are we going to live here now?" Duan Ling asked.

"Yes," Lang Junxia said.

Duan Ling faced the center of the courtyard and started to laugh. Behind him came the soft click of Lang Junxia closing and latching the door, followed by a loud crash as Lang Junxia fell onto the disassembled flower frame in the courtyard and tumbled down onto the ground.

Duan Ling spun around in shock and saw Lang Junxia lying motionless in the snow.

7

"**L**ANG JUNXIA!" Duan Ling shouted, shaking him in a panic, but Lang Junxia remained unresponsive.

A clump of snow fell from the pine trees above and blanketed them both in powder. Duan Ling had no time to think. Fright froze him for a moment before realization spurred him to action: Lang Junxia must have fainted from the cold. Duan Ling didn't know what he'd been through—nor how to explain the blood on Lang Junxia's body—he had to make him better, no matter what.

He dragged Lang Junxia into the hall. It took almost all his energy to move him across the courtyard, but Lang Junxia still showed no signs of waking. Duan Ling called his name several times to no avail; when he held a finger to his nose to check Lang Junxia's breathing, he found it was stable, though his lips were alarmingly pale.

He had to start a fire. Duan Ling rifled through the new residence until he found charcoal and an unused clay stove before the kitchen hearth, which he set up to light a fire in the hall. There was bedding in some of the rooms, and he was carrying a quilt into the main hall when he noticed the track of fresh blood Lang Junxia had left behind him.

The blood trailed back from his unconscious body through the hall and then outdoors; crimson pooled on the threshold and left a clear path under the closed door into the snowy courtyard.

The gory trail would surely continue through the courtyard gates, down the long alley, and onto the main street.

Duan Ling dug through Lang Junxia's belongings but couldn't find any medicine for his wounds—the only item of interest was a small cloth bag containing Duan Ling's birth certificate.

What should he do? Lang Junxia's face was ashen, and he had a high fever; it was obvious he was seriously weakened. When Duan Ling was sick, he knew he had to see a doctor for medicine. During his time with the Duan clan, he'd run everyone's errands and went often to the apothecary to pick up this or that. Steeling himself, he took some silver from Lang Junxia and ran out to find a doctor.

Though it was the quietest period of the night in Shangjing, a mysterious and unsettling force moved through the city. Wu Du—the tall, thin assassin—strolled through the cold wearing a ragged cotton robe and his bamboo hat pulled low, a dagger held loosely between his fingers. He fiddled with it absently as he walked from house to house, pausing on occasion and tilting his head to listen.

A man in black skulked along behind him, looking around suspiciously.

"If you find any clues, don't act on your own," said Wu Du.

The man in black sneered. "Wu Du! Don't forget the general ordered *you* to assist *me*. Where could he have escaped to with those wounds?"

"I wouldn't dream of taking the credit from Zhu-xiong.[6] But if you think I'm a hindrance, Zhu-xiong, by all means, find him yourself," Wu Du replied.

---

6 A word meaning elder brother. It can be attached as a suffix to address a male peer.

The man in black glanced over at Wu Du, then turned and left without another word, disappearing into a residential courtyard. Wu Du hesitated, looking off into the distance for a moment before heading for the market on the main road.

A few streets away, Duan Ling was knocking on the back door of Rongchang Hall. He slipped in alongside a gust of wind and snow.

"The doctor is out seeing patients," the shopkeeper said. "What's the ailment?"

"Bleeding!" Duan Ling exclaimed. "And he's not moving! When will the doctor be back?"

"An injury? What kind of injury?" the shopkeeper asked impatiently. "A man or a woman, how old?"

Duan Ling spoke and gestured, animated by anxiety. But the shopkeeper, drunk and bleary-eyed, only told him that the doctor didn't actually live there, but two streets away. When he'd come to the hall for a drink, a family on East Street had asked for him to help with a difficult labor, so he'd gone to see the laboring woman with his medicine box. The shopkeeper hadn't asked which family it was.

Seeing Duan Ling half crazed with worry, the shopkeeper slurred, "It's all right, it's all right. I'll get you some jinchuang powder and some herbs that can knit wounds and help circulation. Boil them and apply that to the wounds, and he'll be fine after the fever breaks…"

The shopkeeper locked the door and staggered upstairs to collect the herbs while Duan Ling waited behind the counter, uneasy. He recalled once hearing that ginseng cured all diseases, so he scooted a chair over to the medicine cabinet and climbed onto it to find some.

Another knock sounded from the front door.

"Anyone there?" called a deep, hoarse voice.

Duan Ling paused with the lamp held in one hand and a piece of aged ginseng in the other. The door clicked; Duan Ling had watched the shopkeeper lock it, yet the customer walked straight in. Duan Ling clambered down from the cabinet and knelt on the chair, where he set down the lamp and peered over the counter.

The customer was a young man dusted with snow, his left hand tucked in his robes as if holding something. The long, slender fingers of the man's exposed right hand were red from the cold. He leaned his elbow on the counter, angling his head down and looking directly into Duan Ling's eyes. Duan Ling was so short only half his face showed over the counter; he instantly felt intimidated.

The man had a lean face, with defined cheekbones and a sun-burnished complexion, and deep-set eyes bracketed by thick black eyebrows like a downward cursive stroke. On the side of his neck, just below the curve of his jaw, was a black-inked tattoo—the profile of a rare beast in the style of an ancient inscription.

"Where's the doctor?" the young man asked in a low, steady voice. He opened his hand to reveal a shining golden bead caught between his fingers. Duan Ling's gaze dropped to the beautiful bead immediately, surprised. He stared at it for a moment, then looked back up as the young man pinched the golden bead between his fingers and spun it on the smooth surface of the counter.

"The doctor...went to help deliver a baby." Duan Ling was so stunned by the golden bead that he could hardly take his eyes off it. "On East Street...a family was having a difficult labor."

The young man gently flicked the bead so it rolled over to Duan Ling. He gestured for him to take it and asked, "Other than the birth, has anyone else come looking for the doctor today?"

"No one," Duan Ling answered without a second thought.

The sense of danger radiating from the stranger was unmistakable. Duan Ling didn't dare reach for the bead. When something seemed too good to be true, there was certain to be trickery afoot: He'd learned this lesson from his suffering as a child.

"Is the doctor your father?"

"No." Duan Ling edged backward, looking the man up and down.

"What's that in your hand?" The man's gaze rested on the herbs Duan Ling held. Duan Ling obviously couldn't say he was stealing them, so he lifted the herbs into sight and said, "Ginseng for the laboring mother."

The young man went silent.

Duan Ling was afraid the shopkeeper would come downstairs at any moment. "Do you need anything else?"

"No, nothing else." The corner of the man's lips lifted into a wicked smile, and he set his hand back onto the counter, his fingers tapping a rhythm. Instantly, the golden bead unfurled into a centipede with a glittering, golden carapace and a colorful abdomen. The metallic creature shot toward Duan Ling, who shrieked in fear. The man only laughed and reached out to snatch the centipede away, then swept back out through the shop door into the snowy night.

Duan Ling rushed upstairs and found the shopkeeper lying under the medicine cabinet with a loose bag of herbs in his hand, blacked-out drunk. He tiptoed around him to pack up the scattered herbs, found the jinchuang powder he'd mentioned by poring over the labels, and retraced his steps home.

The heavy snow had hidden Lang Junxia's bloody trail. Fortunately, the long street back was bright enough for him to make his way even in the dead of night. The horse was still waiting outside the gate, shivering in the cold. He led the animal around to the stable in the back courtyard, gave it some hay, and murmured, "I'll be back soon."

The instant Duan Ling turned from the horse, he felt himself grabbed from behind. A large, rough hand covered his mouth, muffling his screams.

"Mmngh...*ngh*...!" Duan Ling struggled mightily, but his assailant had a strong grip. The stranger pressed a sharp dagger to the side of Duan Ling's neck, drawing blood. Duan Ling's pupils dilated, and he fell still at once.

"Where is Lang Junxia?" the stranger asked.

Duan Ling's eyes flicked up to the icicles lining the roof. In their icy reflections, he saw that his assailant was a darkly cloaked and masked assassin. He pressed his lips shut, his nerves suddenly calming, and said nothing.

"Show me where he is or I'll kill you!" the assassin hissed.

Duan Ling pointed toward the back courtyard, his thoughts racing. He needed to lure the man away or alert Lang Junxia. The assassin held Duan Ling captive with one hand and hauled him along as he followed the way he pointed. The icy ground was slippery; as they crossed the corridor, Duan Ling opened his mouth wide and bit down as hard as he could on the assassin's hand.

Caught off guard, the man shouted in pain and dropped Duan Ling. He drew his dagger, but Duan Ling had already fallen to the ground and was scrambling away. The assassin followed steadily, knowing he must be going for help.

But Duan Ling was smarter than that—he didn't go toward Lang Junxia at all. Instead, he fled through the corridor and knocked on every door, shouting, "Murderer! Murderer!" before running back toward the stable, hoping to escape before the assassin figured out where Lang Junxia was.

The assassin had originally thought to use Duan Ling as bait, but when he saw the boy sprinting for the gate, he realized he was at a disadvantage. He rushed forward and grabbed for the back of Duan Ling's collar.

From behind a pillar, a glinting sword flashed toward him; the assassin threw up his dagger to parry it. With a *clang*, the dagger snapped into two, and the sword swung up at a sharp angle. Lang Junxia's face was pale and his breathing labored; he lifted his sword again and lurched toward the assassin, but his steps were uneven—the blade missed its target by half an inch.

The assassin danced back, having narrowly escaped being gutted. Lang Junxia staggered, his vision flickering, and once again collapsed to the ground. Yelling, Duan Ling rushed forward to crouch over Lang Junxia's back.

The assassin laughed, cold, and kicked the sword aside. He snatched Duan Ling up by the collar and punched him hard in the face, like he was pounding dough. Duan Ling turned his head aside at the last second, and the bowl-sized fist slammed into his eye socket. Stars burst over his vision, his head buzzing as he fell to the ground.

The assassin wrapped his fist in Lang Junxia's hair and wrenched his head up. He drew another dagger and laid its blade against his throat. "Where is Li Jianhong?" the assassin asked.

Lang Junxia's lips barely moved as he whispered, "I'll tell you if you let the child live…"

Duan Ling felt like his eye had been punched into the back of his skull, but even so, he dragged himself upright and grabbed the sword that had fallen to the ground.

The assassin had sorely underestimated Duan Ling's capacity for taking a beating. The tenacity a person showed in life-or-death situations was often closely related to the amount of physical abuse they'd taken in life. Duan Ling had had his head smashed into walls;

he'd been hit by bricks, slapped around, and punched by adults since he was small. He had honed his skill for withstanding pain and knew that when taking a blow, he should avoid being hit in the nose or temple, and should instead use his eye socket to meet his attacker's fist.

The assassin leaned closer to Lang Junxia's face and saw reflected in his clear eyes what was happening behind his back: Duan Ling hefted Lang Junxia's sword and leapt forward.

In the instant the assassin made to turn for him, Duan Ling thrust the sword directly into the back of the man's neck. The blade sank through with a wet sound, pinning the assassin to the floor.

"I…" The assassin's pupils dilated, eyes wide with disbelief that he was going to die at the hands of a child. His fingers scrabbled through the snow for only a moment—his throat had been pierced from behind, and he died without another sound. Then the light went out of his eyes, and there were only snowflakes between heaven and earth.

Duan Ling had never killed anyone before. His hands and face were spattered with blood, and he stared disbelievingly at the assassin's corpse for a long beat before scrambling toward Lang Junxia and throwing himself across his chest.

Eyes closed, Lang Junxia held Duan Ling in his arms. Duan Ling looked around and saw that the assassin's eyes were still open, staring at them in death. Lang Junxia covered Duan Ling's eyes with his hand, protecting him from the sight.

An hour later, a goshawk circled over the city. A city guard shouted: "Who's there?!"

The assorted guards and soldiers finally spotted the strange young man atop a roof and spurred their horses toward him. The young

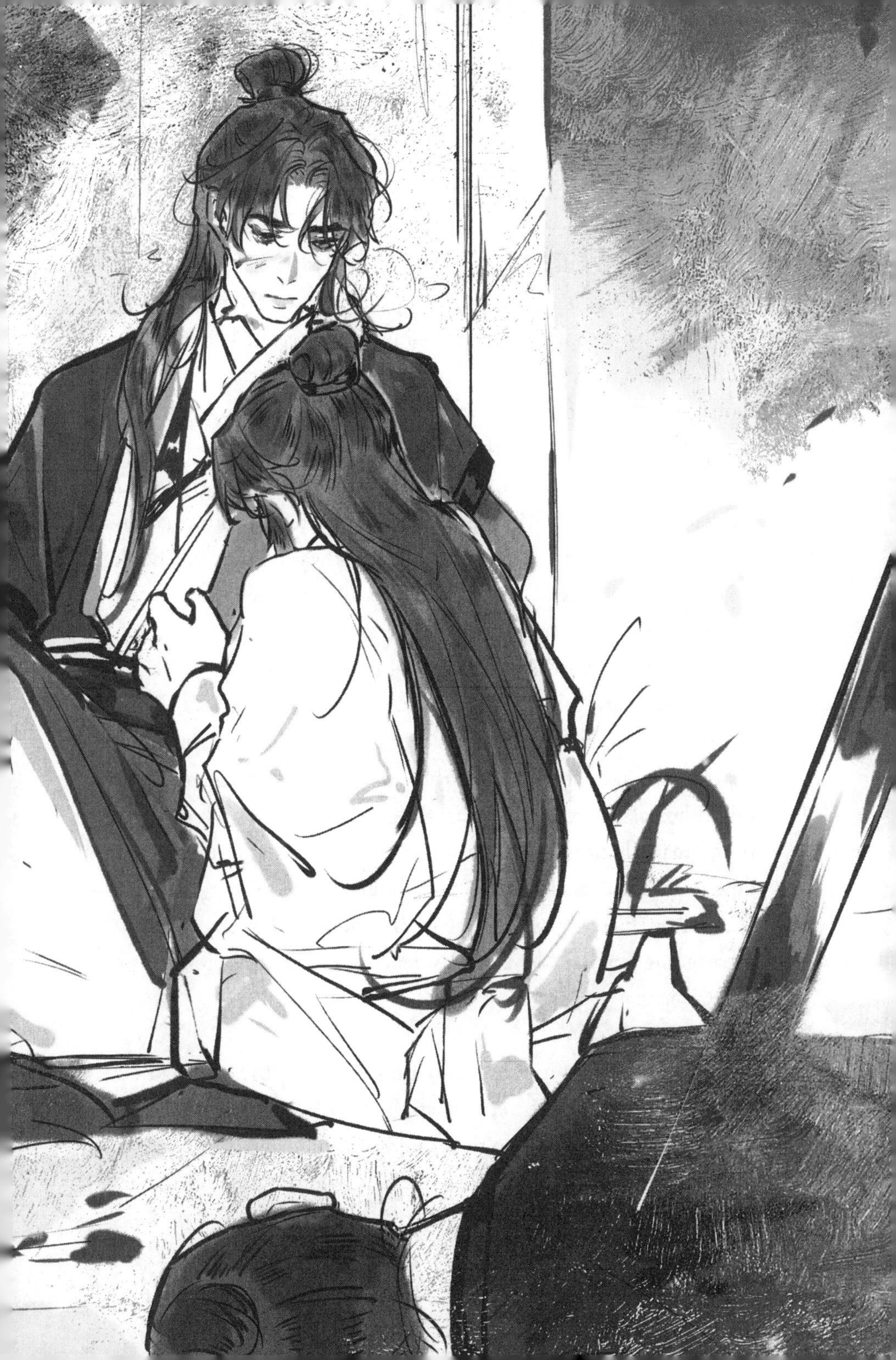

man put two fingers to his lips and whistled several times across the snowy streets, but nobody answered.

Soldiers filled the streets, surging in from all directions as they responded to the call of their fellows' bird whistles. The young man leapt from the rooftop into an alley and fled through the snow, attempting to shake his pursuers—but as soon as he left the alley, more of them followed. He didn't dare stand and fight; his fleeing footsteps were as light as duckweed floating atop water, and he left the shallowest possible footprints in the snow.

Pelting around a corner, he found himself suddenly surrounded by guards and soldiers with bows drawn. Yet before their formation could be completed, the young man spun toward them and shook his robes. Countless tiny, black arrows like gadflies shot out in all directions.

The city guard galloping toward him shouted angrily, "Who dares to be so arrogant in Shangjing?!"

Just as the horse was about to overtake him, the stranger threw his bamboo hat with a flick of the wrist, startling the guard right off his horse. The hat grazed past the guard and spun back into the young man's hand; he wordlessly returned it to his head and fled down another alley, disappearing without a trace.

After briefly reorganizing, the soldiers began to knock on nearby gates, going from residence to residence in search of their quarry's accomplices.

Back in his new home, Duan Ling had lit a fire and hauled Lang Junxia over to the bed. He applied the jinchuang powder as instructed and chopped up the ginseng to boil in a pot of water.

"Where did you get the ginseng?" Lang Junxia asked, his eyes still closed.

"I stole it from the apothecary," Duan Ling said. "Why is someone trying to kill you? Are they bad people?"

"Twelve days ago, I went to the city of Huchang for business, and the assassin Wu Du picked up my trail," Lang Junxia replied. "I intended to take the opportunity to kill him when he followed me, but he was too cunning; I fell for his trap. We fought, and in my haste, I was seriously injured. I used all my strength to shake him off at the foot of the Altyn-Tagh Mountains."

"Wu Du… Is that the name of the man who died?" Duan Ling asked.

"No," Lang Junxia replied, eyes still closed. "The man in black was called Zhu. He was a member of Southern Chen's shadow squad. The shadow squad and Wu Du have long been at odds with one another—Zhu must have hoped to follow me to Shangjing and take the credit for Wu Du's work. I'm sure he never expected to die at your hands in such an unlucky turn of events."

So Lang Junxia hadn't picked him up from school because he was away on business. Where was Huchang? Duan Ling was full of questions, but before he could ask them, Lang Junxia spoke again. "Hide the body in the stable; cover it with hay. Shovel the snow to cover the bloodstains and change your clothes."

Duan Ling was still fearful, but he did as Lang Junxia ordered. When he came to the corpse, its eyes remained wide open. He wondered if the dead man would become a ghost and return to take his life. Just as he finished his last task, removing his bloodstained robes and slipping into a fresh underrobe, the ringing of horse's hooves sounded on the road outside their door.

"City guard! Open up!" came the call.

8

Duan Ling hesitated. Should he open the door or not? Lang Junxia was still lying in bed, and the main gate was already latched. A fist pounded on the door again, and Duan Ling decided to brave the icy wind to open it.

"Oh," the guard said, surprised. "A child? Are there no adults here? Where are your parents?"

"Sick," Duan Ling replied.

"Isn't this kid from Ming Academy?" Another man, likely the guard's superior, peered down at Duan Ling. The child was only wearing his underrobe, and his lips were going blue from cold as he stood shivering behind the gate. As the man dismounted and looked Duan Ling up and down, Duan Ling had the feeling he'd seen him before.

"Where's your father?" he asked. "Do you remember me? Cai Yan's older brother, Cai Wen."

Duan Ling thought for a moment. He remembered Cai Yan, of course, but not this man. "He's sick. Sorry, I don't remember you."

"Can he meet with us?" Cai Wen frowned as he examined the bruise blooming on Duan Ling's eye. Clearly the boy had taken a harsh beating; even his eyelids were swollen. Cai Wen reached out as if to touch his face, and Duan Ling flinched away.

"He's sleeping," Duan Ling said.

He couldn't let Cai Wen or the other guardsmen enter the house, or they might stumble on the assassin's corpse.

Cai Wen, watching Duan Ling shrinking from him while standing barefoot in the winter snow, couldn't bear it any longer. "Forget it; go back inside and rest. Next house!" Cai Wen ordered the soldiers, remounting his horse.

His back swayed as his horse turned; only then did Duan Ling recognize him as the young man who had picked Cai Yan up from school. When the guards had gone, Duan Ling sighed in relief and latched the door. He returned to the bedroom where he'd left Lang Junxia, warm and smelling of ginseng tea, and took the teapot off the stove to cool. Lang Junxia coughed from the bed.

"Who was it?" Lang Junxia asked, his forehead damp with sweat.

"Cai Yan's older brother, Cai Wen."

Lang Junxia closed his eyes again. "Cai Wen—and he left just like that? Who's Cai Yan? You know his younger brother?"

"Yeah," Duan Ling said, lifting the teapot by the handle. He put the spout to Lang Junxia's lips and carefully poured ginseng tea into his mouth. Lang Junxia coughed a few times, then cleared his throat and drank the entire pot.

"Laoshan ginseng." Lang Junxia's voice had grown steadier. "This will keep me alive. The heavens have saved me. Is there more? Brew me another pot."

"There's no more," Duan Ling said. "I'll go steal—er, buy some."

"Don't," Lang Junxia said. "It's too dangerous."

"Then I'll add more water and steep it again for you."

Lang Junxia fell silent.

For some reason, this night stretched on much longer than usual. Duan Ling curled up at the foot of the bed and dozed while the ginseng tea brewed on the little stove. But he roused after a bit and said, "Lang Junxia?"

There was no response.

"Are you going to be all right?" Duan Ling asked, afraid.

"Yeah," Lang Junxia murmured, half asleep. "I'm not dead yet."

Duan Ling felt a wave of relief. The night had grown darker outside, but the stove fire was like a warm sun shining onto them.

"Lang Junxia?" Duan Ling repeated.

"Alive." Lang Junxia's voice sounded like a bellows, as if it rose from deep within his lungs.

Duan Ling fell asleep again, his heavy head knocking down onto the bed.

When he opened his eyes the next morning, the snow had subsided. Duan Ling found himself in bed with Lang Junxia lying beside him, his complexion much improved.

Duan Ling rose on his knees like a puppy and tried to sniff for Lang Junxia's breath. Lang Junxia frowned as the boy nosed around his face and gave a deep sigh. His head felt as if it would split. "What time is it?"

Thank goodness he was speaking again. Duan Ling looked at him with worry. "Are you still feeling bad?"

"Not anymore," Lang Junxia said.

"Then I'll find something to eat," Duan Ling said, his mood lifting.

He clambered from the bed and saw that the courtyard was blanketed in white. He cheered and started outside, wanting to play in the snow right away.

"Put your clothes on first," Lang Junxia said. "Don't catch a cold, you hear me?"

Wrapping himself in a fur-lined coat, Duan Ling took a bamboo pole to knock down the icicles along the eaves of the veranda, laughing loudly. When he turned back to the room, he saw Lang Junxia seated on the bed; he peeled off his outer robe, then cut away his dirtied underrobe, removed his bandages, and began applying ointment to his injuries.

Duan Ling dropped the bamboo pole and ran in. "Are you all better now?"

Lang Junxia nodded. Duan Ling saw that his abdomen was black and blue around his wounds, but the three slashes there—each of a different depth—had already scabbed over. He boiled some water for Lang Junxia, helped him wipe the area clean, and applied more jinchuang powder.

Under the morning light, Duan Ling noticed a strange tattoo on Lang Junxia's tan, muscular arm; it looked like the tigers often engraved into bells. The sight reminded Duan Ling of everything that had unfolded the previous night.

"Why did those men want to kill you?" he asked.

"They're looking for someone, and they think I know where he is," Lang Junxia said.

"Who?"

Lang Junxia looked at Duan Ling, silent. Suddenly, the corners of his mouth lifted and his lashes lowered just a bit. "Don't ask," he said. "Don't ask me anything more. You'll find out in the future."

Duan Ling had been terribly worried, but Lang Junxia was still alive, and so his gloomy mood dissipated. In fact, he found himself quite happy. He sat beside Lang Junxia on the bed, looking at the tiger head tattooed on his arm. "What's this?"

"The White Tiger of the West," Lang Junxia explained. "The west also corresponds to metal among the five elements. As a mythical beast, it reigns over death and warfare; it is the god of weaponry."

Duan Ling didn't understand, so instead he asked, "You know how to use a sword, right? I saw your sword last night. It was very sharp."

Duan Ling got up to retrieve Lang Junxia's sword from where it'd fallen last night, but when he jogged over to the back courtyard, it was no longer there. Abruptly, he remembered the corpse hidden in the stable, and his fear returned. He edged closer to the outbuilding, only to see that the hay had been moved and the body was gone. The sight made all his hair stand on end.

"I got rid of it," Lang Junxia said from behind him. "Don't be afraid. He was from Southern Chen's shadow squad; they've never had a good relationship with Wu Du. We were fortunate it was him you ran into yesterday, and not Wu Du—otherwise, neither of us would be sitting here now."

Duan Ling didn't ask Lang Junxia how he *got rid of* the body. He didn't ask where his bloody clothes had disappeared to, either.

"Go buy something to eat." Lang Junxia handed Duan Ling some money. "Don't say or ask anything else."

By now, it was almost noon. Duan Ling bought steamed buns, both filled and unfilled, rice, and meat from the market. By the time he arrived home with his bounty, Lang Junxia was walking around fine. He shared the buns with Duan Ling for lunch, then said, "We'll make do like this for now. Once I take you back to school, I'll get the house sorted."

"Will you be leaving again?" Duan Ling asked.

"I won't," Lang Junxia said.

"And will you come pick me up on the first day next month?"

"I promise I won't be late again," Lang Junxia said. "Yesterday was my fault."

"Then—" Duan Ling blurted, "can you be my father?"

Startled, Lang Junxia looked at Duan Ling in befuddlement. "You shouldn't go around saying that to just anyone." When Duan Ling frowned at him, Lang Junxia went on, "Your real father will come for you."

Lang Junxia's words pierced him like a bolt of lightning. Duan Ling had been tricked countless times before, by many people, but he had a feeling Lang Junxia wouldn't deceive him. "My father...is still alive?" he asked finally.

"Yes," Lang Junxia replied. "He's still alive."

Duan Ling fired off more questions: "Where is he? He's really alive? Why didn't he ever come before?"

"You can ask him that when you meet him," Lang Junxia said. "He'll come one day. At the least a couple of months, at the most three years. Believe me."

Duan Ling held his bowl with his mouth partway open, looking lost. He was half overjoyed and half terrified at this news. Lang Junxia tugged him over to lean against his shoulder, hugging him close and laying a warm palm on his head.

The snow melted throughout the day. Duan Ling was delighted with his new home. Lang Junxia's injuries were still healing, so he applied some medicine to Duan Ling's left eye and let him loose. He'd hesitated at first over the idea of hiring a servant to look after the house, but Duan Ling didn't care a whit. He ran around with a child's boundless energy, hanging a lantern reading *Duan* on the door and sweeping aside the snow in the courtyard. Like a puppy just brought home, he was curious about everything; his footprints covered every inch of the place, which he explored diligently as if it was a new paradise.

"Can I plant something here?" he asked, squatting in front of a small flowerbed in the courtyard.

"Of course," Lang Junxia said. "The house is yours. But it's too late today. I'll buy you some seeds at the market later."

Duan Ling prodded at the soil seriously. Leaning on a wooden cane by the door, Lang Junxia watched him play for nearly an hour. Dusk had arrived by the time Lang Junxia said, "Come inside. Shangjing is cold; it'll be hard to grow flowers."

Reluctantly, Duan Ling shuffled back in. Lang Junxia was seated before the stove, lighting a fire. "What have you learned so far at Ming Academy?" he asked. "I'll test you."

"In the beginning, the heaven was black and the earth was yellow; the universe was chaos..." Duan Ling began to recite the *Thousand Character Classic*. His short break was nearing its end, and he had to return to his studies the next day. As he continued his recitation, Lang Junxia took a bowl, placed some pig skin in it, and set it on the stove to steam with some water and brown sugar.

When Duan Ling finished reciting the entire *Thousand Character Classic*, Lang Junxia said with surprise, "You already memorized the whole thing."

In truth, Duan Ling had made a few mistakes in the middle, but Lang Junxia didn't point those out. Instead he said, seriously, "Very good—you're an excellent student. I can't take you out to play with this injury, but it's too cold anyway, and there's not much to do around the city. I owe you a reward. When spring arrives next month, I'll take you for an outing."

"You should rest so you can heal," Duan Ling replied. "There's no rush. What are you cooking? I saw sugar. Is it yummy?"

"You'll find out tomorrow," Lang Junxia said.

Duan Ling already knew that no matter what he asked, he wouldn't get any answers from Lang Junxia. He was getting used to it.

During the night, Lang Junxia placed a few handfuls of plum blossoms into several bowls and set them outside.

The next morning, Lang Junxia dropped him off at Ming Academy. Unlike the last time, he didn't hurry off, but stayed to watch Duan Ling as he went inside. Duan Ling was only too pleased to accept this arrangement. Though he didn't want to part, he put on a smile and even said, "It's okay, you can go back now."

But neither left right away. Lang Junxia leaned on his cane and raised an arm, and Duan Ling surged forward to hug him around the waist, burying his face in Lang Junxia's chest.

"Don't tell anyone at the academy about our family affairs." Lang Junxia noticed the porter giving them a curious look, so he draped his arm around Duan Ling, bent lower, and whispered: "Remember, don't say anything. You can only know another person's face, not his heart."

After a few more moments, the two broke apart.

"This is for you," Lang Junxia said, handing Duan Ling a food box. "Eat it quickly. My mother used to make it for me when I was young."

Duan Ling nodded and said his goodbyes. Ever since he'd become Lang Junxia's companion, the two phrases Duan Ling heard him say most were *don't ask anything* and *don't say anything*. Lang Junxia was unbelievably cautious; Duan Ling felt like he was always tiptoeing around secrets, unable to ask any questions.

Fortunately, children have rich imaginations. Duan Ling had already concocted countless theories; they crowded his mind in such profusion that the old ones were rarely fully fleshed out before being replaced by new ones. Lang Junxia's imaginary career had changed many times—from a monster to a vagabond, from a wealthy merchant to a swordsman. He was still thinking about their uninvited guest. The shadow squad had been trying to kill Lang Junxia, so the situation *had* been dangerous, but it seemed safe now. Otherwise, Lang Junxia would have moved them to avoid being discovered again.

Assassins trying to kill him to find someone else: Who could that be? Was it—perhaps—Duan Ling's father?

The instant this thought occurred to him, Duan Ling's pulse began to race. What if his father was an important person, and had asked Lang Junxia to fetch and look after Duan Ling until he could come for him? Then when they met, wouldn't everything finally be explained?

As Duan Ling wandered toward his room holding the food box Lang Junxia had given him, he almost collided with another boy outside the remote courtyard. It was Batu, who had been peering outside the gates.

"What happened?" Batu asked, surprised. "Who hit you in the face?"

"I-it's nothing," Duan Ling stuttered.

He'd intended to go straight back to his room and hadn't expected to run into anyone. Batu reached out to help him carry his things, but Duan Ling refused to let go of the box, worried Batu would take it and look inside. "What are you doing?!" he cried out anxiously.

"Did he hit you?" Batu asked.

"He really didn't..."

"Borjigin!" called a sharp voice behind them—Cai Yan. The other boy gave Batu a cold, threatening stare. Seeing him walking toward them, Batu let go of Duan Ling with a chilly snort.

"Come to my room later," Cai Yan said to Duan Ling. "There's something I want to ask you."

Duan Ling nodded. Batu glanced between Cai Yan and Duan Ling, but Cai Yan didn't say anything more; he figured if Batu knew what was good for him, he wouldn't pester Duan Ling again.

Once Cai Yan turned and left, Duan Ling explained to Batu, "It was my fault. I was careless and bumped into the corner of a table."

"Someone punched you, right at the corner of your eye. I can tell." Duan Ling was speechless, but Batu continued quickly, "Forget it. You Han people are all like this! I'm just a Mongol dog who doesn't know to mind my own business. Fine, I'll leave."

"Batu!" Duan Ling called after him, but the boy stalked off without looking back.

Duan Ling returned to his room and saw that his bedding, which he'd left in the library, had been moved back and placed neatly on his bed. He opened the food box and found that it was filled with candy Lang Junxia had made for him. The brown sugar confection was like a dusky crystal with plum blossoms neatly frozen inside, cut into small pieces and stacked tidily within the box. The longer Duan Ling gazed at it, the less he could bear to eat it. After some thought, he kept one portion for himself and wrapped the rest separately, preparing to give Batu and Cai Yan each a piece.

School had reconvened. Morning classes were paused for the day, and the courtyard was noisy with the children exchanging snacks from home. Cai Yan, however, was not among them. Duan Ling found him standing in the back courtyard of the academy, listening to a teacher's lecture alongside a few older boys.

"Raise your hands high," the teacher said sternly. "Only bend at the waist."

The boys raised their hands in unison, fingers crossed above their heads. The teacher examined them one by one, dissatisfied. "No! Your knees should not bend! When you bow, your knees must remain still! You're bowing, not groveling on your knees."

Cai Yan and the others practiced the motion repeatedly, learning how to make a proper obeisance.

"A gentleman is slow to speak but sharp in his conduct. When the Great Prince of the Northern Court comes, you must distinguish yourself through your actions and not your words," the teacher admonished them.

"Yes, sir," the boys chorused.

From the shadows, Duan Ling watched the whole etiquette lesson. Cai Yan seemed awfully elegant and graceful when performing his obeisance, especially with his tall stature and kind face. Duan Ling imitated him exactly, lifting his hands high and bowing to the wall. When the teacher released them for a break, Cai Yan spotted him waiting and came over.

Duan Ling took the candy from his robes and handed it to him. "This is for you."

Cai Yan accepted the gift without asking what it was, getting straight to the point: "My older brother said he went by your house last night while he was searching the city." Cai Yan's gaze roved over his black eye. "Are you okay?"

Duan Ling hastily nodded, pointing at his face. "I just bumped into something accidentally."

Frowning slightly, Cai Yan said, "Didn't you say your family is in trade?"

Duan Ling looked confused but nodded again. Cai Yan's brother had told him that the Duan residence was shabby, with not a servant in sight. The young master had come barefoot to open the door himself and had been beaten to boot. Cai Yan couldn't help feeling some sympathy for the boy.

"Who do you live with, your father?" Cai Yan asked.

"I..." Duan Ling didn't know how to say it was Lang Junxia, but a word he'd heard before popped up in his mind. He forgot where he'd learned it, but he finished, "Househusband."

There was a long silence. Cai Yan put his hand to his forehead and said, "Where did you hear that from? You can't just say that. He's probably a servant."

Duan Ling nodded.

"And where's your father?" Cai Yan asked again.

"He's doing business in the south," Duan Ling answered, just as Lang Junxia had trained him.

Cai Yan looked at Duan Ling for a long moment. It seemed no matter who he was talking to, the boy was well-behaved and didn't lose his temper, but patiently answered every question. He couldn't help but laugh. "You're a good kid. Oh, well. I just wanted to remind you to associate more with other Han. If you run into any problems with the other kids, just find a Han person nearby. Have you ever been in school before?"

Duan Ling had no idea that the Han people in Shangjing tended to stick to their own social circles, while other peoples did the same. He merely nodded along with whatever Cai Yan said.

Abruptly, Cai Yan changed the subject. "Do you know Ding Zhi from Qionghua House?"

Duan Ling hesitated, but his expression told Cai Yan everything he needed to know.

"Ding Zhi and my brother are fighting right now," Cai Yan confided. "Next time you see her, please ask her to forgive my brother. You don't have to make a special trip for it, though."

As Duan Ling nodded his agreement, they heard the teacher coughing from the inner courtyard. Cai Yan turned to rush back, fearing a punishment—but before he left, he repeated, "If there's anything you don't understand, come and find me."

Duan Ling continued watching the lessons on bowing, following along, until he felt a slight chill in his robes. Remembering he still had another piece of candy that was almost melting by now, he hurried off to look for Batu.

When Duan Ling found him, Batu was wrestling with another tall boy. A group of children crowded around them, cheering. Batu's face was swollen and red; he was shirtless, and his upper body already showed the musculature of a young man. As he collided with, tripped, and flipped the other boy, he caught sight of Duan Ling. Distracted, he was unexpectedly flipped by his opponent in turn and landed flat on the ground.

9

The crowd burst out laughing. Batu's face flushed scarlet with anger. At once, Duan Ling sprang forward to help him up, but Batu brushed him off, standing and storming away. The gathered children peered curiously at Duan Ling.

"Borjigin—" Duan Ling said, hurrying after him. "I have something for you."

Batu spun around and gave Duan Ling a shove. "Don't call me by my surname!"

The plum blossom candy in Duan Ling's hand fell to the ground. Batu slammed the building's door behind him, and Duan Ling flinched.

Everyone laughed again. Duan Ling, embarrassed, had no idea what he'd done to anger Batu. When he saw the young man who'd been wrestling with Batu approaching as if he had something to say, Duan Ling's fear multiplied. Scared someone would pick a fight with him again, he fled.

The tall young man opened his mouth but said nothing as Duan Ling disappeared behind the columns of the walkway.

This was an unwritten rule within Ming Academy: The Han stuck together, and other people did as well. There was neither national hatred nor familial resentment among the children; nor did they think to themselves that those of a different race were, on a fundamental level, much different from themselves. But the Han people presumed the Mongols, Khitan, and Tangut were uncivilized for bathing less often and for having body odor, and read their unruliness as a lack of manners. These peoples, in turn, disliked the Han's pretentious attitudes and posturing.

Unbeknownst to Duan Ling, he had entirely misread the situation: The other young man had only intended to comfort him and offer to teach him how to wrestle. Even if Duan Ling understood his good intentions, however, he would've politely declined.

During the lunch hour, he was surprised to discover that the academy grounds had been thoroughly cleaned. The heavy snow had been swept away, and even the fallen leaves lingering in the flower beds had been removed. The headmaster and other teachers were all dressed in their best robes and lined up neatly before the main gate, as if waiting for someone to arrive.

Is something happening today? Duan Ling wondered, peering curiously around the front courtyard after his meal.

"All of you, go back inside!" a teacher said. "There's still class after lunch, so behave yourselves!"

When the first bell rang in the distance, the children ran back to their rooms to pack up and go to class. Duan Ling's afternoon course was introductory writing; the students first read the *Thousand Character Classic*, then practiced writing the characters in copybooks. Duan Ling had only just dipped his brush into the ink and copied down a couple of characters when he heard voices approaching the Hall of Enlightenment.

"The students practice reading in the morning and writing in the afternoon," a teacher was saying.

"Benevolence, justice, courtesy, wisdom, and sincerity," a deep voice replied. "They should know how to write these five words at the very least."

"Of course," the teacher said. "We've taught them those characters already. Please come this way, Your Excellency."

"Let's see the Hall of Enlightenment first," the deep-voiced man said. Ignoring the teacher trying to guide him, he entered the classroom through the back door.

A tall, strapping man in his forties strode into the Hall of Enlightenment. The teacher, caught off guard, hurriedly told the children: "The Great Prince of the Northern Court is here to see you! Stand and greet him!"

The students, children of many different heights, set down their brushes, stood, and offered their greetings. Some bowed with hands at their sides, some bowed with hands closed before them, and some put their right fist over their chest while bowing; others knelt on one or both knees. The various methods followed the etiquette of the children's own ethnic groups, and together they made up a collection of fantastic oddities. The prince burst into hearty laughter at the sight and offered an approving nod.

"Yes, that's pretty good. You will all be pillars of the country in the future."

Their noble visitor was a leader of the Liao Empire's Northern Court in the Northern Administration, and his name was Yelü Dashi. The emperor of Liao had changed his Khitan title of *Irkin* to *Great Prince*, and this man now commanded the military power of all five of Liao's administrative divisions, second in power only to the emperor himself. He had been inspired this morning to explore the city's academies and walked first through Biyong Academy; then, in the afternoon, he visited Ming Academy to encourage the boys who had come to Shangjing for their studies.

Lang Junxia had never taught Duan Ling how to bow, and so he assumed what he'd learned in the morning would do. He raised his hands above his head and completed a proper obeisance.

"Very good, very good," Yelü Dashi said as he walked past Duan Ling with a smile.

After the children had greeted him, Yelü Dashi asked a few more casual questions before he allowed the teacher to guide him out. Duan Ling stole a longer glance at the Great Prince and saw that his build was strong and powerful, with a full beard, but he seemed good-natured. The moment he exited the room, all the children began talking at once. The noise was so deafening it nearly blew off the roof, but as soon as the teacher returned, silence descended.

"Put your brushes down and line up in the courtyard," the teacher instructed. "Shorter children at the front. Come on, follow me."

Students from all three divisions of Ming Academy lined up in the corridor. Yelü Dashi inspected the whole group once, then began calling children forward one by one to grant them a reward. As the students waited for their names to be called, Duan Ling glanced around, but he didn't see Batu anywhere.

The boy Batu had been wrestling with stood at the back of the next line over. Noticing Duan Ling scanning the crowd, he guessed whom he was looking for. "He's not here."

"Why not?" Duan Ling asked.

The young man shook his head, then gestured toward the east wing with a shrug, as if to say there was nothing he could do about it.

"Is he sick?"

"N-no. H-he just said h-he doesn't w-want to come."

The other boy, Duan Ling realized, had a stutter. When the gathered children heard him speak, two whole classes snickered. The teacher glowered back with disapproval, and the line of children went quiet again.

Duan Ling waited until the teacher turned his head to slip from the line, trotting along the corridor in search of Batu.

He found him sitting in the courtyard, the plum blossom dessert he'd given him laid out on the table. His back was turned to Duan Ling, and so he didn't notice his approach; he carefully blew away the dirt from the confection's oilpaper covering, then unwrapped it and folded the paper neatly to put away in his robes.

Just as he opened his mouth to eat the treat, Duan Ling called out, "Batu!"

Batu was so startled he nearly choked on the candy. Duan Ling rushed forward to thump on his back. After he swallowed, Batu got up to find some water.

"The Great Prince is here," Duan Ling said, following him. "And he's giving us rewards for nothing. Are you not going to go?"

"I'm not a dog. I don't accept gifts from the Khitan," Batu said. "You can go back."

Batu crossed the threshold into his room, and Duan Ling leaned in through the window. "Why not?"

"Well, because I don't want them. You shouldn't take them, either. Come in here; there's something I want to say to you."

Duan Ling felt torn. While he did want the Great Prince's reward—even if he didn't quite know what it meant—his instincts told him Batu was right. When he was in Runan, he never picked up any scraps the serving girls threw to him, even if he was starving. There was no special reason; it was simply his nature, a stubbornness engraved into his heart since the day he was born.

"Then I don't want the reward either," Duan Ling announced.

Batu lay on his bed and scooted over to one side, then patted the pillow, inviting Duan Ling to lie down and take an afternoon nap with him. Instead Duan Ling paused, glanced around, and headed off back down the corridor.

"Hey! Where are you going?" Batu got up, chasing him outside.

"I'm just going to take a look."

He didn't want the reward—but it was okay to see what it was, right?

He soon found out: It was a weasel-hair brush and one silver tael per child.

Batu and Duan Ling hid in the back courtyard and spied on several servants carrying wicker baskets full of brushes. They weren't as nice as the one Lang Junxia had bought for Duan Ling.

Batu tossed his arm over Duan Ling's shoulders and said, "Let's go."

Suddenly, one of the taller, thinner servants turned around, giving Duan Ling a glimpse of his face. Duan Ling had the strange feeling he'd seen him somewhere before.

The memory struck like lightning: the man with the golden centipede he'd seen at the apothecary! But his neck tattoo was gone now. Was it really the same man?

"Let's go," Batu said. "Or do you want it after all?"

"Wait a minute," Duan Ling said, thinking hard.

Why would this man be at Ming Academy—and why was he hauling baskets around in the back courtyard?

Wu Du removed the brushes from a basket and carried them into the front courtyard. Duan Ling knit his brows and moved to follow him. Impatient with his dawdling, Batu yanked Duan Ling back behind the corridor wall. Wu Du turned his head slightly at the noise and saw only Batu out of the corner of his eye.

Batu had distinct features—a high nose and deep-set, faintly blue eyes—and he was wearing Mongol clothing. Assuming it was just a curious child looking around, Wu Du didn't spare his watcher another thought. He walked briskly toward the lines of children, scanning their faces one by one.

When he didn't find the one he was looking for, he crossed to stand by the window at the side of the hall, eavesdropping with his arms folded.

Within the hall, a group of older children, including Cai Yan, stood in rows to greet Yelü Dashi.

"Very good," Yelü Dashi said, clearly satisfied with what he saw.

The teacher called their names one at a time, and each student came forward to bow and kowtow to Yelü Dashi, who then took one tael and a brush from the guard beside him and handed them to the young man as encouragement in his studies.

"Where is the child from the Helian family?" Yelü Dashi asked the teacher, seeming to remember something.

"Helian Bo! Helian Bo!" the teacher called out in a hurry. The stuttering young man who had wrestled with Batu ran in, bumping into the teacher on the way.

Yelü Dashi nodded toward the boy. "Have you gotten used to life in Shangjing?"

"T-to answer Your Excellency," the young man named Helian Bo said. "I-I'm used to it now. Thank you for your grace."

Before Yelü Dashi could reply, Helian Bo knelt and kowtowed, knocking his head on the floor loudly three times. Yelü Dashi was quite pleased, and his hearty laughter carried into the courtyard outside. He helped the boy up, placed the tael and brush in his palm, and curled the boy's fingers over them as he affectionately patted the back of his hand.

Helian Bo nodded once, then turned and left. The instant he was out of sight of the hall, he threw the gifts into the flowerbed in a fury and stomped on the brush until it splintered into pieces. Just as he was about to leave, Batu waved him over from their hiding place. Helian Bo furrowed his brow, looked around, and ran toward Batu.

Back in the hall, Yelü Dashi continued, "What about the child from the Borjigin family?"

The teacher called again, but Batu only ducked down lower, Duan Ling beside him. Beside the window, Wu Du turned his head, narrowed his eyes, and once more observed the gathered young men through the latticed window.

The teacher left to find Batu, but he still hadn't returned after a long wait. Since the other boys were still standing around, Yelü Dashi asked, "Han Jieli is here, right?"

The chubby boy from the Han family stepped forward. "Yes, Your Excellency." He bowed to Yelü Dashi, but he did not kneel.

"You've gained weight again." Yelü Dashi laughed. "At this rate, you'll catch up to your father in no time."

The other students laughed with the prince. Han Jieli blushed but said nothing.

"Study well," Yelü Dashi said warmly.

"That guy is weird," Duan Ling said.

"Wh-who?" Helian Bo asked, confused.

Duan Ling pointed to where the servant he saw earlier was standing by the window. "The guy with the sword."

Helian Bo and Batu gave him shocked looks. Realizing he'd said too much, Duan Ling shut his mouth, but Batu pressed him: "An assassin—you've seen him before?"

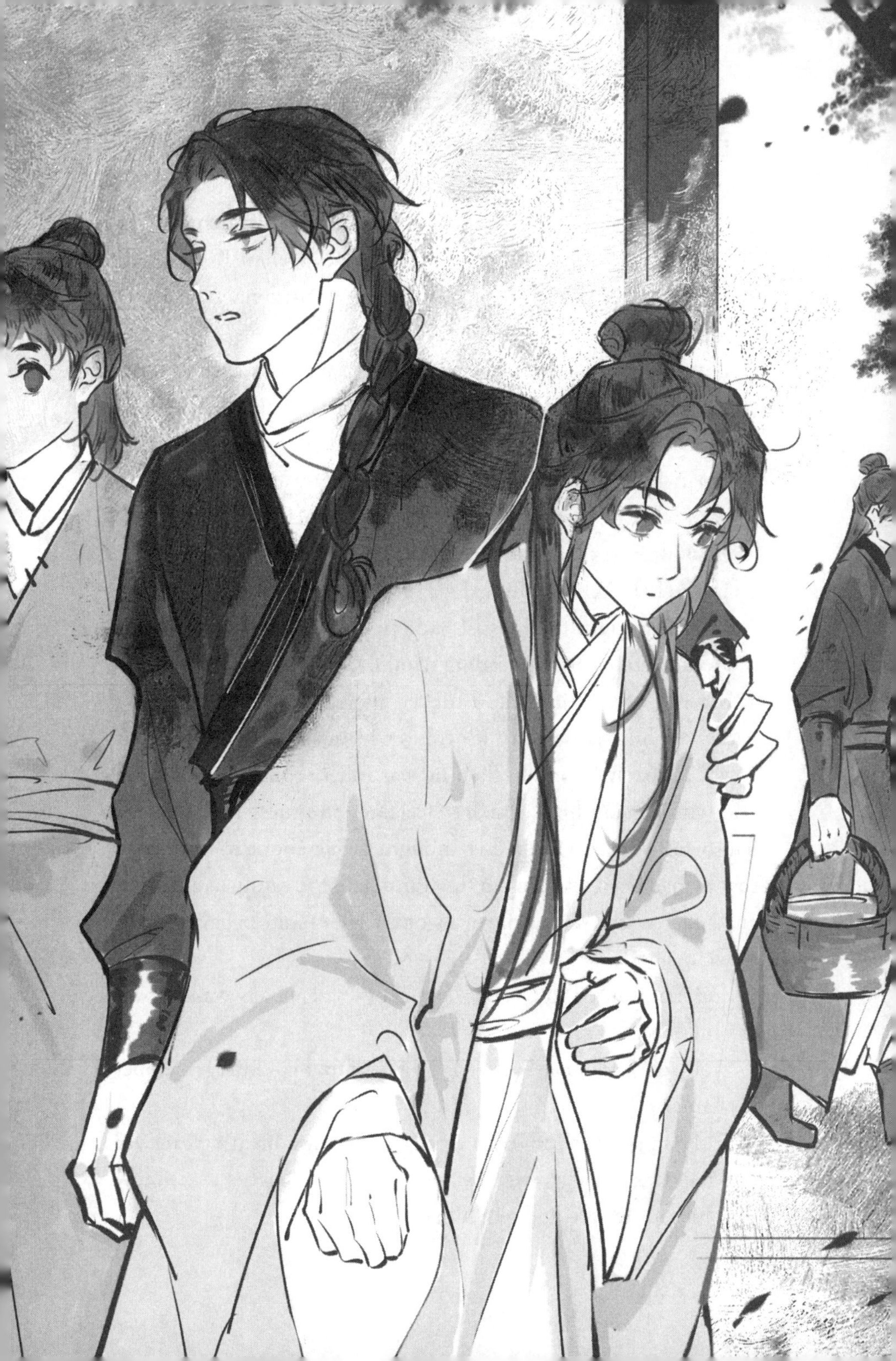

Duan Ling immediately waved a hand. "No, I haven't seen him before. Doesn't he look like he carries a sword?"

Batu and Helian Bo observed the man for a moment before Helian Bo said, "Th-th-that m-man i-i-is..." Helian Bo was too panicked to speak clearly, instead patting Batu's hand. "Hand! Hand!"

Batu noticed his hands as well. "He's a martial artist, and his sword is hidden on his back! He's definitely an assassin—Duan Ling, you were right!"

Duan Ling had hit the bullseye entirely by accident. He had no idea what this man was doing at the school. Maybe he was an assassin by profession, but worked as an errand runner part-time?

In the hall, Yelü Dashi had waited some time, but the bastard from the Borjigin family still hadn't appeared. He gestured for the teacher to continue reading names. Cai Yan stood nervously at the end of the line—he'd tucked the confection Duan Ling had given him earlier into his robes without much thought, but it was a frozen dessert. When he was in the courtyard learning etiquette, or standing outside to welcome the guests, the weather had been cold and he hadn't thought twice about it—but now that he had been standing in the warm hall, the candy had melted. The sugar-water seeped into his outer robes and began to drip down his body.

Cai Yan wanted to die, but Yelü Dashi had already walked over to him.

"You are..." Yelü Dashi thought for a bit, but couldn't remember his name.

Cai Yan greeted him respectfully and drew a breath to answer, but Yelü Dashi had already lost interest in this Han boy; he simply gave him his reward and sent him on his way.

The students waiting outside watched as Cai Yan ran from the room and across the corridor, leaving brown-red splotches on the floor behind him.

Wu Du frowned slightly and followed a few steps behind Cai Yan. The young man ducked behind some rockery and untied his robes, then removed the oilpaper wrapper from his pocket. It was soaking wet; when he opened it, there was a handful of damp plum blossoms inside.

Cai Yan nearly lost his mind. While he was wiping down his outer robe in frustration, a voice sounded behind him: "Did a Xianbei person make this plum blossom candy for you?"

He was about to turn when a hand clamped over his nose and mouth. He fainted without making a sound.

"He's taking that Cai dog away!" Batu stared, dumbfounded. "Is that guy the Cai clan's enemy?"

"D-do we save him?" Helian Bo asked.

The three boys looked at each other, completely befuddled. But Duan Ling knew this man was dangerous—without wasting another moment, he chased after him with Helian Bo and Batu right on his heels. They followed as Wu Du made his way through the corridor. When he arrived at the inner courtyard, he heard footsteps approaching: Yelü Dashi's guards on patrol. Wu Du deposited the unconscious Cai Yan behind a tree and stood straight, his head lowered and hands as his side, as the guards passed.

"Come on!" Batu whispered.

He led Helian Bo and Duan Ling around the edge of the courtyard. Duan Ling started over to go rescue Cai Yan right away, but Helian Bo grabbed him and dragged him back. They conversed in frantic whispers as they ran.

"Are we not going to tell the headmaster?" Duan Ling hissed.

"And wait for him to call for help?" Batu whispered back. "The Cai dog's body will be cold by then!"

"Wait! Wait! H-he w-wants..." Helian Bo stuttered more when he was nervous; Duan Ling and Batu listened anxiously, wishing they could upend him and pour out all his words at once. He finally gave up and pointed toward the inner courtyard.

Duan Ling said, "Does he mean... Should we find the prince instead?"

Helian Bo nodded hastily, but Batu waved a hand. "That Yelü dog doesn't care about Han lives. He only cares about himself."

By the time he'd said it, Helian Bo had arrived at the same conclusion. He nodded again, saying, "Right."

Worriedly, Duan Ling asked, "Then what should we do?"

"Helian speaks too slowly," Batu said. "You go to the city guard headquarters and get this Cai dog's brother. Helian and I will think of a way to save him."

"But I don't know where that is," Duan Ling protested.

Batu had no words. After a moment, he resigned himself to his fate and said, "I'll go, then. You two follow him."

Wu Du had hefted Cai Yan's limp body again, prepared to flee. Duan Ling and Helian Bo were about to follow him out of the corridor when suddenly Duan Ling's collar wrenched taut, and he was dragged behind the corridor wall.

Before he could scream, a hand covered his mouth; he jerked his head around and saw a masked man wearing a dark cloak. Helian Bo kept his wits about him and leapt forward to help Duan Ling, but he'd made it only a step when the masked man nonchalantly jabbed an acupoint at the base of his throat, and he collapsed, unable to speak or move.

As the masked man held Duan Ling in his arms, Duan Ling caught a whiff of a familiar scent. The man nudged Duan Ling to the side, where Helian Bo couldn't see him, and brought a finger to his lips. The corners of his lips beneath the mask lifted slightly.

Duan Ling didn't so much as breathe.

The masked man patted Helian Bo once, unsealing his acupoints. Without a word, he ran from the courtyard to hunt down the unlucky Wu Du.

10

THE MASKED MAN sprang at his target from behind the tree, smiling coldly. His sword produced countless mirrored afterimages that completely surrounded Wu Du. With no other avenue of escape, Wu Du was forced to retreat to the roof of the school's stables. He drew his own blade with a mocking smile.

The masked man's sword flashed toward Wu Du's throat.

Wu Du's smile didn't waver. He abandoned his defense and directed his blade toward the unconscious Cai Yan. But to his surprise, the masked man ignored Cai Yan entirely, his blade sweeping unhesitatingly toward Wu Du's unprotected neck. Instantly, Wu Du knew he'd miscalculated: Even if he killed Cai Yan, his assailant's sword would run him through. He swiftly changed tactics, but he'd already lost his advantage; when he ducked his head to the side, the masked man followed with a sideways slash that left a bloody wound across Wu Du's face.

Turning, Wu Du attempted to break away, but the masked man followed close as a shadow. The boy in his hands was clearly useless as a hostage—Wu Du dropped the youth and raised his sword. As the two blades clashed, Wu Du's was knocked from his hand, spinning off in a wide arc and embedding itself in a wooden pillar on the roof of the stable. The masked man tossed his sword aside and thrust his palms toward Wu Du's abdomen.

The impact was silent, but held all the force in the masked man's body. Wu Du's insides spasmed, and he spat blood as he fell backward.

A momentary misjudgment had almost cost Wu Du his life—but as he crashed into the stable roof, he flicked his left hand and dispersed a handful of poisonous powder into the air. The masked man held his breath, grabbed his sword, and leapt after Wu Du, who emerged from the poisonous cloud to retrieve his sword from the pillar. Wu Du turned and staggered toward his pursuer.

The masked man landed on the courtyard wall, his cloak fluttering, as Wu Du caught up to him. Both crossed onto the roof of Ming Academy, leaping across the gap directly over the guards' heads. The masked man's movements seemed sluggish, and Wu Du was still fighting though the palm strike had injured him badly. Their feet slipped on the icy roof as they landed, dislodging and shattering tiles.

The noise alerted the guards, who finally looked up.

Duan Ling and Helian Bo seized their chance. They raced forward from their hiding place, grabbing Cai Yan and carrying him back into the corridor.

By the time the guard lifted his head, Wu Du and the masked man had already disappeared. Stepping lightly with qinggong,[7] they flew over eaves and walls, landing silently on the roof of the main hall. The wound on Wu Du's face was still bleeding freely.

He and the masked man stared each other down. Neither was arrogant enough to make the first move—both knew that, this time, only one would come out alive.

The masked man asked, hoarse, "How did you figure it out?"

Wu Du laughed. "After seeing you rush back to Shangjing as soon as we parted ways, I left you alive as bait for a bigger fish. What else

---

7   Literally "lightness technique," the martial arts skill of moving swiftly and lightly through the air.

could you be doing here but protecting his descendants? If he had a child, they'd be around this age."

"Even the most careful men will make mistakes. I see you're still one step ahead, Wu-xiong," the masked man replied.

"You can protect him for now, but not for a lifetime," Wu Du said.

"I will protect him as long as I can. You've lost today."

Wu Du sneered. "Don't be so sure."

Without warning, the masked man summoned his inner force and stomped down. The rooftiles buckled beneath the wave of energy. Wu Du's expression shifted, but he had no time to jump to safety. He crashed down into the main hall with the falling tile, the masked man right behind him.

Yelü Dashi was still passing out rewards when the roof collapsed in a vivid demonstration of the Han proverb "wealthy men ought not sit beneath treacherous eaves." The two assassins tumbled down together, and the hall erupted into chaos. The Great Prince roared, the guards shouted, the headmaster cried out, the children wet themselves in fright—a hundred different reactions painted a lively scene.

"Who—?!"

"Assassin!"

"Protect His Excellency!"

But Yelü Dashi was no weakling himself—he made a quick decision, flipping the table and throwing it toward the intruders.

Wu Du and the masked man soundlessly separated and jumped up, each flying toward a window. The masked man fled east and Wu Du fled west. The guards drew their bows, and a volley of arrows flew after them, nipping at their heels.

In the space of an instant, arrows sailed past glittering icicles, and a drop of water plinked to the ground. The masked man touched down on the rockery in the front courtyard. The archery skills of the Khitan people were unparalleled, and the arrows had all been aimed at his vitals; he narrowed his eyes, and the onrushing arrows dwindled to a hundred sharp points in his vision. Spreading his arms and stepping onto the rockery, the masked man backflipped into the air like a falcon spreading its wings, avoiding all the arrows and landing nimbly on the far side of the courtyard wall.

On the other side of the school grounds, Wu Du fled up the wall, arrows whistling toward him. He landed on the top with one foot and used his momentum to whip himself around, his flaring robe catching the arrows instead of his body. Channeling his inner force, he flung the arrows back, sending them streaking in all directions.

By the time the guards ran into the outer courtyard, Wu Du had vanished without a trace.

The pounding of hooves came from the other side of the wall, and Cai Wen rode into the alley leading his soldiers. Batu saw Wu Du leap down to the ground and shouted, "That's him!"

The guards charged. Wu Du, injured, didn't dare keep fighting; he fled deeper into the alley. Yet as he turned into another narrow lane, more soldiers appeared. The city guards running down the main road along the river were gaining ground, threatening to outflank him. Out of options, Wu Du leapt into the air, drew his sword from the scabbard in an arc of light, and crashed into the frozen river.

With a thunderous *crack*, the river ice split, and Wu Du disappeared into the dark water.

Back at Ming Academy, in a remote courtyard, Duan Ling and Helian Bo were shaking the unconscious Cai Yan.

"Cai Yan!" Duan Ling cried out.

"Water," Helian Bo said shortly, and handed Duan Ling some to give to Cai Yan.

Without a sound, the masked man appeared right beside them. Helian Bo started and tried to tug Duan Ling away, but Duan Ling waved his hand—*it's all right*—as the masked man leaned forward and checked Cai Yan's breath and pulse. Duan Ling opened his mouth to speak, but the masked man laid his other hand over his lips.

Cai Wen's voice sounded from the other side of the wall. The masked man pointed at Cai Yan and shook a finger at Duan Ling—Cai Yan would be fine. With that, the man scaled the wall, disappearing from sight seconds before Cai Wen rushed into the courtyard.

Yelü Dashi was furious. That afternoon, he closed Ming Academy to question all the children. Everyone was exhausted, and many children couldn't stop crying.

Batu had gone for backup; he hadn't seen the masked man who fought Wu Du. Duan Ling had already told his version of the story three times. Of course, he didn't dare mention Lang Junxia, so he left out some particular details. He explained that when he went to find Batu, he stumbled upon Cai Yan being kidnapped. The second mysterious assassin had appeared after that, and everyone had witnessed the rest.

Even when Cai Yan woke up, he couldn't provide any more information. Yelü Dashi listened in himself, but when he tried to check their stories against Helian Bo's, the boy stuttered so much the prince could hardly understand a word. Yelü Dashi would rather listen to Duan Ling repeat his story ten times over than patiently await Helian Bo's story once, so Duan Ling and Cai Yan's recountings were the ones taken and recorded. Cai Wen's investigation turned up nothing useful. Everyone was confused, and eventually, they gave up.

The interrogation had exhausted Duan Ling, and he didn't have much appetite for dinner. He went back to his remote courtyard room to sleep, but only tossed and turned. The day's events were still racing through his mind. He'd lain in bed restless for some time when a graceful flute melody picked up outside and floated through his window. Wrapped in that delicate melody, Duan Ling calmed bit by bit, and at last fell into a deep sleep.

The next day, everything returned to normal, save for the dark smudges under Cai Yan's eyes. Duan Ling tried to check on him, but Cai Yan only nodded at his inquiry. Cai Yan had no idea whom his family might have offended; all he could tell Duan Ling was that his older brother had discovered an unconscious servant behind the Hall of Ink, whose clothes the assassin had disguised himself in to sneak inside.

Why had the assassin entered the school at this particular time to kidnap someone? What's more, why Cai Yan? As for the second man with the mask, Cai Wen couldn't figure out who he was either. Later, the guards found another hole in the river ice outside the city and concluded the assassin had emerged from the water and escaped.

Later that night, at Qionghua House, Lang Junxia mixed medicinal powders together, turned his back to the mirror, and began applying the medicine to his injuries. To one side of him sat a folding screen, and beyond it, six girls in splendid attire, including Ding Zhi. These were Qionghua's finest courtesans: Orchid, Peony, Hibiscus, Jasmine, Gardenia, and Angelica.

One of the girls was lighting hand stoves while another was offering tea, colorfully dancing around a noble-looking lady in the hall—the head of Qionghua House, whom Ding Zhi called *Madam*.

"You and that child have uncommonly good luck," the madam said lightly. "Why don't you find a place to hide for a few days, then move again?"

Lang Junxia's muscular, bare-shouldered silhouette moved in shadow on the screen. "Instead of skulking around," he said, "it's better to be prepared and lie in wait."

"That child must be blessed by the heavens. To think Wu Du was the one who came this time…" the madam mused. "Zhu of the shadow squad was highly skilled. It was purely by chance that he died at the hands of a child. Fate is at play, to be sure. But next time, it may not be Wu Du who comes."

"Even if it's Changliu-jun, so what?" Lang Junxia asked as he put down the saucer of medicine.

"Don't underestimate the enemy," the madam said calmly. "Wu Du is proficient with poison, but he's otherwise an outlier among those in your trade. He knocks people out with his tricks if possible and spares those who can be spared. Whenever he goes out to kill, he lets more people go than he makes enemies—and he often lets them live out of sheer pity. A softhearted person like him isn't qualified to be called an assassin."

Lang Junxia had finished changing his bandages. He slipped his outer robe on and tied his belt, then emerged from behind the screen.

The madam was dressed in dark red brocade, embroidered with lifelike cranes spreading their wings. Her features hinted at a heritage in the Western Regions; her eyebrows were so dark there was a sheen of blue, and her eyes were like the jade pools of mountain springs. She was the most beautiful flower in Qionghua House, and though she was the madam, she had yet to reach thirty years of age.

"I doubt Changliu-jun will come," Lang Junxia said.

"You've always been bold," she replied flatly.

"The emperor of Southern Chen's days are numbered," Lang Junxia continued as if she hadn't spoken. "The outcome of their northern expedition was a foregone conclusion; within three years, Southern Chen's military will be pinned south of Yubi Pass. Zhao Kui and Mu Kuangda will be mired in internal strife. At that point, neither Wu Du nor Changliu-jun will dare leave their masters' sides." Lang Junxia paused. "Shangjing is the territory of Liao. Surely they have better things to do than send a famed assassin thousands of miles away just to find a single child of unknown origins."

The madam regarded him in silence. Lang Junxia had no more to say; he nodded to the madam and took his leave from Qionghua House.

Many nights later, in Southern Chen, Zhao Kui sat within the hall of the general's estate, casting a long shadow across the floor.

"Spare his life," he said.

"What?" Wu Du said, thinking he'd heard incorrectly.

He'd returned from Shangjing in a miserable state. He'd neither discovered the location of Li Jianhong nor killed the legendary Nameless Assassin. In the end, he'd brought back only one piece of useful information.

Zhao Kui sat with his back to the dim light that illuminated Wu Du's face. The assassin's expression carried complicated emotions.

"Who else knows about this?" Zhao Kui asked.

Wu Du shook his head. "Zhu lost his life, and the other assassins from the shadow squad failed to sneak into Shangjing in the first place. This is information only I was able to infer. But I don't understand…"

"His Majesty hasn't much time left," Zhao Kui said, his tone measured. "The fourth prince has no children, and Li Jianhong's whereabouts remain unknown. Mu Kuangda aims to seize control of the court, and if we don't have a trump card, he'll be difficult to manage. So—pretend this incident never happened."

CHAPTER TEN

Wu Du nodded his understanding. "General, I didn't search for the third prince outside Huchang—I headed for Shangjing instead. Prime Minister Mu...may have already put two and two together."

Zhao Kui's smile was chilly. "Even if Mu Kuangda knows, he won't send Changliu-jun off to Shangjing. He can't sleep soundly without Changliu-jun's protection. Not to mention, after your little excursion, the city will be heavily guarded; he won't have the opportunity to sneak in."

Shangjing remained under martial law for ten days. Guards patrolled Ming Academy and observed the children, such that the teachers were afraid of even breathing too loudly.

After this incident, Cai Yan and Duan Ling grew steadily closer. Cai Yan occasionally let Duan Ling ask him questions about his homework, and if there was anything Duan Ling didn't understand, he would explain it and urge him to take his studies more seriously.

The city guards withdrew on the final day of the first month. That day, more relatives waited outside the gate to pick up children than usual; everyone was worried after the assassination attempt. The alleys were packed with carriages, and many of the officials' vehicles were guarded by soldiers.

"Duan family—Duan-shaoye," the porter called out. "Are you here?"

Lang Junxia had been the first to arrive, waiting by the door before it was the proper time.

"Here, I'm here!" Duan Ling rushed to the porter, handed over his name plaque, and threw himself at Lang Junxia, who hugged him firmly with one arm.

"Let's go home," Lang Junxia said. As he grasped Duan Ling's hand to lead him away, Duan Ling couldn't help gazing backward through the lattice of the academy gates. Batu stood in the outer courtyard, watching him from afar.

Lang Junxia guessed what was holding Duan Ling back. He stopped and asked, "Are you friends with the Borjigin child?"

Duan Ling nodded.

"Should we invite him to our house for dinner?"

"Can we?" Duan Ling replied.

"He's your friend. Of course we can."

"Batu!" Duan Ling yelled. "Come to my house tonight; let's leave together!"

Batu waved him off. Duan Ling waited, but even after the alley had almost cleared, Batu hadn't emerged. Assuming no one would be picking Batu up this time either, Duan Ling shouted again, "Come on!"

Still Batu didn't answer him. Instead, he picked up the iron rod he'd used to strike the bell last time and turned away toward the inner courtyard. The setting sun shone on them from the entrance of the alley, and Duan Ling's shoulders slumped.

As soon as they got home, however, Duan Ling's melancholy evaporated. Lang Junxia had prepared a small feast and spread the dishes out on the table. Duan Ling cheered as he sat down, eager to dig in without even washing his hands; Lang Junxia held him back and wiped his grubby little paws with a wet towel.

"I'm not a very good cook," Lang Junxia said. "Unlike Zheng Yan. When you eat better things in the future, you won't miss this. Please make do for now."

Who is Zheng Yan? Duan Ling thought fleetingly. But his curiosity was much less important than stuffing his mouth full of food, and any further questions flew right out of his head.

A sharp knock sounded on their door. Lang Junxia frowned.

"Duan Ling!" Batu shouted from outside.

Duan Ling swallowed his mouthful and ran out to let him inside. Batu's woolen coat had been unwashed for days; it was dirty, with leaves hanging from it. As Duan Ling opened the door, he said, "That Cai dog's brother was right: You really do live here. Here you go." He handed Duan Ling a bag of snacks.

"How did you sneak out?" Duan Ling asked.

"I have my ways, of course," Batu said mysteriously.

"Then come in and eat; hurry up."

Duan Ling tried to pull Batu inside, but Batu dug in his heels at the doorway. They tugged fruitlessly at each other until Lang Junxia came up behind Duan Ling and said, "Come in and have a cup of tea."

Batu gave up his resistance and came inside the house.

Lang Junxia laid chopsticks out for him. "I already ate," Batu said. "I'm just here to talk to him."

"Have fun, you two," Lang Junxia said, and stepped outside.

Watching Lang Junxia take his food and move a stool over to sit just beyond the door, Duan Ling was slightly disappointed. He was about to call out to him when Batu said, "Go ahead and eat."

Though Batu looked enviously at the table laden with food, he only sipped the cup of tea he held. Duan Ling tried again to persuade him to have a bite, but Batu insisted he'd eaten at the academy; Duan Ling reluctantly gave up. The two half-grown boys chatted for a while, talking and laughing. Duan Ling had been progressing rapidly in his studies and had recently graduated to the Hall of Ink. He would begin intermediate classes after returning from the short break.

When Lang Junxia had finished eating as well, Duan Ling rummaged through his own things for clothes to loan to Batu and dragged him out to a nearby bathhouse. Batu was reluctant, but he was aware his body odor had grown too strong—earlier, when he'd gone to the Cai residence for directions, he had received more than one contemptuous look. He gave in, letting Duan Ling tow him along as they walked behind Lang Junxia.

Finally, the two of them were soaking in the bathhouse. Batu had given up his woolen coat to be washed and dried by the servants while he played in the water with Duan Ling. Lang Junxia called someone over to shave the downy fuzz off Batu's face and trim his nails, but he washed Duan Ling himself.

"Your eyes are like lake water," Duan Ling said as the two of them faced the mirror. "They're so pretty. I wish I had blue eyes too."

"You envy my blue eyes, but I envy your black ones," Batu said.

"Blue eyes have their advantages, while black eyes have theirs too," Lang Junxia said casually. "Everyone has their own fate. There's no need for envy."

Duan Ling nodded. At the time, he didn't understand at all what Lang Junxia meant—but much later, this comment surfaced often in his memories of himself and Batu.

As the night grew deeper, the three returned to the courtyard residence. Batu shrugged on his half-dry woolen coat and said to Duan Ling, "I'm heading back."

"Stay here for the night," Duan Ling protested.

Waving him off, Batu scampered away before Duan Ling could insist. Duan Ling watched him walk off down the road in silence.

Batu cut through the alley to arrive outside Ming Academy, then crawled in through a gap in the garden fence and pushed a flowerpot housing a sacred lily back into its proper place to block the hole again. He returned, alone, to the library to sleep.

"You can be friends with the Borjigin boy," Lang Junxia warned Duan Ling that evening, "but you shouldn't imitate how he deals with others."

Duan Ling nodded.

All young people loved to play. It wasn't that no one at the academy wanted to befriend Duan Ling, but he always sat apart, following Lang Junxia's careful teachings to the smallest note. His childhood had taught him to be wary—he feared losing what he'd gained, and feared even more bringing trouble to his father, far away. Thus he stayed alone in his remote courtyard and didn't try to make friends.

Duan Ling's world centered on Lang Junxia, and on the father he'd never met.

At first, the other children thought he was shy and didn't have the courage to join them. But over time, they realized Duan Ling simply had a solitary nature, and they slowly accepted his habits. The atmosphere in Shangjing was carefree and easygoing, and Khitan attitudes were liberal; everyone respected each other's preferences. When other students bumped into Duan Ling on occasion, they would nod, and Duan Ling would return it politely, pausing and straightening his clothes just as the teachers had taught him.

They were nodding acquaintances in the truest sense. His classmates chuckled at first, thinking it a novelty. But when his habit continued, they began to think Duan Ling had a crisp and refreshing presence, and admired his elegance when he greeted others—thus, for a time, proper etiquette became popular throughout the academy. Only Cai Yan perceived him differently, and though neither boy acknowledged it aloud, they were both aware. His brother, Cai Wen, met with Duan Ling on several more occasions, and he, too, very much liked the boy's quiet seriousness. When Duan Ling joined the Hall of Ink, his deskmate turned out to be the tall, stuttering Helian Bo. He was a boy of few words, silent most of the time, and his company suited Duan Ling's own quiet temperament perfectly.

Before they knew it, the days grew longer, the snow melted, and winter gave way to spring. Duan Ling was always one of the first at the gate when it came time to leave the academy, and after that first school break, Lang Junxia was never late again. Duan Ling felt as if someone was always watching over him while he was at his studies.

As the weather warmed, Duan Ling felt himself distracted and drowsy during afternoon classes. On this day, he had dozed off on his desk and only woke when a plum bounced right off his head.

"Ow!" he yelped.

Duan Ling looked up and saw a figure flash across the wall, then disappear without a trace. He returned his focus to his calligraphy practice. He had completed the introductory curriculum in a scant three months, quickly surpassing the other children in the Hall of Ink. Soon after, he was assigned to another class, where he read more books and learned new, different subjects including astronomy, numerology, and several traditional forms of poetry. He applied himself diligently to all of them.

The warm spring nights blossomed with an alluring atmosphere. Duan Ling often felt a strange stirring in his heart on these evenings, and what came to his mind's eye was what he'd seen his first night in Shangjing: Lang Junxia's strong, masculine form in the room of Qionghua House.

The melodious notes of a flute sounded from beyond the walls of his remote courtyard. Crossing the spring night with its hundreds of flowers in bloom, the song seemed to be speaking directly to Duan Ling. He felt somehow certain that it must be Lang Junxia playing the flute, though he couldn't see him. Wearing only his underrobe, Duan Ling ran out under the moon and stood barefoot until the sound slowly faded. Only then did he return to his bed, but once he lay down, he tossed and turned, unable to fall asleep.

In the blink of an eye, half a year had passed. Just as he'd promised, Lang Junxia never traveled far again and kept the Duan residence in good order. Every time Duan Ling had a break, he took him out: riding horses across the wide-open grassland, watching herds of cattle and sheep, sitting at the bottom of the Altyn-Tagh Mountains and drinking the cold alpine meltwater while fishing in the river.

Occasionally they brought Batu along. Duan Ling often felt that he was very happy, but Batu didn't seem to want to share in his happiness. Over time, he began finding excuses to distance himself from Duan Ling. When Duan Ling consulted Lang Junxia, the man advised him that everyone had their own private thoughts—sometimes, there was no need to force things.

Every time Duan Ling came home, he asked: "Has my dad come yet?"

"Soon," Lang Junxia said to Duan Ling when he asked. "He won't abandon you."

Duan Ling asked the question routinely, seeming to find comfort in this routine answer. Lang Junxia admonished him again, "You must study hard so as not to disappoint your father."

The Duan residence remained snug and tidy, and Duan Ling planted an array of medicinal herbs in the flower garden. Some survived, while others did not. Lang Junxia asked him, puzzled, "Why are you planting so many herbs?"

"It's fun," Duan Ling said, wiping sweat from his brow.

"Do you want to learn medicine?" Lang Junxia asked.

Duan Ling mulled that over. Perhaps because his childhood had been full of injury and illness, he was always on edge. Human life was finite, and everyone would face death one day, so, yes, he was interested in treating diseases and saving lives. He often supplemented his reading with medical compendiums on identifying herbs.

"Don't study medicine," Lang Junxia advised him. "Your father has high hopes for you. In the future you will achieve great things."

"I'll think about it," Duan Ling said stubbornly.

"Since you like plants and flowers, why not plant this?" Lang Junxia asked, pointing to a peach tree sapling. He had bought it especially for Duan Ling in the market, shipped all the way from the south. Fertile southern Jiangnan was filled with peach blossoms in the spring, but the trees had trouble surviving in Shangjing.

Lang Junxia planted the sapling with Duan Ling, then dusted off his hands. "When the tree flowers, your father will come."

"Really?" Duan Ling asked.

Remembering this promise, he tended the peach tree with utmost care. But the tree wasn't suited to the climate or the local soil, and looked sickly year-round. When spring arrived again, it formed a few buds, but they all withered before blooming.

Autumn came once more. On the outskirts of Shangjing, grass covered the ground like rust, and a strong wind blew from the other side of the mountains. Lang Junxia stopped by the bright band of the river and gazed into the distance, leading his horse along. After all this time, Duan Ling had more or less forgotten distant Runan. After his ascension from the Hall of Enlightenment to the Hall of Ink, and from there to the Chamber of Tomes, the number of Mongol, Khitan, and Tangut children among his fellow students decreased, while the number of Han children increased. From his classmates, he also learned a great deal that Lang Junxia hadn't taught him; for example, that most of the Han people in Shangjing came from the south, and that the headmaster had once been a great scholar in Southern Chen. Qionghua House, he discovered, was where the officials of the Northern and Southern Courts of Liao joined one another to have fun and drink, and the girls there had been brought from the south by its founder.

Many Han in Shangjing dreamed of their homeland in Southern Chen; in their dreams, willow catkins flurried and peach blossoms flowered. Though peach trees rarely survived in Shangjing, many tried planting them, and though the Han people's books were difficult, many tried reading them.

Borjigin Batu, Helian Bo, Wuerlan... His classmates at Ming Academy had fathers with a special identity, called *hostage*. The Cai, Lin, and Zhao boys... Their families also had a special identity, called *Southern Court official*.

Everyone missed their hometown. Though nobody said it aloud, they all believed in their hearts that they would one day return.

11

On the students' final day at Ming Academy, the headmaster gave each of them a dragon stone carved with their name in Han on the front and Khitan on the back. From the head seat of the main hall, the headmaster took a leisurely sip of his tea and said, "These rocks are harvested from Mount Yuheng. Do not forget whence they came."

The students—about a dozen in number—bowed toward the headmaster. As of that moment, they had completed their studies at Ming Academy. When the sixth month came, they would bring their recommendation letter signed by the headmaster and the teachers and sit for Biyong Academy's entrance exam.

Later, as he held the recommendation letter in hand, a strange feeling came over Duan Ling.

"Am I Han?" he asked Lang Junxia.

"Of course you are." Lang Junxia was cleaning fish in the kitchen. In his forever-nonchalant tone, he said, "You are a Han among the Han."

Duan Ling was no longer the naive child he had once been; now, he noticed the weight behind Lang Junxia's words. "What do you mean by that?"

"I mean that you're Han," Lang Junxia replied easily. "Now go study."

"But my surname is Duan—that's not one of the four major houses of the Central Plains," Duan Ling pushed.

"You'll understand one day," was Lang Junxia's only response.

Duan Ling tucked his hands in his sleeves and watched from the side as Lang Junxia prepared the fish. Lang Junxia's hands were dexterous, and he effortlessly sliced pieces thinner than paper. Duan Ling started forward to help, but Lang Junxia held up a hand.

"A gentleman does not enter the kitchen. Go read your books."

Duan Ling deflated at the rote command. But after living with Lang Junxia for so long, obedience had become second nature. He strolled into the yard, where he picked up a long stick.

"When will you teach me martial arts?" Duan Ling asked, swinging the stick a few times. "You promised after I graduated from Ming Academy, you'd teach me how to ride and shoot, and hand-to-hand combat."

"'The swordsman transgresses the law by way of martial arts,'" Lang Junxia replied. "What's so good about learning to fight? Only illiterate roughnecks practice martial arts. You'll attract nothing but trouble."

"'And the scholar transgresses by way of books.'"[8] Duan Ling finished the adage, then countered, "Yet everyone studies the Four Books and Five Classics."

Lang Junxia was stumped. Duan Ling was no longer a child who listened to his every word without question; he was intelligent and clear-eyed, and the wheels in his brain turned speedily during debates. Now, even Lang Junxia lost the argument sometimes.

"If I don't learn martial arts, I'll be no more than meat on someone else's chopping block—I'll get my ass kicked," Duan Ling reasoned with great seriousness.

---

8   Lines from "The Five Vermin," a chapter in Han Feizi, by Warring States era Legalist philosopher Han Fei.

"In this life, there will be those whose role is to protect you," Lang Junxia replied, wiping his hands. "Put down the sword and pick up the brush; the kingly way—the natural order of society—will be your weapon. One can only do a single thing well in life, yet you want to learn medicine *and* martial arts on top of everything else. You'd be spreading yourself too thin."

"Borjigin said I can't depend on anyone but myself," Duan Ling said.

Lang Junxia's lips quirked upward at the corners. "Not even me?"

"Of course you'll protect me," Duan Ling said. "But what if... What if you fall into danger? How will I protect *you*?"

"Failure to protect you would be a dereliction of my duty," Lang Junxia replied simply. "Should such a thing happen, even if I didn't die in the process, someone would eliminate me—which would be fine. After I'm gone, there will still be plenty of others who will shield you from harm—"

Whatever he planned to say next was cut off as Duan Ling caught him from behind and rubbed his head against his back. "That won't happen. I'll be your shield," Duan Ling declared. Then he turned and left the kitchen.

Sunlight spilled across the chopping board. Without noticing, Lang Junxia had lightly cut his finger with the knife in his hand.

In the back courtyard, Duan Ling straightened the laundry poles and began hanging their freshly washed pants and underclothes to dry. Lang Junxia had ultimately decided against hiring any servants to take care of them—instead, he'd taken on everything himself. While Duan Ling was in school, Lang Junxia visited from time to time and brought him goods from home. And during break, Lang Junxia ensured that Duan Ling lacked for nothing. Sometimes, curiosity struck Duan Ling and he would ask Lang Junxia where his money came from, but Lang Junxia's answer was always the same: "It's not something you need to worry about."

It was early spring, and Duan Ling felt too sluggish for studying. A strange, burgeoning sensation made him fidget restlessly at his desk. Lang Junxia knelt beside him helping grind ink and light incense; he even prepared Duan Ling a hot towel to wipe his hands. Yet the second he left, Duan Ling tiptoed out of the study to his flowerbed instead, picking up a trowel to tend to his plants.

As a child in Runan, Duan Ling had often watched the gardener at work: planting flowers, pruning branches, and maneuvering the greenery. Gradually, he'd developed a love for cultivating growing things. After unsuccessfully attempting to talk him out of this hobby a few times, Lang Junxia had relented—provided that his studies weren't affected.

Study, study, study… Nothing but study… Duan Ling didn't mind studying, but studying too much would bore anyone. Cai Yan was two years older than him and had already entered Biyong Academy, while Batu had no mind for higher learning and had disappeared to who knew where without so much as a goodbye after graduating. Duan Ling had gone to his house to call on him a few times but never managed to see him. His house was dark and gloomy, and more than a little frightening. Batu's father had glowered at Duan Ling and told him never to come there again, for no other reason than that he was Han. It was a great contrast to Helian Bo's mother, who was cordial to Duan Ling because the Han and Tangut peoples shared a friendly relationship. She'd tug on Duan Ling's hand while she asked after his well-being and thank him for caring for her stuttering son.

Having graduated from Ming Academy but not yet matriculated into Biyong Academy, Duan Ling found himself idle and spent most of his time at home tending his garden. On this day, he had cautiously dug out a peony seedling and transferred it to a different plot when Lang Junxia's voice rang out behind him: "We'll hire a gardener one of these days; this is distracting you from your studies."

Duan Ling nearly snapped the stem of the seedling in surprise, then replied, "I can tend to the garden myself."

"The entrance exam is in the sixth month," Lang Junxia said, frowning. "You certainly look distracted."

"I'll study more in a bit," Duan Ling said, stretching.

"Perhaps I should find a ruler too," Lang Junxia added. "With no one to smack your palms outside the classroom and keep you in line, you'll start slacking."

Duan Ling laughed heartily at that. Lang Junxia never hit him; even his reprimands were measured, with rarely any sharp peaks of joy or sorrow. He only stood, silent, like the bamboo framing the outdoor corridors.

"Or maybe we should go spend a night at Qionghua House?" Lang Junxia suggested.

Duan Ling flushed scarlet immediately. Many students at Ming Academy were adolescents and spoke frankly of the affairs between a man and a woman. Once, Batu and Helian Bo had even snuck Duan Ling out of school, crawling under the garden fence and creeping into Qionghua House, where they witnessed Ding Zhi waiting on Cai Yan's elder brother and pouring him wine.

Since then Duan Ling had learned, more or less, what kind of place Qionghua House was. Cheeks still warm, he turned to go inside.

"Why are you blushing?" Lang Junxia asked.

Spring days were lazy; after returning to his room, Duan Ling watched Lang Junxia's shadow moving to and fro through the corridors and couldn't help dozing off. He napped until nightfall, then couldn't fall asleep after dinner, tossing and turning in his bed.

"Want some water?" Lang Junxia asked from the other side of his door. Duan Ling hadn't slept in the same bed as Lang Junxia for years, and usually only heard minor movements from the next room over once in a while.

Duan Ling hummed noncommittally. Sensing that Lang Junxia had sat down instead of leaving, he rolled onto his side and murmured, half awake, "Are you not going to bed?"

"Can't sleep," Lang Junxia answered. "I'll sit here for a bit."

The next day dawned bright and sunny. After Lang Junxia rose and dressed, he called through the door, "Duan Ling, I'm going out for some business. I'll be away for the day, back by evening."

Duan Ling mumbled a response, still dozing. When the warm sunlight filtering through the window landed on his face, he twitched his head aside to dodge its rays. The sun crept further over, and Duan Ling moved again too, maneuvering here and there whenever the sun shifted to avoid the light.

Outside the window, a man silently watched Duan Ling. He was dressed in coarse linen, travel-worn, and his chapped lips were quivering.

"That is my son," Li Jianhong said.

"Yes, Your Highness," Lang Junxia responded. He dug a yellowed birth certificate from his breast pocket and presented it to Li Jianhong with both hands. Li Jianhong didn't take it, nor cast it a single glance.

Quietly, Lang Junxia continued, "The princess consort traveled southward from Yubi Pass and returned to the Duan family. She was with child when she arrived. After Shangzi fell, the princess consort didn't dare reveal the little highness's true identity. The birth was difficult… Only the child survived."

Li Jianhong's exposed wrists were covered in blade scars, and there was another that snaked beneath his ear. When he'd embarked on his life as a fugitive many years before, hunted across the land by the assassins of Southern Chen, he had been alone. He had endured hardships no ordinary person could withstand. And in these recent years, fearing he would implicate his only son, he hadn't dared recklessly travel north.

After recovering from his initial injuries, he'd disappeared without a trace from the Xianbei's sacred mountain—also Lang Junxia's hometown—and entered Goryeo, where he snuck into a merchant caravan and traveled to Western Liang. He'd waited until Southern Chen's imperial court believed him dead before leaving Western Liang for Shangjing.

The journey had devoured too much of his time, taking so long that in the end the only thing propelling him forward was an elusive scrap of faith. When he finally arrived at the place he'd agreed upon with Lang Junxia, he couldn't take another step; he hardly believed he'd made it, and he didn't dare guess what awaited him behind the door of this small courtyard residence. In all likelihood, it would be nothing, and as soon as he knocked, only a fate of eternal solitude would greet him.

But heaven had shown him mercy—had left him a solitary light on his pitch-black road, a boat on the vast river of life and death. And although the light was dim and flickering, it brightened his entire life. The moment he laid eyes on Duan Ling, it was as though he was somehow saved. Li Jianhong's eyes were like deep pools of chilly autumn waters, and his powerful build exuded an invisible might, yet in that moment his gaze held only tenderness.

"My son has his mother's eyes," Li Jianhong said. "His lips are my father's; they're the Li family's lips."

"Yes, Your Highness," Lang Junxia answered.

Li Jianhong continued to watch, unblinking, as Duan Ling slept. The boy had grown significantly over the five years since he'd left Runan. He was handsome, with gently curved lips and a high, straight nose—exactly the same as Li Jianhong's.

"He'll be thirteen this year," Lang Junxia said, still holding the certificate. "His birthday is the sixth of the twelfth month."

"Yes, that sounds right," Li Jianhong said, almost to himself. "Xiaowan left me to travel south in the second month of that year."

"This subordinate was incapable and made one mistake after another," Lang Junxia said. "I was not able to protect the princess consort, nor assist Your Highness. The night I rode to Huchang in search of Your Highness, I was hindered by Wu Du—"

"No," Li Jianhong said emphatically. "Lang Junxia, any mistakes you might have made are void as of this moment."

Duan Ling rolled over again, and sunlight spilled across his youthful face. Li Jianhong stepped forward, unable to help himself, and nearly ran into the window lattice.

As he watched Duan Ling, he was like an exhausted traveler who'd trudged through miles of desert under a blazing sun, discovering an oasis as he teetered on the verge of death. Yet despite his overflowing longing, he was also filled with fear—scared that, with another step forward, he would find that the boy was nothing more than a mirage, shimmering at the edge of the world.

12

Duan Ling wallowed in bed until the sun was shining so brilliantly he could no longer escape it.

"Lang Junxia!" he called out, finally roused by the heat.

Outside his window, Lang Junxia stirred. Li Jianhong stopped him, wagging two outstretched fingers. With the two same fingers, he plucked Duan Ling's birth certificate from Lang Junxia's hands and folded it neatly—still sparing not a glance at its contents—before handing it back to him and gesturing for Lang Junxia to keep it.

Within the room, Duan Ling had finally remembered that Lang Junxia had said he'd be away on business today. He rolled out of bed and dressed himself. After washing his face and donning an outer robe, he left his room, yawning as he crossed the courtyard.

"Per your orders, sir, the little highness was enrolled in Ming Academy," Lang Junxia said quietly where they still stood in the shadows. "His Highness is exceedingly intelligent; he has read many books and can already compose his own essays."

Li Jianhong didn't respond to his report. He hurried down the long corridor, shadowing Duan Ling's steps and stopping behind a door when he saw Duan Ling had gone inside. Duan Ling was searching the kitchen for something to eat, and moments later, he re-emerged with the food box Lang Junxia had prepared for him.

"Has he learned martial arts?" Li Jianhong asked.

"He's always pestering me to teach him, but I didn't dare delay his studies," Lang Junxia answered.

Li Jianhong was silent for a while. His gaze had been trained on Duan Ling the whole time, never straying once, and the rims of his eyes had gone unexpectedly red.

"Your Highness?" Lang Junxia ventured.

Li Jianhong took a single step forward, then appeared to freeze in place—or even cower back, scared to approach the boy. He had faced battalions of thousands fearlessly, yet in that moment, he quailed before his own son.

"Does he hate me?" he asked.

"Never," Lang Junxia answered. "He's waited for your return all this time. I always told him Your Highness would return when the peach tree bloomed."

On his side of the door, Li Jianhong raised a hand to push it open, but he didn't dare breach that final barrier. Even his breath seemed to shudder.

As Duan Ling ate his lunch, he noticed a bird had flown inside; he fed it a few grains of rice from his own bowl. The sight made Li Jianhong chuckle.

Lang Junxia quietly added, "He's already read a bit of the Four Books and Five Classics, but it was too much too fast, and quickly abandoned. The teachers at Biyong Academy will need to explain and dissect the text for him. Also, his writing is good; he has been copying the script of the renowned calligrapher, Madam Wei. Outside of his studies, he's read miscellaneous texts like those of Sun Tzu and Sima, as well as *Wuzi*, and he's partial to *The Book of Songs* and other books of old poems."

"Princess Duanping would love my son," Li Jianhong muttered. "Arts, math... His interests span a wide range of disciplines."

Once his meal was done, Duan Ling cleaned up after himself and stretched, then went to sit and daydream in the courtyard. The sun beamed its gold light upon his fresh and youthful visage, which brimmed with the vitality of spring. Though he appeared to be sitting thoughtlessly, his head was filled with all sorts of things: studying and practicing his calligraphy one minute, his own little flowerbed world the next.

"He loves spicy food, much like yourself," Lang Junxia continued. "And he also loves gardening. He acquired some techniques from the Duan family in Runan. But his interests are too broad. This subject dared not teach them all, and only provided him select knowledge. Usually, my focus has been to supervise his studies."

"Does my son fancy any girls here in Shangjing?" Li Jianhong asked.

Lang Junxia shook his head.

It was rare for Lang Junxia to be gone all day. With no one watching over his shoulder, Duan Ling decided to first tend to his flowerbed. The peach tree had finally bloomed, and was even blooming well. There were many more flowering branches than there had been the previous year. Delighted, Duan Ling gasped and hurried back inside to find a wooden case for collecting the fallen petals. After tucking them safely away, he proceeded to water the herbs.

As he put down the watering can, Duan Ling sensed someone behind him.

"Didn't you go out?" Duan Ling asked without turning.

He glanced around and froze. A strange man stood in the courtyard. Rather than being scared, however, Duan Ling was curious.

Is this the new gardener? he wondered. *Did Lang Junxia actually hire someone? He doesn't look like a gardener, though.*

The stranger was taller and broader than Lang Junxia, with a darker complexion than most of those in Shangjing. He had a strong jawline and a sharp nose, but soft, gentle lips. His deep-set eyes, black and bright, sparkled like stars. Though he appeared careworn, he was more handsome than any man Duan Ling had ever seen in Shangjing, and he radiated a sense of comforting solidity.

He removed the bamboo hat on his head. His ink-black eyes, spirited yet hopeful, were red around the rims as he looked at Duan Ling.

Duan Ling felt an odd sense of familiarity, as though he'd met this man before in his dreams.

"Did you grow all this?" Li Jianhong asked.

When Duan Ling nodded, Li Jianhong slowly stepped forward.

Taking a seat on a small stool in front of the flowerbed, Duan Ling considered his garden's bounty, then looked over at Li Jianhong, who knelt down beside him, bringing their eyes level. Li Jianhong gazed at the flowerbed for a moment before turning back toward Duan Ling.

"What plants are these?" Li Jianhong asked.

"This is medicinal peony, and this is spatholobus; there's boneset, basil..."

As Duan Ling introduced his little garden, Li Jianhong's gaze never once left his face. Abruptly, he started chuckling, and Duan Ling—puzzled—briefly laughed along with him.

Yet soon he asked: "Why are you crying?"

Li Jianhong shook his head, unable to speak. Duan Ling reached out and wiped the man's tears with his own sleeves, then offered his seat for Li Jianhong to rest on. Li Jianhong settled crosslegged behind Duan Ling as the youth turned the earth with his trowel.

"Do you have any worms?" Duan Ling asked. "It's spring now, so I wanted to put some in the soil."

"I'll go dig some up for you tomorrow," Li Jianhong answered.

"I have to go study now," Duan Ling said, rising to go back inside. Li Jianhong followed him.

Duan Ling had assumed he was the new gardener, but the man really didn't look like one. "Are you Lang Junxia's friend?" he ventured. "He's not home now; he had some business to take care of today and won't be back until tonight."

When Li Jianhong nodded, Duan Ling invited him to the study and poured him a cup of tea.

"Seaside Snowdrop," Li Jianhong observed, identifying the tea.

"You can tell? I bought it in the city," Duan Ling said with a smile, handing him a warm towel. "Here—to wipe your face."

"What books have you been studying recently?" Li Jianhong asked conversationally.

"*The Annals*," Duan Ling answered.

"Which part?"

"I skipped *The Zuo Commentary*," Duan Ling said, flipping his book open. "I'm currently on *The Guliang Commentary*, but the headmaster said my understanding is still shallow."

Li Jianhong smiled. "Try reading *The Annotations of the Thirteen Classics* alongside it."

Duan Ling dug the suggested book out from a pile and beckoned Li Jianhong over. "I borrowed this from the Chengkang shop. Are you a scholar as well?"

After taking a sip of tea, Li Jianhong answered, "No, my readings are also shallow. I didn't finish the entirety of the Four Books and Five Classics, and I'm no good at composing essays. The ancestors' wisdom shouldn't be lost, though. You're doing very well in this regard."

"Are you Han?" Duan Ling asked, curious.

The sun spilled its light over Li Jianhong where he sat. Despite his threadbare clothes, he exuded an air of noble authority that defied easy description. With a solemn countenance, he told Duan Ling: "Yes. My family once produced a sage in ancient times."

Shocked, Duan Ling asked, "Who?"

"Take a guess," Li Jianhong said.

"Might I ask your surname?" Duan Ling asked.

Li Jianhong chuckled. "My surname is Li."

"'High winds last not all morning, heavy rains last not all day,'" Duan Ling recited.

Li Jianhong nodded. "'If heaven and earth cannot eternity make, how can man find a lasting way?' Correct. It was Li Er."[9] When Duan Ling gaped at him, Li Jianhong added, "Among myself and my three brothers, I've studied the least. In this, I often felt ashamed before our ancestors."

Duan Ling had to laugh. "But you must be incredible in your other endeavors. Is that a sword you're carrying?"

He had noticed a long case beside Li Jianhong; Li Jianhong placed the case on the table and opened it to show him.

Duan Ling was shocked again by what was inside. "Is this your sword?"

"Do you like it?" Li Jianhong asked.

---

9   Li Er, better known as Laozi, is the founder of Daoism and a central figure in Chinese culture. He is the author of Dao De Jing, the foundational text of Daoism. The quoted lines are from Chapter 23 of Dao De Jing.

Inside the case lay a heavy black sword almost as tall as Duan Ling himself. A yin-yang symbol was carved into the hilt, while the blade's body had been etched with strange characters. Though it looked old, the edges gleamed as sharply as if it were newly forged. Duan Ling reached toward it, and Li Jianhong caught his wrist with two fingers, staying his hand. He laid his hand over Duan Ling's, holding it lightly.

"This forty-pound sword might be made from meteoric iron, but it cuts through metal like mud. You can easily lose a finger if you're not careful."

Duan Ling laughed, and Li Jianhong guided his hand instead to the hilt. The sword thrummed when he made contact, as if alive.

"What's its name?" Duan Ling asked.

"Some call it the Guardian of the Realm," Li Jianhong said, "but *I* call it Nameless. In the previous dynasty, it was a saber, and at that time it was called the Nameless Saber. Later, when the land fell into the hands of foreign invaders, the Rouran artisans reforged the Nameless Saber into five separate weapons and distributed them across their various tribes. Later, it fell into the hands of the Loulan Kingdom."

Duan Ling sat quietly, absorbed by the tale.

"After that, our dynasty—Southern Chen—defeated the Loulan Kingdom. The five weapons were reclaimed and forged together to become this sword. Reinforced by the refined metal of the west and thoroughly tempered, Nameless can cleave mountains and rivers; it can sunder the land itself. It symbolizes the heavenly way, the natural order of the universe—it is the sword of the Han people."

Duan Ling nodded and withdrew his hand, then closed the case. "Lang Junxia also has a very sharp sword."

"His sword is called Chilling Edge," Li Jianhong explained. "Lang Junxia's Chilling Edge, Wu Du's Flashblade, Changliu-jun's Sunstreak, Zheng Yan's Violet-Gold Lightning, Xunchun's Cleaver of the Land, and Master Kongming's Ender of the Profane are all famous swords from the previous dynasty. Of these people, Zheng Yan, Changliu-jun, Wu Du, and Lang Junxia are assassins."

"What about you? Where are you from? Are you also an assassin?" Duan Ling held a deep curiosity about this strange wandering swordsman.

Li Jianhong shook his head. "I come from the south. Have you ever been?"

"I lived in Runan when I was little, but that's it," Duan Ling replied. "Since we moved to Shangjing, I haven't been anywhere else."

"These are places from the old homeland, but I lived in Xichuan once," Li Jianhong said. "It had bustling streets that stretched ten miles across the city, and its green waters flowed like emerald ribbons. The starlit Mount Yuheng of the west is forever enveloped in mist, and the dissolute Jiang Prefectural City never sleeps."

Seeing Duan Ling's jaw drop at these stories, Li Jianhong added: "Jiangnan is also much different from Shangjing. The trees are a deeper shade of green than you see here, and when spring comes, the city is awash in peach blossoms. And the sea—it's boundless."

"You've been to all those places?" Duan Ling asked in amazement.

Li Jianhong nodded, smiling. "And Diannan in the south. The beauty of Diannan is akin to an immortal realm; it's forever spring there, and never snows. The lakes at the foot of its snowy mountains are crisp and clear like mirrors. There's Yubi Pass as well, in the north. Once autumn arrives, it's an endless grove of maple trees."

The pictures he painted filled Duan Ling with yearning. "I'd love to see all those places myself one day."

"If you want to go, I can take you. Tomorrow," Li Jianhong stated.

After a brief moment of speechlessness, Duan Ling asked incredulously, "Really?"

"Of course," Li Jianhong said to Duan Ling, utterly serious. "The sky will be our blanket, the ground our mat. We can go wherever you wish."

"But I have to study," Duan Ling said, caught between bafflement and laughter. "And I've got to…to rank in the imperial exams first. Lang Junxia won't let me go on a trip like that."

"He won't be able to stop you," Li Jianhong said. "Whatever you desire, I can give it to you. Tell him tonight where you want to go, and we'll depart tomorrow. You want to learn martial arts? I can teach you that too. And if you never want to study again, then leave it behind."

Duan Ling was dumbfounded. His first thought was that the man was teasing him, but the way he spoke, with such earnest feeling, allowed no room for doubt. Thirteen was so young—how could he remain calm when playfulness was in a boy's nature? But after a moment's excitement, Duan Ling gave up on the idea; he knew he couldn't just up and leave.

"Maybe…not," he said.

"Why not?" Li Jianhong asked, his gaze intent.

"I'm waiting for someone," Duan Ling said. "Lang Junxia told me he would come."

"And who are you waiting for?"

After a brief pause, Duan Ling replied, "My dad. Lang Junxia said he's an incredible man."

As the sun tilted toward the west, time appeared to stand still. Beyond the window, a peach blossom abandoned its branch and twirled gracefully to alight on the pond. A fish broke the water's surface with a delicate splash.

Li Jianhong carefully withdrew an object from his waist pouch and set it on the table with a muted *clink*. He slid it slowly toward Duan Ling.

"Is this what you were waiting for?" he asked, voice rough.

Duan Ling's breath caught. On the table before him was a crystalline jade arc with three words etched upon its surface.

Trembling, Duan Ling unfastened the red string holding the pouch around his neck and retrieved the other half of the arc. As he joined the two pieces, they formed a perfect jade ring carved with intricate cloud patterns, eagle feathers, and coiled dragons; the complete pendant displayed a verse of six words:

The Golden Age; the Beautiful Land.

13

The setting sun cast Lang Junxia's long shadow across the floor. Its fading light filtered through the cracks in the walls and fell upon the dark bricks in patches, like the flickering torchlight of frontier beacons.

"Lang Junxia! Lang Junxia!" Duan Ling yelled as he tore down the corridors toward him. "My dad is back!"

With a muted smile, Lang Junxia turned to face Duan Ling and nodded.

Still catching his breath, Duan Ling panted, "He—"

"I know," Lang Junxia said.

"He said his surname is Li, and mine is too," Duan Ling said, his brow creased. "He's not called Duan Sheng."

"You've grown up, Duan Ling," Lang Junxia said. When Duan Ling gave him a confused look, he continued: "I'll be leaving tonight on business."

"You're going out again already? But you just came back," Duan Ling said.

Lang Junxia didn't explain further, only extending a hand. When Duan Ling stepped closer, bemused, he pulled the youth into a hug.

"This is good," Lang Junxia said.

The embrace was quick. As they parted, Lang Junxia straightened Duan Ling's posture—then swept his robes aside and knelt before him.

"Hey!" Duan Ling moved to pull him up at once, but Lang Junxia merely gestured for him to be still before kowtowing.

"This is farewell," Lang Junxia said.

"Hang on!" Finally realizing what was happening, Duan Ling exclaimed, "You're leaving?! But where are you going? Dad—Dad!"

Lang Junxia looked up from where he knelt, gazing at Duan Ling and taking his hand. "Yes. I went to Runan to find you, and I was fortunate to accomplish my mission. Now that you've been reunited with your father, my duty is done, and my work here in Shangjing must come to an end."

"D-don't go! Didn't you say you'd stay with me?"

"We will surely meet again—in several months, perhaps, or a year at most," Lang Junxia replied. "But you'll have His Hi...your dad to take care of you. You can ask for the whole of the Central Plains and he will give it to you. To you, I'm already... I have more important things to take care of."

"Lang Junxia, please don't go!" Duan Ling begged, the rims of his eyes reddening.

Lang Junxia rose to his feet. He smiled and said, "Duan Ling, I am but a passing visitor in your life. From now on, listen to your father. If there is anyone in this world who will treat you sincerely without deception, who will disregard his own life to save yours and do his utmost to plan for your future, it is him, and no one else."

"No, you can't leave! At least tell me where you're going, and how many days it'll be until you come back!" Clinging to Lang Junxia's hand in a death grip, Duan Ling tried to drag him back inside the house—but Lang Junxia stood firm, as unmoving as a mountain.

Li Jianhong's voice rang out from behind them. "Your dad is sending him to investigate something. I can't rest easy until this matter is made clear."

Lang Junxia swiftly made to kneel again, but Li Jianhong motioned for him to forgo formalities. Solemnly, Lang Junxia said, "Duan Ling, be good. I will come back."

Miserable, Duan Ling reluctantly let go.

"When you're in the south, do not mention me," Li Jianhong instructed Lang Junxia.

"Yes, sir."

Before Duan Ling could find his own words, Li Jianhong commanded Lang Junxia, "Go on, then. Before the city gates close for the night."

Lang Junxia bowed. "This subject will take his leave."

"Can't you leave tomorrow instead?" Duan Ling tried to ask.

But Lang Junxia had already vanished down the corridor in a gust of wind.

"Wait!" Duan Ling called out. "I'll pack some…"

He whirled, flustered and wanting to prepare something for Lang Junxia, but he'd hardly begun when he heard the sound of hooves beyond the courtyard—Lang Junxia had left without delay. Duan Ling ran out the door holding a hastily packed bag, his robes flapping in the spring night's breeze as he chased after him, crying in panic, "Lang Junxia! Lang Junxia!"

Before Duan Ling could process it, Lang Junxia was gone. Everything had happened so quickly, and all of it combined was more than anything Duan Ling had endured for the past five years. As Lang Junxia's horse disappeared from view, Duan Ling stopped in his tracks, dazed. Li Jianhong had come, but Lang Junxia had left. Like the wax and wane of the moon's light, or the rise and fall of tide, this parting was both sudden and inevitable.

Brows locked in a deep furrow, Li Jianhong watched Duan Ling for a moment, then reached out, as if to draw him close. Overwhelmed by his grief, Duan Ling didn't seem to notice—he merely stood panting, his face red and his tears threatening to spill. Li Jianhong was immediately caught off guard—he could handle anything save for his son's tears.

Flustered, Li Jianhong said, "Dad really does have a mission for him... But we could delay it a few days? Or forget the whole thing..."

"No, it's okay. I understand," Duan Ling sobbed out, wiping his eyes.

"Don't cry," Li Jianhong pleaded. "It pains me to see you cry."

This sentiment stumped Duan Ling, enough to pause his tears. Li Jianhong swept him up and carried him back home. Li Jianhong coaxed his son, trying all manner of ideas to lift him from his low mood. It didn't take long for Duan Ling to come around—all it took was Li Jianhong promising him, over dinner, that he would call Lang Junxia to return and serve Duan Ling alone once his mission was accomplished.

"Really?" Duan Ling asked.

"If that's what you want, of course. It's your call," Li Jianhong said.

But the word *serve* didn't sit right with Duan Ling; it was too heavy. He'd seen how the noble and affluent ordered their servants about. His relationship with Lang Junxia wasn't like that. While Lang Junxia had called himself a retainer, their relationship was in truth quite different.

"Though I had him fetch and take care of you, I don't want to see my son turn into a little Lang Junxia," Li Jianhong said.

"But Lang Junxia is a very, very good person," Duan Ling replied.

"Mm-hmm," Li Jianhong hummed noncommittally. "A very, very good person who nearly stabbed your dad to death a couple times. But yes, aside from that, he's not a bad fellow." After a pause,

Li Jianhong said, "In this life, you'll meet many others aside from Lang Junxia, and you must learn how to discern whether they are genuine, or whether they are false and fawning."

"I don't really understand—but I know he's been genuine to me," Duan Ling replied.

"Judge someone by their eyes," Li Jianhong said. "Those who sincerely befriend you will often speak without thinking; they'll show you their true colors without any guile. And the present cannot be the only factor by which you come to know someone. He has a background, a past."

"But the headmaster said that family background doesn't determine anything," Duan Ling countered.

"I don't mean family background; a hero is not determined by their birth," Li Jianhong explained. "But their background—their life experiences—will determine at least half of any person's character."

Duan Ling realized that, indeed, Lang Junxia had never told him anything about his past. Despite his frequent queries, Lang Junxia always remained tight-lipped on the subject. At last, Duan Ling said, "But Lang Junxia has been very, very good to me. So his background can't be that bad. He's a...um, to me at least, he's a good person."

Although Lang Junxia's departure saddened Duan Ling deeply, he quickly grew accustomed to Li Jianhong's presence. Lang Junxia had chided him to study and taken care of his daily needs, but he'd been quiet on the ways of the outside world; in comparison, Li Jianhong seemed to hardly ever stop talking. Over dinner he instructed Duan Ling not to talk with his mouth full, and to swallow first before speaking—but for any and every one of Duan Ling's questions, he had a patient, thorough answer. He never stifled Duan Ling's curiosity with a *Stop asking, you'll understand one day.*

After they'd finished eating, Li Jianhong took over Lang Junxia's role and sat beside the well to draw water for dishes and laundry as though it was the most natural thing in the world. Duan Ling rested a bit before brewing Li Jianhong a pot of tea. Then, realizing Li Jianhong might need to bathe after his travels, he brought out the soap and other necessities—as well as a set of new robes Lang Junxia had never worn—and waited to accompany him to the bathhouse.

The lights in Shangjing's bathhouse were never extinguished. The establishment provided dried fruit snacks and sweet rice wine, and a storyteller often plied his trade on the first floor. Bathing at home in the winter was no easy affair, and so Lang Junxia had often brought Duan Ling here in the colder months. Holding Li Jianhong's hand, Duan Ling led him inside with easy familiarity; standing on tiptoe, he began counting out coins on the reception counter, ready to order scrubbing service. Li Jianhong watched him from behind, a smile dancing in his eyes. Looking around to admire the brilliantly lit hall, Li Jianhong said, "Your dad doesn't need that service; no need to order it."

Duan Ling figured Li Jianhong wasn't used to being waited on by others and decided he'd do the job himself—but when Li Jianhong stripped off his clothes, baring his muscular body, Duan Ling's eyes widened at the sight.

Li Jianhong was covered in scars. One particularly conspicuous gash streaked across his toned abdomen; there was the telltale pockmark of an arrow on his chest, and an old burn scar marred a portion of his broad back.

His father released a long breath as he settled down into the warm water. They were currently the only guests in this tub. Though he had the coarse cloth ready, Duan Ling was at a loss on where to start scrubbing.

"I've seen my share of battles, and that's how I obtained these scars. Don't be afraid, son," Li Jianhong said.

"How… How did you get this one?" Duan Ling asked, placing a hand just below Li Jianhong's ribs.

"That was a saber wound from Nayantuo's assassination attempt."

"Who's that?"

"Supposedly the number one swordsman of the Western Regions, but now he's just another corpse," Li Jianhong said, nonchalant. "A sword's wound for a saber's: He stabbed me in the stomach, so I stabbed him in the throat. Fair trade."

"What about this one?" Duan Ling asked, indicating the arrow scar.

Li Jianhong turned to show Duan Ling his back and said, "Your dad was locked in close combat with the Mongols at Yubi Pass. Jebe shot through my armor and left this scar."

"Where's Jebe now?"

"He escaped alive… But he won't be for much longer," Li Jianhong answered. "The patch on the back was burned by hot oil. You can scrub as hard as you want, though; it doesn't hurt."

As Duan Ling ran the cloth over Li Jianhong's body, he silently counted all the scars, large and small. Although Li Jianhong's body was a tapestry of wounds, the marks didn't frighten Duan Ling. Instead, each and every scar seemed to complement Li Jianhong's fit and masculine physique, enhancing his rugged charm and adding to his magnetism.

"Did you see this one, Son?" Li Jianhong tilted his head and beckoned Duan Ling for a closer look. His nose was tall and straight, and his skin was a healthy bronze; he directed Duan Ling's attention to the corner of his eye, where there was a barely visible scar.

Brushing his fingers over it, Duan Ling asked, "How did you get it?"

"Your mother's fine work," Li Jianhong said with a chuckle.

He plucked a piece of cheese from the snack plate beside the tub and fed it to Duan Ling. Holding him with one arm, Li Jianhong pressed his forehead to Duan Ling and nuzzled hard. It felt nice; Duan Ling relaxed as Li Jianhong hugged him close, their skin warm against each other as they soaked.

"What'd she do that for?" Duan Ling asked.

"I told her to go, and she refused," Li Jianhong said. "That night, she grabbed the Xiongnu king Kursu's vase from my tent and smashed it on your dad's face—truly vicious. I think you resemble your mom a little in this. She was usually harmless, but could do anything when cornered."

Duan Ling was struck momentarily speechless. "And then what? Did you fight back?"

"Of course not. How could I?" Li Jianhong said. He sighed and hugged him tighter, as though he was embracing his entire world. "Did you ever meet her?"

Duan Ling turned and laid his head on Li Jianhong's chest. "No."

After the bath, Li Jianhong donned the set of new green robes, though Lang Junxia's clothes appeared a size too small on him. He hoisted Duan Ling on his back for their languid stroll home along the deserted bluestone path in the spring breeze. Late spring in Shangjing had unfurled like a maiden lazily stretching her limbs after sleep. Pear blossoms drifted through the air, weaving through moonlight before settling softly on the path below.

Leaning against Li Jianhong's broad back, Duan Ling grew sleepy. He murmured, "Dad."

"Hm?" Li Jianhong seemed to be lost in thought.

Though Duan Ling had met Li Jianhong for the first time today, it was as if—strangely—they had known each other all along. A tacit understanding seemed imprinted deep in their souls, a familiarity that somehow didn't require any pleasantries: No self-introductions nor probing questions were necessary between them. Duan Ling felt as if Li Jianhong had been by his side for the past dozen years, like his absence had only been because he had gone out for the day to the market—but by evening, he had returned.

Duan Ling's worries had evaporated, leaving behind a sense of present safety—a certainty that, now that he'd found him, his father would never leave again. It was as if, across the vast world, Duan Ling had been destined from birth to belong with him, and to follow in his footsteps.

"Dad, how old are you?" Duan Ling asked.

"Twenty-nine," Li Jianhong answered. "I wasn't much older than you when I met your mom; just about sixteen."

"Was my mom beautiful?"

"Of course she was," Li Jianhong replied easily. "When she smiled, she could melt the hardest frost and turn even the most desolate desert into a fertile paradise. When I saw her at Qixue Springs, it was love at first sight. How else could you have come to be?"

"Then…"

"Hm?"

Duan Ling stopped himself. He thought his father might be sad if he continued.

Li Jianhong asked him instead, "Did the Duan family treat you poorly when you lived in Runan?"

After a brief moment of silence, Duan Ling offered a white lie: "No, they were good to me, because they knew you were coming."

Li Jianhong grunted an affirmative. "Lang Junxia betrayed me three times, and tens of thousands died as a result. He's reckless; his temperament has burdened him his entire life. And at the end of the day, if it hadn't been for his impulsive actions, your dad and mom and you—we wouldn't have been separated for so many years."

Duan Ling was speechless.

"Fortunately, not all his humanity was lost, and he brought you out of Runan. I suppose that's also karma," Li Jianhong said. "I promised he could atone for his sins if he protected you well. Otherwise, I swore the sword Nameless would hunt him to the ends of the earth, and that he'd never be able to show his face again in this lifetime."

His father described a Lang Junxia that Duan Ling had never known. "What did he do?"

"It's a long story." Li Jianhong thought briefly, then said, "I'll tell you another day, when we have more time. If you still consider him a good person after learning of his past deeds, I won't try to convince you otherwise. So—do you still want to hear about it?"

Duan Ling couldn't believe his ears, but he trusted that his father wouldn't lie to him. He nodded.

"But you must be tired after today. Sleep first," Li Jianhong said.

Once home, Li Jianhong laid Duan Ling down in his bed. But when he turned to go, Duan Ling tugged on his sleeve and stared up at him with wide, unblinking eyes. Li Jianhong was puzzled—yet when he figured out Duan Ling's unspoken request, he smiled. He removed his robes, leaving him bare-chested and wearing only his knee-length underpants, and lay down next to Duan Ling.

Blearily hugging him around the waist, Duan Ling fell asleep with his head pillowed on his father's arm.

A gale tore through the pine grove like a million-man army, splitting trunks and cracking branches. Spilled blood, the anguished cries of comrades in their final moments on a distant

CHAPTER THIRTEEN

battlefield—once again, they coalesced into a boundless nightmare to assault the dreamer in this midnight hour.

With a primal shout, Li Jianhong bolted upright in bed.

The commotion shocked Duan Ling awake. "Dad!" he yelped, scrambling up. Beside him, Li Jianhong panted harshly, soaked in sweat.

"Dad? Are you okay?" Duan Ling asked anxiously.

"Just a nightmare. I'm fine," Li Jianhong replied. His heart was still racing. "Did I scare you?"

"What were you dreaming about?" Duan Ling had once also suffered frequent nightmares of the beatings he'd endured as a child, but the trauma of Runan had faded as the years passed.

"Killing." Eyes closed, Li Jianhong finished, "And my dead comrades."

Duan Ling kneaded the acupoint on his father's hand that would help soothe his nerves. Gradually, Li Jianhong calmed; he lay back down, though his eyes remained open, staring vacantly into space. Tucked back beneath his arm with his head pillowed on his chest, Duan Ling toyed with the jade arc that hung around Li Jianhong's neck. Trying to console his father, he said, "It'll get better with time."

"My son, do you also have nightmares?" Li Jianhong asked, regaining himself.

"I used to," Duan Ling said, absorbed in playing with the pendant.

"What about?"

Duan Ling hesitated. He didn't dare tell Li Jianhong about his past abuse—and it *was* in the past, after all. In the end, he replied, "I dreamed about Mom."

"You never met your mother. It must've been the pain of birth you dreamed about—but birth, illness, old age, and death are things all mortals suffer. Everything will be all right, eventually," Li Jianhong comforted him.

"I don't have nightmares anymore," Duan Ling said. "I'll buy you some tranquilizing medicine tomorrow; it'll help you sleep."

"To think there's someone in my Li family who knows the art of medicine." Li Jianhong chuckled and rolled over. He hugged Duan Ling closer, until Duan Ling's nose was pressed against his chest. "What do you want to be in the future? A doctor?"

"I don't know. Lang Junxia said—"

Duan Ling was about to say that Lang Junxia had taught him to study seriously, so as to accomplish great things and not disappoint his father. But Li Jianhong cut him off. "My son needn't care what others say. He can be whatever he wants, and do as he will in the future."

It was the first time Duan Ling had ever heard such advice. Back at Ming Academy, everyone from the headmaster up above to the servants down below believed that life's purpose was fighting one's way to the top. As they said: Just as water flows down, a man must rise, and all skills—whether in scholarship or martial arts—must be paid to the emperor.

Li Jianhong neatened his son's bangs and met his eyes. "My son, if you want to be a doctor, or learn martial arts, or even take up Daoist cultivation or beg for alms as a wandering monk, do it, as long as it makes you happy."

Duan Ling laughed. No one had ever told him he could be a monk if he wanted to.

Turning solemn again, Li Jianhong said, "Earlier this afternoon you talked about your studies so seriously, but I'm guessing, deep down, you still prefer fun over books. Tell me, do you not want to study?"

"It's not really about whether I want to or not," Duan Ling said after some thought. "Studying is necessary. But I do like gardening more."

His father nodded. "Becoming a gardener one day is also a good path."

"The headmaster said all is inferior except scholarship, which is the superior pursuit."

Li Jianhong heaved a sigh. "Academia has its good points, but if you're really not interested, your dad won't force you. What I want is for you to live a happy life."

"Then as of tomorrow, I'll change my profession to gardening."

Smiling again, Duan Ling closed his eyes and pressed them to the jade arc hung around his father's neck. It was warm from his body heat. Li Jianhong grinned at his son's response. Holding Duan Ling, he, too, closed his eyes and lowered his head, taking in the scent of fresh soap in his son's hair.

Before Duan Ling knew it, he had fallen asleep once more.

It was morning when Duan Ling next opened his eyes. Li Jianhong was training in the courtyard, his upper body bare. The long staff he wielded sliced through the air, stirring up a flurry of peach blossoms from the ground and scattering them in a brilliant spray of pink.

Yawning, Duan Ling wandered out of the room. When he looked again, Li Jianhong had switched to bare-handed boxing—shear, push, wrist flip, palm down. His face, brows knit in concentration, was exceptionally handsome.

Duan Ling watched him a little longer, until Li Jianhong ended his practice.

"Do you want to learn?" he asked.

When Duan Ling nodded, he began to walk him through the steps.

"But I've never practiced the horse stance before; my core is weak," Duan Ling said partway through.

"Don't worry about that," Li Jianhong replied. "It's fine as long as you're happy."

Imitating his father, Duan Ling tried a set of punches. Li Jianhong didn't correct his form and only showed him a few more rough basics.

"That's good enough for now," Li Jianhong said. "You can practice more if you're interested. That's what they call keeping it simple."

Duan Ling laughed; this attitude fit him perfectly. Once he started to fatigue, Li Jianhong adjourned for breakfast. After the meal, Duan Ling waited for the usual instruction—*Go study*—but it never came. Li Jianhong showed no signs of pushing him to open his books.

"Dad, I want to tend to my garden," Duan Ling said.

Li Jianhong waved a hand, telling him to do as he pleased, and so Duan Ling went to fuss over his plants. Meanwhile, Li Jianhong cut some bamboo to construct a watering channel. But even without anyone to supervise him, Duan Ling ended up feeling uneasy. After he'd absentmindedly worked in his flowerbed a while, he returned to studying.

Sitting outside the study holding a bowl of tea, Li Jianhong watched the clouds drifting past overhead. He asked, "Conscience eating at you?"

"Yeah," Duan Ling replied. "It didn't feel right."

"Seems you do want to be a scholar after all," Li Jianhong said.

Duan Ling ducked his head sheepishly.

Days passed just this way. Once he moved into the courtyard residence, Li Jianhong never forced Duan Ling to do this or that— he could pursue whatever his heart desired, even if what he desired was doing nothing at all. He could laze around and space out while drinking tea if he wanted. But Duan Ling's temperament had always been thus: He was reluctant if forced into doing something, but when no one pestered him, he'd end up bored. Duan Ling studied of his own accord without Li Jianhong's urging. When he took a break, he'd mimic Li Jianhong's boxing techniques in an attempt to learn martial arts.

As for Li Jianhong, he couldn't bear to leave Duan Ling for a second, even to shop for groceries. He refused to allow Duan Ling out of his sight. They slept together at night, and stayed in the same room during the day.

In his waking moments, Li Jianhong was always pensive. Eventually, Duan Ling couldn't hold back his curiosity any longer. "Dad, what are you thinking about?"

"I'm thinking about my son," Li Jianhong replied.

Duan Ling laughed. He put his book down and went over to bother his father. Although Li Jianhong's brows were perpetually drawn by unresolvable troubles, his eyes were infinitely gentle whenever he gazed at Duan Ling. Sandwiching Li Jianhong's face with his hands and pushing his head playfully from side to side, Duan Ling said, "You're unhappy. Is something troubling you?"

He had sensed a certain heaviness in his father's abstraction. Aside from the first few days after they'd met, Li Jianhong had seemed constantly preoccupied.

"Yes," Li Jianhong admitted. "I've been thinking about what I can provide you."

"You can provide me with Five Rivers to the Sea's jasper-jade dumplings," Duan Ling said with a grin.

"That's for certain," Li Jianhong agreed. But as he took Duan Ling's hand to lead him out for a good meal, he added, "But feeding you isn't what troubles me."

Duan Ling looked a question at Li Jianhong.

"Does my son wish to go home?" Li Jianhong asked.

At this, Duan Ling finally understood. It was just as he'd heard from everyone at Ming Academy—all Han wished to go home.

Li Jianhong continued, "There's something I want to give you—something that belongs to you in the first place."

"But I'm already very satisfied," Duan Ling said. "People should learn to be satisfied with what they have if they want to be happy, right? Lang—" Duan Ling cut himself off when he remembered Lang Junxia was gone. Almost to himself, he muttered, "Oh—he's not back yet."

Though Lang Junxia had been gone a long time already, Duan Ling had never gotten used to his absence, catching himself over and over thinking he was still home. What was the business he'd been charged with? And why hadn't he returned, even after so long? *When is Lang Junxia coming back?* had replaced his daily question of *When is my dad coming back?* But despite his yearning, Duan Ling sensed his father didn't necessarily appreciate him saying Lang Junxia's name so often. Every time Duan Ling mentioned him, Li Jianhong seemed to brim with jealousy.

But to his surprise, Li Jianhong answered: "He's preparing the new house to welcome you home."

14

Duan Ling missed Lang Junxia, but he came to understand that if Lang Junxia hadn't left, his father wouldn't have come. Some people come; some people go. As Lang Junxia had once told him: Life will always bear some regret or another, and you can't always have everything you want.

As it was, many things were as if the heavens themselves had arranged them on his behalf.

To Duan Ling's surprise, whenever he voiced questions arising from his studies, Li Jianhong generally had the answers. Moreover, the solutions he provided derived from a system entirely his own, completely different from what the teachers had taught. Duan Ling was floored.

"Dad, didn't you say you weren't a scholar?" Duan Ling asked.

"There's a limit to life, but not knowledge—who in the world would dare proclaim themselves truly well-read?" Li Jianhong replied. "All we learn are but fragments and pieces of a greater whole. The more you know, the less you understand."

Duan Ling nodded, though he didn't quite grasp his meaning. After reading his books a little while longer, he asked another question: "Dad, Confucius says 'The noble man is in awe of three things.' What does that mean?"

"The three things noble men are in awe of are the Mandate of Heaven, great men, and the words of the sages. Petty people do not know the Mandate of Heaven, and therefore are not in awe of it," Li Jianhong answered. Gazing toward the interior of the courtyard, he added in a casual aside, "'Awe' in this context does not imply *fear* but rather *respect*. Only by honoring the will of heaven can we find true peace."

"Then what is the Mandate of Heaven?" Duan Ling asked.

"Everyone has a purpose they must fulfill in life," Li Jianhong said. "It's predestined from the moment you're born. Some are meant to farm, some to fight wars, and others are born to rule nations. Each person's path is unique to themselves."

"How do I know what mine is?"

"It's perfectly reasonable not to know." Li Jianhong set down his bowl and heaved a sigh. "Your dad doesn't know his, either. 'Self-reliant at thirty; self-aware at forty; knowing fate at fifty'—and so the sages say we won't know until then."

"That's so long," Duan Ling said, baffled.

"It is," Li Jianhong agreed. "We spend the first half of our lives ignorant and naive, bumping into hurdle after hurdle in search of our fate. Truly, what a waste of time."

After Li Jianhong rose and left, Duan Ling pondered what he'd said—it was so much more interesting than the teachers' lessons.

Moments later, Li Jianhong reappeared at the door, now wrapped in a mantle for the drizzle outside and holding a small bag.

"Aren't you going to Ming Academy today? Or will you keep studying a while longer?"

"Oh!" Duan Ling exclaimed, remembering that it was essay-collection day. He was to retrieve the final essay he'd composed for

Ming Academy, have it stamped by the headmaster, and then submit it to Biyong Academy. He'd nearly forgotten—but Li Jianhong remembered everything about him. Heading out on horseback, the pair planned to collect the essay and register for the entrance exam at the new school before heading out of the city for a wandering afternoon.

Shangjing's Biyong Academy was situated on Zhenghe Street, a bustling road full of people and horses traveling to and fro. A long queue of noble and affluent students had already formed outside the school. Dressed in their simpler clothing, Duan Ling and his father observed the crowd from the side.

"Do you envy their glossy horses and glamorous carriages?" Li Jianhong asked.

Duan Ling shook his head. Many of those waiting had been his classmates at Ming Academy for years; he simply hadn't realized they all came from such prominent backgrounds.

"The headmaster taught us to accept poverty and be our own king."

Li Jianhong nodded. "The headmaster spouts loads of nonsense, but at least he got that one right."

Laughing, Duan Ling waded through the crowd to register his name and collect his examinee number. Li Jianhong pulled his hood down, covering half of his face, and stood in the shadows, scrutinizing every passerby.

Cai Yan's voice rang out: "Duan Ling! What're you waiting for? Come over here!"

Although Duan Ling had studied at Ming Academy for several years, he'd rarely befriended anyone. Moreover, he'd roomed in one of the school's more remote courtyards on Lang Junxia's request, which granted him few chance meetings with his peers. The only other students he'd become familiar with were Cai Yan, whom he'd met on his first day, Borjigin Batu, and Helian Bo, whom he'd occasionally stood outside class with, sharing punishment.

Cai Yan waved at Duan Ling. His older brother had accompanied him, so Li Jianhong approached as well to make his greeting, hands cupped in salute.

"Thank you for looking after Duan Ling," Li Jianhong said.

Cai Wen smiled and returned the courtesy. "It was nothing."

Hooking an arm around Duan Ling's shoulders, Cai Yan pulled him into his spot in the line, and the two boys caught up as they waited. Duan Ling rarely encountered Cai Wen; the sight of the young captain reminded him of that winter day long ago, when Lang Junxia had been injured. When Duan Ling had returned to Ming Academy a few days later, Cai Yan had sought him out and consoled him, thinking he'd been beaten at home due to his swollen right eye.

Otherwise, the two hadn't often shared the same classes. Cai Yan had already started on the Four Books and Five Classics as well as composing essays in the Chamber of Tomes when Duan Ling enrolled at the school. When Duan Ling had at last moved up to join him, he'd spent only a few short months as Cai Yan's classmate before his older brother hired a tutor for him to study with at home, and Cai Yan had left the school.

Although the two didn't see each other often, Duan Ling knew a bit about Cai Yan's family affairs. Cai Wen was the older brother, but the two were not born of the same mother. Since Cai Wen took care of Cai Yan's daily necessities in the same way Lang Junxia had taken care of Duan Ling's, the two brothers were close. Cai Yan and his brother had run into Duan Ling and Lang Junxia twice while out and about: once during the Mid-Autumn Festival, and once while on an outing by the water during the Double Third Festival. But because Ding Zhi seemed to fancy Lang Junxia much more than Cai Wen, meetings between the two were somewhat awkward.

On this day, Cai Wen wore casual robes the blue of the sky. He was handsome, and he radiated the air of a soldier, as sharp as a newly forged sword. The adults talked idly on the sidelines while the boys queued together, their conversation revolving around the boys' studies. Duan Ling had forgotten to properly introduce his father to Cai Wen, but compared to Lang Junxia's distant demeanor, Cai Wen thought Li Jianhong seemed more polite.

When the subject of Lang Junxia was raised, Li Jianhong answered with nonchalance, "A servant. I didn't want him getting too involved, so once my business was finished and I came north, I sent him back south to take care of things there."

Cai Wen nodded. "I hear you work in trade, Duan-xiong?"

Li Jianhong returned his nod. "It's not easy," he admitted. "I'm thinking of giving it up for something new. I have great ambition, but in this turbulent world, I find myself stymied at every turn. I suppose I'll sit idle for now and watch over my son as he grows, then go from there."

"Judging by your eloquence, I don't imagine you will sit idly by, Duan-xiong," said Cai Wen, smiling. "You're far too modest."

Li Jianhong was humbly dressed, yet his every word and gesture exuded sophistication, not at all the crass mannerisms of a nouveau riche merchant. In recent years, throngs of people from all classes—including the wealthy—had poured into Shangjing, seeking temporary haven in the city. Cai Wen found Li Jianhong to be an unusual character, but as he was already acquainted with Duan Ling, he didn't think much further on it.

Cai Yan spotted another boy in the crowd. "Helian Bo!"

Duan Ling also grinned. "Helian Bo!"

The boy who'd once stood outside the classroom with Duan Ling as punishment had grown. At fourteen, he was exceptionally tall; his complexion was dark, his brow deep, and his features sharply defined. But although he was quietly imposing at first glance, he still spoke with a stutter.

"You're here too! Come here!" Cai Yan beckoned.

Helian Bo, clad in the style of Western Liang, nodded to Duan Ling and Cai Yan and promptly joined them in line. He dismissed the steward following along behind him.

"Have you seen Borjigin?" Cai Yan asked offhandedly.

Helian Bo shook his head, then looked toward the unfamiliar Li Jianhong.

"This is my dad," Duan Ling said, finally recalling his manners.

Helian Bo put his hands together in greeting, and Li Jianhong returned the courtesy with a nod. When Duan Ling glanced back, he noticed a carriage parked on the side of the road. Helian Bo pointed at it and said shortly, "My mom."

Helian Bo's mother had brought him to register for the entrance exam, but according to the customs of Shangjing, a female relative could not show her face. Thus he'd come to queue up by himself. He cupped his hands toward the group in a gesture of apology.

The boys chatted until it was their turn. Duan Ling urged the other two to go ahead, but Helian Bo gestured politely for him to step forward. Both he and Cai Yan allowed Duan Ling—the youngest among them—to enter first.

"If Duan Ling is free, he's welcome to come to our house," Cai Wen was saying to Li Jianhong. "I hired a teacher from the south; he can tutor Duan Ling on the simpler readings in advance."

"I'd be very glad to accept. Much obliged," Li Jianhong replied.

Cai Wen genially waved off his thanks. When Duan Ling re-emerged from the academy with his stamped papers, Li Jianhong bade Cai Wen farewell and went to pay the entrance exam fee with his son. As they left the school, Duan Ling peered over his shoulder several times, though his friends had already disappeared.

"Are you looking for another of your friends?" Li Jianhong asked.

"Batu isn't here," Duan Ling replied. "He said he would come register for the exam today."

Li Jianhong was quiet a moment. "Do you have any other friends?"

"They're the ones who treat me best," Duan Ling said. "But their families all keep them on a tight leash."

"Ah, I forgot to ask: Was Lang Junxia very strict with you?"

Duan Ling shook his head. Though he and Lang Junxia had been apart for some time now, he cherished the memories of the time they'd spent together. Certainly there had been times when Duan Ling had wanted to play and have fun, yet the thought of disappointing Lang Junxia had held him back. But it was different for his friends. He could tell that Cai Yan, Helian Bo, and many of his other classmates weren't happy; they lived as though a dark cloud loomed over their heads.

"Helian Bo and the others…" Duan Ling began. "I don't know how to describe it, but they act like—act like… Hmm."

"Like a ghost is following them around, forcing them to study. And even when they laugh, they can't laugh too loudly?" Li Jianhong supplied.

"Yeah," Duan Ling said, chuckling.

"They're mature for their age," Li Jianhong said. "Unlike you."

Duan Ling sighed.

"They're the sons of hostages, so of course they understand more about such things."

"I know. But is being a hostage really so scary?" Duan Ling asked.

They strolled hand in hand down the street. Li Jianhong explained, "Helian Bo is the son of Helian Luan, of the royal house of Western Liang. Borjigin is a descendant of Great Yuan's Kiyat clan. Those brothers, Cai Wen and Cai Yan, are the sons of Khitan women. Their father is Minister Cai, of the Cai clan, which came north to serve as officials in Liao. In other words, all their fathers are foreigners—and in most cases, carry royal blood. They live as hostages here in exchange for peace between their nations, but the moment a war breaks out, they'll be killed."

Duan Ling was shocked. "Who's Southern Chen's hostage?"

"No one, because the Han are tough," Li Jianhong said. "Many of your peers at Ming Academy are the sons of officials in Liao's Southern Court. If any officials threaten to rebel or join the enemy forces, the emperor of Liao will kill their sons. Know a kid surnamed Han?"

"Yes!" Duan Ling immediately remembered one Young Master Han.

"He's actually Khitan. His father is the Grand Preceptor of the Southern Court," Li Jianhong said.

Duan Ling nodded. They came to a stop where the street intersected with Zagas Barikh Alley. Duan Ling peered down it. "I want to check on Batu's house."

Li Jianhong and Duan Ling entered the alley, where they discovered a group of Liao soldiers patrolling the area and questioning all passersby. Duan Ling and Li Jianhong didn't escape their notice. "Who are you?" a soldier barked.

"I'm—" But before Duan Ling could answer, Li Jianhong squeezed his shoulder.

"I encountered Captain Cai outside Biyong Academy earlier when I took my son to register for exams," Li Jianhong said nonchalantly. "The Borjigin child was absent, so the captain sent me to ask after him."

"This has nothing to do with Cai Wen," the officer said. "You can tell him to mind his own business."

Li Jianhong nodded and led Duan Ling away, his brow creasing.

"Why are they—?" Duan Ling began.

Li Jianhong pressed a finger to Duan Ling's lips, forbidding further questions.

By the time they got home, Duan Ling had put the strange incident behind him. He worked in his garden for a while, until he noticed Li Jianhong lying on the reclining chair in the courtyard with his eyes closed.

"Dad," Duan Ling called over. He was about to tell Li Jianhong to sleep inside when his father opened his eyes and beckoned Duan Ling over. Duan Ling pattered over and sprawled on top of him.

With one arm around Duan Ling, Li Jianhong caught his son's hands and said lightly, "What's this? Always wiping your muddy paws all over your dad's face?"

Duan Ling cheekily wiped his hands on Li Jianhong's robe instead. "I'm hungry," he said.

"What are you craving? We can go out now," Li Jianhong replied, but when Duan Ling began to wriggle away to go wash his hands, he didn't loosen his hold. He studied the boy's face and gazed into his eyes. "Before we go, let's talk. Are you and the Borjigin boy good friends?"

Li Jianhong's expression was serious. Worried he disapproved of him being friends with Batu, Duan Ling paused as he searched for his answer. Li Jianhong added, "Just say *yes* if he is, *no* if he isn't. What, do you think I'll bite your head off over it?"

"He is," Duan Ling answered.

"A man needs a friend or two in his life," Li Jianhong said. "Now go wash your hands."

Later that evening, Li Jianhong took Duan Ling to the best restaurant in Liao. As he leaned over the establishment's railing looking out, Duan Ling said, "Dad, I heard Batu's father beats him. He never comes to see me anymore, either."

"He doesn't come see you because he's been locked up," Li Jianhong said absently. "His dad Kuchi has always had a nasty temper. Being sent to Shangjing as a hostage and facing scorn from every direction—all he has left to amuse himself with is beating his own children."

"Then how come there are guards outside blocking people from going in?" Duan Ling asked.

"They're worried he'll run." Li Jianhong turned his gaze to the building across the street—which happened to be the Borjigin residence. A great number of soldiers surrounded it, on guard. "Tensions are building at the border of Yuan and Liao," Li Jianhong explained. "War might break out as soon as this month."

"How do you know?" Duan Ling asked.

"A guess," Li Jianhong said. "Spring has returned to the vast lands north of the Altyn-Tagh. The Mongols have waited the entire winter, and now they must send their forces south or starve."

"What happens if there's a war? Will Batu be in danger?" Duan Ling asked in alarm.

"The emperor of Liao is young. Although the empress dowager acts as regent, the military is in the hands of the Great Prince of the Northern Court, Yelü Dashi. Borjigin's fate will depend on his mood. If he suffers a defeat and feels sour about it, perhaps he comes back to seek trouble with the Borjigins. If the fancy takes him, he very well may behead them all."

This revelation upset Duan Ling greatly, and he was tense with worry the entire walk back.

Once they'd arrived home, and after thinking on it for a bit, Li Jianhong asked, "Well, do you want to save him?"

"How?" Duan Ling asked. "Dad, you can rescue him?"

Without looking up from where he was washing his face in the courtyard, Li Jianhong said, "Not me—you."

"How would I do that?"

His face now cleaned, Li Jianhong walked to the veranda to wipe his hands dry. "Indeed, how *would* you do that? We'll have to give the matter some thought."

Duan Ling was briefly speechless. "If only Lang Junxia was here. Three people are better than two—"

"We don't need Lang Junxia," Li Jianhong said in a serious tone. "Your dad is, at the very least, the number one swordsman of Southern Chen. It wounds me to be compared to an assassin by my son all day, every day."

Duan Ling was once again speechless. After some hesitation, he began: "Then—"

"Come, you can think of something," Li Jianhong prompted. "Have you never studied the art of war, or listened to any storytellers? You're given a great warrior—now what do you do with him? Will you use him as a mule or a dog? What have you got?"

Duan Ling couldn't help but laugh, but Li Jianhong pulled a long face.

"What are you laughing about? The great warrior doesn't work for just anyone—you're the only one whose command he'll listen to. And you'll have to pay him handsomely when the job is done." Li Jianhong mimed rubbing coins together, indicating that he expected some reward upon their return.

Ignoring Duan Ling's shocked expression, he turned on his heel and left to do the laundry. Duan Ling sat there, dazed, for more than a moment. When he finally realized Li Jianhong's intent, an intense thrill coursed through him, and he ran back inside to retrieve his brush and paper.

"Dad!"

"Yes, my son," Li Jianhong responded, continuing to wash their clothes.

Duan Ling came running, a map flapping in his hand. Drawn upon it was a neat outline of the Borjigin residence, with routes sketched around it and little figures signifying the guards outside.

"A battle map," Li Jianhong said approvingly. "Why make it so pretty? Just draw some triangles and you're good to go."

Duan Ling nodded and explained, "We'll have to smuggle them out, then find a way to get them out of the city when the city gates open tomorrow morning. This here is their house. Weren't we having tea across from it just this afternoon?"

"Hm. And where do we hide them after we fetch them out of their residence? Our house?" Li Jianhong asked.

"Our house is too far from the city gates," Duan Ling said. "And we don't even have a cellar. It wouldn't be easy to hide anyone here, and if the guards discover they've escaped, they'll search door to door and block all the exits out of the city."

Li Jianhong chuckled. "Very clever."

"The main concern is the city locking down tomorrow morning, so we'll hide them—*here*!" Duan Ling said, pointing at a spot on the map. "It's close to the city gate, and we can send them out without anyone knowing!"

"Done! That's just what we'll do," Li Jianhong said. "Once your dad dumps the garbage, we'll embark on the rescue."

Chasing after him, Duan Ling exclaimed, "You didn't even look where I pointed! It's Ming Academy!"

After Li Jianhong hung the laundry and tossed the garbage, he said, "Ming Academy is familiar terrain for you, so of course it's the best choice. Let's go."

"Huh? Are we not putting on masks? Don't assassins all cover their faces?" Duan Ling asked.

"Only useless trash mask their faces," Li Jianhong stated.

"Then…" Duan Ling didn't wish to drag Li Jianhong down in this operation and promptly handed him the map. "Follow this route—"

"I won't remember it."

Li Jianhong hoisted Duan Ling onto his back and, with two powerful leaps, scaled the wall. On the third, he touched down on the roof and dashed across its sloping tiles as if they were level ground, vanishing into the dark night. Duan Ling nearly yelped, but thankfully caught himself. After a few more strides, Li Jianhong dropped back down to the ground and ran past a number of alleyways with Duan Ling still on his back. Taking a shortcut, they vaulted over a wall into someone's courtyard and heard the sharp barks of the family's dog.

"Oh ho, what a fearsome creature," Li Jianhong commented. "More ferocious than Kublai."

Duan Ling didn't know what to say.

In the blink of an eye, they arrived at the side street of the Borjigins' residence. "Come here, duck down," said Li Jianhong. Perched kneeling on top of the roof with one arm around Duan Ling's waist, Li Jianhong motioned for him to hang on to the tile at the end of the roof ridge and stand steady.

"Dad, we forgot to bring your sword," Duan Ling said. "Should we go back and get it?"

"No need." Li Jianhong looked up at the moon; it was the fifteenth of the month, and its full, round face illuminated the earth. "What a bright night," he muttered to himself.

"There's some shadow over there that might cover you," Duan Ling said, pointing toward a spot within the walls of the residence. Li Jianhong grunted acknowledgment. Liao soldiers passed through the alleyway below, and Duan Ling pointed down, signaling to Li Jianhong to be careful.

In a low voice, Li Jianhong said, "Wait here."

He stuffed a bag of snacks into Duan Ling's hands and mimed that he could munch on them if he was bored. But how could Duan Ling be hungry at a time like this? Before he could react, Li Jianhong had dropped out of sight.

As the Liao patrol rounded the corner, Li Jianhong crept silently up behind the final soldier in line and delivered a swift chop to his neck. The soldier crumpled, and Li Jianhong whisked him back into the shadows. With practiced efficiency, he stripped the man of his quiver and bow, a length of rope, and the saber at his waist. He weighed the saber in his hand, then tossed it over his head. Duan Ling, practically vibrating with nerves, reached out to catch it and missed.

Li Jianhong threw the saber again, and Duan Ling missed again. At last, on the third try, he finally caught the blade. Li Jianhong gave him a big thumbs-up for a job well done.

Duan Ling sweated nervously in embarrassment.

15

LI JIANHONG BOUNDED back up the wall. He pulled a few arrows out of his pilfered quiver, snapped off the arrowheads to leave the ends blunt, and nocked one onto the bow. Duan Ling's heart leapt into his throat.

An arrow whistled through the air, striking something in a tree in the garden with a muted *thud*. Li Jianhong shifted his aim to another tree and released three more arrows in rapid succession. The hidden sentinels perched among the foliage were instantly knocked unconscious, their bodies slumped and dangling from the branches. Li Jianhong rejoined Duan Ling on the roof and crouched down against the tiles, one hand gripping the corrugated edge. His long, lithe form melded seamlessly into the darkness.

"The guards are about to change shifts; we can go down now," Duan Ling whispered. "We have five minutes at most. Should I wait here for you, Dad?"

Li Jianhong took the saber from Duan Ling. "We won't be returning via the rooftops. Get ready to jump!"

Flinging the rope he'd acquired from the Liao soldier, Li Jianhong looped one end securely around the corner of the eaves. Duan Ling clung to him tightly, and together they swung across the rooftops, flying over the heads of the guards below until they landed in the Borjigins' yard.

The instant their feet hit the ground, Li Jianhong swung the still-sheathed saber. His movement was a blur, and before Duan Ling had even registered their presence, two Liao soldiers crumpled to the ground in front of him. Li Jianhong grabbed his hand again and ran another few strides.

"Jump again!" he instructed.

Duan Ling obeyed without hesitation, and the pair hopped over the garden fence, landing in the corridor beyond. With one hand holding Duan Ling's and the other gripping the saber, Li Jianhong effortlessly dispatched several more soldiers as they moved through the shadows. Liao guards also roamed inside the residence; Li Jianhong pulled Duan Ling close, then ducked below a window.

The hall on the other side was brightly lit, and the murmur of voices spilled into the night. Li Jianhong glanced at Duan Ling and saw his son's eyes shining with admiration, though he was clearly too afraid to speak. Noticing a smudge of dirt on Duan Ling's face, Li Jianhong reached out and gently wiped it away.

Duan Ling recognized one of the raised voices inside as Batu's. He was speaking Mongolian and sounded agitated; the sound of a cup shattering punctuated the end of his sentence.

"Is that him?" Li Jianhong asked.

"Yes!" Duan Ling whispered.

Still firmly holding Duan Ling's hand, Li Jianhong rose and crept toward the door. With swift precision, he sidestepped, then darted forward and delivered a swift palm strike to the back of the soldier guarding the entrance. The blow knocked the soldier out in an instant, then sent him flying soundlessly to the back of the garden.

"Batu!" Duan Ling hollered as he dashed into the hall, followed by Li Jianhong.

More guards awaited them inside.

The heated quarrel between Batu and his father came to an abrupt end. Duan Ling froze in shock at the sight of the guards, then spun around, intending to run back to Li Jianhong. He got no further before Li Jianhong stepped into the hall. His father flung a handful of wooden chess pieces with lethal precision; the makeshift weapons struck the four guards in a quick flurry, and they dropped to the ground.

"Duan Ling?!" Batu was equally shocked.

"Let's go!" Duan Ling exclaimed. "We've come to rescue you!"

Simply seeing Duan Ling was more effective than any words could be; Batu glanced at his father and resolutely ran over to his friend.

"Wait here while I go pack some stuff," Batu said.

"There's no time!" Duan Ling hissed anxiously.

Batu's father, Borjigin Kuchi, followed them out. Li Jianhong gave him a curt nod, gesturing him ahead with all politeness—escape was the most important thing at the moment.

Batu stopped in the hallway with Duan Ling still tugging on his hand. "Okay," he said decisively. "Let's go."

"Let's find your mom first," Duan Ling said.

Batu had begun to move forward again, but he stopped at Duan Ling's words, casting his eyes to the ground. Puzzled, Duan Ling swung their clasped hands; Batu squeezed his in response. After a short silence, Batu looked up and said, "She already left."

Duan Ling felt a great surge of relief; escaping with two people was far safer than three. He glanced over his shoulder at Li Jianhong, who pointed toward the back courtyard.

The guards along the way had all already been knocked out by Li Jianhong. The sight of the unconscious soldiers strewn across the ground seemed to enrage Kuchi. He unsheathed the blade at his waist, ready to cut the bodies to pieces, but Li Jianhong blocked his way with his borrowed saber.

"Shh." Li Jianhong hushed him, motioning that he shouldn't create more trouble.

Kuchi gave him a hard look.

Li Jianhong swiftly turned and sprinted from the back courtyard, putting down another pair of guards, and the four escaped down the small alleyway.

"Ambush!" a guard cried out behind them.

Duan Ling's timing was impeccable. As the new guards arrived for their shift and discovered the chaos inside, they raised the alarm; the mounted soldiers patrolling outside ran over to surround the building. With those oncoming troops, Kuchi finally found a target for his pent-up anger. He rushed ahead and delivered a powerful punch directly to the head of a warhorse, the force of the blow so immense it knocked both horse and rider to the ground.

Arrows whizzed through the narrow alleyway. Kuchi fought as he retreated, but at the sound of Li Jianhong's whistle, he veered down a footpath to escape rather than staying to confront the soldiers.

The streets around the residence devolved into mayhem.

"This way," Duan Ling hissed to the group.

Duan Ling and Batu pelted at frantic speed down the alley, their hands tightly clasped, as the guards closed in. Li Jianhong dashed ahead, grabbed both boys by the backs of their collars, and vaulted over the wall into a stranger's courtyard. He kept running, scaling the courtyard's opposite wall to make their escape, and in a heartbeat, they'd left the main street. Kuchi, out of breath, stumbled and fell behind.

CHAPTER FIFTEEN

Another troop of soldiers emerged from a cross street.

"Stay where you are!"

"Outflank him!"

As Batu turned back toward his father, Li Jianhong caught him and held him back.

"Let me go!" he raged.

Without missing a beat, Li Jianhong shoved Batu to the side and—leaving Duan Ling clinging tightly to Batu to prevent a rescue attempt—leapt back over the wall. Arrows sang through the air, followed by terrible cries. Duan Ling clapped a hand over Batu's mouth, both their hearts pounding in their chests.

They heard Li Jianhong say something in Mongolian, and the door of the courtyard swung open. The two men slipped inside, to the great relief of Duan Ling and Batu. Kuchi was unharmed, though panting harshly, and he continued to eye Li Jianhong.

Li Jianhong kicked open the door of the household they'd entered and strutted inside. A woman, roused by the commotion, screamed at the sight of him. She quieted speedily, however, when Li Jianhong pointed his saber at her and nudged her back onto her bed.

"Just passing through," he said, sounding a perfect gentleman, before ducking back into the yard to pick up Duan Ling.

Caught between laughter and tears at his father's display, Duan Ling beckoned Batu to hurry over, only to see Kuchi already carrying him on his back. The group made their way through the house and exited via the front entrance, weaving through the streets as they made their escape under the cover of night.

"Where do we go now?" Li Jianhong asked.

Now that they'd lost their tail, Duan Ling led the group to the back garden of Ming Academy. It wasn't a holiday, so the school was occupied by staff and students—but at this hour, the boys ought to be in bed in their respective dormitories. The flowerpot was moved aside, and Batu crawled through the hole first, followed by Duan Ling. Li Jianhong simply scaled the high wall in a few leaps, and they all followed Duan Ling to the library. With practiced familiarity, Batu retrieved the library's spare key from under another flowerpot and let them into the building.

At last, they'd reached their destination. Duan Ling, whose nerves had been strung taut throughout the escape, collapsed by a long table to catch his breath. Batu lit a lamp, and its flame began to warm the cool spring night air. Yet before the flame had a chance to grow, Li Jianhong snuffed it with a sharp flick of his fingers.

"We'll wait here until morning," Li Jianhong said without turning, closing each window of the library. "I'll think of a way to send you both from the city."

"Who's this?" Batu asked Duan Ling.

"My dad." Duan Ling produced the bag of snacks from his robes. "Hungry?"

Batu shook his head, but Duan Ling urged him, "Eat. You'll need energy to escape in the morning."

The room was pitch-black save for a sliver of bright moonlight filtering through the window lattice, which cast a soft glow on Duan Ling's face. Batu gazed at him, entranced. After a moment, he reached out to gently brush his fingers across Duan Ling's cheek.

"What's wrong?" Duan Ling felt Batu was acting strangely, and it frightened him a little. There seemed to be no reason for Batu to behave this way.

"It's nothing," Batu said. "Where's Helian?"

"Everyone else is fine," Duan Ling replied. "I saw them earlier today. There's no time to say goodbye, but I'll tell them on your behalf."

"What if people find out you helped us?" Batu frowned.

"It'll be all right," Duan Ling reassured him, catching his hand again. "My dad is seriously strong. And no one will know it's him who helped anyway."

Heaving a sigh, Batu leaned back against a bookshelf and closed his eyes in exhaustion.

"Batu, are you okay?" Duan Ling shook the hand he was holding.

Batu silently shook his head. Duan Ling shifted and made room for him to rest his head on his thighs. Li Jianhong came over and gave each of the boys' heads a pat before draping an outer robe over them. The robe was Kuchi's, still speckled with blood.

Across the room, Kuchi said something in Mongolian. Duan Ling didn't understand the words, but Batu's eyes widened. Li Jianhong answered Kuchi in the same tongue, and the two men began to converse. The Mongolian language was brusque and direct; listening to them speak in hushed tones, it sounded as if they were either plotting or bargaining. Duan Ling hadn't known his father could speak a foreign language, but seeing Batu listening in quietly, he gave him a nudge. "Can you hear what they're saying?" he asked.

"My dad and your dad knew each other a long time ago," Batu explained. "They were enemies."

Duan Ling was taken aback, his mouth gaping in disbelief. At last, Kuchi said something that made Batu sit upright in alarm. He stared at Duan Ling in disbelief.

Shocked, Batu stammered, "You—you're..."

Duan Ling looked back at him in confusion. "What?"

"Batu!" Kuchi snapped, and Batu shut his mouth.

"What, what is it?" Duan Ling asked, anxious.

"Son," Li Jianhong called out. Silence filled the room until he added, "Come sit over here with me."

As Li Jianhong turned to face the boys, Duan Ling felt an indescribable prickle of danger. He glanced between Batu and Li Jianhong, uncomprehending. Batu, having already released his hand, gestured for him to go on. Father and son settled on the floor next to a shelf cluttered with scrolls and books. Meanwhile, Kuchi approached Batu and, after blowing out a long sigh, sat down beside him.

"Sleepy?" Li Jianhong asked Duan Ling.

He was, but he felt he couldn't close his eyes just yet. He didn't know what his father intended. The matched pairs of fathers and sons were separated by the wide desk, just as Duan Ling and Batu had been that first night together in the library. The only thing missing was the lamp glowing on the desk, which had been replaced with silver moonlight. Duan Ling buried his head in Li Jianhong's shoulder and rubbed his face hard. Though struggling to stay awake, he shook his head *no*.

"The Mongols are currently besieging the city of Huchang," Li Jianhong told him. "Once we escort your friend out of Shangjing, he'll be out of danger. You can relax."

Duan Ling responded with a nasal "Mn." When he noticed Batu still staring at him in shock, he looked up at Li Jianhong. "What were you and Batu's dad talking about?"

"I asked him for a favor," Li Jianhong replied. "Something that will help me send you back south in the future."

Duan Ling made a confused noise. What could Batu and his father possibly have to do with him returning to the south?

"Do you want to go back to the south?" Li Jianhong asked. "Would you rather live here in the north with me, or go back to our homeland?"

"If I go south, will you come back with me?" Duan Ling asked after a pause.

Li Jianhong's lips quirked in a smile. "What if I say I won't?"

"Then I won't go either," Duan Ling said.

"I will," Li Jianhong promised. "Wherever you go, your dad will go too."

With that confirmed, Duan Ling felt better. "Mn. Then I want to."

Li Jianhong didn't respond. He turned his head to gaze at Batu and his father, as though Duan Ling's answer had proven a certain point.

"All human souls yearn for home. Even if your son was born and raised in an enemy state, Mongol blood flows in his veins," Li Jianhong said, slow and sure, looking at Kuchi. He then asked, "Batu, have you ever been to your homeland?"

Batu jolted, whipping his head around to look at Kuchi. Before he could translate what Li Jianhong had said into Mongolian for his father, Kuchi laid a hand on the top of his son's head, indicating that he understood. In rusty Han, Kuchi said, "Your son wants to go back too. But you—have little hope. You, no hope."

"Your son has never been to that blue pearl in the high steppes of the Hulunbuir Grasslands, yet he has seen it over and over in his dreams. That longing is built into him, like an instinct," Li Jianhong said. "My son, too, yearns for the willows on the shores of West Lake and the raging rivers south of Mount Yuheng."

Batu thought for a moment, then translated Li Jianhong's words into rapid Mongolian. Kuchi stared intently at Li Jianhong, as though considering an extremely difficult proposition.

"After tonight, the world will be theirs," Li Jianhong concluded. "I will not force you, of course. Whether you agree to my proposal or not, you may leave as you will when the sun rises. This is not a transaction, and I will not hold your debt to me over your head. But I hope you will consider the idea carefully."

16

KUCHI FELL INTO a deep silence. Li Jianhong reclined against the wall with an arm around Duan Ling and closed his eyes to rest, saving his energy for their escape in the morning.

Duan Ling briefly drifted off, curled up in Li Jianhong's arms, but he stirred again minutes later. When he looked toward the other end of the room, he found Batu still awake, looking as if he hadn't slept a wink. A wave of melancholy washed over Duan Ling as he realized they would soon be separated, perhaps never to meet again in all their lives.

Noticing Duan Ling had woken up, Batu waved him over before bending down and crawling under the table. Duan Ling followed suit, squirming away from Li Jianhong's embrace and ducking under the table as well. But the boys were children no longer; now, the space under the table was too cramped to fit their gangly adolescent bodies.

Batu held a sheathed bone dagger, which he placed on the floor beneath the table. He mouthed, *For you*.

Duan Ling couldn't speak.

Batu flicked the knife with his fingers, sending it skidding in Duan Ling's direction, and gestured for him to take it. Duan Ling was at a loss; he had nothing to give in return, and had never anticipated saying goodbye under such circumstances. Nonetheless, Batu gazed earnestly at him, waiting—and after a long moment, Duan Ling finally accepted his offering.

A moment later, Kuchi roused himself and yanked on Batu's collar, pulling him back with a stern look that said as clearly as any words, *Stop causing trouble*. Batu, flustered by the interruption, thrashed in his father's grip.

Li Jianhong opened his eyes as well. Duan Ling was about to nervously return the dagger when Li Jianhong said, "Take it. It's a token of promise."

When the first rays of sunlight began to filter into the library, Li Jianhong rose to his feet. "Let's go."

Dawn was breaking, a pale smear across the horizon. In the back courtyard, Li Jianhong found a large empty wagon meant for household goods and donned a wide bamboo hat. He beckoned Batu to climb in first, then loaded the wagon bed with hay. Kuchi approached, paused for a moment, then raised a hand. Li Jianhong mirrored the gesture, and the two struck palms thrice in a wordless exchange before Kuchi, too, climbed into the wagon and ducked under the hay.

Li Jianhong vaulted into the driver's seat. When he noticed Duan Ling's curious gaze, he explained, "To clap hands in promise means you've made a vow never to be broken."

"What did you vow to do?" Duan Ling asked.

Li Jianhong's horse was tied up in the academy's back alley. Quickly, he hitched the animal to the wagon and cracked the whip to set them in motion. Leaning down to Duan Ling's ear, he whispered, "Once they return to their homeland, Batu's father will deploy troops to Jiangjun Ridge and encroach on Liao's border."

Duan Ling realized at once that Li Jianhong was executing a small step in a much larger plan. "And then?"

CHAPTER SIXTEEN

"And then your dad will leverage this assault to strike a deal with Yelü Dashi," Li Jianhong replied breezily. "We'll need a bit of luck to pass through the city gates today—let's see how the heavens feel about us two. *Hyah!*"

Li Jianhong steered the large hay wagon toward the main city gates, where a swarm of carriages had already gathered. Merchants outside the city were eager to enter, while travelers inside were equally eager to depart, creating a snarl of carts and horses. The guards were out in force, questioning everyone and methodically inspecting the cargo of each vehicle.

"We'll wait here until the traffic clears a bit," Li Jianhong said, parking the wagon on the roadside. Keeping an eye on the guards in the distance, he lowered his hat and laid several copper coins in his palm.

"Are we buying breakfast?" Duan Ling asked.

"Nope. These are weapons," Li Jianhong answered. He spread his fingers to show Duan Ling the pile of copper coins, then closed his fingers over them.

When Duan Ling saw that Li Jianhong was thinking of fighting their way through the gates, he said nervously, "There's no way the guards won't pursue us."

"It's a last resort. We should be prepared for anything," Li Jianhong said.

He lapsed back into silence, seemingly waiting on someone or something. Finally, an ornately decorated carriage came into view—one that belonged, he remembered with a start, to Qionghua House. It was traveling down the main street toward them, on its way out of the city.

"Qionghua House's carriage?" Li Jianhong's brows shot up in surprise.

"Yeah. Lang Junxia is friends with them. Do you know them too, Dad?" Duan Ling asked.

Li Jianhong contemplated, then murmured, "Qionghua House... Never mind, it's worth the risk. Son, I need you to get on that carriage and show the one inside something."

Per Li Jianhong's instructions, Duan Ling hopped off the wagon and scampered over to Qionghua House's carriage. Li Jianhong tugged the rim of his bamboo hat down, once again covering half his handsome face. As Duan Ling approached, the curtain of the carriage was drawn aside to allow him entry. Yet when he climbed in, the person seated within was not Ding Zhi, but instead what appeared to be a strange young noblewoman.

"Who are you?" Duan Ling asked.

"Shouldn't I be the one asking you that?" she replied. "Who are *you*?"

The maiden beside her burst into laughter. "What's this? You climbed into our carriage without even knowing who was inside?"

Perhaps it was on account of Duan Ling's fair, jade-like looks that the woman didn't throw him out of the carriage immediately, only examining his face with care.

After a moment's hesitation, Duan Ling said nervously, "My dad told me to come and show you something."

He fished his pouch from his robes, untied the red string, and showed the woman the white jade pendant inside. She blanched, rendered speechless as her breath caught in her throat. Voice quavering, she asked, "What...what did you say? Your father? Then you—"

"You can only look, not touch," Duan Ling said when she reached out with a trembling hand. He flashed the jade arc once more in front of her face before tucking it away again, quick and careful.

"Madam?" the maiden said, concerned.

As polite as he knew how to be, Duan Ling raised his cupped hands in salute and bowed to the woman with grand ceremony. Then he said, "My dad requests a favor, my lady."

"You flatter me. You can simply call me *Madam*, Gongzi," the woman said, rising to her feet. She extended her arms, her expansive sleeves sweeping wide, and returned the courtesy with the same solemnity.

Shortly thereafter, Qionghua House's carriage began rolling once more, turning past an unassuming little wagon. Li Jianhong followed close behind them with his hay. When they arrived at the city gates, a fair and delicate hand reached from behind the curtains to show a token of passage.

"The wagon behind us is our cargo."

The carriage's curtain drew back to reveal the madam's profile, and she cast a single glance at the guards, who nodded with haste and parted to give way. Leisurely, Li Jianhong drove his wagon along behind the carriage, and they left the city without any trouble at all. Once the carriage and wagon reached the official highway, Duan Ling ducked under the curtain and ran back to Li Jianhong; Li Jianhong whispered some words in his ear, and Duan Ling returned to the carriage.

"My dad says thank you, Madam, for your assistance. He is indebted to you. When he returns to Shangjing, he will surely visit Qionghua House for a drink."

"He is too kind," the madam said, pulling the curtains aside as if to dismount the carriage. Duan Ling held up a hand.

Repeating what Li Jianhong taught him, Duan Ling said, "We shouldn't tarry here long, so we won't bother you further, Madam."

"A million blessings unto you, Gongzi," the woman replied in a languid tone. "Heaven bless our Great Chen."

Spring painted the land in vibrant colors. The grass grew lush and warblers danced through the air; soft fluff from reeds rustling at the edge of the fields drifted across the sky like an endless river, sweeping through the season of renewal. In this fine, bright sunshine, Duan Ling felt a solemn sense of hope.

"Heaven bless our Great Chen," he mumbled to himself. The words seemed to carry an indisputable rightness.

"You can come out now," Li Jianhong called to the back of the wagon.

Batu and Kuchi were exhausted after the previous night's flight, and had been dozing in the hay. Duan Ling returned to the driver's seat and tucked himself under Li Jianhong's arm. He glanced backward every so often, but Batu showed no sign of wanting to talk again. As the wagon rocked leisurely down the road, Duan Ling, too, drifted to sleep amid the vernal breeze.

From deep within his slumber, he heard Batu's voice saying, "Don't wake him."

Duan Ling shifted slightly and felt someone stroke his groggy head.

When he awoke some time later, he was lying in the back of the hay-filled wagon, which had been parked atop a hill. Li Jianhong reclined in the wagon bed beside him with a stalk dangling from his lips, idly watching the pristine white clouds travel across the vast spring sky. A light wind brushed Duan Ling's face, and he yawned and stretched in Li Jianhong's arms. Li Jianhong pressed a loving kiss on his forehead as he stirred.

"Where's Batu?" Duan Ling asked with a jolt, suddenly awake.

"Gone." Li Jianhong put his arm around his son's shoulders. "That barbarian brat wanted you to be his anda. He's smart, I'll give him that."

"What's an anda?" Duan Ling asked.

"Blood brothers joined through life and death," Li Jianhong replied. "Thank god we didn't have anything good to give for the vow, or we would've been swindled."

Melancholic, Duan Ling asked, "Dad, do you think I'll see Batu again?"

"All things in this world are brought together by fate. Fate is the wind, and people are like the clouds you see before you: They come and they go. You'll have more friends; don't be too sad," Li Jianhong consoled him.

Duan Ling hummed in response. Somehow, Li Jianhong's words did make him feel a bit better.

"Will you go too?" Duan Ling asked. The thought of separating from his father depressed him again immediately.

But Li Jianhong burst out laughing. "Before I answer, cough up my handsome payment."

Oh yeah, Duan Ling thought. He'd forgotten all about their deal. "What do you want?"

Li Jianhong studied him for a moment, then chuckled. "Why are you rubbing your hands together like that? Plotting to murder your dad?"

Duan Ling laughed too; his dad was hilarious.

Once they quieted down, Li Jianhong said, "Grab a stalk of hay and come clean your dad's ears."

Duan Ling had Li Jianhong rest his head on his thighs, focusing on his task. Seeing him with his eyes closed, Duan Ling couldn't tell if Li Jianhong was dozing or thinking.

"Son."

"Hm?"

"What do you think of your dad's skills?"

"Formidable," Duan Ling said sincerely.

"Well, since I'm formidable, I can live however I want—so of course I won't leave my son. What would be the point of mastering all those skills otherwise?" Li Jianhong said.

In a more serious tone, Duan Ling said, "But if you go drink at Qionghua House, maybe you'll take a fancy to one of the girls. If you fancy a girl, you'll remarry, and if you remarry, you'll have another son. Then you won't want me anymore."

Li Jianhong was taken aback. "Are you jealous, kid?"

Duan Ling laughed, a little embarrassed. He was just talking; Li Jianhong knew he wasn't really serious.

Nonetheless, Li Jianhong answered him seriously: "I won't. Dad owes you. No one will ever take your place, as long as I live."

Duan Ling's hand jerked, and Li Jianhong yelped. "Ow! Careful."

The interjection instantly dispersed Duan Ling's complicated mood, and he leaned down to carefully pick at Li Jianhong's ears anew.

"In this day and age, forget about our wives in the harem. Even our own children have to fight for favor, huh," Li Jianhong commented.

Duan Ling didn't know how to respond. He felt his dad was constantly teasing him.

"I get it," Li Jianhong continued evenly. "In the past, I used to fight with your fourth uncle for favor too. It's all too common."

"Fourth uncle?" Duan Ling asked.

Ears now satisfactorily cleaned, Li Jianhong sat back up. He unfastened the horse from the traces and patted the animal's back. "Since we're out, shall we go for a ride?" he asked.

Attention once more diverted, Duan Ling cheered; Li Jianhong would only make the suggestion if he wanted to do it as well. He ran over to the horse and waited for Li Jianhong to help him mount.

"Are we spending the night out of the city?" he asked.

"Up to you," Li Jianhong replied.

"Will we go back to the home you mentioned in the south? Is our old house there?"

"I suppose it was," Li Jianhong said. "But not anymore. Do you want to go back? Are you feeling cooped up in Shangjing?"

Li Jianhong held Duan Ling from behind as they rode southward at an unhurried pace, enjoying the fine spring day. The sun shone brightly, the breeze was gentle, and life flourished all around them. Though a month had passed since Li Jianhong arrived in Shangjing, this would be their first journey together.

"Where are we going?" Duan Ling asked.

"To meet one of your dad's old friends and ask him a few questions," Li Jianhong replied.

Intrigued, Duan Ling asked, "About what?"

"About the Mandate of Heaven."

17

LIFE WITH LI JIANHONG was easy and unrestrained. The vault of the sky arched overhead and the world seemed endless beneath it; it didn't matter where they were going. Sometimes, Li Jianhong let Duan Ling take the reins as the horse galloped across the plains. Duan Ling could hardly contain his excitement.

"Do you know how to ride?" Li Jianhong asked, amused.

In truth, Duan Ling had never ridden a horse on his own before—but though he wanted to try, the idea of riding without Li Jianhong was a little scary.

"Only one way to learn!" Li Jianhong said. He slid off the horse and slapped its rear.

The animal instantly whinnied and sprang into a gallop, prompting Duan Ling to scream over his shoulder: "*Dad!*"

Li Jianhong only waved and brought his fingers to his lips to give a sharp whistle. The warhorse dashed ahead at top speed, bounding over a small stream as if taking flight. Duan Ling screamed the entire way. At first the uncontrolled ride was thrilling, but when he looked back and realized he could no longer see Li Jianhong, panic seized him. He tried to turn the horse around to no avail, which only alarmed him further.

"Stop!" he cried. "Dad! Dad, where are you?!"

The warhorse plunged into a stand of trees, nearly whipping Duan Ling off its back. Clinging to the horse's neck for dear life, Duan Ling bawled, "Dad! Where are you?!"

There was another piercing whistle, and Li Jianhong appeared from behind a tree, regarding his son with a grin. Duan Ling had nearly fainted from fear; he hurriedly dismounted and flung himself at Li Jianhong for a firm hug.

"His name is Skychaser," Li Jianhong said, patting the steed. The horse bowed his head, snorting, and rubbed his neck against Duan Ling. Only then did he finally exhale in relief.

"He's a Wusun horse," Li Jianhong said. Holding Duan Ling's hand in one of his and taking the reins with the other, he explained, "Your dad saved the Wusun king once, at the foot of the Qilian Mountains. The tribe gave me this horse as thanks."

"He's so fast," Duan Ling said. "He almost threw me off his back."

"He saved my life when I was escaping the snowfields," Li Jianhong said.

Noon had arrived, and as the pair walked under the shadows of the woods, Duan Ling saw many fruits he couldn't name.

"What's that?" he asked, pointing at one.

With a casual glance, Li Jianhong answered, "Ground cherry. It's too sour. Don't pick just any wild fruit or fungus—the brighter the color, the more potent the poison."

"I won't," Duan Ling promised. "What kind of tree is that?"

Duan Ling was preternaturally curious, and he was gradually coming to realize an important fact: No matter what question he asked, Li Jianhong always supplied a convincing answer. This was a great contrast to Lang Junxia, who had only one response, which was, *Don't ask. You'll learn in the future.*

"Euphrates poplar," Li Jianhong answered. "Looks like a willow when it's young, extremely tolerant of dry weather when grown."

Li Jianhong, Duan Ling thought, knew everything. *Why bother studying books when all I have to do is ask Dad?*

"Are we camping out here tonight?" he asked.

"Certainly not." Li Jianhong looked stern. "I should think my son can enjoy a hot meal in Huaide before sunset."

"What's that?" Duan Ling asked.

"A city in Xin Prefecture," Li Jianhong said.

"Where's Xin Prefecture?" Duan Ling was utterly clueless about anything outside Shangjing.

"The founding emperor of Liao established Shangjing as their capital, and the Shangjing highway is one of their nineteen highways. The southbound roads reach Xin Prefecture, and south of that is the Great Wall."

Duan Ling had at least heard of the Great Wall. "And past the Great Wall is Yubi Pass. Going south from there would take you through the Zhili region. Keep traveling south on the Hebei Highway, and it'll be…"

"Indeed." Li Jianhong stepped over some fallen branches and replied, "Then you'll pass through the city of Shangzi, and then Runan…all of which are now part of Liao's territory."

"And Chen is even further south than that?" Duan Ling asked.

"The lands north and south of the Yangtze belong to Chen." Seeming to recall some distant memory, Li Jianhong sighed. "Chen territory now only covers Xichuan, Jiangnan, Jiang Prefecture, and a few others."

"You said we'll go back to Southern Chen in the future. Did you mean it?" Duan Ling pressed.

"You really want to return?" Li Jianhong asked him.

Before they'd noticed, they emerged from the woods. Li Jianhong hoisted Duan Ling, helping him climb onto the horse while he pulled on the reins, and led the horse along the banks of a stream.

Swaying atop the horse, Duan Ling said, "The headmaster told us the south is beautiful. It's too bad I've never been."

Imagining a faraway paradise he hadn't ever seen was too much to ask of him.

"Everyone who travels far afield remains a guest; they all long for home," Li Jianhong said, swinging up into the saddle behind Duan Ling. "The south yearns for the north, and likewise, the north yearns for the south. The Han all think this way. So yes, the south is beautiful."

During his five years in Shangjing, Duan Ling had come to understand certain truths. He knew that when the iron cavalry of Liao rode southward, the Han people had to abandon their homes and cling to survival. And he knew that deep down, every Han in Shangjing longed for the day they could return.

"Was our home also destroyed when the Liao army marched south?" he asked.

"What?" Li Jianhong was momentarily dumbfounded; the question had broken his train of thought. As the horse trotted steadily onward, Li Jianhong stroked Duan Ling's head, and said, "Our home is still standing, but there's not much left of it."

"Do we have more family?" Duan Ling had never imagined having relatives, but today, he came to the abrupt realization that he was no different from his schoolmates in this regard. He had a father, a mother; he had uncles and aunts somewhere, like the "fourth uncle" his dad had mentioned earlier.

"Your fourth uncle and fifth aunt are both still around," Li Jianhong said. "I'll tell you about them now, but you must engrave this in your heart: Don't ever talk about this with anyone else."

When Duan Ling nodded, Li Jianhong continued, "I'm the third son in my family. My eldest brother passed before he came of age, and my second eldest sister—who was common-born—also passed young. Fourth Brother is still in Xichuan, though he is without heirs. Your fifth aunt married into a family in Jiangnan."

"What about *your* dad—my grandfather?" Duan Ling asked.

"He's still around," Li Jianhong replied. "But he likes your fourth uncle, not me... *Hup!*"

Duan Ling understood now—if his own father shunned him, that would explain Li Jianhong's mixed feelings about the south. He sensed Li Jianhong's reluctance to speak on the past and was mature enough not to pry any further.

In Jiang Prefecture, on the cusp between spring and summer, shrubs of snowball viburnum bloomed in abundance, bursting with splendor. In the springtime landscape, a solitary mountain was set against a clear sky, such a pure shade of blue it seemed freshly cleansed. The glistening mountain lakes reflected the occasional vibrant colors of a paper kite soaring above them. When the string snapped, the kite disappeared into the woods, following the flight of the birds.

Lang Junxia, clad in a long, sky-blue robe, walked along the winding gallery road with his horse. He passed by Jiang Prefectural City but did not enter. After drinking but a single handful of the waters of the south, straight from the Yangtze, he boarded a long-haul ship going north. The vessel would sail inland along the great river and enter the four-river region at the foot of Mount Yuheng, bypassing the most difficult road through Shu, before arriving at the capital of Southern Chen.

Throughout his journey, he hardly spoke a word. When the travelers disembarked at last at their final destination, he followed the throng off the ship and stopped at the riverbank, where he again bent down and cupped a handful of water to drink.

After three months, Lang Junxia had finally arrived at Xichuan.

The capital's walls were draped in lush greenery; when autumn arrived, they would bloom splendidly with hibiscus. After passing through the city gates, he made his way to a bookshop in the west end of the city, where he effortlessly dispatched the rusted lock on its main gate. Layers of dust mantled every surface of the establishment. Lang Junxia settled his horse with some hay in the courtyard, then removed his bag and opened the door to the interior of the building. Yet he hadn't even crossed the threshold when he stopped in his tracks.

In the dim light, a masked assassin stood waiting, as if he'd been there all this time—or perhaps as if he'd just arrived.

The assassin cut a towering figure, six feet tall, with a sword gripped firmly in one hand. No less imposing than Li Jianhong, he stood like a mountain in the abandoned hall, his eyes fixed intently on Lang Junxia.

"Hello," was the assassin's first line.

Lang Junxia put a hand on the hilt of his sword.

"My name is Changliu-jun." This was his second line. He slowly pulled down his mask, revealing a handsome face.

"I've come to kill you." This was Changliu-jun's third and final line.

Lang Junxia drew his sword without waiting for Changliu-jun to strike, but Changliu-jun was poised to preempt him. Before Lang Junxia's blade was fully unsheathed, the sharp qi of Changliu-jun's divine weapon was flashing before his eyes.

It was the closest Lang Junxia had ever come to death.

But even the meticulously prepared Changliu-jun hadn't anticipated that—despite his planning—Lang Junxia would evade the strike that should have killed him. Lang Junxia raised his sheath and slammed the half-drawn sword back in, trapping Changliu-jun's blade with a resounding *clang* amid the powerful tremors of Lang Junxia's inner force.

The move came at immense cost to Lang Junxia. He swung his sheathed sword and spun, dragging Changliu-jun with raw strength to reverse their positions. The second they came to a stop, each struck out with a palm: Lang Junxia with his left and Changliu-jun with his right.

Their palms collided, and Changliu-jun's rock-crushing force dissolved before Lang Junxia's supple response, redirected instead toward the nearest wall. With a terrible rumble, the wall collapsed as it absorbed the force of Changliu-jun's blow.

Alas, Lang Junxia's left hand was not as powerful as his right; blood gushed from his hand. He fled, crashing through the main gate, and disappeared into the bustle of the market.

Changliu-jun stepped forward and bent to pick up a finger that lay curled on the ground. After retrieving it, he put his bamboo hat on anew.

When he returned to the prime minister's residence, he tossed the severed pinkie to the dog in the yard to eat. He stored his sword in his room, then made his way down the winding corridors to the study.

Mu Kuangda was in the middle of drafting a memorial to the throne, imploring the emperor to abdicate and enjoy his old age, when Changliu-jun approached him from behind.

"I have failed my mission."

"I imagine he wouldn't have gotten away if you didn't make that little three-line speech you always give," Mu Kuangda replied mildly. "Did you injure him?"

"He lost the pinkie on his left hand," Changliu-jun answered.

"I'll send a letter to inform the general. I'm sure he'll be delighted," Mu Kuangda said.

Deep in the northern Altyn-Tagh Mountains lay Huaide Province, a vast region crucial for passage through the range to reach Shangjing. Its villages were scattered across the mountains' slopes, linked to the provincial capital by a network of winding, cobweb-like paths. Spring was in full bloom, and the mountains teemed with valuable flora and fauna, which turned Huaide into a popular trading hub.

Duan Ling had only ever been in Runan and Shangjing; as he looked around this new city, his eyes sparkled with curiosity. He craned his neck to take in every detail as he and Li Jianhong passed through the village marketplaces on horseback.

"Hey! You want a tiger pelt or bones?"

"Where're you from?"

"Buy some candy?"

Duan Ling glanced back at Li Jianhong, not daring to answer any peddling merchants, until Li Jianhong said, "What? Don't look at me; your dad'll get you whatever you want."

"But I'm not allowed to speak to strangers, am I?" Duan Ling asked.

Li Jianhong laughed. "There's no such rule. Speak if you want to speak; talk to whomever you want."

And so, when Duan Ling came to an herb stall stocked with exotic plants from deep within the mountains and an object the size of a goose egg caught his attention, he asked, "What's this? A bezoar?"

Li Jianhong cast the item the briefest glance before handing over the money.

CHAPTER SEVENTEEN

As Li Jianhong led the horse through the market, he said, "It's not that you can't speak to strangers. But you have to know what to say and what not to say in order to protect yourself."

Understanding that Li Jianhong was teaching him more about the ways of the world, Duan Ling answered with an affirmative hum.

"The same rice feeds hundreds of kinds of people. Even if you mean no harm to anyone else, it doesn't mean no one means harm to you," Li Jianhong added.

"Then how do I know what to say and what not to say?" Duan Ling asked.

"When you have no mission to discharge, you can say anything. But you must observe the person you're talking to, and guard against any malicious intentions they might have. Do not speak about wealth to the poor; do not speak about poverty to the rich; do not flaunt your ambitions to men, and do not exhibit lust when speaking to women," Li Jianhong answered. "When you do have a mission, do not easily allow others to learn your identity. You must be on constant guard. When necessary, you may have to fabricate new identities according to your situation. Crowded places like inns are hotbeds for rumor; keep a tight lip on any important matters. Irrelevant persons, especially tavern managers and waiters, must never learn the reason you're there."

Duan Ling nodded, though he didn't entirely understand.

"Lastly, when it comes down to it, you must never succumb to avarice during your travels," Li Jianhong concluded. "If you don't covet what doesn't belong to you, you'll save yourself a lot of trouble."

He took Duan Ling to an inn for a rest, requesting a room for one night. Li Jianhong dutifully retrieved his identity papers for the inn manager to inspect, but due to the complicated political situation in Liao and the many tribes holding different documents who crossed through the region, the manager didn't look closely before instructing his staff to open one of their best rooms.

Lying in bed with Duan Ling tucked against his side, Li Jianhong appeared lost in thought. Duan Ling asked, "Dad, are we going back on the road tomorrow?"

"Don't want to travel anymore?" Li Jianhong asked.

"No." Duan Ling shook his head, feeling drowsy. "Let's keep going."

Li Jianhong leaned down and dropped a kiss on Duan Ling's head, and Duan Ling wriggled around to bury his head in his father's shoulder.

"What is it? Getting cranky?" Li Jianhong asked. Duan Ling responded by digging his head harder into his chest. "Oh, I see. Being cute, are you?"

Wrapping both his arms around Duan Ling, Li Jianhong pinned his son down and tickled him until the bed creaked with their play. Duan Ling struggled hard, but he laughed harder. When the tickling finally stopped, Li Jianhong stared into Duan Ling's eyes. He took his son's hand and pressed it against his own cheek, closing his eyes in reverie. Lids heavy, Duan Ling gazed up at Li Jianhong's face, his hand brushing over his cheek and lips. Then, with his head lolling against his father's shoulder, he fell asleep.

By the time Duan Ling opened his eyes, awoken by noise outside, it was morning. Thinking blearily that the commotion came from authorities ready to apprehend them, he jolted alert. "What's happening?"

"It's nothing to do with us," Li Jianhong answered. Since Duan Ling was awake, he rose and wet a towel for him to wash up.

In a single night, Huaide had transformed into a scene of mayhem. Crowds filled the streets as families fled along the northeast road.

"The Mongols are coming!"

CHAPTER SEVENTEEN

"Go! Everyone, this way!"

Duan Ling had never witnessed such a sight. As the father and son ate their noodles in the ground floor restaurant of the inn, Duan Ling watched the swarms of refugees congesting the main road with growing alarm. The flow of people was endless, stretching as far as the eye could see, but Li Jianhong seemed unbothered.

"Shoo! Don't come in here!" barked the inn manager in displeasure, sending the waiter to chase refugees out of his establishment. The world was turbulent, and without money, the road was hard. Duan Ling stole look after look toward the doorway, until a boy his own age ducked into the inn with a smaller boy in tow.

Duan Ling held a flatbread out to the older boy. "You want one? Have a rest."

"Out! Both of you!" the waiter yelled at the dirty-faced brothers.

Li Jianhong shot the waiter a look, which promptly shut him up.

"Please give it to my little brother instead," the youth said with a bow. "Thank you so much, sir. May you have safe travels."

The sight made Duan Ling's heart clench. The older boy knew his manners and took up only the smallest possible corner of the restaurant as he let his little brother eat. Li Jianhong took another piece of flatbread, spread it to dip in the mutton soup, and handed it to Duan Ling.

"Where are you kids from?" Li Jianhong asked casually.

"Huchang," the older child replied.

"Oh? Has the city been breached?" Li Jianhong asked.

"Close to it," the child said. "The Mongols are at the gates. Everyone's fleeing to Shangjing for fear Huchang will be razed. My lord, could you spare us some water?"

Li Jianhong poured him a bowl of tea. The boy swallowed a few large mouthfuls before giving the rest to his little brother.

"Where are your parents?" Duan Ling asked.

"We lost them on the road," he said. "If you're heading north, can you ask around—"

"We're heading east," Li Jianhong said. "But don't worry. The Mongols haven't come this far south yet. Your parents should be all right."

The older boy nodded. "Be careful in the east as well. The Yuan cavalry is all over the mountains."

"Come on," Li Jianhong beckoned Duan Ling once they finished their food. He paid for their room and board and led Duan Ling out of the inn.

The pair mounted Skychaser, detoured around the main road, and sped away east.

18

"Is there going to be a war?" Duan Ling asked.

Skychaser stopped halfway up a hill, and the two looked down. The city of Huaide had become a sea of refugees as citizens from the nearby cities of Huchang and Jinde streamed into the provincial capital. From there, they hoped to continue westward across the Altyn-Tagh and reach Shangjing, or further on, Yubi Pass.

"Yes," Li Jianhong replied.

"Then what about Batu and his dad?" Duan Ling asked.

"The Mongols have been raising their army for a long time. If the fight didn't start at Jiangjun Ridge, then it makes sense it would be here and now. Whether you saved Batu or not, war would've broken out; if you hadn't, it would've merely meant the vain sacrifice of their lives."

Duan Ling had never witnessed anything like this exodus. "Who will win?"

"Hard to say," Li Jianhong replied. "Who do you want to win?"

Although Shangjing was within the domain of the Liao Empire, Duan Ling had lived there for five years and saw it as his second home. In his heart, he hoped the Liao Empire would prevail—but when two nations clashed in war, victory and defeat were not determined by human wishes alone.

"Dad, do we have to leave too?" Duan Ling asked.

"I don't know yet," Li Jianhong replied. "But we'll find out soon enough. Come."

With that, he wheeled the horse around and spurred Skychaser to a gallop down the road, entering the rocky paths of the mountain range.

They hadn't traveled far before Duan Ling cried out in alarm, "Dad!"

Li Jianhong's gaze followed Duan Ling's pointing finger. Fog from the mountain streams filled the morning air, and through the mist, a Yuan cavalry squadron passed into view. When they moved on moments later, the bodies of several Liao soldiers remained on the ground behind them. There had obviously been a clash just now.

"How long have we been on the road?" Li Jianhong asked, dismounting to examine the fallen soldiers.

"Almost two hours," Duan Ling answered, nervous. "How is the Mongol army here already?"

"Here, take these." Li Jianhong tossed Duan Ling the quivers, crossbow, and longbow he had relieved from the dead Liao soldiers, then swung back onto the horse. He weighed the crossbow in his hand. "A vanguard unit. They're planning to go around the Altyn-Tagh to ambush Huaide. Can you still see them? Count how many riders there are."

"Five, ten…" While Li Jianhong tested the crossbow, Duan Ling counted the troops ahead. "Maybe a hundred of them."

Li Jianhong taught Duan Ling how to pull the crossbow's trigger and had him fire a few test shots before instructing him to carry it on his back. He settled the longbow on his own shoulder.

"Don't panic when you encounter the enemy's vanguard on the road," he said. Duan Ling nodded in understanding, and he continued, "Hide yourself first—then measure the enemy's strength, your own strength, the terrain, the weather, and the people involved. In this moment the enemy is in the light, and you are in the shadow; if you have at least a sixty percent chance of success, you can risk launching a sneak attack."

"But there's only two of us," Duan Ling pointed out.

"King Wei of Qi asked Sun Tzu: 'Is there any way to fight one against ten?'" Li Jianhong said. "And do you remember what your textbook said?"

"Yes!" Duan Ling had read this passage before in *The Art of War*, and so he answered, "'Catch the enemy off guard; attack where they are unprepared'!"

Li Jianhong smirked. "Then let's go!"

He pressed his knees to Skychaser's sides to spur him forward, and the horse streaked toward the enemy like lightning, galloping through the hills and forests as though they were flat ground.

"Take the reins," Li Jianhong said. When Duan Ling did, he cried, "Turn!"

Duan Ling yanked on the reins, turning Skychaser's head. Li Jianhong pressed his feet firmly down into the stirrups, his long, fit body rising from the horse, longbow in hand. He drew the bowstring taut and released it; a muffled *thwack* followed, and Li Jianhong returned to his seat in the saddle.

"Turn again!" he instructed.

Duan Ling shook the reins and Li Jianhong loosed three more arrows in quick succession. The cries of the Mongol riders rang through the trees as they fell from their horses. Another three-beat set of arrows and screams followed. Then another.

"You must be fast, ruthless, and precise between the first and second ambush," Li Jianhong said beside Duan Ling's ear, teaching him as they went. "This will confuse the enemy and sow apprehension in their ranks because their opponent's numbers are unknown. If you release only one arrow, they'll assume there is only one opponent."

"Got it," Duan Ling said.

They crossed a stream in their unrelenting pursuit of the cavalry vanguard, tailing them. Sure enough, the Yuan cavalry stopped and entered into an uneasy formation, afraid to advance recklessly.

"What do we do now?" Duan Ling asked.

Li Jianhong took a flint from his breast pocket. "'Favorable timing is inferior to favorable terrain; favorable terrain is inferior to favorable relationships.' Who said this?"

"I think it was Mengzi,"[10] Duan Ling said.

Focusing on striking the flint, Li Jianhong said, "Correct. We must take full advantage of the landscape. Since they are in formation inside the forest, we'll smoke them out."

At this time of the year, the woods were dense with overgrown shrubs, and the forest floor was strewn with fallen leaves, all shrouded in heavy layers of spring fog so that the terrain ranged from damp to dry. Li Jianhong set the dry leaves beneath him alight. The fire crackled as the wind stoked it, billowing an immense amount of white smoke that blew into the forest.

"See how that man is dressed differently from the others?" Li Jianhong said. "He's the zuut jurtchi—the captain of this unit."

Although the Yuan squadron was coughing loudly, they remained calm, shouting to one another as they retreated from the forest. But the white smoke had already spread, reducing visibility to near zero.

A warhorse burst out of the smoke. Duan Ling, gripping the reins, charged into the enemy formation, while Li Jianhong wielded

---

10   A Confucian philosopher from the Zhou dynasty during the Warring States period. This quote is an excerpt from the chapter "Gongsun Chou II" in Mengzi, the philosopher's eponymous collection of writings.

anti-cavalry sabers with both hands, cleaving through the enemy troops. Blood spattered on all sides as they trampled their way through the brush.

"Now, throw the rope!" Li Jianhong called.

Duan Ling cast a lasso around the jurtchi's neck with perfect accuracy, but the soldier's solid weight nearly yanked him off the horse. Quick-handed, Li Jianhong caught the rope and steadied Duan Ling as Skychaser carried the pair out of the encircling troops, arrows raining down around them.

Once they'd broken free of the enemy ranks and gone further up the mountain, Skychaser slowed to a trot—still dragging the jurtchi on the ground behind them. The man had a death grip on the rope around his neck, keeping it from tightening. Duan Ling panted for breath.

"Yuan's military rules are strict: If the zuut jurtchi dies, the jurtchi of the next division down will take over," Li Jianhong said. "Don't even think about taking hostages. No soldier will fall for that."

"Then why...why did we capture him?" Duan Ling was still huffing, and his heart hadn't stopped pounding. He glanced backward again and again.

Borrowing the horse's momentum, Li Jianhong tossed the rope up and wrapped it around a tree branch several times, then secured it with a firm knot, leaving the jurtchi dangling in midair. The two then rode off to a higher vantage point, where they stopped to observe from a distance.

"This tactic is called 'guarding the corpse to strike the reinforcements,'" Li Jianhong said. "Watch."

As Yuan riders charged from the dense woods to rescue their captain, Li Jianhong nocked six arrows to the bow and released them all the moment the troops reached the captive.

The arrows flew like deadly shooting stars, felling the enemies and their horses. His face turning a deep red, the jurtchi thrashed as the Yuan riders were thrown into chaos. It took them mere seconds to spot Li Jianhong atop the hill, but he had situated himself carefully upwind; their arrows foundered before they reached him, and they were forced to draw back. Li Jianhong shot arrow after arrow after their retreating forces, killing several dozen men as if cutting grass.

Duan Ling's heart was racing as he watched.

"Do you understand?" Li Jianhong asked.

"I...I think so," Duan Ling said with a nod, though his eyes were bright with fear.

"Don't be scared," Li Jianhong soothed him and bent to press a comforting kiss beside Duan Ling's ear. "We may be killing people, but we're also saving people. If you'd ever witnessed the Yuan army massacring a city, you would understand that this handful of arrows has saved innumerable lives."

"I know," Duan Ling said. He'd heard many such tragic stories of Yuan armies butchering innocents—but this didn't make the scene before him any less of a shock.

"Don't be afraid to take a life," Li Jianhong said. "Just believe that you are right."

Between sentences, Li Jianhong let two more arrows fly, killing two more Yuan soldiers. The riders no longer dared to advance, and—anguished beyond measure—retreated beyond the range of fire and watched helplessly as their leader died a slow death by hanging.

"Understand, these men's hands are soaked in blood," he continued. "The reason I strangled him with the rope is so he couldn't cry out and alert his fellows, or sacrifice himself by telling his comrades to leave."

"Okay." Duan Ling's voice trembled.

The Yuan riders' eyes were all bloodshot, but none dared advance anymore. Li Jianhong shot one last arrow, severing the rope from a hundred paces. The jurtchi dropped ten feet to the ground from the tree branch, and Li Jianhong turned the horse away, disappearing over the crest of the hill.

The Yuan soldiers rushed forward to save their captain—but just as Duan Ling was about to ask if they were going to leave just like that, Li Jianhong wheeled around and regained the hilltop. In these final volleys, he shot multiple arrows at once, raining missiles down on the squadron in a deadly torrent. Terrible cries echoed across the hills as bodies blanketed the fields and blood flowed like a river. The remaining soldiers fled, not daring to remain another moment.

"And that's what we call 'deception,'" Li Jianhong said. "There's no such thing as too much deception in war."

Duan Ling sat utterly speechless.

At last, Li Jianhong shot a single, final arrow into the jurtchi, ensuring the end of his life. "Let's go."

Employing ambush and deception, Li Jianhong had eliminated nearly half the Yuan's hundred-man vanguard squadron. The surviving troops, huddled like frightened birds, were too afraid to make any reckless moves. As Skychaser left the hills and galloped down through the woods, the soldiers' dying screams echoed in Duan Ling's ears.

"I don't wish for you to kill innocents," Li Jianhong said suddenly. "But more than that, I don't wish you to be indecisive and defenseless in the face of danger. Sometimes, when a person can't make up their mind, it's not because they can't do it—but because they don't *want* to. Kill those who deserve to die; save those who deserve to live. It was

Mengzi who said, 'Despite thousands who wish to stop me, I will move forward.' No one but you can decide your guilt."

Li Jianhong's voice was deep and gentle, and it dispersed the agonized cries from Duan Ling's mind. By now, the sun had fully risen, and the dappled light filtering through the forest leaves shimmered past their bodies like millions of shooting stars in the night sky.

"My son, use your eyes. See the truth clearly: Life is miserable and short. To live in this world, you must face many cruelties."

Skychaser burst out of the forest. The sun beat down on them, blazing like fire, its brilliance scouring the land and dispelling all traces of gloom. A sea of clouds rolled below them, from which rose a range of mountain peaks, the two riders on their single horse like a lone boat drifting across a vast ocean.

With a casual calm, Li Jianhong said, "When you're standing high enough, everything else will fall away. You need only heed what's in here…" He pressed a hand to the left side of Duan Ling's chest. "Listen to your heart, and do not fear."

Duan Ling's eyes reflected the rolling clouds and the jagged teeth of the mountains. In that moment, he felt it: how small he was under his father's protection. Yet despite his insignificance, he still stood at the highest point in the world. All the lives passing below him were mere fleeting reflections, rising and falling with the sea of mist beneath his feet.

Li Jianhong eased the horse's pace, and they trotted along the path that wound around the summit.

"I'm not scared," Duan Ling declared.

"I know you've killed before, to save Lang Junxia," Li Jianhong said. "But you haven't learned yet that sometimes, you kill to protect people you've never met. Those people will never know what you've sacrificed for them in distant lands, and will likely never thank you once in their entire lives. But I think, even without their thanks, you'll still make the sacrifice and do what you must, won't you?"

"Yes," Duan Ling said, nodding.

As they came around the summit, a temple rose into view at the end of the long stretch of mountain peaks. Under that flame-like sun, it was burning in a great conflagration.

"It's on fire!" Duan Ling exclaimed.

"Damn. We're too late," Li Jianhong said under his breath.

"Do we go help?" Duan Ling asked.

"Hopefully we still can!" Li Jianhong spurred the horse into a furious gallop down the winding mountain path, speeding toward the temple.

19

It was an ancient Buddhist temple, four centuries old. Master Malika, the founder, had come east to sow the seeds of Buddhism across the steppes and Central Plains, tirelessly teaching the sutras into his old age—whereupon he once again crossed the border with a single walking stick, hiking across the westernmost peaks of the Xianbei Mountains in hopes of reaching the distant north. Yet for reasons unknown, upon reaching this mountain's highest peak, he had stopped to build this temple. According to the legends of the Khitan people, it was a place not even birds could reach on their wings. For centuries, it had been known as the Northern Temple.

Later, when Liao's founding emperor marched his army south to invade the Central Plains, he prayed for success at the Northern Temple on multiple occasions. After his triumph in the Battle of Huai River, the Liao Empire established capitals in Shangjing and Zhongjing, and a new grand temple was constructed in the latter. This temple was designated the center of national worship and named the Northern Daming Temple; monks from the Northern Temple were invited to serve there and bring their sacred sutras. Even so, many monks chose to remain within the remote Northern Temple.

And at this moment, this very same Northern Temple was ablaze, the bodies of its monks strewn over its grounds. The Yuan army was brazenly searching the buildings, and what monks were left alive stood guard at the entrance of the main hall, wielding their staffs.

With a sharp whinny, Skychaser leapt across the sea of fire and kicked open the front gates. The commotion alerted the nearest Yuan soldiers, who turned to yell toward the rest of the troops.

In a single swift motion, Li Jianhong leaned to one side and loosed four arrows, then whipped the bow in his hands to the other side to shoot two more, felling all the Yuan soldiers posted outside the temple gates in the space of a breath.

"Block the gates!" he shouted to the monks.

The Yuan army was caught off guard by the arrival of aid. Yet when they saw the reinforcements were but one man riding double with a single boy, they became fearless and drew their sabers to charge. As the leading soldier lifted his blade to slash down on Li Jianhong's back, Duan Ling yanked the horse around and pulled the trigger of his crossbow, shooting a bolt straight into the soldier's right eye. The man let out a terrible howl as he collapsed to the ground.

"Amitabha—" sighed a voice from within the main hall.

The pair dismounted and fought their way into the yard on foot. Li Jianhong shielded Duan Ling as he struck and parried the attacks of the Yuan soldiers. The strength of these men was much greater than that of the vanguard they had encountered before—these were obviously part of the army's main forces.

Li Jianhong turned his head to block another strike when Duan Ling cried, "Dad, above you!"

A burning wooden beam had collapsed, crashing toward Li Jianhong's head. Li Jianhong caught it and swung the massive, fiery beam. It whipped up the air as he spun around, smashing the blades from the Yuan soldiers' hands and sending their bodies flying out of the courtyard, coughing blood.

Duan Ling released bolt after bolt from the stairway as the guardian monks rushed to pick up pot covers and planks to cover him. Li Jianhong bent low and swung the giant beam once more, forcing the gathered Yuan soldiers to scramble back as he unleashed a mighty roar. His cry was so powerful it sounded like the collapse of the mighty Mount Tai, setting everyone's eardrums vibrating painfully. Thrusting both hands forward, he used the beam to shove the Yuan soldiers through the open gates of the monastery, his fearsome strength sweeping them from the courtyard like leaves. With one last formidable strike, he shattered the burning beam; it exploded into sharp, flaming fragments that shot into the crowd of Yuan soldiers. With nowhere else to go, the remaining troops were driven over the cliff's edge.

Amid the lingering screams, Li Jianhong finally turned to face the monks. "Everyone, onto the walls and ready your arrows. Shoot any that dare attack!"

The handful of remaining guardian monks took their positions at the highest points of the courtyard wall, while the errand runners picked up buckets to continue extinguishing the devastating fires inside the Northern Temple.

"Which general is outside?" asked a hoarse, elderly voice. "The flames of war will soon rise; all is uncertain, yet there exists someone who remembers this old man. I can feel your great kindness. Please, come inside for a chat."

Duan Ling glanced up at his father, remembering Li Jianhong had taken him on this trip in the first place to meet an old friend. Li Jianhong nodded, confirming his guess.

"That's right," he said. "The old man has a bad temper, so try not to talk too much in front of him. If you plan to insult him, hide behind me first."

Amused, Duan Ling nodded back. Li Jianhong straightened Duan Ling's clothes before taking his hand and leading him inside the hall.

The temple hall was dim, and remnant fires crackled nearby. As Li Jianhong and Duan Ling entered, a novice monk—a young child—approached with a copper basin so they might clean their hands. After washing, father and son accepted the proffered incense and bowed thrice to the Buddha statue. The discipline monk struck the copper alms bowl with a mallet, drawing out a melodious clang.

"Please step this way," the monk said.

Li Jianhong passed through a second set of doors, entering the depths of the temple. At the top of a set of low stairs stood an inner hall with its doors flung open, and at the center, an old monk sat on a prayer cushion. Eight guardian monks flanked him on either side, holding their staffs and murmuring the sutras as they sat.

"I see. So it is His Highness the prince," said the old monk coolly. "Please forgive this weak old man for being unable to stand and welcome you."

His Highness? Duan Ling turned to Li Jianhong in shock, but his father was entirely unaffected.

"This is my son," he said. He looked at Duan Ling. "Son, go over and greet Master Kongming."

Duan Ling approached and made a proper obeisance with both hands raised above his head—just as he'd been taught by the headmaster.

The old monk—Master Kongming—smelled like ash and decay; bits of his robes had been singed away. He extended a hand toward Duan Ling. Uncertain, Duan Ling glanced back at his father, who shooed him forward. Duan Ling moved closer and knelt before Master Kongming, and the old monk placed a hand on his forehead.

"I bestow blessings unto you," Kongming said. "And therefore will you bestow blessings unto the people. May heaven bless your Great Chen—never mind. Forget it."

Duan Ling was struck speechless.

Kongming turned to Li Jianhong. "Your Highness, please speak your mind."

He waved a hand, and the guardian monks rose to their feet and exited the room. They closed the doors behind them, leaving Li Jianhong, Duan Ling, and Master Kongming alone.

Duan Ling saw that Master Kongming's left hand was charred black, the skin cracked like coal to reveal raw scarlet flesh beneath— yet he showed no sign of being in pain. With his uninjured hand, the old monk pulled over another prayer cushion. Duan Ling handed the cushion to his father and knelt behind him on the floor.

"I've come a long way, yet you're as inhospitable as ever, Master Kongming," Li Jianhong said. "At least offer me a cup of tea to soothe my dry throat."

"I never imagined I would meet you again at a time like this, Your Highness," Kongming said. "The grudges we shared in the past feel as if they're from a lifetime ago. But although you have let them go, Your Highness, this old man has not."

"A man of the cloth must let go what he should let go," Li Jianhong said. "Cheer up, Master Kongming. Isn't it only a sword?"

A young novice monk offered Li Jianhong tea; he sipped it before passing the bowl to Duan Ling. Parched, Duan Ling downed half of it in one gulp. As he listened to the conversation between the adults, his mind circled back to that address of *His Highness the prince*. The words by themselves weren't anything shocking; after all, most of the students at Ming Academy were the sons of either royalty or nobility. Helian Bo, Batu, and the other children of hostages were all apparently some form of royalty—but his father had once told him that they were Han. And if his father was a prince of the Han, didn't that mean his father's father was the emperor?! The thought rocked Duan Ling to his core.

Yet despite this revelation, Duan Ling's impression of his father was fundamentally unchanged. He was still himself, and Duan Ling was too.

"I was presented with an opportunity," Li Jianhong began, "and I released a tiger back to his mountain. I don't yet know if this will be a good or a bad thing, but I figured it was time for a visit. I've come with three questions to ask you, Master Kongming."

Kongming had possessed a violent temper in his youth, and it remained uncurbed in his old age. "Your Highness, you may have three questions for this old man, but this old man would like you to answer one of mine first," the old monk said. "What do you mean you released a tiger back to his mountain?"

"I helped the Borjigin hostages escape Shangjing," Li Jianhong replied.

Master Kongming easily guessed the rest. "Hmm. Yuan has invaded Liao, but the Great Prince of the Northern Court has no illustrious record of victories. He won't be able to hold off Kublai's great army. Upon returning to Shangjing in defeat, he would surely kill Kuchi to vent his anger. What you've done may be considered a good thing. It is time you washed your hands of blood, Your Highness."

Li Jianhong sighed. "Not quite yet. In exchange for his and his son's lives, Kuchi will ask Kublai for a battalion to station at

Yubi Pass in alliance with the Han. At the very least, this will obstruct reinforcements from Southern Chen to Liao...if such a force even exists. This plan holds nothing but advantages for Yuan—Ögedei doesn't want to face a war on two fronts, after all. Once the Yuan army surrounds Shangjing, I can make an offer to Yelü Dashi: I'll provide assistance in fighting the Mongols, and I'll promise an alliance with the Liao Empire once I return to Xichuan and reclaim the throne. In return, I'll request he deploy his army to help me fight in the south. It's the best way to earn Liao's trust."

"Then you have decided to return to the south, Your Highness?" Master Kongming stared intently into Li Jianhong's eyes.

"This I have not decided—which is why I've come to the Northern Temple. While I'm here, will Master Kongming please give my son a name?" Li Jianhong said.

Master Kongming shifted his gaze to Duan Ling and appraised him for a long moment. Duan Ling hadn't understood much of what Li Jianhong said, but he sensed that Master Kongming disagreed with his plans. It seemed a rift already existed between them.

"The Li family lacks heirs," Li Jianhong said. "The only one to enter the clan book in this generation is my son. He used his mother's surname in his childhood, with the single given name *Ling*. I've come to request a blessing from Master Kongming, that he may grow up strong and live a life free of misfortune."

"How can one ever be free of misfortune in life?" Master Kongming remarked. "According to naming tradition, your family's current generation name should contain the *cao* radical—*grass*. What do you think of the name Li Ruo, from the divine tree Ruomu?"

As Li Jianhong contemplated the name's sound, Master Kongming added, "In the far east stands Fusang; in the far west stands Ruomu. The day begins at the top of one tree and ends at the other. Having endured the storms, it fears neither wind nor rain, and ultimately becomes fine building material for grand houses—a blessing to the realm."

"Thank you, Master, for the name," Li Jianhong said. He shot a glance at Duan Ling, who quickly bowed.

"Thank you, Master, for the name," Duan Ling echoed.

Master Kongming regarded Duan Ling again, quietly.

"There is one more question I'd like an answer to, Master Kongming," said Li Jianhong.

Narrowing his eyes, Master Kongming said, "Speak freely."

"I want to know—can I rebuild Southern Chen's empire and restore my great country?" Li Jianhong asked.

Master Kongming's reply was tepid. "And if this old man says you can't? Will you give up, Your Highness?"

Duan Ling blinked, listening with bated breath. He understood only vaguely what Li Jianhong meant by this question. Were they really going back to the south?

Li Jianhong flashed a smile. "You're right, Master Kongming. I've gotten impatient."

"Now allow me to ask you, Your Highness," Master Kongming said. "After the battle at Jiangjun Ridge, you vanished from the world for years. Why return now?"

"My son wants to return to his homeland. That's all," Li Jianhong replied.

"Dad!" Duan Ling exclaimed. Li Jianhong turned and locked eyes with him. After the time he'd spent with his father, Duan Ling could guess Li Jianhong's intentions. "I just want us to be alive and well," Duan Ling said. "We don't have to go back."

"In that regard, my son can relax," Li Jianhong said.

"Your Highness, you are one of the most sensible people in this world," Master Kongming said. "Thorough, prudent, and almost undefeatable. But from what I see…" He trailed off, shaking his head.

Li Jianhong's expression darkened, but Master Kongming continued. "Naturally, there is no place you cannot go, and nothing you cannot achieve. I only pray that I am mistaken. Regardless, you will only accomplish half of what you intend—the other half of Southern Chen's future must rest on the young prince's shoulders."

At this, the crease in Li Jianhong's brow eased, and he grew contemplative. After a pause he said, "The world thrives when the universe renews itself, an endless cycle of rebirth and new beginnings. The mantle of responsibility would have always come to him. My third question need not be asked. No one in this world can truly divine another's fate—least of all the fate of my son."

"Right or wrong, success or failure, all abide by nature's law," Master Kongming said. "The cycle of karma is absolute. Thus, by what he does, a man holds his own fate in his hands."

Li Jianhong said nothing for a moment. Duan Ling sensed a looming darkness, like the shadow a dying man manifested. Frightened, he shuffled closer to Li Jianhong, who reached out and drew him close.

"Master?" Li Jianhong prompted after a time.

"Before we say farewell, I will gift you with a phrase, Your Highness," Master Kongming said slowly. "The unbending is easily broken; the unyielding is easily dishonored. The sun declines once it reaches its zenith; the moon wanes once full. Remember this well."

Duan Ling stared at Master Kongming.

Li Jianhong began, "I imagine Master Kongming has no more use for the sword the Northern Temple has been safeguarding. Why don't y—"

"You're too late." Master Kongming closed his eyes, his voice grave. "It was stolen away by my traitorous shidi.[11] The Northern Temple has been dishonored. If one day the opportunity presents itself, I pray you'll help this old man dispose of him and restore the Ender of the Profane to its proper place. All my life, I have been unable to escape the profane..."

His speech ground to a halt. Duan Ling gasped in shock as Master Kongming slumped backward and collapsed heavily onto the floor. The sun filtering through the cracked ceiling of the temple cast its light over Master Kongming's unmoving body. He had passed away.

---

11   Younger martial brother, used for younger disciples or classmates.

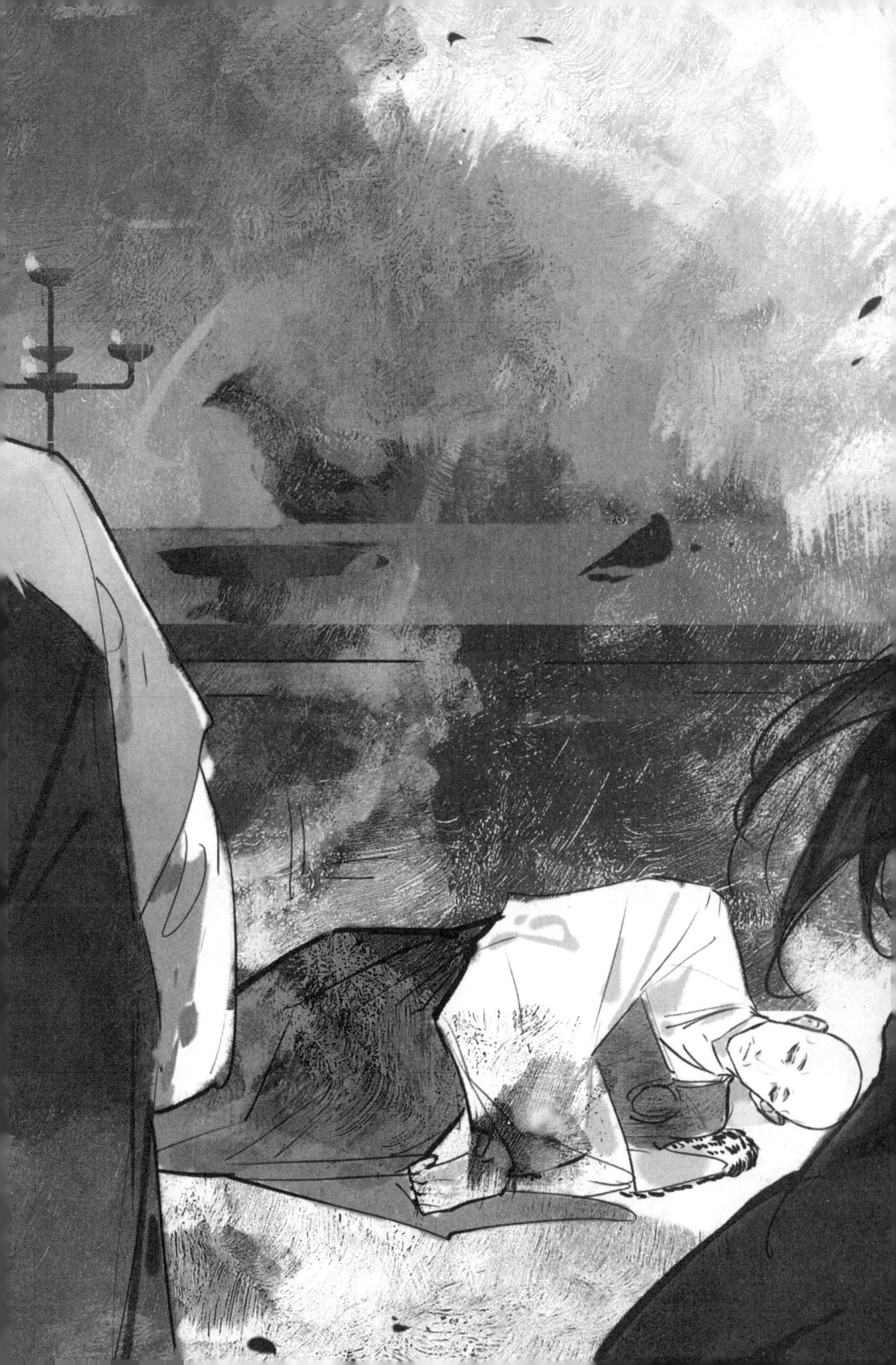

20

"Is there really no one in this world capable of killing Li Jianhong?" Mu Kuangda heaved a long sigh. Behind him stood the masked Changliu-jun, and before him sat Grand General Zhao Kui, dressed in scholarly robes and practicing his calligraphy. Wu Du stood off to one side of the study, silent.

"It's not that no one is capable, but that those who are capable may not do so," Zhao Kui replied. "Wu Du, Changliu-jun, Zheng Yan, the Nameless Assassin—all are bound by the Guardian. They cannot raise their blades to him so long as he wields that sword."

Zhao Kui swept his brush, stroke by stroke, down the paper, his characters as vigorous as a tempest of blades. Darkly, he continued, "Since Nayantuo's death, finding another who can rival Li Jianhong has proven difficult."

"No matter how strong the man is, he is human. And all humans have weaknesses," Mu Kuangda replied dismissively. "When someone is too confident that everything is under their control, it inevitably leads to unforeseen variables."

"Perhaps the Nameless Assassin will become his variable," Zhao Kui mused. "That man betrayed his teacher and slaughtered his entire sect. Even now, no justification has ever been given. Based on Wu Du's report, I've been able to track him down; his home village lies at the far reaches of the Xianbei Mountains. When Li Jianhong was running for his life, he hid there for a time."

Mu Kuangda raised the teacup to his lips and took a sip, casting his gaze into the outer corridor. "I fear I can't do anything about him, so I will have to leave the matter to you, General."

Zhao Kui set down his brush. "There's another man who might be a match for Li Jianhong," he said, looking up at Mu Kuangda. "But as I've been unable to move him, I will have to leave that matter to *you*, Your Excellency."

Contemplating, Mu Kuangda didn't respond.

"Back when Master Wangbei was fatally wounded by Nayantuo, he left the Ender in the hands of Kongming," Zhao Kui said. "Kongming has a shidi who is a lay monk. When he defected from the monastery, he took the blade." Zhao Kui paused and sighed. "I've no hopes for Wu Du and Changliu-jun at this point; we can kill anyone in the world except Li Jianhong. But the Nameless Assassin must have come with an important mission. Yuan has declared war against Liao. If all goes as expected and the flames of war rise in the next few months, Li Jianhong is certain to show himself."

Mu Kuangda remained silent for a long time, lost in thought.

The vanguard of Yuan's southward invasion army took the city of Huchang, sending a shockwave across the Liao Empire and spurring a mass exodus toward Shangjing. By the fifteenth of the sixth month, nearly thirty thousand refugees had gathered outside the northern capital's walls. Li Jianhong and Duan Ling traveled back via the official highway and arrived at the city gates.

"Who's there?! Show your travel papers. You will be searched!" barked the guard.

CHAPTER TWENTY

Li Jianhong turned his horse and whistled up at the top of the city wall. Cai Wen, who commanded the city's defense, saw them at once and instructed that the side door be opened for their passage.

"Make sure to thank him," Li Jianhong said. Duan Ling cupped his hands in salute toward Cai Wen from a distance. Cai Wen cupped his hands back, returning the courtesy. Occupied as he was by his duties, he hadn't time to ask when the father and son had left the city, nor for what purpose.

Although they'd been gone only a few short days, it felt like a lifetime since they'd been home. The second Duan Ling had stepped out of the door to rescue Batu, he'd unknowingly embarked on a momentous road. Overnight, he had become Southern Chen royalty. His father was the number one warrior of the frontier, the Han's god of war...yet because of the shifting political climate in Southern Chen, Li Jianhong had been forced to leave his homeland and drift aimlessly through the world. Now the two of them only had each other to depend on.

This dramatic revelation made his past seem foreign, while simultaneously casting all Duan Ling's memories in a new light. Lang Junxia's enigmatic attitude, his father's sudden arrival—all of it now made sense. A great undertaking awaited him in his future; he understood everything he hadn't before.

He sat on the veranda, looking out at the courtyard while lost in thought.

"Dad," he said at last.

"Yes, Son?" Li Jianhong replied, watering Duan Ling's flowerbed as if this day was no different from any other.

Duan Ling fell silent. Once the flowerbed was watered, Li Jianhong began preparations for dinner, drawing water to steam rice and then taking a seat beside the well to descale the fish.

Everything had happened too fast—Duan Ling didn't know what to think, or what to do. Watching Li Jianhong's back as he worked, he was shocked to realize that the man he knew as his father was not the same man that Master Kongming, Lang Junxia, or Qionghua House's madam knew. It felt like a dream.

As Li Jianhong scraped the fish clean of scales, he glanced back at Duan Ling. "Hungry? Dinner will be served soon, just half an hour."

"Dad. What should I do now?" Duan Ling asked, perplexed.

Li Jianhong was, for a moment, taken aback. Then he chuckled and carried the cleaned fish into the kitchen. Duan Ling scurried after him, watching as he oiled the wok.

"Do whatever you want," Li Jianhong answered breezily. "All those past grudges are my business. They are not your shackles."

"But your business is my business," Duan Ling said. "What does a prince do?"

Li Jianhong moved in front of Duan Ling and gestured for him to stand back, out of range of the splattering oil. He slipped the fish into the wok from the edge, and it crackled in the hot oil, filling the house with its delicious aroma.

"Your fourth uncle has no children," Li Jianhong said in a conversational tone. "And even if he does in the future, Southern Chen's throne will be yours. You're no prince—you're the emperor."

Duan Ling found himself speechless.

Without turning, Li Jianhong struck the edge of the wok, sending the fried fish spinning in the pan; with a flick of his fingers, the sizzling fish flipped over so its golden, crispy side faced upward. "You learn how to be an emperor by studying," Li Jianhong said, smiling. "Learn well, and when you ascend the throne, you won't be flustered and lost. Remember what my old ancestor said?"

"Governing a great country…" Duan Ling looked at the fish in the wok. "…is like cooking a small fish."[12]

"Just so," Li Jianhong agreed, then observed: "Looks like all that studying paid off after all."

"But I don't know how to *do* anything," Duan Ling said.

Li Jianhong added half a ladleful of water and sprinkled in the green onions, ginger, and garlic. Wiping his hands, he said, "Learn, then, Your Majesty. Go get the bowls; dinner is served!"

Li Jianhong swept Duan Ling up in his arms and dropped him outside the main hall to retrieve the cutlery and set the table.

As they ate, Li Jianhong turned serious again. "In your free time, think about what you want to do when you become emperor."

Duan Ling nodded, highly amused.

"Before anything is settled, just think about it on your own—keep all this to yourself. You don't want to incur anyone's jealousy," Li Jianhong advised. "After all, most people don't get to become emperors."

Duan Ling burst out laughing. Although they were discussing the concept out in the open now, the reality still felt very far away. Later that night, Li Jianhong sat stargazing on the veranda, hugging a knee, while Duan Ling flipped through his books to review for the upcoming exam. When he fell asleep at his desk, Li Jianhong carefully gathered him up and carried him to bed, the father and son pair lying together.

Days passed, and the weather grew gradually warmer.

"The educated must possess resolve and breadth of mind…" As Duan Ling recited from Confucius's *Analects*, he couldn't help stealing a glance at Li Jianhong, who was reading on the side.

---

[12] From Chapter 60 of Dao De Jing by Laozi; an adage that means interfering too much will spoil the undertaking.

"...For he bears grave responsibility, and the journey is long," Li Jianhong nonchalantly finished the verse.

Duan Ling dutifully echoed: "For he bears grave responsibility, and the journey is long."

As he studied, questions propagated in his mind. His father was alone, with only Lang Junxia at his command, while Southern Chen possessed vast territories and an army hundreds of thousands strong. Could his father reclaim the throne by dint of his royal status alone?

"Dad, do you know Yelü Dashi?" Duan Ling asked.

"I do, but he likes to pretend he doesn't know me," Li Jianhong said.

"Huh?" Duan Ling was baffled.

Li Jianhong smirked. "Think of it like this: When someone gets beaten up, they go out of their way to avoid the one who gave them the beating. It's the same basic idea."

Duan Ling was speechless for a second. "Then will he make trouble for you?"

After spending a few days doing a great deal of thinking, Duan Ling had come to understand just how sensitive his father's position was. If he found himself alone, his enemies might very well come knocking.

"He won't," Li Jianhong replied. "I was his enemy in the past, but not anymore. Yelü Dashi is a cunning man; he always sails with the wind. Besides, he doesn't even know I'm here."

"So what do we do about the south?" Duan Ling asked.

"I've been thinking it over." Li Jianhong paused, then said, "Everything comes down to borrowing an army, forming an alliance, and wooing Liao into fighting Yuan. If Yelü Dashi is willing to lend me an army of ten thousand, taking down Zhao Kui will be a simple matter."

"Will he, though?" Duan Ling asked.

"That's what we need to work on," Li Jianhong replied. "What we need is an offer he absolutely can't refuse. That's part of the plan I was discussing with Batu's dad the other day. I told him to station his army at Yubi Pass and prevent Southern Chen's army from crossing it. That way, Shangjing can only seek reinforcements from the southwest."

"You could leave me here as a hostage, just like Batu…"

Li Jianhong's face fell, and his voice became stern. "No. And don't ever say that again. Am I that kind of man in your eyes?"

Duan Ling shook his head. Another short moment later, he stole a glance at Li Jianhong, and—sensing he was still angry—shuffled nearer. Li Jianhong turned and put his arm around him.

Lighthearted again, he said, "Yelü Dashi must never know your identity." When Duan Ling gave an affirmative hum, Li Jianhong continued, "I'll discuss any developments with you, so don't worry too much about these things."

Duan Ling nodded and returned to reviewing for his exam, still curled in Li Jianhong's arms, while Li Jianhong studied a yellowing map spread across the desk. The word *Liao* had been written on it in large strokes. This map delineated the Liao Empire's entire territory in the north, stretching from Yubi Pass in the south to the Huai River in the north.

For many days thereafter, Li Jianhong ruminated upon his plans. Duan Ling's entrance exam day was fast approaching. Strangely, Duan Ling felt as if he'd grown up overnight. He didn't much care for what he used to like anymore, and no longer did he fuss about going out to have fun. Something more important now awaited him.

Maybe this was what they called the Mandate of Heaven. Powerful new feelings were burgeoning inside him, and his admiration of his father knew no bounds. However, he was also gradually realizing that, although his father belonged to him, he simultaneously shouldered an inescapable responsibility for countless others. Perhaps this was the kingly way the headmaster spoke of—and, he now understood, this kingly way belonged to them both.

Once this notion occurred to him, Duan Ling did his utmost to avoid troubling or interrupting Li Jianhong during his long periods of reflection.

Summer arrived, bringing with it the relentless cacophony of cicadas. The season was dry and cool in Shangjing, the air crisp and refreshing. As Duan Ling strode down the corridor with a bag slung over his shoulder, he called out to Li Jianhong, who was drinking tea inside the main hall: "Dad, I'm off to the entrance exam."

Li Jianhong's gaze upon him held a tangle of feelings, but the foremost among them was warmth. "Look at you, all grown up," he said.

Duan Ling stood in the courtyard, bathed in the brilliant summer sun. For some reason, his father's words made him a little sad.

"But I like how you are now." Li Jianhong stood up with a smile. "Shall we?"

Duan Ling hadn't wanted Li Jianhong to waste any time worrying over mundane affairs, but his father was mindful of it all. Everything Duan Ling needed had been packed in a bag and set aside. Putting down his tea cup and picking up the bag, Li Jianhong accompanied Duan Ling to Biyong Academy.

It was the first exam Duan Ling had attended in his life, and in truth, he was nervous.

"Don't worry," Li Jianhong said. "If you fail, I'll just spend a little money to get you admitted so you can play around."

Duan Ling laughed, the joke chasing his nerves away. When they arrived, Biyong Academy was bustling with examinees, the air filled with noise. Li Jianhong found Duan Ling's seat among the crowd and bade him to sit.

"I'll wait for you at the top of that tree outside," he whispered to Duan Ling.

Duan Ling was speechless. Feeling rather embarrassed, he murmured back, "It's fine; you can just go home."

Many people moved to and fro across the school grounds, and no one paid them any mind. Li Jianhong set Duan Ling's paper, ink, and brush upon the table and said, "In the future, you'll face plenty more grand occasions; just write whatever for the exam. You don't need to prove your abilities here. I already believe in you, so don't take it too seriously."

What Li Jianhong meant suddenly clicked, and Duan Ling nodded at his father. All skills, whether in scholarship or martial arts, must be paid to the emperor. Well, he was to someday become the emperor—so what was there to worry about? Li Jianhong was probably trying to say he shouldn't exert too much effort, lest he stand out and bring unwanted attention to himself.

With a hearty thumbs-up, Li Jianhong left him to his exam.

21

The entrance exam was held in Biyong Academy's courtyard. A solemn air hung over the grounds, a stark contrast to the lively atmosphere of Ming Academy. When the students crossed the threshold of this higher institution, they unconsciously adopted a more restrained and serious demeanor as well.

Flowers bloomed riotously inside the courtyard, complementing the clear blue sky; the scene had the look of an exceptionally beautiful painting. Teachers walked down the rows and distributed test scrolls among the students. The entrance exam would only take half a day. Duan Ling stole a glance at the trees over the wall of the courtyard, wondering which one hid Li Jianhong. After surveying the treetops yet failing to locate him, Duan Ling threw himself into completing his exam.

Two hours later, when Duan Ling was nearly halfway through the exam, he rubbed his hands and glanced up—and spotted Li Jianhong just outside the wall. He was perched on the branch of a nearby tree, swinging an irreverent leg and eating a red, sugar-crusted tanghulu.

Duan Ling was at a loss for words.

Li Jianhong waved a second tanghulu skewer, assuring him that he hadn't been left out and that he should focus on his exam.

Both baffled and amused, Duan Ling realized Li Jianhong must have just returned to the academy. Where had he gone? He couldn't have spent two whole hours climbing in and out of a tree, right?

Another two hours later, under the scorching afternoon sun, the proctor declared, "Collect the scrolls!"

Like a pot of water coming to a boil, activity bubbled through the courtyard as the examinees all began talking at once. The proctor cleared his throat, and the noise died down; the students quickly got the hint to stand and bow to the exam proctor. "Thank you, sir," they chorused, and began exiting the grounds in an orderly fashion.

The instant Duan Ling emerged, he ran toward the tree outside the courtyard, but when he looked up, its branches were empty. Confused, he glanced left and right—only to be suddenly swung into the air by a laughing Li Jianhong, who hoisted him over his shoulder to carry him away.

"Let's go have a bath. I'm taking you out for some fun later tonight," Li Jianhong said.

"The scores will be announced first thing in the morning!" Duan Ling reminded him.

"Not a problem. We'll be back by bedtime."

The father and son had lunch out and returned home after a detour to the bathhouse. Using the fact that they'd woken up too early as an excuse, Li Jianhong managed to coax Duan Ling to take a nap. By the time he woke, it was sunset.

Upon seeing that Duan Ling was awake, Li Jianhong retrieved a set of clothes. The robes were lavishly made, using the finest black brocade and embroidered with White Tiger patterns. Everything, down to the belts and boots, was brand new.

"When did you have this made?" Duan Ling asked, surprised.

"I ordered it a long time ago," Li Jianhong said. "But I went to retrieve it during your exam."

"What do you mean, a long time ago?" Duan Ling put on the new robes and considered himself in the mirror. He almost didn't recognize his reflection. The clothes had been tailored based on the measurements of his old outfits. The White Tiger, embroidered in shimmering silver thread, appeared almost alive against the rich black brocade. "What kind of outfit is this?"

"These are the robes of a prince," Li Jianhong explained. "The emperor's robes are embroidered with a dragon, and the prince's robes are embroidered with the White Tiger of the West. The White Tiger is the god of war, symbolizing control of the military and protection of the nation. That's also why the tally wielded by generals is called the tiger tally."

Li Jianhong himself changed into a set of long robes practically identical to his son's. Duan Ling's eyes lit up at the sight of his father in the mirror.

"How do I look?" Li Jianhong asked, casual.

"Good... Really, really good..." Duan Ling barely recognized his father.

Since the day they'd met, Li Jianhong had rarely paid any mind to his appearance, usually dressing in simple linens with his hair loosely tied. But now, in his princely robes, he exuded a completely different aura. Simply standing there, he appeared regal and handsome, radiating the commanding presence of a ruler descended from heaven to preside over his realm.

"Where are we going dressed like this?" Duan Ling asked.

"Somewhere you'd rather not go," Li Jianhong said. "Qionghua House."

Duan Ling's face twitched, and his expression soured—they'd gotten dressed up in formal robes to go to a brothel? Despite his age, Duan Ling had already learned many things unfit for a child's ears.

"I knew you'd react like that," Li Jianhong said, laughing with amusement. "We're going to see an old friend, nothing else."

Duan Ling was dubious. "Really?"

Still chuckling, Li Jianhong said, "You can keep an eye on me the entire time. If I say anything that upsets you, just smack me."

"All right, you said it…" Duan Ling peered suspiciously at Li Jianhong. His father was honestly too handsome.

"And lastly, we can't quite go like this." Li Jianhong retrieved two masks from the table and placed one on Duan Ling's face.

Duan Ling was thoroughly perplexed. The masks were made of leather and extended up to their hairlines. They concealed much of their faces, but left Li Jianhong's straight nose and gentle lips exposed, giving him a captivating air of mystery. Once Duan Ling properly fastened his own mask, Li Jianhong instructed him to take out his jade arc and tie it onto the buckle at his waist. He then gave Duan Ling his own pendant with a pointed look.

Duan Ling tied the jade arc onto his father's waist.

"Let's go," Li Jianhong said, picking up Duan Ling's hand.

The two departed into the twilight. Outside the door, a carriage was waiting. The driver drew the curtains aside and motioned for them to climb in.

"Did anyone see this carriage come here?" Li Jianhong asked from inside the coach.

"Rest assured, sir, I was discreet," replied the driver.

The carriage meandered through the alleyways, turning this way and that, never following any of the usual routes. After crossing two main streets, it dove into another small alley, then passed through the west end of the city where many officials resided before returning to a major street again, rambling on, unhurried, until it finally stopped at the back entrance of Qionghua House.

The summer nights were stifling, with overcast skies that obscured the moon and a choking air of unease—the tension of oncoming war. No chatter or laughter emanated from the windows of Qionghua House, only the glow of the brightly colored lanterns that hung in its hallways.

"Greetings, Your Highness."

Holding a lantern, Ding Zhi personally welcomed the two guests and led them down the corridor from the back entrance, keeping to the edges of the hallway. As Li Jianhong and Duan Ling walked hand in hand through the corridor, every servant they passed dropped to their knees and kowtowed.

"Greetings, Your Highness."

"Greetings, Your Highness."

Duan Ling was rendered speechless by this reception.

"Are you hungry?" Li Jianhong asked without turning. Duan Ling quickly shook his head, but Li Jianhong pressed on, "You must be. We'll sit down in a moment and you can eat something."

"Greetings, Your Highness."

As though Qionghua House were abloom, from the main hall emerged the remaining five ladies, who knelt before Li Jianhong with low, reverent bows. Standing at the center of the hall was the madam, dressed in a formal robe the vibrant red and gold of a phoenix. When Li Jianhong entered, she approached him, sweeping open her expansive sleeves and folding her hands in a curtsy.

"Greetings, Your Highness. And greetings to the young prince," the madam said in a solemn voice.

"Rise," Li Jianhong said at last.

Although he spoke only one word, it radiated authority.

The six ladies parted to make way for their guests, and Li Jianhong pushed Duan Ling into the seat of honor, while he himself took the seat beside it. Xu Lan, who took her name from the orchid, approached with a tea platter, and Qiu Jin, named for hibiscus, offered a cup to the madam—who placed it by Li Jianhong's hand. Li Jianhong took a sip before breezily passing it to Duan Ling; the madam offered a second cup to Li Jianhong for himself.

"Xunchun," Li Jianhong said.

"Yes, Your Highness," the madam answered.

Duan Ling vaguely recalled having heard this name before, but couldn't quite remember where—and his attention was quickly diverted back to Li Jianhong's conversation.

"Have you called him?" Li Jianhong asked.

"Qiu Jin has already sent the invitation. I'm sure he'll come tonight." Xunchun's lashes remained lowered, and she spoke in a quiet, even tone.

"Who else is here?" Li Jianhong asked.

"A city guard by the name of Cai Wen. He's listening to music and drinking with the child from the Southern Court," Xunchun replied. "I have their room under watch; they will not interrupt the meeting."

"Bring us something to eat; the young prince is hungry," Li Jianhong ordered, ending the exchange.

Xunchun and the five ladies bowed out of the room.

All the ceremony made Duan Ling uneasy, and Li Jianhong hadn't supplied any immediate explanation. The pair sat in silence, each lost in their own thoughts, in the hall redolent with the scent of sandalwood incense.

After a moment, Li Jianhong suddenly said: "If one day I'm not around anymore, would you miss me?"

Duan Ling turned his gaze upon his father. Li Jianhong met it, but his eyes were far away.

"I would," Duan Ling said. "Are you leaving? When?"

Over the past few days, Duan Ling had been grappling with a strong feeling—a mix of intuition and conjecture. If Li Jianhong planned to fight to reclaim the south, he wouldn't have much time to spend with his son—nor was he likely to bring Duan Ling along with a marching army.

The corners of Li Jianhong's lips quirked. "Well, no. But once you enter Biyong Academy, you'll only come home every so often. I'm going to miss you."

He reached out to gently push Duan Ling's mask up onto his forehead and gazed at his face. Duan Ling did the same, mirroring his father. The thought of boarding at Biyong Academy had been plaguing him too. Every time he was reminded, it filled him with reluctance.

Cupping Duan Ling's face, Li Jianhong said, "I have to take every chance to look at you now, so when I leave for war, I'll be able to remember your face while I lie awake in my tent at night."

Duan Ling didn't respond, though his eyes began to burn. Biyong Academy would release the exam results the next morning; if he'd successfully passed into the school, he would move into the dormitory that same afternoon. Biyong Academy was stricter than Ming Academy: They allowed their students to go home only once a month. Although his father had only been with him for a short few months, the time they'd spent together had thoroughly erased all the pain Duan Ling suffered before, all the tears he'd cried, as if they had never been. It felt as though everything he'd gone through in the past had been worth it for the days they now shared.

The sweet melody of a flute floated in from beyond the hall. It was as gentle as flower petals fluttering down in the tranquil night, carried by the wind and dancing in the air.

"I've heard this song before," Duan Ling said, surprised.

It was the same tune he'd heard played somewhere outside his rooms at Ming Academy—except this time, the melody was even sweeter.

"'Joyful Reunion,'" Li Jianhong murmured, gazing deeply into Duan Ling's bright eyes. "'The woodland flowers shed spring colors before their time.' The work of the last ruler of the Tang dynasty, after his country fell. Life is unpredictable, leaving much to be desired."

Duan Ling leaned into Li Jianhong's chest. Something told him this was an unusual night. Li Jianhong hadn't brought him to Qionghua House for simple entertainment—judging by his father's conversation with Xunchun earlier, someone else would be joining them.

Li Jianhong stroked Duan Ling's head, breathing in the clean scent of his hair. Outside, they heard someone softly murmur "Madam"; the flute stopped, and the sound of footsteps soon followed.

"Your Highness," came Xunchun's voice.

"Enter," Li Jianhong said.

The doors of the hall swung open, and Ding Zhi entered with a tray of refreshments—the same treats the young woman had prepared for Duan Ling on his first day in Shangjing, but more exquisitely crafted.

"He has arrived," Xunchun said.

"Bring him in after a few minutes," Li Jianhong instructed.

Xunchun bowed. As she turned to exit the room, Li Jianhong called, "Qionghua—meaning *snowball viburnum*, a blossom that gathers the eight fairies. But of your house's eight—orchid, peony, hibiscus, angelica, jasmine, gardenia, crab apple, and azalea—why are there only six of you here?"

"To answer Your Highness, our crab apple and azalea—Qin Tang and Su Juan—have passed away," Xunchun replied.

Li Jianhong stirred at this. "When? Where?"

"The day Liao breached the former capital," Xunchun said. "The seventeenth of next month will be the anniversary of their death."

Li Jianhong nodded. "Was that you playing the flute?"

"Yes." Xunchun's eyes remained downcast as she answered each question. Li Jianhong lapsed into silence, and Xunchun quietly left the room.

When Duan Ling had eaten his fill of treats, Li Jianhong straightened his mask and instructed him to sit behind the nearby folding screen. Shortly thereafter, the tap of footsteps came outside the door.

"Your Excellency," they heard Xunchun say.

"I shouldn't be here tonight," Yelü Dashi said, his words slightly slurred with inebriation. "Insisting on inviting me for a drink at this hour—is there something major the madam wishes to discuss with me?"

At the sound of Yelü Dashi's voice, Duan Ling tensed. He poked his head out from around the screen to peek at the door. Li Jianhong chuckled lightly and put a hand on Duan Ling's head, stuffing him back behind the partition and bringing a finger to his lips.

Xunchun's placid reply drifted in. "It's not my place to speak on state affairs. Truth be told, the reason I've invited Your Excellency here tonight is because there is a guest who wishes to meet you."

"Oh?" Yelü Dashi sounded curious. His large form cast a shadow on the window. "Who?"

"He is inside. Your Excellency will know him when you meet," Xunchun replied, approaching the door and opening it herself. She did not enter.

Puzzled, Yelü Dashi peered inside, his expression mildly dazed.

Masked, Li Jianhong reclined on the short divan before the screen, one leg propped on the tea table and an elbow resting on his bent knee. He spared not a glance at Yelü Dashi, only taking a leisurely sip of his tea and saying in a mild voice, "Long time no see, Yelü-xiong."

22

Yelü Dashi hadn't recognized Li Jianhong with his mask, but as soon as he heard that voice, he sobered immediately and took a step back. "Guards!"

Several guards heeded his call, surrounding Yelü Dashi in a defensive circle. Li Jianhong set his tea down and said, almost to himself, "Why so nervous, Yelü-xiong? As it is, I'm worse off than a stray dog."

The surprise had shaken Yelü Dashi's composure, but as he remastered himself—and realized Li Jianhong was alone inside the hall—he turned a scrutinizing stare on Xunchun.

"You... Your Qionghua House is actually..."

"This humble servant does not know this guest," Xunchun replied calmly, untroubled by the implied accusation. "He came and refused to leave until he met with you, Your Excellency. I pray you will forgive me."

"Come in for a drink," Li Jianhong said. "Whether what lies between us is favor or grudge, life is forever changeable—why take trivial past disagreements to heart?"

Yelü Dashi snorted, but he didn't dally any longer, stepping forward into the room. Xunchun closed the door behind him, and when his servants tried to follow, she blocked their entry with an extended hand, indicating that they shouldn't intrude on the meeting.

"Wait outside," Yelü Dashi called out. "No one is to enter without my orders."

Rain drizzled through the black night in Xichuan, misting over the city. In the depths of a narrow alleyway, Lang Junxia was cornered by surrounding soldiers with no path of escape. He leaned against a wall, panting harshly. His hand, now missing a finger, had swollen and turned an abnormal shade of blackish-blue, the skin glistening with an unhealthy sheen.

"Sometimes I wonder…" came a voice behind the soldiers. Mantle flapping in the wind, Zhao Kui strode into view, his sure steps splashing through the puddles. He stopped and stood before Lang Junxia with a casual air of command, hands clasped behind his back. A soldier raised his torch to illuminate Lang Junxia's face. "…What exactly Li Jianhong did to make you so devoted?"

"A man like me must throw my lot in with someone," Lang Junxia replied coolly. "If not you, then him. All you lords and princes come and go like mayflies. What difference does it make who I choose?"

Every soldier in the narrow alley had their crossbows trained on Lang Junxia, and more bolts bristled from the walls of the residential courtyards and rooftops. Zhao Kui had mobilized upward of a thousand men in Xichuan to capture him, weaving a net so tight there truly was no way out.

"Li Jianhong's days are numbered," Zhao Kui said. "Join me instead. Leave the darkness and step into the light, and you will have my personal respect. To say any more would be pointless."

Lang Junxia drew in a slow breath, closed his eyes, and exhaled. "Given Changliu-jun's enviable combat skills, I didn't think he'd resort to poison," he breathed out, his voice dark.

Zhao Kui turned on his heel. His subordinates rushed in to apprehend Lang Junxia and dragged him away.

"Have a drink," Li Jianhong said, inviting Yelü Dashi to take a seat. "And do forgive me for masking my face."

He filled the cups with wine and tossed back his first in a gesture of apology. Yelü Dashi didn't touch his cup, only rapping the table with his knuckles a few times.

"The one behind the screen is my son," Li Jianhong said, answering his unvoiced question.

Yelü Dashi eyed the screen. Duan Ling hesitated, uncertain whether he should come out; after a moment, Yelü Dashi saw the shadow on the screen bend forward in a bow. Only then did he take his cup, toss back the wine, and place it on the table rim-down, rejecting more drink.

"They say you are the boldest among the Han," Yelü Dashi slurred, his face flushed red with the drinks he'd consumed before coming to Qionghua House. "What are you thinking, coming to Shangjing at a time like this?"

"The world is vast, but I've a home I cannot return to," Li Jianhong replied easily. "I don't wish to mix in with the Mongols, so I've no choice but to settle in Shangjing."

"Settle?" Yelü Dashi said, incredulous. Realizing this nemesis of his had somehow snuck into his territory without a word, he couldn't resist asking, "Where do you live?" He narrowed his eyes and scrutinized Li Jianhong. Abruptly, he remembered the strange matter of the assassin from years ago. "That time at Ming Academy!" he exclaimed in shock.

"Correct," Li Jianhong said. "One of the men involved was my subordinate. The other was an assassin Zhao Kui sent to kill my son."

Shooting to his feet, Yelü Dashi paced back and forth in the hall. Unruffled, Li Jianhong turned the man's cup back over. "How about another?"

Yelü Dashi spun around to face him. "What do you want?"

"You know the political situation in Southern Chen," Li Jianhong said. "Zhao Kui stripped me of military power, and my father issued the order to have me detained and interrogated in Xichuan. Sometimes, things are exactly as they appear. Come. Drink."

Yelü Dashi was still dubious. He heaved a long sigh, and said, "Leave. Shangjing has no place for you."

"Will you call for your subordinates and have me tied up and sent back to Xichuan?" Li Jianhong said, nonchalant.

"As if I could hold you," Yelü Dashi said. After a brief pause, he admitted his uselessness: "Come and go however you please, then; Shangjing's defenses pose no challenge to you. What more do you want?"

"I've come to save you," Li Jianhong stated impassively. "Your end is nigh."

Yelü Dashi whirled and glared at Li Jianhong.

"Yuan is marching south. Their armies have already breached Huchang; they're regrouping in the mountains as we speak. It's a matter of days before they arrive at the walls of Shangjing," Li Jianhong said. "You have Shulü Jin defending the north road and Wang Ping defending the south, but your two generals can't stop Borjigin's iron cavalry. Now that Kuchi's escaped, he will most certainly come seeking vengeance against you."

At this, Yelü Dashi burst out laughing. "Li Jianhong, I see you still love making pronouncements of doom."

Disregarding Yelü Dashi's dismissive response, Li Jianhong continued in a cooler tone, "Han Weiyong has been waiting a long time for this moment. Unless I miss my guess, his son is currently on his way to Zhongjing to 'seek higher learning.'"

Yelü Dashi paused.

"When the Yuan army breaches the north and south roads and moves to slaughter the city, your reinforcements will never come." Li Jianhong spread his hands. "My patience is limited. Yelü-xiong, will you or will you not drink this cup of wine?"

After a protracted silence, Yelü Dashi slowly sat back down. "I have controlled the Northern Court for twenty-two years," he said deliberately. "Long ago, I advised the late emperor that anywhere the Han people go will surely become embroiled in schemes and chaos."

He closed his eyes and drank the wine.

"Kuchi is guarding the road south of Yubi Pass," Li Jianhong said. "I don't need to tell you what that means. Drink this third cup of wine, and tomorrow, lend me an army of ten thousand. I will flatten the Yuan army for you, then march south and reclaim Xichuan."

Li Jianhong topped off their cups and picked Yelü Dashi's up with three fingers, placing it in front of him.

"As always, I will drink first to show my respect." Without sparing Yelü Dashi a second glance, Li Jianhong gestured toward the cup. "Yelü-xiong, if you please."

But Yelü Dashi didn't lift the cup. He sat on the other end of the divan, his elbow propped on the small table between them. After a pause, he leaned forward and stared into Li Jianhong's eyes. "Do you know why Zhao Kui wants to kill you?"

"I don't hate Zhao Kui—that's the honest truth," Li Jianhong said. "No deep grudge exists between us. We each have our own path to walk; it's all fair competition. But if he's thinking of overthrowing the Li family, that, of course, is a rather different story."

The sound of a commotion came from outside. Yelü Dashi's expression shifted as Li Jianhong turned toward the door.

"You can't go in." It was Xunchun's voice. "The Great Prince is meeting a guest inside."

"Your Excellency," Cai Wen's breathless voice called out. "Please return to the Northern Court at once. Messengers have come from the north and south roads!"

Yelü Dashi's face changed color. Li Jianhong said not a word more; having made his report, Cai Wen, too, fell silent and left.

They heard Xunchun's voice, muffled on the other side of the door: "Bring His Excellency's horse."

She opened the door, and Yelü Dashi leapt to his feet.

"How long has it been since our last battle?" Li Jianhong asked.

"Five years," Yelü Dashi said, his expression stormy as he marched toward the door. The third cup of wine remained untouched on the table.

"Farewell," Li Jianhong said. "Take care."

When Yelü Dashi heard this, he stopped in his tracks, turned, and stalked back toward Li Jianhong. Li Jianhong had already risen to his feet. Stately in his brocade robe, he stood with hands clasped behind his back and looked at the Great Prince.

Yelü Dashi paused again, indecisive, and turned to leave. Yet just as his toes touched the threshold he again turned back. Li Jianhong couldn't help but laugh. Duan Ling poked a curious head out from behind the screen to study Yelü Dashi and was pushed back by Li Jianhong.

"You and your son have been in Shangjing for a while now," Yelü Dashi said.

"Yes," Li Jianhong confirmed. "But I will never give him to you. You need only know that he is in the city. Do not think of testing me on this, Yelü-xiong."

Yelü Dashi studied Li Jianhong for a moment, then walked to the table, picked up the cup, and tossed back the wine before throwing the cup down to shatter on the floor. Li Jianhong gestured his thanks and sent Yelü Dashi on his way.

Only after Yelü Dashi's footsteps faded did Duan Ling crawl out from behind the screen.

"Did you understand all that?" Li Jianhong asked him.

"Not really," Duan Ling admitted, shaking his head.

"Stomach full?" Li Jianhong asked. When Duan Ling nodded, he said, "Then let's go home."

That night, Li Jianhong couldn't sleep; he held Duan Ling and talked nonstop. Through this, Duan Ling came to grasp a bit of the political landscape. The three kingdoms—Liao, Chen, and Yuan—all kept each other in check. When one became too strong, the other two would quietly ally to curb its influence. The Battle of Huai River was one such conflict between Liao and Chen, with Yuan acting as a check from the sidelines. Conversely, when Liao grew too powerful, Chen borrowed Yuan's support to drain the Liao's military strength.

Now that the Yuan armies had returned to the field, Chen's stance was crucial. The humiliation of Shangzi had never been repaid, and given what Li Jianhong knew of Zhao Kui, his preference would be to sit by and watch Yuan and Liao destroy each other. However, it was equally likely that Southern Chen would join forces with Yuan. If such an alliance formed, it would deal a devastating blow to

Liao's power. What Yelü Dashi was facing was a war with impossible odds, with himself as the central target.

As Duan Ling drifted off, he heard himself ask, "But what if you change your mind?"

"If I was someone who reneged on my word, Xunchun wouldn't have played that song outside the room," Li Jianhong replied.

But Duan Ling didn't hear him. He didn't know that this song was one only the Han understood. That sorrowful lament bade the listener never to forget the humiliation of their defeat at Shangzi.

"I don't hate Li Jianhong," Zhao Kui stated. "Exactly the opposite, in fact. I admire him greatly. In all our Chen Empire's four hundred years of history, we've never produced another military genius to rival him."

Zhao Kui and Wu Du watched as Lang Junxia's poisoned blood was purged from multiple cuts made to his swollen arm. Since he'd been brought back to the general's residence, Lang Junxia had maintained his usual stoic silence. Wu Du stared at him contemptuously, his brows knit in a frown, as though watching a rat in a trap.

"Remove his fetters," Zhao Kui instructed.

A subordinate approached and freed Lang Junxia from his restraints. Zhao Kui sat and took a sip of tea before continuing. "Do you know why I want to kill Li Jianhong?"

Lang Junxia remained silent.

Zhao Kui wasn't expecting a response. He went on, "In the seventeenth year of Qingyuan, the Central Plains conscripted 270,000 men and levied a tax of 414,000 taels of silver. By the nineteenth year, the conscription had risen to 330,000 men with a tax of 360,000 taels. In the twenty-seventh year, 360,000 men were conscripted—but the tax dropped to 190,000 taels. Throughout these years, Jiang Prefecture contributed the most recruits, followed by Yi, Yang, and Jiao Prefectures. More and more men were drafted each year, but the taxes, in comparison, were dropping. Over that ten-year period, nearly a million men were sent to the freezing north to die in endless wars. Countless young men, barely sixteen years of age, lost their lives at Yubi Pass, never to return to their homeland in this life."

Lang Junxia stared down into the basin filled with his blood and saw the blue skies outside the window reflected on its surface.

"And what was left behind? Miles of abandoned farmland and years of grassroots uprisings across the south," Zhao Kui said. "Li Jianhong certainly is a military genius, but unfortunately, we've no more food or men left to send to the front lines." Zhao Kui rose and said to Lang Junxia, "He was born at the wrong time, and therefore he must die."

"You didn't have to tell me all this," Lang Junxia said, disinterested. "In the eyes of an assassin, who our target is doesn't matter; only whether they live or die. Even if you heal me, I will not be grateful."

"I'm not trying to recruit you," Zhao Kui replied. "Once you're well enough, you may leave if you wish."

"If you intend to come back and kill the Grand General, by all means, try. We'll see who's the better assassin," Wu Du interjected. Lang Junxia looked back at him in stony silence.

"But before you leave here, there's someone I want you to meet," Zhao Kui said.

Lang Junxia's brow creased.

"This way, please." Zhao Kui led Lang Junxia to the main hall of the general's residence. Inside sat an old woman, drinking butter tea.

Lang Junxia was struck speechless.

"I've heard you were once engaged to a girl from the Feilian family," Zhao Kui said.

Ignoring him, Lang Junxia said something in the Xianbei tongue. The old woman set down her tea bowl and looked up with rheumy eyes, reaching her hands out in Lang Junxia's direction. Lang Junxia darted forward and caught her hand with his intact one, tucking the arm with the missing pinkie behind his back. Dropping to one knee, he touched his forehead to the old woman's hand.

The old woman smiled broadly and replied to Lang Junxia in the same tongue. He drew in a deep breath but didn't answer her, only patting her hand in a gesture of comfort.

"I'll leave you two to catch up," Zhao Kui said. He closed the door behind him, leaving Lang Junxia to his own devices. Arms crossed over his chest, Wu Du followed Zhao Kui out.

Halfway down the corridor, Zhao Kui asked, "How long does she have left?"

"Not even fifteen minutes," Wu Du replied. "When we come back later, that man will have killed the old hag with a single stroke of his sword."

Zhao Kui shook his head with a smile. "I don't think he will."

"Someone who could wipe out his entire sect has no attachment to old acquaintances," Wu Du pointed out.

Zhao Kui stopped in his stride, gazing up at the sky. "Following intel from the shadow squad's report, I sent men to track him down in the Xianbei Mountains. They searched a number of villages. In the end, they found that someone had laid a bouquet of a type of flower that only blooms on cliffsides before the tomb of a girl who was once engaged to him. Nameless Assassin—no, Wuluohou Mu—I never guessed you'd be of Xianbei royal descent."

He nodded to himself, perhaps in surprise, or perhaps in regret, and continued on his way.

23

THE FOLLOWING DAY, torrential rain battered Shangjing; lightning flashed and thunder boomed. Pedestrians waded through puddles traversing the streets, and horses kicked up muddy water as they cantered down the roads. Wearing his usual linen robes paired with a set of wooden clogs, Li Jianhong had rolled up his pant legs to trek down the street. He carried Duan Ling on his back, and Duan Ling held the umbrella for them both.

They were on their way to check the exam results.

Everyone who stood before the posted bulletin was a servant, save for this father and son. They craned their necks to look up at the large board filled with names.

"My name's there," Duan Ling exclaimed. "The eighth one! I came in eighth!"

"Aha! Of course my son did well," Li Jianhong said.

Li Jianhong chuckled at the way Duan Ling was crying "Eighth! Eighth!" as he carried him inside Biyong Academy. The porter approached as they entered.

"Servants are not permitted inside. We have our own people who will look after your young master."

"This is my dad," Duan Ling told the porter.

Doubtful, the porter looked Li Jianhong up and down a few times, then finally let them in. Both were soaked to the skin.

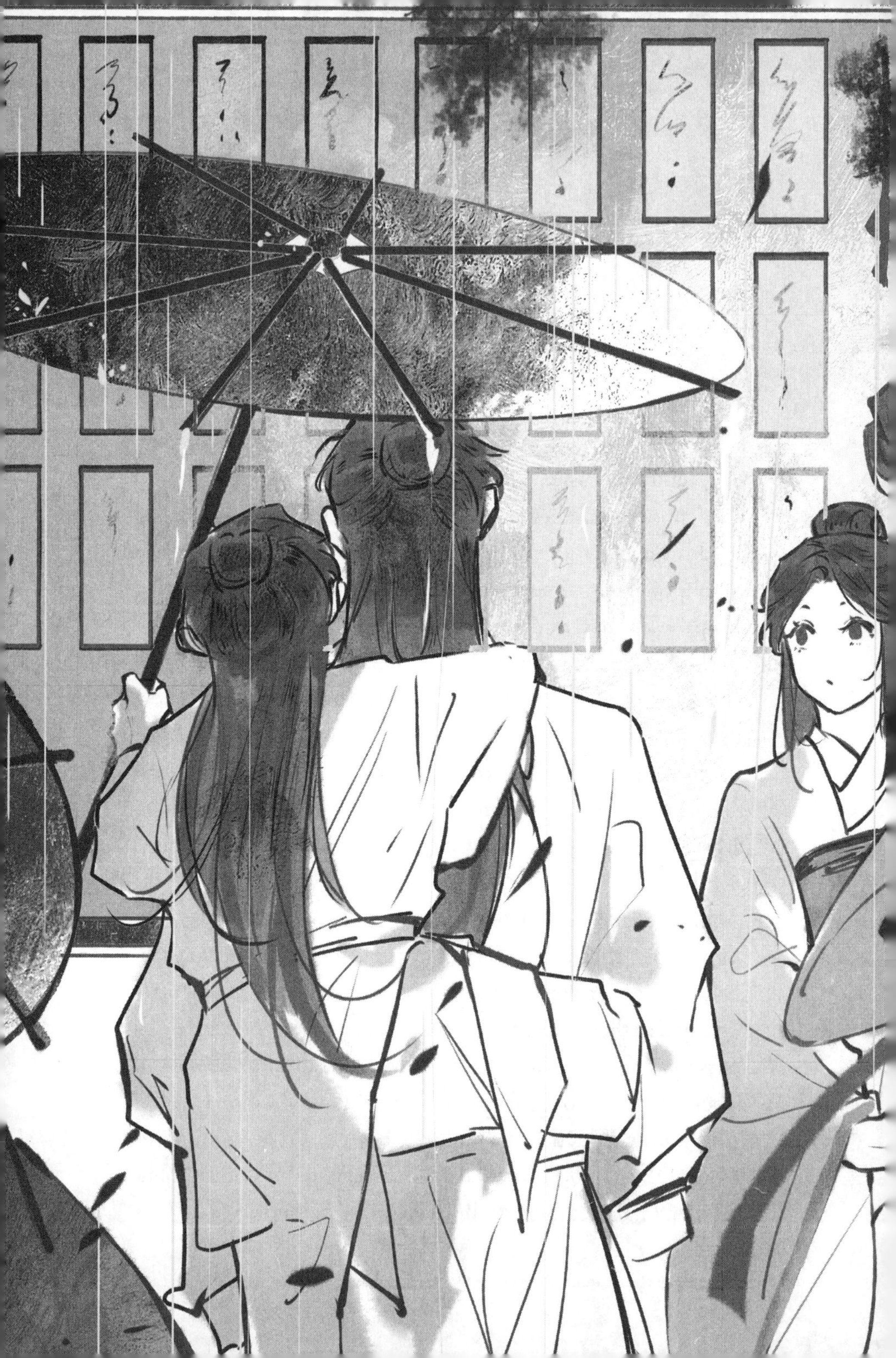

CHAPTER TWENTY-THREE

The students of Biyong Academy weren't due to report until after noon, so they were early. Duan Ling collected his name plaque, signed in, and went to find his room in the dormitories. Once the rain eased slightly, Li Jianhong told him to stay in the room while he made a trip back home to collect the rest of his things.

Later, with the bed made and blankets folded—and after they'd had some ginger broth to chase away the cold—Duan Ling said to his father, "Why don't you go home? They'll serve us dinner here, like at Ming Academy."

Li Jianhong nodded. As more and more students had arrived at the school, he'd put on his bamboo hat to cover his face as he leaned in through the window to talk to Duan Ling.

"Keep an eye on your things, Son," Li Jianhong admonished. "Don't just leave them anywhere. School isn't like home; no one will help you if you lose anything."

"Don't worry, Dad."

"And make sure you eat properly—don't skip meals."

The schoolyard was filling with boys arriving to sign in, all greeting each other just beyond the dormitory. With another soft "Don't worry," Duan Ling led Li Jianhong by the hand to the back entrance to see him off. He was reluctant to say goodbye, but he knew that if he didn't hold back his tears, Li Jianhong would carry on lecturing forever.

"Go on home, Dad," Duan Ling said. "I can take care of myself."

Though it had only been a few months since Li Jianhong had come into his life, Duan Ling had entirely forgotten how he'd managed by himself back at Ming Academy.

"Enjoy yourself at school. Don't worry about me; I'll come visit you when I'm free," Li Jianhong said.

Duan Ling nodded—then suddenly dashed forward and hugged Li Jianhong around the waist. He buried his head against his chest and nuzzled him, then let go, turning and jogging away without another word.

Li Jianhong was left standing in the empty back courtyard, watching the space where his son had vanished.

"Don't take it too hard," the porter said. "Your son is on his way to earning scholarly honors. Go home, now. Go on."

Li Jianhong heaved a long sigh, his wooden clogs clicking against the bluestone path as he left the academy behind.

From the other side of the courtyard walls, Duan Ling chased along after Li Jianhong with red-rimmed eyes, craning his neck to keep sight of his father through the windows as he ran and only stopping when he disappeared from view at last. He rubbed his eyes, standing at a corner, and went to join the other students.

After the rain stopped, the skies cleared, leaving the night air crisp and clean. When Duan Ling returned to his room, he found Cai Wen making up the other bed as Cai Yan watched with his arms crossed.

"Don't just put your things anywhere," Cai Wen chided. "This isn't home. No one will help you if you lose them."

Duan Ling couldn't help but laugh when he heard that. At the sound, Cai Wen turned his head and nodded at him. "Take care of each other, you two."

He approached Cai Wen, and the two patted each other on the back in greeting. After leaving his little brother a few more admonitions and a bit of money, Cai Wen left as well.

"You made it," Cai Yan said.

CHAPTER TWENTY-THREE

Duan Ling had seen Cai Yan's name in the top place on the bulletin, so he'd known he would be coming to school. But he hadn't expected they'd be rooming together.

"Helian Bo is in the building across from us," Cai Yan added. "He's got a single room."

Duan Ling ran over to greet Helian Bo. The other boy's response was a simple nod. "Batu, l-left."

Nodding as well, Duan Ling answered, "Yeah. He'll be fine."

Helian Bo laughed. Then he pointed at himself and walked his two fingers across the air toward the dining hall.

Understanding at once, Duan Ling said, "Let's go eat."

Most of the boys at Biyong Academy were familiar faces. The boy from the Han family hadn't come—apparently, he'd returned to the Southern Court's capital of Zhongjing. Yet curiously, as they now entered Biyong Academy after many months apart, it felt as though everyone had been tagged with a strange magic talisman—one that made them all more mature overnight, calling each other *xiong* and cupping their hands to each other in greeting as they nodded with a smile.

Reuniting with his peers over dinner briefly washed away the sadness of parting with his father. But as he lay in bed afterward, Duan Ling felt the pang of loneliness creep up again. He tossed and turned, missing the warmth of his father's body, a comforting heat beneath his underrobes. He missed resting his head on his chest and feeling the steady rhythm of his breath, the strong beat of his heart.

"Mosquitoes?" Cai Yan asked.

"No," Duan Ling replied, and stopped moving, lest he disturb Cai Yan's rest. It was their first time spending the night in the same room, and Duan Ling wanted to be careful to not bother him.

He heard Cai Yan pipe up again: "Homesick?"

"Of course not," Duan Ling said. "Didn't I also stay alone back at Ming Academy?"

"Mm-hmm. What happened to your househusband? Is he not back yet?"

As he recalled their silly past exchange, laughter bubbled up in Duan Ling. "No, my dad came back and sent him off to run some errands."

Cai Yan turned his head and peered at Duan Ling. Moonlight filtered into the room, casting a soft glow over him and illuminating his handsome face. Duan Ling couldn't help staring.

"We don't look very alike, do we?" Cai Yan said.

"What?" Duan Ling asked, confused.

"Me and my brother," he said. "Everyone usually comments on it."

This thought hadn't occurred to Duan Ling—he'd only been musing that Cai Yan looked more grown up. But upon hearing him, Duan Ling hummed, "Mn."

"We have different moms," Cai Yan elaborated.

"Ah."

Cai Wen had thick eyebrows and large eyes, while Cai Yan had delicate, refined features that lent him a dignified and scholarly air. Although he maintained a cool and indifferent attitude toward others, he had always looked out for Duan Ling—if only because Duan Ling posed no threat to him. In this way, Cai Yan fancied himself to be protecting the weak.

As they looked at each other, a wavering tune drifted in.

"Is someone playing a flute outside?" Baffled, Duan Ling crawled out of bed and opened the back window, welcoming in the fragrance of a summer night's flowers.

Sitting up as well, Cai Yan looked out into the distance. The notes were arduously played, as if a beginner was trying hard to remember the fingering while also keeping their breath steady, and was thus blowing so hard that the music became an unbearable cacophony. As they listened closer, the melody seemed to be accompanied by the wet sound of spit clogging the finger holes.

Cai Yan was speechless, as was Duan Ling.

"...'Joyful Reunion'?" Duan Ling finally figured out what the song was supposed to be. "It's 'Joyful Reunion'!"

Palm covering his face, Cai Yan commented, "This is the worst song I've ever heard."

The player outside continued, but the terrible technique was making Duan Ling miserable on his behalf; he wished desperately that he could take over to help him out. Yet the flutist was undeterred; the melody grew louder and more enthusiastic, self-indulgent to the extreme.

"Who the hell is that?" The awful music was giving Cai Yan goosebumps.

Duan Ling snorted, trying not to laugh. He could guess who it was, but he didn't dare expose the unfortunate player.

"Quiet!" Helian Bo yelled from the building next door, having finally had enough. He flung open the window and threw a flowerpot in the direction of the music.

"We're trying to sleep!" Cai Yan shouted.

At last, the flutist fell silent. Duan Ling, however, didn't close the window.

"All right, time for bed. We've got an early start tomorrow," Cai Yan said.

Duan Ling tucked himself in, curling up with his blankets and closing his eyes as his drifting mind wandered back to Li Jianhong. In his dream, a fallen blossom fluttered through the air and swirled inside through the open window, alighting upon his pillow. A pebble tapped the window frame with a soft *tock*, and the window swung shut.

"The Way of Great Learning is found in the manifestation of one's radiant virtue..."

"Knowing where to stop leads to stability, and with stability comes tranquility..."

"All things have their beginning and end; all affairs have their start and finish. Knowing the natural order of things draws one closer to the Way of Great Learning."[13]

Biyong Academy was overseen by four officials: the chancellor, two directors of study, and a director of student affairs. The chancellor was a plump, affable man of middle age, and chief of all affairs concerning the academy. Given that the academy officials presided over the highest scholarly institution within the empire, they reported directly to the Southern Court. There were also multiple professors of the Five Classics teaching at the academy, as well as a few teaching assistants. All of the institution's personnel, from the chancellor down to these assistants, were ranked court officials of the Liao Empire, though they were also Han. Whenever students encountered them in the hallways, they were to stop and bow courteously, and the chancellor or professors would nod and hum their acknowledgment. In this, Han and Khitan were easily differentiable—the Han grunted a nasal "Mn," while the Khitan said "Oh."

For Duan Ling, a new life had begun. From his first teachings of "In the beginning, the heaven was black and the earth was

---

13 Excerpts from Great Learning, attributed to Zengzi, a scholar during the Zhou dynasty. This is one of the Four Books in Confucianism.

yellow; the universe was chaos," Duan Ling had come far. He now learned, "The way of Great Learning is found in the manifestation of one's radiant virtue," along with "When three walk together, one must be my teacher,"[14] and "Fatty meats in your kitchen, strong horses in your stables, yet the people starve, their bodies strewn in the wild."[15] Neither the summer sun nor his peers had changed, but Duan Ling nevertheless felt as if everything was different.

Aside from reading and composing essays, Biyong Academy also required the practice of the six arts: ceremony, music, archery, chariotry, calligraphy, and mathematics—though chariotry had long since been replaced with horseback riding. Every morning, Duan Ling was expected to assemble with his peers on the drill grounds for archery practice. Most scholarly institutions in the Chen Empire didn't teach horsemanship or archery, but unfortunately for the students here, the Liao Empire valued martial prowess and placed more emphasis on military strategy than scholarship.

On their very first day on the horses, a student fell and broke his arm, then ran back to his room crying and howling in pain. Duan Ling quaked with fear, terrified he'd be trampled into a pancake under the horse's hooves. Fortunately, Li Jianhong had at least taught him how to mount a horse, so he easily hopped astride and steadied himself in the saddle.

"Well done! I can see you've ridden before," praised the instructor. "Off! You—your turn!"

Cai Yan mounted next. Almost the moment he was seated, the horse spooked and threw him off into the dirt. As Duan Ling hurried forward to help him stand, a stranger rushed onto the drill grounds and whispered in the instructor's ear. Whatever news he'd heard

---

14 *Excerpt from Book 7 of The Analects by Confucius.*
15 *Excerpt from the chapter "King Hui of Liang I" in Mengzi, an anthology attributed to the philosopher of the same name.*

seemed to give him a great shock. He strode off to find the chancellor, leaving the young men at the stable whispering among themselves, abandoned on the drill grounds with one very confused horse.

"Are we done with riding, then?" someone asked.

The boys complained as they rolled their sore shoulders and arms, eager to go back to their dorms to lie down.

In the distance came a muffled *boom*, and the thunder of hooves raced past on the streets outside the school grounds.

"What's happening?" Duan Ling wondered aloud.

Cai Yan wasn't any wiser.

The chancellor bustled onto the drill grounds soon after, mouth set in a deep frown. "Classes are canceled for the day. Everyone, return to your rooms and stay there. Do not come out until you're told."

The boys burst into excited chatter. The director of study scolded: "Quiet!"

The group immediately settled. The chancellor bent first in courtesy, and the students returned his bow before filing out of the drill grounds.

Lessons were clearly done for the day. The students returned to their rooms, but they didn't stay there, flitting from doorway to doorway in the dormitories to discuss what might have caused the cancelations. Helian Bo came to Duan Ling's building and waved for his attention.

"Wh-what?" Helian Bo said, the rest of his question implicit in his stare: *What's going on?*

"We're going to be at war," Cai Yan answered from the courtyard, applying a damp towel to his dirtied face.

Before he'd finished his sentence, another muffled *boom* echoed from the distance and jolted Duan Ling. The students all began yelling, and Duan Ling pulled Helian Bo over. "Come here!"

CHAPTER TWENTY-THREE

Realizing what Duan Ling intended, Helian Bo crouched down, bracing his arms on his knees, and allowed Duan Ling to step onto his shoulder to scale the wall. Cai Yan followed a moment later, and together, the two boys pulled Helian Bo up behind them. Once all three were on the wall, they climbed higher, onto the dormitory roof, then hopped across the eaves to the roof of the main hall. From this height, the entire city lay sprawled before them, its rooftops and houses stretching into the distance.

Where the rooftops ended, giant boulders were flying over the city walls, making the strange booming sounds they'd heard.

"The fighting's started!" Helian Bo exclaimed.

"The fighting's started," Cai Yan mumbled to himself, a deep furrow between his brows. "Is it the Mongols? Have they reached the city walls?"

Duan Ling was silent. He thought of his father and Yelü Dashi's negotiation the other night—everything had seemed to be within Li Jianhong's grasp then. Where was he now?

"The fighting's started," Duan Ling said at last, unsure what to feel.

Catapults sent more giant boulders flying into the city. The city guard ran through Shangjing's streets like a many-forked river, streaming in all directions to defend each city gate.

"Your brother is strong—I'm sure he'll be fine," Duan Ling consoled Cai Yan, remembering that Cai Wen was an officer in the city guard.

Cai Yan gave a noncommittal grunt, nodding. Realizing he'd gone overboard with his excitement, Helian Bo patted Cai Yan's shoulder.

"Let's climb higher," Duan Ling suggested. "I wonder how the north gate is faring."

The three scurried across the rooftops and finally scaled the library. The library building was three stories tall, and perched on its high railings, they gazed out into the distance. The view here was much better. Smoke was rising outside the city, where the Yuan army had gathered in immense numbers. Liao troops were mobilizing inside the city walls.

"Do you think we'll be able to defend the gates?" Cai Yan asked Helian Bo.

When Helian Bo shook his head *no*, Cai Yan pressed further, "Your people have fought the Mongols before. What are they like?"

Helian Bo remained silent, shaking his head again.

"Don't worry. We'll definitely hold the gates," Duan Ling said.

"Thank goodness Batu already left. Otherwise, he'd be killed for sure after all this," Cai Yan remarked.

Recalling their friend, all three boys sighed. Batu's escape had nothing to do with whether the Yuan general Ögedei would lay siege to Shangjing, but had he not fled the capital that night, he and his father Kuchi would surely have died under Yelü Dashi's blade. The thought made Duan Ling wonder: If he himself had become Yelü Dashi's hostage, and his father was the one at the head of the army, would his father stop his march on the city?

"Who's up there?!" bellowed a city guard from below.

Oops. They'd been discovered. Flustered, the boys tried to scamper off—but they could see the chancellor beckoning them amiably from the courtyard below. "Easy, easy. You won't be punished; just don't fall."

After the three slowly made their way back to the ground, the chancellor instructed them, equally amiably, "Now kneel right there. Don't stand until I say otherwise."

Duan Ling was dumbstruck.

The three boys knelt in the yard as the chancellor paced beside them, his hands clasped behind his back.

After a quarter of an hour, he asked the youths solemnly, "Every citizen bears responsibility for the rise and fall of their nation. Do you know what you can do for the country?"

None of them dared respond, lest they be punished with the ruler. Unlike Ming Academy, Biyong Academy rarely used the switch to discipline students—but at the moment, Duan Ling would much rather suffer a beating than continue listening to the chancellor's relentless nagging.

An officer of the guard came over. "Lord Tang."

"Stay here and reflect on your actions," Chancellor Tang instructed.

As soon as he walked away, the three boys shuffled over in unison, craning their necks to watch him disappear around the corner.

Helian Bo scrambled to his feet. "Go."

"Maybe we should kneel a bit longer..." Duan Ling said.

Cai Yan pulled him up. "We're at *war*—what're you kneeling for? Let's go, let's go!"

24

As they passed through the back corridor, the three boys paused to listen beneath a window. The Yuan forces were currently gathered outside the east gate of Shangjing, but if that failed, there was no telling whether they would redirect their attack to the north gate. Biyong Academy was close to the north gate; the city guard who had come was suggesting Chancellor Tang either move lessons elsewhere or suspend them entirely for a time.

"Isn't the imperial palace in the north end of the city too?" Duan Ling asked.

"The emperor doesn't stay there much."

According to Cai Yan, the imperial Yelü clan spent very little time in Shangjing over the course of a year. The imperial palace here was more of a holiday palace. When the Liao Empire had established its five capitals after the Battle of Huai River, the founding emperor had spent most of his time in Zhongjing, in Henan Prefecture. The Southern Administration had also located their offices there.

"Classes must go on," Chancellor Tang said thoughtfully. "Young men are hot-blooded, and their fathers are busy either fighting the war or attending court. If left at loose ends, who knows what dangerous mischief they'll get up to?"

"Then we shall do as you say, Chancellor Tang," replied the messenger from the city guard. "Officer Cai gave me orders before he left to protect Biyong Academy in case you didn't agree to relocate."

"What home is there to go back to when the country is torn? Who can truly remain untouched by battle?" Chancellor Tang replied. "Go back and tell Captain Cai this: There is no need to worry over these trifles. Focus on fighting the war. We may be scholars, but we can take care of ourselves."

With that, the guard was dismissed. Chancellor Tang returned to the inner courtyard and could only shake his head when he found the boys had already slipped away.

A fiery glow lit up the southeastern night sky—the battle had begun outside the city. Duan Ling couldn't bring himself to climb the wall again; he merely stood in the courtyard, looking worriedly into the distance. Everyone gossiped over dinner, excitedly swapping wild rumors. After the meal, Chancellor Tang came to the dining hall to personally take attendance and warned them sternly that any students who snuck out at night would be expelled.

When the students filed back out into the inner courtyard, however, a clamor arose. The situation outside the city was taking a dire turn, and Yelü Dashi had assumed command. He'd clashed with the Mongol forces three times and come back wounded; fear had immediately spread throughout the city. Now, the families had arrived to retrieve their sons.

Chancellor Tang maintained his usual calm demeanor. "Everyone, please go home. Tell your mistresses that their requests will not be heeded. Biyong Academy answers only to the Northern and Southern Courts. If you have any doubts, send your masters. Most of them attended school here themselves."

CHAPTER TWENTY-FOUR

Chancellor Tang's words stayed the servants at the gates. Outside, they were consumed by anxiety; inside, homesick children looked back with forlorn eyes. The distance between them was barely a few paces, yet crossing Biyong Academy's threshold was as difficult as traversing the silver river of the Milky Way.

Less than an hour after the servants went back to their respective houses, a din rose again at the gates. This time it was the women of the households who'd come in person, with a different plan. They detoured their carriages around the main gates, driving around the academy walls instead. Dismounting at the square windows, they poked their bleak and anxious faces through the lattices. "My son! My precious boy!" they cried one after another, wailing as if their hearts would break.

Though he saw a boy standing before every window like a row of prisoners receiving visitation, Duan Ling didn't join them. He didn't think Li Jianhong would be outside. The previous night's flute melody was still on his mind as he strolled into the inner courtyard, but this time, no one had come to play it.

As the bright moon shone down over the earth, the sounds of battle outside the city died down. Even the Yuan army had to sleep. Duan Ling didn't go to bed, but merely rested against the parasol tree in the courtyard, eyes vacant, and sighed.

"The moon is so beautiful tonight. Why do you sigh at it, Your Majesty?" came Li Jianhong's voice.

Duan Ling's eyes lit up. Laughing, he scrambled to his feet. Li Jianhong, clad in military robes, dropped down from the tree. Duan Ling's first instinct was to throw himself into his father's arms, but things had changed—he was a student of Biyong Academy, and there were many things he used to do that embarrassed him now, so he simply beamed.

Li Jianhong's black sparring robe made him look even more dashing and free-spirited than usual. Watching Duan Ling, he found his son's joy infectious.

"What are you doing here?" Duan Ling was delighted, yet he didn't quite know what to say.

"You know what," Li Jianhong replied with a straight face.

Only then did Duan Ling run over and grab Li Jianhong in a tight hug.

"All right, all right," Li Jianhong said. "Careful, or your friends might see."

Duan Ling let go, a little embarrassed.

"For you," Li Jianhong said, unstrapping a sword from his side.

"Where did you get this?" Duan Ling asked, unsheathing it.

"I borrowed it from an old friend," Li Jianhong told him. "Come, let your dad teach you a few moves."

Duan Ling had badgered Lang Junxia nonstop to teach him how to wield a sword, but Lang Junxia had steadfastly refused. He'd only shown him a few simple moves: draw, thrust, and block. Yet now Li Jianhong had not only brought him a sword, he was even going to teach him to use it. Duan Ling couldn't have asked for anything more.

"You already know how to draw, thrust, and block," Li Jianhong said quietly, so as not to be overheard.

"Yes," said Duan Ling.

"Now let me teach you the flick, stab, spin, and circle parry."

Li Jianhong demonstrated the moves for him, then broke them down step by step as he practiced.

"Got it?" he asked. When Duan Ling nodded, he said, "Now put the sword down. We'll learn hand-to-hand combat."

Li Jianhong held up his open palms. As he broke down each form, Duan Ling recognized them as the same ones Li Jianhong had taught him before. He was thoroughly attentive in his instruction, patiently sparring with Duan Ling over and over again—now picking up the sword, now switching back to palms—until both styles wove seamlessly together. Duan Ling fought clumsily, often forgetting one technique after learning the next. Li Jianhong stepped lightly, rolling onto the balls of his feet, then hooked a finger, signaling Duan Ling to mirror his footsteps. Together they turned, thrust their palms out, and drew their swords.

When Li Jianhong swept his blade through the air, it flickered like rippling water. His technique was effortless, and when he struck with his fist, the movement held his singular focus. Li Jianhong followed up with another turn, then drew his sword and struck out with a palm. Duan Ling watched in awe.

"Try again." Li Jianhong smiled and patted his head.

Duan Ling followed him in sequence: sword, palm, sword, step.

"Excellent," said Li Jianhong. "You've got talent; you've picked up the important points."

Fundamentally, wielding a sword was the combination of many small moves used in concert. Duan Ling had never noticed this before, but as Li Jianhong began with him from the basics, he saw new depths to the martial arts that made them no less worthy a pursuit than the literary ones.

By the time Li Jianhong ended the lesson, four hours later, Duan Ling was soaked in sweat. Within this time, apart from teaching him sword techniques, Li Jianhong had mentioned nothing else. Not until he was about to leave did he say, "It's late; you should hurry back to your bed and sleep. I'll be going now."

"Dad!" Duan Ling cried in disappointment, but Li Jianhong had already hopped onto the wall and disappeared behind the crown of the parasol tree, leaving Duan Ling speechless and alone.

To avoid being caught in the conflict, students were told to be ready to gather at a moment's notice. They no longer held classes all together, for fear that if boulders began to fly, they'd all be killed in one fell swoop.

The monthly break came in the blink of an eye, yet the chancellor insisted that they stay at the academy, as it was no safer for them at home.

With the country in crisis, the students were of course concerned, but their fear was balanced by the joy of canceled classes. Only Cai Yan worried without end, and his broodiness spread to Duan Ling.

"I'm worried about that idiot," Cai Yan finally admitted. "What about you? What are you worried about?"

Duan Ling didn't dare reveal that he was worried about his father—although given Li Jianhong's battle prowess, there was no real cause for concern. Instead he asked, "What idiot?"

"My brother. My common-born brother who always gives too much of himself to others."

"It won't help to dwell on it," Duan Ling consoled him.

Cai Yan paced back and forth in the hall. "I want to take a look outside."

"Don't. It's too dangerous," Duan Ling told him, setting down the book in his hands.

A great rumbling came from outside: The Yuan army had begun their assault on the north gate. Boulders smashed into the city walls. The walls were too high for the catapults to fling the heavy stones over them, but still people flooded the streets and stared in the direction of the noise in horror.

"Don't be scared," said Duan Ling. "They can't hit us here."

No sooner had he spoken than the Yuan army changed tactics. This time it was not stones, but bundles of cloth showering down into the city like sparks from fireworks. A dozen such bundles fell into the academy grounds, and they hit the earth with a series of clanks, oozing blood.

Shrieks of horror broke out in Biyong Academy. Heads—they were severed heads, still clad in their city guard helmets, necks ragged where they'd parted from bodies. The other boys screamed, while Cai Yan howled in distress.

"What are you yelling about!" Chancellor Tang roared, and they all fell silent.

"Pick them up and bring them into the main hall," he ordered, regaining his composure.

The boys, quaking, picked the severed heads up by the hair and threw them into a basket in the main hall. Duan Ling was bolder than the rest, carrying the heads in his hands. The chancellor instructed the students to form a straight line in front of the basket, a queue that trailed out of the main hall. He bade them bow three times to the heads, then ordered the director to take them to the city guard headquarters. As Duan Ling turned away, he saw emotion shining in the chancellor's eyes. Many things in the world didn't need to be put into words to make a lasting impression in Duan Ling's heart.

During dinner, every boy was weighed down by the terror that more things would fly over the walls and crush them to death. The chancellor, however, remained steadfast. "Return to your dormitories and get some sleep. Nothing will happen overnight," he told them.

That evening, Biyong Academy was as silent as a tomb. There were no voices, no lights. Dark clouds shrouded the moon. Duan Ling rose quietly, groped for the sword beneath his bed, and padded toward the door.

"Where are you going?" Cai Yan asked in the darkness.

"Can't sleep. I'm going to take a walk."

"I'll go with you." Cai Yan made to rise from his bed, but Duan Ling quickly assured him he was fine on his own. Cai Yan settled back down without pressing the matter.

But, left alone, Cai Yan tossed and turned. Unable to fall asleep, he got up, opened the doors, and stepped out. "Duan Ling?" he called.

Duan Ling was nowhere in sight. Panic shot through Cai Yan, and he ran off barefoot in search. As he hurried down the corridor, he heard Duan Ling's voice a short distance away. A lamp sat on a wall of the inner courtyard, casting its light on a man over six feet tall. He was crouched down, hands planted on his knees, his face drawn so close to Duan Ling's as he spoke that they were practically touching.

"When are you going to scare them off?" Duan Ling was asking.

"Wait for Liqiu, the start of autumn," said the man.

"Why?"

"Autumn is the season of metal, and metal is the element that imparts bloodlust to troops," Li Jianhong explained. "It's the best time to do battle."

Duan Ling considered this in silence.

"One and a half more months," Li Jianhong said. "Come, let's review yesterday's lesson."

Duan Ling reluctantly picked up the sword. He missed his father terribly, but when he was here, there was barely any time to talk.

Li Jianhong answered questions only briefly before urging Duan Ling to practice his sword techniques.

"Can't we skip lessons today?" Duan Ling asked. What he most wanted was to sit in his father's lap, lay his head back on his father's chest, and chat—even if they didn't speak, as long as Li Jianhong was close, all his fears dissipated.

"No way," Li Jianhong said seriously. "Don't tell me you don't want to learn these techniques. Many would die for the chance, that's for certain—but even if they all got on their knees and begged, the only person I want to teach is you."

A smile crossed Duan Ling's face.

"Plus, if I don't teach you properly, I won't be able to focus on fighting the war," Li Jianhong added.

"Then...after we finish our lesson, can you stay a bit longer?"

"Your dad's busy these days," Li Jianhong said softly, shaking his head. "Why—is there something you want to tell me?"

"I'm scared," said Duan Ling.

"Of what?" asked Li Jianhong. "You have a sword in your hands and me by your side. I haven't always protected you, but you're safe within Biyong Academy. Don't be afraid."

Duan Ling put down the sword. Somewhat puzzled, Li Jianhong nonetheless sat down and patted his knee for Duan Ling to come sit. He wrapped his arms around his son, and Duan Ling leaned back against his chest, telling him about the fright they'd had earlier that day. Li Jianhong merely smiled and recited in a low humming tone:

"Oh, our swords still at our belts, our Qin bows on our arms;
Oh, our heads torn from our shoulders, but our hearts remain as one...
Oh, our bodies may be dead, but our spirits still live on;
Oh, our souls stand firm, unwavering, phantom heroes are we."

His voice was rich and resonant, pleasing to the ear. Duan Ling, too, had studied and knew the significance of "Hymn to the Fallen."[16] Reminded of its words now, he no longer felt as troubled.

Li Jianhong arched a brow at Duan Ling—*Understand?*

A complicated feeling swelled in Duan Ling's chest. Together in the stillness of the night, Li Jianhong's simple recitation had connected Duan Ling's soul with the cycle of life, with sorrow, with the manifestation of all things in the world, with their rise and fall—yet Duan Ling didn't feel he was being preached to.

"Up now. Time to practice," Li Jianhong said, rising to his feet.

Duan Ling retrieved his sword and demonstrated the forms he'd learned the previous night. Li Jianhong bade him repeat it several times, correcting his mistakes.

"Hey, young master behind the pillar over there," Li Jianhong suddenly remarked in a casual tone. "You won't learn anything peeping like that. You're better off going back to bed."

Duan Ling paused, confused, as Cai Yan scurried out from the shadows, gawking at Li Jianhong.

"Uncle, please teach me!" he cried.

Duan Ling jumped in shock as Cai Yan ran up to Li Jianhong and sank to his knees before him. He stepped forward at once to help his friend up, but Li Jianhong blocked him with an arm.

---

16 Part of "Nine Songs" from The Songs of Chu, a collection of ancient elegies noted for recording mythology and rituals related to ghosts and deities in the early southern Central Plains.

25

"Why do you wish to learn the sword?" Li Jianhong asked.

"I'm Cai Yan, of the Cai clan."

Li Jianhong frowned. "Your name and family mean nothing to me. I only want to know why you need to learn the sword."

"My brother is an officer in the city guard. I'm worried for his safety. I want to learn to fight too, so I can help him."

Struck by a memory, Li Jianhong turned to Duan Ling. "Is his brother the Cai Wen who knocked on our gates that snowy day?"

Duan Ling nodded that he was.

"I owe your brother a favor, so I'll return it to you," Li Jianhong said to Cai Yan. "But you must remember—no matter what skills you manage to learn, you must never use them against my son."

"Dad, we're friends," Duan Ling insisted.

"Go find a stick and use it as your sword for now. Follow what we do from behind," Li Jianhong said.

Nodding, Cai Yan did as instructed, taking his place behind Duan Ling. Li Jianhong acted as if he wasn't there, teaching Duan Ling the techniques one at a time as usual. Duan Ling learned incrementally more from this lesson, building on the last. After two hours, Li Jianhong vanished in a flicker—just as he had the night before.

Cai Yan nodded to Duan Ling in thanks. Duan Ling smiled back, sheepish. He thought Li Jianhong had been rather rude to Cai Yan, though Cai Yan himself didn't seem to mind.

"What's your dad's sword style called?" he asked Duan Ling.

"I don't know," Duan Ling said, at a loss.

Cai Yan was instantly livelier, as if he'd unearthed a glimmer of hope. "I'll find a sword tomorrow, but first let me see yours."

Duan Ling handed him the sword, and Cai Yan studied it. Its sheath was crusted with jewels; there was no doubt that it was highly prized, though the two boys had no idea of its provenance.

"It's a good sword," Cai Yan finally said.

Day by day, the war ground onward. It was Duan Ling's first time living through such a conflict, and it struck him as a strange experience. At first everyone had panicked, but as the Yuan forces laid siege to the city, they slowly grew accustomed to it. Even Biyong Academy became laxer in its rules. The day after the sword lesson, Cai Yan stole a ceremonial sword from the library to use for the moment, and at night, he waited together with Duan Ling for Li Jianhong.

When asked what style he was teaching, Li Jianhong replied, "One I came up with," before urging Duan Ling into his lessons.

For the past few days, Duan Ling had been feeling an acute pain in his shoulder, and his arms were often too sore to lift. When he complained of it to Li Jianhong, his father circulated vital qi through his body and massaged Duan Ling with a light touch. Miraculously, when Duan Ling woke the following morning, the soreness was gone.

Li Jianhong always came and went in a rush, and since Cai Yan was with him now, there was no good time for Duan Ling to ask what else Li Jianhong was doing. But this, too, was something he quickly became accustomed to. He contented himself with merely seeing Li Jianhong every day.

Life in Shangjing changed over the course of the month. Though the schoolboys knew little of what happened beyond the academy's walls, they felt these changes through tiny, daily details. For instance: They could no longer eat until they were full, and were limited to a single bowl of rice. Lunch became a thin porridge, and no meat was served at dinner, only vegetables.

After a month under Yuan siege, the city was running out of food.

When Li Jianhong visited next, he threw Duan Ling a parcel of roasted meat. "Eat up."

Duan Ling sat and ate, sharing with Cai Yan. As he waited for them to finish eating, Li Jianhong asked Duan Ling what he'd learned that day and which books he read. When Duan Ling had finished, he continued giving sword lessons.

The fighting became more urgent by the day, and Shangjing buzzed with restlessness. The day families were due to pick up their children arrived, but with the chaos of battle all around, the chancellor decided they should stay in Biyong Academy. Arrows flew over the walls around the east, south, and west gates; only the north gate was safe. Even when their parents pleaded until they were hoarse, the chancellor remained good-natured but firm: The students must stay, and there was nothing that could be said to change things.

The first rain of autumn began to fall at dusk. For dinner, there was only a watery porridge. A dense crowd of family members gathered on the other side of Biyong Academy's outer walls, passing food to their children through the windows. Most of it was cured pork belly wrapped in flatbread. Even the merchants and officials—rich in coin but poor in goods—no longer had fresh meat. They could only offer the rice, bread, and preserved meat left in their dwindling pantries.

After eating their bowls of porridge and salted vegetables, Duan Ling and Cai Yan looked out at the crowd from the corridor, still hungry, but Cai Wen did not come. Every time he heard hooves on the path, Cai Yan ran through the rain to the latticed window and searched the street outside. When he saw that it wasn't Cai Wen, he could do nothing but step aside and let another student take his place. Again and again, he looked for his brother in vain, until his hope curdled into despair and then anger.

"I'm going to bed," he declared. "Wake me up when your dad comes."

Before Duan Ling could offer any words of comfort, Cai Yan stalked off back to bed, pale and sullen. Duan Ling paced a few circuits around the courtyard until, an hour after the sky had turned dark, a lantern peeped through the window of the wall.

"Cai Yan!" a man yelled, "Cai Yan!"

"Wait!" Duan Ling called back, running over. "I'll go wake him up."

The man outside the window was not Cai Wen but another city guard. "Captain Cai sent me with food for his brother. Please pass it to him," he told Duan Ling. "The captain can't come today."

Duan Ling took the parcel of smoked meat wrapped in paper. The paper was stamped with the official seal of the city guard—leftover rations. Duan Ling scampered back to the dormitory and shook Cai Yan awake. "Cai Yan, your brother came," he lied.

Cai Yan groaned. Duan Ling quickly felt his forehead and discovered he had a fever.

"Where?" Cai Yan asked weakly. "Is he still alive?"

"He's well. He says eat more, and that he'll come visit some other day."

Cai Yan nodded feebly. The only thing that mattered was that Cai Wen was alive. He turned his head toward Duan Ling and asked, "Is he going to fight outside the city?"

Duan Ling took his pulse. "I don't know," he said, shaking his head. "I'm going to find you some medicine. Lie down."

Rain dampened Duan Ling's shoulders as he left the inner courtyard. Aside from the steady drizzle, Shangjing was deathly still.

A whistle called to him from behind, lilting like birdsong before it came to a sudden stop. Duan Ling's face broke into a smile as he sprinted back into the inner courtyard. The whistler strode forward, scooped him up by the waist, and carried him laughing underneath the eaves of the veranda.

Today, Li Jianhong looked grand, clad in a full suit of armor. His mail, crafted of tiny metal plates, glistened like dragon scales, and he wore an ornate qilin helmet fastened under his chin by a red cord. Setting his bronze sword and halberd on the ground, Li Jianhong turned and leaned back against the veranda railing to sit shoulder to shoulder with Duan Ling. Their figures, one large and one small, made a stark contrast.

"Wow!" exclaimed Duan Ling.

"Shh…"

"What is this?" Duan Ling touched his father's armor, then tugged at the glove on his hand curiously.

"A gauntlet," Li Jianhong explained, pulling it off to show him. Duan Ling moved on to touch his helmet, and Li Jianhong warned, "Don't take it off; just look at it like this. It's hard to put back on."

"What are these?" Duan Ling pointed down.

"Boots?" Li Jianhong said, amused.

"But why do they have metal spikes?" Duan Ling had never seen armor like this up close. Clad in his shining mail, his father was so mighty it nearly took Duan Ling's breath away.

"They're to stab enemy horses in a melee," Li Jianhong explained.

"Are you going into battle?" Duan Ling asked. "Can you really fight in such heavy armor?"

Shoving off with his left foot, Li Jianhong leapt into the air, swept his halberd several times, twirled, and landed again in a cross-legged seat. He took out a paper-wrapped parcel and handed it to Duan Ling. "Eat. We're skipping sword practice today."

Inside the package was a pile of neatly sliced pieces of crispy roasted pork. Duan Ling wolfed them down, occasionally holding a piece up to Li Jianhong's lips.

"I've had fine wines," Li Jianhong said when the pork was gone, "and my share of every delicacy across the land. I've waited a month and a half, and today, I shall leave the city to eradicate those barbarians."

Duan Ling's brows instantly knit in worry. Li Jianhong ruffled his hair and said in a serious voice, "Dad has been teaching you sword techniques this past month and a half, all for today. Do you remember them?"

Duan Ling nodded. "I can fight alongside you! Let's go!"

"Your Majesty, what on earth are you thinking?" Li Jianhong exclaimed in bewilderment, clapping a hand to his forehead. "A royal expedition? It hasn't come to that!"

"We should fight as one. Do I get armor too?"

Li Jianhong poked Duan Ling with a finger. "Tonight *I* shall leave the city, not you. Around midnight, Yelü Dashi and I will each take half our forces to raid the enemy camp and burn their rations. Understood?"

"Then what am I supposed to do?" Duan Ling asked, confused.

"When I leave to set fire to the enemy camp, there'll be no one here to protect you. If anything should happen... It's a very small chance, but it is a chance. You absolutely must not lower your guard. Keep your eyes and ears open."

Duan Ling nodded. "Then, what should I do?"

"Take up Kublai's sword—"

"Where is it?"

Li Jianhong was at a loss for words. He tapped Duan Ling's sword with an expression that said, *What am I going to do with you?*

"Right here. Kublai Khan gave it to Ögedei, and your very own father stole it from the general the first day he had it."

"Oh." Duan Ling could only nod again.

"If anyone comes looking for trouble, assess them carefully," Li Jianhong instructed. "If you can cut them down, do so. If you can't, run and hide. Understood?"

"What will happen to Biyong Academy?" Duan Ling asked.

"Most likely nothing. But if something does, no matter what happens, don't try to show off. I can't take you with me to burn the enemy camp, so my son, you must protect your life at all costs. If you die...your father won't be able to go on."

"Okay, okay..." Duan Ling understood.

Li Jianhong was confident he could force the Mongols to retreat, but he didn't know if they would launch a last desperate attack. He couldn't stay behind to guard his son, so instead he'd spent a month and a half teaching him some rough basics. As he was still just learning, Duan Ling couldn't possibly hack down a whole host—but if danger came to his doorstep, he could at least protect himself and flee while the enemy underestimated him.

Another thousand times, Li Jianhong drilled into Duan Ling what to do if the north gate fell and the Yuan forces breached the city—what to do in case of fire; what to do if arrows began to fly; what to do if boulders started falling; what to do if the city walls collapsed. All potentialities large and small, he asked Duan Ling to repeat back to him until he was satisfied he'd truly committed them to memory. He even drew a map and planned an escape route for him. Li Jianhong spoke as if the Yuan forces were already at the gates of Biyong Academy and were merely waiting for him to start the drill.

"How likely are they to invade the city?" Duan Ling asked, increasingly anxious.

"Very unlikely. But if there's even a slight chance..." Li Jianhong stressed again, "You must not let your guard down, even for a moment."

Duan Ling lapsed into a nervous silence.

"If anything happens to you..."

"You won't be able to go on," he finished for his father.

The first time Li Jianhong had said those words, Duan Ling had been incredibly moved, but after having them hammered into his head again and again, they'd become rote.

"Exactly," Li Jianhong said, raising his hand. "Strike, and seal the promise that you'll stay alive."

Duan Ling clapped his father's hand thrice, and Li Jianhong continued, "Your father's going off to war. I'll be back at dawn, and tomorrow, I'll bring you home."

He threw his arms around Li Jianhong's neck, and Li Jianhong laughed. "You're thirteen already," Li Jianhong said, chuckling. "Don't drag out goodbyes."

Only then did Duan Ling let go of him. Li Jianhong briskly hopped the fence of the inner courtyard and swung astride his horse. Duan Ling scrambled up the fence and propped his chin on it to see his father, halberd strapped to his back and sword case tied to Skychaser's saddle.

"Get back down before you fall," he said.

"Be careful!" Duan Ling called.

Legs tight against his horse's sides, Li Jianhong leaned toward Duan Ling. He raised one leg for balance and pressed a kiss to his son's forehead. Duan Ling kissed his cheek in return, and Li Jianhong spurred his steed forward with a cry and a toss of the reins. Man and horse became one with the wind, disappearing into the distance along the dark alley.

26

Duan Ling collected some herbs from the school's stores and went back to decoct some medicine for Cai Yan.

"Did he come?" Cai Yan groaned weakly.

"Who, my dad? Yeah."

"Okay."

"We didn't have sword practice today," Duan Ling continued.

Cai Yan let out a long, slow breath. Duan Ling poured the medicine into a bowl to let it cool.

While Duan Ling had been speaking to his father, he had taken the cloth pouch on its red cord out from his robes. Now, as Duan Ling helped Cai Yan sit up to drink the medicine, it swung back and forth, dangling from his neck.

"I heard on the first day you came to Ming Academy, you got in a fight with Batu because of this"—Cai Yan took the pouch in hand—"this piece of jade?"

"Mm-hmm," Duan Ling said. "Drink your medicine."

"Batu always wondered what was inside, but he didn't dare bother you about it after that," Cai Yan said, smiling. He rubbed the jade through the cloth before slipping it back into Duan Ling's underrobe. "Half of a jade disc."

"A jade arc," Duan Ling confirmed.

Cai Yan drank the medicine and lay down.

"I made you a strong decoction. You should sleep soundly tonight and wake up feeling better."

That night, Duan Ling went to bed with his sword under his pillow, but sleep eluded him. Scenes of his mighty father fighting in gleaming armor flashed through his head: scenes of him slicing off heads, of his flawless bow shots.

At midnight, Cai Yan was still feverish, gasping for breath in his bed. Dark clouds shrouded the moon, and the rain had resumed. Horses splashed through the puddles in the silent streets outside, their hooves a quiet rumble as they passed by. Duan Ling sat up and peered out the window. He sensed that there were many soldiers close by, on their way out the north gate—but the sound was different, more muffled than the usual thunder of warhorses.

It was an ambush brigade, four thousand strong, their horses' hooves wrapped in cloth. With Li Jianhong in the lead, they snuck through the north gate and soundlessly circled around a hill toward the Yuan troops camped to the city's east.

At the same time, the Yuan forces were looping around the south, intending to attack the west gate. In the dense, dripping woods outside the city, Yelü Dashi and Li Jianhong waited, both clad in armor.

"You were right," Yelü Dashi said. "They fell for the fake report."

"Right now, my greatest concern is that the defenses outside of our north and west gates are undermanned."

"I don't like the idea of putting our main force on the walls. Anyway, Ögedei isn't that smart."

"Yelü Dashi, maybe I'm being overcautious, but you must order Cai Wen to station a battalion at the west gate for defense."

Yelü Dashi stared him down. "Li Jianhong, I'm the commanding general here," he reminded him. "Split the troops!"

Li Jianhong was forced to let it go. He and Yelü Dashi each took two thousand men as they stealthily crept down the hill toward the enemy's rear from both directions. The last month of holding the city against the siege was all for the sake of this single night. By joint agreement, Li Jianhong and Yelü Dashi had decided to engage the Mongols in a battle of attrition, waiting until Liqiu and then sending out a messenger with fake plans. As expected, the Yuan troops intercepted the missive and acted on the planted information.

The Yuan troops, already rallied around the west gate, set up their siege ladders with hardly a sound. On the other side of the wall, Cai Wen ordered the city guards to aim their glinting arrows high.

Li Jianhong led his troop of elite soldiers in a steady march toward the Yuan army's rear, their footsteps drumming a dull beat on the earth.

"Attack!" he shouted.

With a battle cry, two thousand brave soldiers of the advance squad rushed toward the Yuan army's main camp.

Jars of crude oil exploded in a roar of flame. Horses whinnied in terror, the provision tents caught fire, and the horizon glowed red. A Mongol soldier raced onto a gong platform with his torch held high, ready to beat it for a retreat. Li Jianhong, galloping at full speed, loosed an arrow; blood splattered as the soldier collapsed onto the gong.

"Attack!" Yelü Dashi and his soldiers surrounded the Yuan army, lighting their oil reserves on fire. Flames licked into the night sky.

At the city walls, Ögedei, the commander of the Yuan army, was ordering batches of flaming oil jars to be launched into Shangjing.

Flames erupted there too. The wall garrison loosed their arrows, and Mongol corpses littered the ground. A messenger sprinted in from the army's rear, announcing that the main camp was under attack as boulders and arrows poured down from the city walls—they had fallen into the enemy's trap.

Roaring, Ögedei abandoned the wall and charged toward the rear with his army. Yelü Dashi attacked from the flank, but the finely trained Yuan forces fluidly shifted formations to protect the siege brigade.

Yelü Dashi cursed at Ögedei in Khitan, and Ögedei cursed back in Mongolian.

"Forget the insults!" Li Jianhong raged. "Shut up and kill him!"

Leaving the Yuan army's main camp to burn, Li Jianhong led his own troops into the fray. The plain outside the west gate immediately became a bloodbath. The Mongols were hemmed in on three sides, leaving the south their only avenue of escape. Yet unexpectedly, Ögedei made the daring decision to break through Yelü Dashi's lines.

Li Jianhong cursed inwardly when he saw the Yuan formation shifting again. An arrow arced through the air and shot the Mongol messenger with the commander's orders dead on his horse, but it was too late: Fifty thousand soldiers turned as if they were a single titanic organism. On one flank, they fought off Li Jianhong's troops with their lives, while on the other, Ögedei rallied his main force and charged toward Yelü Dashi.

The Mongols rushed forward like a tidal wave, catching Yelü Dashi off guard. His soldiers scattered in disarray as their formation split from the center. Li Jianhong's battalion pierced through the Mongols like a dagger as Yelü Dashi, shot by an arrow, listed in the saddle.

At the last moment, Li Jianhong thrust his halberd through Yelü Dashi's clothes, raising him back up on the horse.

"Open the gates!" Li Jianhong bellowed.

The doors of the south gate swung open, and the twenty thousand troops hidden behind it finally sprang out, but Ögedei had already fled in the direction of the north gate. Without hesitation, Li Jianhong galloped in through the south gate, cutting a path straight through Shangjing to ambush Ögedei on the other side of the city.

The Liao army was more than twenty thousand strong, while the Yuan army, depleted by nearly ten thousand casualties over the past weeks, still had around forty thousand. The two forces clashed fiercely at the north and west gates as Ögedei's vanguard approached the north. Flaming jars of oil flew in all directions, and the buildings surrounding the north gate were swallowed by a sea of flames.

The fiery missiles traced bright arcs through the sky as they fell onto the grounds of Biyong Academy, where they smashed on impact. Flames splashed over the buildings and courtyards.

Duan Ling jolted awake to the sound of screams. Doors were flung open, and boys ran barefooted out of their rooms. Duan Ling snatched up his sword. By the time he shook Cai Yan awake, flames were licking at the threshold.

"The Yuan army's breached the gate!" a boy shouted.

"Don't panic!" Duan Ling yelled back, jumping out the window. "Head west!"

All the boys in the dormitories near Duan Ling came running.

"We should stand and fight!" one yelled. "The city's been breached; we can't surrender!"

"How?!" Duan Ling shouted back. "Do you plan to catch their swords with your bare hands? Run, don't try to be a hero!" When they continued squabbling, Duan Ling said, "Stay then! I'm going!"

"I'm! Going!" Helian Bo echoed.

"Wait! Wait!" The boys chased after Duan Ling. "What about the chancellor?"

"Don't worry about him!" Duan Ling declared. "Protect your own lives first!"

"Grab bows and arrows!" one boy called.

"I'll pick them up somewhere!" Duan Ling responded.

Chancellor Tang finally appeared. "Don't panic," he ordered. "Evacuate through the back alley. Stay away from the fires and gather at Ming Academy!"

Following his directions, many boys streamed into the alley. Duan Ling looked around, remembering the escape route his father had given him. Instead of heading toward Ming Academy, he beckoned his companions and turned back the other way, intending to run for the west district.

Hoping to capture all of Ögedei's men in one fell swoop during the night, Yelü Dashi had deployed all his troops, leaving the north feebly defended. It took less than a quarter of an hour for the Yuan army to penetrate the city there, trampling over the corpses of Khitan soldiers and horses.

At the same time, Cai Wen was rushing at breakneck speed toward the north gate with a battalion of the city guard to provide reinforcement. Two thousand Mongols had already breached the walls, flooding Shangjing's streets and alleyways. Women and children, old and young—all were killed on sight. Within the space of a heartbeat, corpses littered the city streets; houses burned and then collapsed in on themselves. The city guard fought the Yuan invaders with their lives, forcing them back toward the gate.

Behind Duan Ling, Biyong Academy burned. The servants, lugging buckets of water to put out the flames, were shot dead by the

Yuan cavalrymen before they could empty their pails. With no more time to search for people, Duan Ling turned and drew his sword, blade flashing, just as the nearest soldier brandished his saber and hacked down at him from the saddle, aiming to split the boy in two. Duan Ling swung up on drilled instinct, meeting his strike head-on. The two blades crossed, and the soldier's arm dropped to the ground as the rest of his body tumbled from the horse.

"Run!" Duan Ling yelled.

The boys ran out of the alley and found the streets in chaos. Buildings burned on both sides of the street, with bodies of both the Yuan forces and the defending city guard strewn over the ground.

"Retreat! Everyone, back into the alley!" Cai Yan ordered.

Helian Bo, Cai Yan, and Duan Ling scavenged bows and arrows from the fallen soldiers, heedless of whether they belonged to the Khitan or the Mongols. They retreated back into the alleyway, picking up wooden boards and bucket lids to use as shields; from behind them, several students shot arrows into the streets with no aim whatsoever.

"I got one!" a boy shouted excitedly.

"Ge! Ge!"[17] Cai Yan called, watching the numbers of the city guard dwindle.

Without warning, a Mongol cavalryman rammed through their ragged line of defense. Duan Ling turned in a flash and stabbed his sword into the horse's leg. The horse and soldier both fell, and the soldier cried out in a strange language as he drew his saber, surging back up to slash at his assailant. Duan Ling turned aside again, and the soldier's blade cut through empty air as Duan Ling and Cai Yan thrust their blades out in tandem. The man died instantly, one blade through his chest and another through his back.

---

17 *An address for an older brother or an older male friend.*

More and more Yuan soldiers, having overpowered the city guard, swarmed toward the alleyway. Duan Ling cursed under his breath.

"Run?" Cai Yan asked.

"No! As soon as we run, they'll shoot! Get back, back!"

The Mongols charged the boys' line over and over on their horses. Just as their defense was about to break, a roar came from the end of the alley:

"Ögedei!"

Li Jianhong's voice shook the heavens and earth.

Duan Ling watched, wide-eyed, as Skychaser leapt off the roof of a house with enough force to bring it down behind him. On his back was Li Jianhong in blood-smeared armor, shearing a path down the alley with the Guardian in his left hand and halberd in his right. He cut the Mongol soldiers down in a breath, a terrifying god of war. Blood misted the air as a horse was hacked in two along with its rider.

Li Jianhong wheeled Skychaser around and galloped out of the alley, joining the reinforcements from the city guard in repelling the invading Mongols at the north gate.

The tides of battle turned once more. Duan Ling waited until his peers had all escaped the alley. Li Jianhong had disappeared in a flash, and what remained before Duan Ling were the Mongol and Khitan soldiers on the front lines. The Mongols were being pushed out through the north gate step by step, while the Khitan soldiers sat high on their horses in flashing armor, each looking as heroic as Li Jianhong.

Duan Ling had opened his mouth to call out for his father when Helian Bo yanked him out of the path of a horse charging from behind.

"Let's go!" Cai Yan shouted.

A dozen boys pelted down the main street into the west district. As much as he worried for his father, Duan Ling didn't dare to get in his way—not to mention, Cai Yan was still sick. The group ducked into a small alley. Hoofbeats thudded close by, and three Yuan soldiers spotted them from the other end of the alley, spurring their horses toward the students and raising their bows. While the other boys screamed in terror, Duan Ling charged down the alley toward the horses. Helian Bo and Cai Yan ran after him with their makeshift shields, providing cover from the rain of arrows. Yet before Duan Ling reached them, there were three consecutive thuds as the Mongol soldiers dropped from their horses.

Skychaser skidded to a halt at the mouth of the alleyway. The sky was beginning to pale with the first light of dawn, but the cries of battle showed no signs of stopping.

"Take the alley to the west district," Li Jianhong told them. "Go through Ming Academy. Don't light any lamps."

The boys filed through the back gates of an unattended house. Duan Ling took up the rear, turning back to look at Li Jianhong.

"I happened to see a group of boys go into the alley," Li Jianhong said quietly. He was short of breath, but didn't get off his horse. "I thought something was off, so I came for a look, thinking I should save everyone I could. Thank the heavens I did."

Tears streamed down Duan Ling's cheeks, though he couldn't explain why. Li Jianhong pointed toward the house, urging him to go on, quickly.

"I'm off," he told Duan Ling.

27

WITH A FINAL NOD to his father, Duan Ling ran off to catch up with the other boys.

As they left the north gate behind, the clamor died down and the roads emptied. Still, the boys remained wary, unsure how the battle was progressing. When their flight brought them close to the Cai residence, Cai Yan suggested, "Let's take cover at my house."

The boys, tired and hungry, nodded their agreement and followed Cai Yan inside.

Famished, Cai Yan called for the servants to find something for them to eat—but no one answered. The whole residence was a mess, having apparently been looted. Duan Ling poked around the inner courtyard and saw a dead Mongol in a corner with an arrow sticking out of his back. He seemed to have fled there after being shot, and his body was still warm.

"There's a dead guy in the corner," Duan Ling said calmly before taking a sip of water.

"Leave it," Cai Yan replied. "Everyone, come to the front hall."

Despite turning the Cai family's kitchen upside down, Helian Bo found not a scrap of food. The stove was ice-cold, obviously unlit for many days. All they could do was fetch a bit of water to drink from the well. A few of the boys picked leaves in the courtyard to chew on.

"Drink more," Duan Ling urged. "Water will fill your stomach. And peel off the bark—that'll keep you full too."

They had been going hungry for ages, and were all relying on one another. Duan Ling laid his hand on Cai Yan's forehead and found him still feverish.

Helian Bo fell asleep and snored, a trail of drool stretching from his mouth. Duan Ling grabbed a pillow and lay down next to him, his hand over the hilt of his sword as he slept. Cai Yan sprawled across the table; the other boys spread themselves out across the floor of the front hall.

Eventually, the sound of hooves rang out on the stone outside. Everyone startled awake like birds at the twang of a bow, leaping to their feet. Duan Ling gripped his sword and stood behind the doors, surveying the courtyard. A soldier in the uniform of the city guard had come, his face caked with blood.

"Is anyone inside?" he yelled.

Duan Ling kept hidden out of fear it was a deserter who'd come to rob the place, but Helian Bo burst through the doors. Thankfully, the soldier announced, "The battle's over. Come get rations at the drill grounds outside the city guard headquarters."

Everyone exclaimed in joy. Helian Bo ran up to the soldier. "Th-th-the M-M-Mongols l-left..."

The soldier had no patience for his stuttering and turned to be on his way. Still in their underrobes, the boys roared with giddy laughter, gazing at each other like they'd just been reborn.

Despite wolfing down the pork his father had brought the prior evening, Duan Ling was so hungry he was dizzy with it. The effort of keeping everyone in the group together and walking back across half the city after the rain tired them to their bones; they only arrived at the guard headquarters at sunset.

The flames had been put out around the north gate, but Shangjing looked like a ransacked city. Injured soldiers lay everywhere on the drill ground outside the city guard headquarters, wailing in pain, pieces of their armor strewn about. Duan Ling's heart broke at the sight. He turned to look for Li Jianhong among the rallied soldiers, and as if by some curious connection, his eyes were immediately drawn to his father.

Li Jianhong was deep in conversation with an injured Yelü Dashi in front of the gates of the city guard headquarters, his armor coated with coppery blood. Duan Ling was about to run up to him when— though Li Jianhong never moved his eyes away from Yelü Dashi and his face remained stern—his father gently wagged a finger in Duan Ling's direction.

He understood at once: Li Jianhong didn't want Yelü Dashi to see him. Duan Ling turned away and found Cai Yan running frantically around the camp. Soldiers were being carried into tents on stretchers, one by one.

"Where's my brother?" Cai Yan asked urgently.

"Cai-gongzi," a soldier called out. Cai Yan and Duan Ling approached, and the man handed Cai Yan a flatbread. "Have a bite first."

Cai Yan accepted the flatbread but handed it to Duan Ling. Stashing it in his robes, Duan Ling followed him into a white tent where injured soldiers lay in untidy rows. Cai Yan came to a halt. The soldier led them to the far end of the tent where a body had been laid out, veiled in a white cloth.

Without a word, Cai Yan fell to his knees before it. He peeled back the cloth to reveal Cai Wen's dirty, bloodstained face. An arrow shaft, now snapped in half, had pierced him through; the cold hand at his side still clutched the fletched end.

"He was always bad at fighting," Cai Yan told Duan Ling. "Yelü Dashi only promoted him because of our father. I begged your dad to teach me the sword so I could teach him how to defend himself."

As soon as the last word left his lips, he swayed and fainted into Duan Ling's lap.

Duan Ling wiped away his tears. Concerned that Cai Yan would see his brother's body and be struck down by grief again if he woke up in the casualties' tent, Duan Ling painstakingly carried him out in his arms. The soldiers outside all tensed at the sight. One came up to Cai Yan and felt his forehead—burning hot. As he was the little brother of the captain who had given his life for the empire, they ordered the medic to see to him first.

The doctor prescribed a list of fever-reducing herbs. Duan Ling borrowed a crock and decocted Cai Yan's medicine on a stove the soldiers lit for him, then fed him the decoction through a reed straw.

After Duan Ling spent a whole evening tending to Cai Yan, a city guard came up to him. "Hey, you two—go to Ming Academy. The masters of Biyong Academy are gathered there now."

He drove them there in a borrowed flatbed cart. It was deep in the night when they arrived; Cai Yan's condition had improved, but he still had a low fever and mumbled incoherently in his sleep from time to time. Helian Bo had also returned from the drill ground, and many other boys from Biyong Academy had returned as well. A few who hadn't fled in time when the Mongols invaded had been killed in the fray, but thankfully, the rest had escaped unscathed. Chancellor Tang, too, was still among the living.

Duan Ling greeted the headmaster, who was telling stories to a group of Ming Academy's younger students in the library.

"...then, Guan Zhong shot Bai-gongzi,"[18] he was saying, "and with a cry, Bai-gongzi fell over in the carriage."

Duan Ling sat on his knees behind the rows of children. His eyes roved from the lamp next to the headmaster to the hanging scroll illuminated by it: *A Thousand Miles of Rivers and Mountains*. He thought of the day he'd parted with Batu. The rise of one power and the fall of another, the never-ending cycle of life and death—what was it all if not a fleeting dream?

The next morning Cai Yan finally woke, and an exhausted Duan Ling finally fell asleep. Some time later, he was roused by a hand shaking his shoulder:

"Hey," Cai Yan said, "It's time to eat."

It was the third day after the Mongols had left Shangjing, and order was finally restored. The teachers distributed pitifully meager rations. As they ate, a boy named Huyan Na scurried over and announced, "The chancellor wants everyone to go downstairs."

Duan Ling helped Cai Yan navigate the staircase to where the chancellor had set up a meeting space in an ancillary hall of Ming Academy.

"Roll call," Chancellor Tang announced. "When you hear your name, go out and wait in the entry hall. Xiao Rong..."

"Here," said the student. Chancellor Tang put a stroke beside his name. He went down the list until he called a name and got no answer. "Is he here?"

---

18 A story of true friendship and forgiveness dating to China's Spring and Autumn period: Guan Zhong and his friend Bao Shuya each tutored a son of Duke Xiang of Qi who fled the state during a coup. When both princes sought to return and claim the dukedom, Guan Zhong attempted to assassinate Bao Shuya's student, Prince Xiaobai, but failed. When Prince Xiaobai became Duke Huan of Qi, he planned to execute Guan Zhong. Bao Shuya persuaded Duke Huan to make Guan Zhong his chancellor instead. Guan Zhong's reforms helped Qi become one of the most powerful feudal states.

"No," said another boy.

"When was he last seen?" Chancellor Tang asked.

"He was shot by the Mongols," the boy said.

"I see..." Chancellor Tang circled the name. He fell silent for a long time before resuming the roll call.

"Helian Bo."

"Here." Helian Bo took a step forward.

Chancellor Tang nodded and pointed outside. "Your mother is here to pick you up. Go home and wait for the notice to come back to school."

Helian Bo cast a questioning glance at Duan Ling, who waved him on; Li Jianhong would come for him.

"Cai Yan," Chancellor Tang said. "Are you here?"

Cai Yan didn't respond, so Duan Ling spoke for him: "He's here."

"Wait in the garden. Your family will come pick you up," the chancellor instructed him.

"I have no family," said Cai Yan. "My brother is dead."

"Then go home on your own for now and wait for the notice to come back to school."

Cai Yan turned and walked out. When Duan Ling moved to follow, the chancellor's gaze alighted on him.

"Duan Ling?"

"Yes?"

"Go with him," said Chancellor Tang. "Take Cai Yan home."

Nodding, Duan Ling stepped out of the main hall after him into the dawn light. They sat together, waiting as Duan Ling had done many times before. Back then, when he had been waiting for Lang Junxia with wistful yearning, Cai Wen had ridden by on his towering horse and whistled to them from outside. Batu had also been there, waiting for a father who never came. He would hover until the crowd thinned out, then grab his bedding from the dormitory and move to the library for the night.

The alley bustled with the parents of students from both Biyong and Ming Academies, all crowding the gates with dirty faces and bloodstained robes, ready to collect their children.

"Mom..."

"Your dad is gone..."

Sobs and cries rose on all sides. Some parents yelled, "Step aside! Step aside!" as they cut through the crowd, tossed a wooden name plaque at the gatekeeper, and whisked their child away.

Eyes falling shut, Cai Yan dozed against the pillar.

"Cai Yan?" *Come to my home,* Duan Ling wanted to say to him. "You can go on. Let me sleep a while."

All Duan Ling could do was take off his outer robe and drape it over him.

And then Li Jianhong was waiting on the other side of the fence. Bathed in the early morning light, once again wearing his coarse robes and bamboo hat, he smiled at Duan Ling.

Duan Ling rose gingerly and ran over to the fence. "Did you finish everything you had to do?"

"Why aren't you wearing your outer robe?" Li Jianhong asked. "What if you catch a cold? Come on, let's go."

"I don't have my name plaque. I have to get the chancellor to sign me out."

"I need someone's signature to pick up my own son? What kind of logic is that? Wait there," Li Jianhong huffed, about to leap the wall.

Duan Ling stopped him with a "Shh." He cast a glance behind him at Cai Yan and turned back to speak, but Li Jianhong held up a hand, signifying he understood. He waved to indicate they could talk about it once they left, so Duan Ling went to look for the chancellor to write him a note.

When he returned, he shook Cai Yan awake. Cai Yan blinked open a pair of soulless eyes, staring at Duan Ling without recognition. Duan Ling checked his forehead—still warm.

"Come home with me," Duan Ling said. "Come on."

"Huh?" Cai Yan muttered.

Duan Ling felt miserable seeing him like this, but he didn't know what to say. Eventually, Li Jianhong joined them as well. He glanced down at Cai Yan, who had closed his eyes again, lifeless. Duan Ling grabbed his hands and pulled him onto his feet, and Li Jianhong bent over, scooped Cai Yan up, and carried him home with them.

That night, they ate better than they had in weeks. After tucking Cai Yan into bed, Duan Ling went to draw water for his father's bath. He found Li Jianhong sitting naked on a stool in front of the well. With the dappled moonlight shining on his toned upper body, he brought to mind a leopard just returned from a hunt. As Duan Ling scrubbed his back and chest clean, the coppery smell of blood slowly dispersed on the wind. Li Jianhong put his hands—stained black with dried blood—into the water basin.

"Dad…" Duan Ling began, lifting the basin and pouring water over Li Jianhong's head.

"Yes, my son," Li Jianhong said. "There are some things one must do—even if it means going through hell, even if you know death is certain. Don't make his grief your own."

"Mn."

Duan Ling knelt behind Li Jianhong, turning his face, and hugged him around the waist. He rested his head on Li Jianhong's back, sighing.

"We'll be able to go back soon, I promise," Li Jianhong said.

When they climbed into bed that night, Li Jianhong pulled the blanket up over both of them.

"It would be nice if there were no more wars," Duan Ling said, staring up at the canopy overhead.

"Your fourth uncle often said the same thing. Every time I returned victorious, I'd think of it."

Duan Ling turned over, pressed himself up against Li Jianhong's arm, and fell asleep.

When Cai Yan woke the next day, his fever had broken, although he still felt weak and listless. He rolled over to get out of bed and heard Duan Ling and Li Jianhong talking in the courtyard.

"Jump like this," Li Jianhong was saying, "first from the flowerpot to the bamboo fence, then onto the wall. Go on."

Li Jianhong demonstrated, reaching the top of the wall effortlessly. But when Duan Ling tried the same move, he smacked face-first into the wall every time. Li Jianhong laughed.

"I can't jump that high!" Duan Ling cried. "I'm not you!"

Duan Ling was at the age where his voice cracked when it rose, scratchy like a duck's.

"I can't jump that high! Dad! Pull me up!" Li Jianhong mimicked.

Duan Ling wanted to be angry at his mockery, but his lips twitched in amusement. He found himself powerless to respond. Li Jianhong was grabbing Duan Ling around the ribs to give him a boost when he heard Cai Yan getting out of bed.

"Feeling better?" he called over to the boy.

Cai Yan nodded, and Li Jianhong gestured for Duan Ling to go help him. The three ate breakfast together at the table; Cai Yan was completely silent throughout. After he finished eating, he set down his chopsticks and said, "I'm sorry to have troubled you. Thank you for taking care of me; I'll be going now."

"Why don't y—" Duan Ling began.

"You're going home?" Li Jianhong cut in.

Cai Yan nodded. "I have to collect my brother's body and check on the house. I can't leave it empty."

Li Jianhong nodded, casting a sidelong look at Duan Ling. Remembering his father's words from that morning, Duan Ling said, "Well—take care of yourself. I'll drop by to check on you in a few days."

"Thanks."

Cai Yan sank into a deep bow. Duan Ling hurriedly stood to return the bow, but Cai Yan was already on his feet, speeding through the corridor to return home. He closed the main gate behind him on his way out.

28

There are some things *one must do, even if it means going through hell, even if you know death is certain.*

But couldn't Cai Wen have done something else?

Li Jianhong's answer would have been: *No. He had no other choice.*

Cai Ye—Cai Yan and Cai Wen's father—had once been a great scholar of the Central Plains. When the emperor of Liao had taken Shangjing, Cai Ye had surrendered with the city and later became one of the main contributors in forming the government of Liao's Southern Administration. However, he was soon caught up in a revenge plot concocted by spies of Southern Chen and executed on false charges by the emperor of Liao. His death left his sons, the two brothers, with only each other to rely on, as there weren't many left in the Cai clan in the south. When Yelü Dashi later redressed the injustice done to Cai Ye, the problem of where to put his sons became a critical one.

Everyone dreaded allowing Cai Ye's sons entry into the Southern Administration—but the Han clan and Empress Dowager Xiao had a firm grip on the Northern Administration and would never let Yelü Dashi introduce his own people. Thus the only suitable solution was to place Cai Wen in a military post. Perhaps he could become a general—but that wouldn't do either, as he had a younger brother at home to care for. And so Cai Wen was assigned the position of captain of Shangjing's city guard and given a round of encouragement.

The Cai clan had no military background and did not raise their sons to shoot or ride. Cai Wen was forced to devote his blood, sweat, and tears to his physical training—but since he'd missed the critical years of childhood where his bones and muscles were still malleable, he could never become a great warrior. In times of peace, this presented no issue, but as soon as the country was thrown into crisis, the outcome was inevitable. When developing their plan of action, Li Jianhong had confirmed Cai Wen's role over and over with Yelü Dashi, but Yelü Dashi's decision was this: Though Cai Wen's capabilities as a warrior might fall short, as a soldier, he was loyal to the core, and would defend Shangjing with his life.

And so his life he gave—a life of one common-born son in exchange for proof of the Cai clan's unwavering loyalty to Yelü Dashi and Cai Yan's shining future prospects.

"This too will pass," Li Jianhong told his son. "There are some things you must do, even if it means certain death. That's what it means to be a man."

After the chaos of war, Shangjing gradually returned to normal. Biyong Academy, which had burned during the siege, was busy organizing and salvaging their collection of books and granted its students the interim time off. Three days later, Chancellor Tang appointed a new location for the students to attend daytime classes. At night, they would continue to return to their family homes.

The sight of Cai Yan weighed on Duan Ling's heart, but he remembered his father's lesson: As Cai Yan didn't bring up his brother's death, Duan Ling didn't ask, and they carried on as usual. Cai Yan became more reserved, seldom speaking to his peers—and of the few words he spared for Duan Ling, most were about school. Once classes concluded, he would grab his bag and head straight home.

Duan Ling attended school during the morning and learned martial arts from Li Jianhong at home in the afternoon. He had begun to feel a pressing sense of urgency and cursed himself for wasting so much time in the past.

When would he reach his father's level? He dwelled often on this question but never asked it aloud. Instead he changed it to: "When will I become as good as Lang Junxia?"

"Out of all the people in the world," Li Jianhong said, polishing Duan Ling's sword, "there are only four great assassins. You're not going to be an assassin, so why do you want to be like him?"

His question rendered Duan Ling speechless.

"Every little bit you learn matters," Li Jianhong continued. "But to be a good martial artist, you mustn't only learn technique—you must also practice diligently. A master can only guide the way. The rest is up to you."

Duan Ling murmured his acknowledgment.

Over the course of a few months, he became significantly more confident. Perhaps he was far from matching the skill of absurd outliers like Lang Junxia or Wu Du, but after learning how to summon his inner force, he could finally leap onto the wall, though not with ease.

Winter came again, and Duan Ling counted down the days. If Yelü Dashi kept his word, it would soon be time for Li Jianhong to leave—but Duan Ling didn't ask, and Li Jianhong didn't mention it. When the first snow fell late in the season, covering Shangjing in a blanket of white, the director of studies sent out letters announcing that Biyong Academy would be repaired by spring, and all would be as it was before. At the start of the third month, they would return to school.

That day, after Li Jianhong finished teaching him, Duan Ling performed the closing form. Nearly nine months had passed since his martial arts lessons began, yet Duan Ling had only learned the one sword style. While he was practicing with single-minded focus in the courtyard, a visitor arrived.

"He's defected," Duan Ling heard from the entrance. He recognized Xunchun's voice.

When Duan Ling poked his head into the corridor, Li Jianhong pointed him back to the courtyard—*Keep practicing; don't stick your nose where it doesn't belong.*

Li Jianhong replied, "I told him before he left that he could go undercover if necessary."

Xunchun did not reply. Though she was hidden from Duan Ling by the stone spirit screen, she cast a shadow across the snow.

"I'll be leaving everything here to you for the next few years. Your revenge will come in due time," Li Jianhong said. After a pause, he continued, "But that time is not now."

Xunchun sighed.

"Unless I come in person, don't let anyone take him away."

"Understood," Xunchun said.

In the snowy courtyard, Duan Ling heard a rustling as if Xunchun was rummaging through her robes. "This is the letter my master gave me for my shidi on the day he and I went our separate ways. It has passed from one hand to another for eleven years, and still, in the end, it has not reached him."

"How old is he now?" Li Jianhong asked casually.

"Sixteen when he made a name for himself. Nineteen when he pledged service to Zhao Kui. If he ever finds his way back onto the right path, please spare him, Your Highness."

"Putting aside whether he has lost his way, capable men choose the right leader to serve," Li Jianhong said with no change in tone.

"Every man has his own destiny. Kill or be killed—that is simply the way of it. He is a man of sentiment, unlike Lang Junxia. If he pledges his allegiance to me, I shall make great use of him. You may go."

Xunchun curtsied and saw herself out.

Li Jianhong turned back to the courtyard. Duan Ling looked over at the same time with the sword in his hands, and they regarded each other in silence.

"I have to go," Li Jianhong said at last.

"For how long?" Duan Ling asked.

"A year. Two, at most."

"Oh."

Duan Ling returned to his practice, and Li Jianhong walked down the corridor into the main hall. Duan Ling had known this day would come, so he felt no shock, only unhappiness. After moving through his forms a few more times, he looked back and found Li Jianhong watching him silently from the center of the main hall.

Snowflakes drifted between father and son, and it was as if time drifted with them.

Li Jianhong laughed. "You may not be the best emperor in history, but you will at the very least be the best-looking one."

Duan Ling laughed too, embarrassed. Now that he had begun to gain his adult height, he exhibited the might inherited from Li Jianhong in every move, though without the same flashiness. The main hall and the outer courtyard might as well have been split by a mirror, each a reflection of the other—on one side Duan Ling, still tinged with the freshness of youth, and on the other, Li Jianhong with the solid composure of a grown man.

"I want to go with you," Duan Ling blurted out before he could stop himself. "But I know I'll just be a burden. I really…"

"Stop. Say no more." Li Jianhong waved his hand. "Another word from you, and your dad won't be able to go. I never wanted to leave to begin with."

At some point, Duan Ling had become too self-conscious to hug Li Jianhong. Over the past year he'd matured so much—more than he had in all the time before—and it was all thanks to being around his father. From him, Duan Ling had learned how to think and act as an adult would.

This winter had been the coldest in Shangjing in a decade, and two feet of snow piled up in the courtyard and blocked their front gates. That night, after lighting the stove in the main hall, Li Jianhong began to teach Duan Ling about the court officials, politics, and other inner workings of Southern Chen. While Southern Chen's government followed the system of the Three Departments and Six Ministries, real power in the court currently lay in the hands of its two greatest civil and military officials: The first, Zhao Kui, was a meritorious general celebrated for his heroic deeds in the Battle of Huai River. When the Chen army had been routed, it was General Zhao who had escorted the imperial Li clan safely to Xichuan. The second, Mu Kuangda, was born to Jingchuan gentry and had achieved the top score in the imperial examination. After taking office, he'd stabilized the government of Southern Chen and eventually became its central pillar.

After the imperial capital moved to Xichuan, however, the emperor's health had begun to decline. He had refused to name a crown prince; instead the fourth prince, Li Yanqiu, had aided his father in court affairs while the third prince, Li Jianhong, had defended the borders. By all rights, the title of crown prince ought to have been bestowed on the eldest son, and so, as the eldest surviving prince, Li Jianhong should have succeeded his father as emperor. Initially, Li Jianhong had strong ties to the military, and Zhao Kui had been his staunchest supporter—but eventually, Zhao Kui withdrew his backing.

"Why?" Duan Ling asked.

"My 'excessive belligerence,' and 'insatiable greed for glory,'" Li Jianhong said. "The court feared that if I became emperor, I would exhaust our army with endless military expeditions and bring the empire to ruin. But look at things now: The Liao Empire is no longer our greatest enemy; they have been part of the Central Plains for too long. The Khitan are no different from the Han now—but there is a wolf further north looking with hunger at the south. We must set aside our blood feud and ally with Liao to fight Yuan. If we continue to clash, we will both fall to the Borjigins, and they are as vicious as jackals. Every city they conquer, they bathe in blood."

Li Jianhong also taught him the history and structure of the Liao Empire. After establishing a foothold in the Central Plains, the Liao Empire had divided itself into the Northern and Southern Administrations. The Southern Administration was made up of mostly Han ministers, whereas the Northern Administration consisted of all Khitan ministers, with one Han exception.

The Northern Administration was further divided into the Northern and Southern Courts. Both had military authority and wielded authority over the governance of the Liao Empire. This division of power had given rise to two opposing pillars of the state. In the Southern Court there was Grand Preceptor Han Weiyong, the only minister of Han ethnicity, who enjoyed the backing of Empress Dowager Xiao—and in the Northern Court, there was the Great Prince, Yelü Dashi.

Years ago, Han Weiyong's son, Han Jieli, had arrived in Shangjing to attend Ming Academy and serve as a hostage. But when he graduated, the boy, wary of Yelü Dashi, found an immediate excuse to leave the city.

"Yelü Dashi was the tiger of the north in his youth," Li Jianhong said. "But he succumbed to a life of comfort as he aged, letting indulgence in wine and women weaken him. When I fought with him outside the city, the man was shot off his horse. Any fool can see what will become of the Liao Empire with leaders like this."

"Is the wine in Qionghua House…" Duan Ling still remembered Lang Junxia refusing to let him drink when he first arrived in Shangjing.

"The wine is not fatally poisoned," Li Jianhong told him. "But over time, it will waste you away. Qionghua House's ultimate target was never Yelü Dashi, but Han Weiyong and the former emperor of Liao. It's too bad old man Yelü Longxu died before they could get to him. Their little emperor, Yelü Zongzhen, is kept on a tight leash by Empress Dowager Xiao and hasn't come to Shangjing in many years. He won't be found anywhere near Qionghua House, let alone come often enough to give them a chance."

Li Jianhong paused briefly. "Borjigin Batu, Yelü Zongzhen, Cai Yan, Helian Bo, Han Jieli—all of them might be your enemies someday."

Duan Ling fell into a long silence.

"Your dad'll take care of as many of them as I can," Li Jianhong continued. "And when I go back to the south, I will not take the throne myself. Your grandfather is dying and can no longer manage the affairs of the court. I will force him to pass the throne instead to your fourth uncle, and in turn, your fourth uncle will declare you crown prince. No one else is suitable to hold this title."

"But what about you?" Duan Ling asked.

"Your dad can't be emperor, but I'll still have to break your fourth uncle free from Mu Kuangda and Zhao Kui's control."

"Is my fourth uncle doing all right?"

"He's a chronically ill medicine jar with no power over the ministers. Mu Kuangda may have the court and the populace under his thumb, but he'll be easy enough to defeat. The real nuisance is Zhao Kui, who holds the military."

"Why?" Duan Ling asked. "I figured Mu Kuangda would be harder to defeat."

"Because Mu Kuangda is smart," said Li Jianhong. "He's a member of the literati; he doesn't have the gall to overthrow the dynasty and declare himself emperor. He merely has to pull the strings behind your fourth uncle and he can get whatever he wants; he can be an emperor in the shadows. But Zhao Kui is different—the general desires the title for himself."

"Because he's a warrior." Duan Ling understood now.

Li Jianhong nodded. "The seed of treason was buried in his heart after the Battle of Huai River. Since then, he's bestowed generous gifts upon his subordinates, recruited soldiers, bought horses, and raised private armies—all for the sake of declaring himself emperor. As long as I live, he cannot be at ease. Zhao Kui is a formidable opponent."

It was the first time Duan Ling heard his father refer to anyone as such. From their conversation, he received the broadest sense of how difficult an opponent Zhao Kui would be; only Li Jianhong understood the gritty details. At times like these, Duan Ling wished he could grow up faster and be of more help—yet at the same time, he knew even if he spent his whole life studying the art of war, he would never leave his father's shadow.

The words Lang Junxia had said, as well as the words he'd left unsaid, suddenly became clear: *What's the use of learning how to fight? You'll never surpass your father. To achieve great deeds and improve the lives of people, you must study.*

29

Shangjing during winter was a frozen city. Duan Ling welcomed his fourteenth year by lighting a string of red firecrackers, and on the eve of the new year, he and Li Jianhong sat cross-legged facing one another.

"This is our first New Year's Eve together," Li Jianhong said, smiling as he poured wine for Duan Ling. "Have a little bit. Remember, you can drink wine, but never too much."

"Dad, let me toast you." Duan Ling had outgrown his crisp childhood voice. "To a swift victory."

As they drank together, Li Jianhong regarded Duan Ling's face in the lamplight. "You've grown up."

Duan Ling emptied his cup and released a long sigh. *Actually, I don't want to grow up at all,* he thought. But instead he asked, "Isn't that a good thing?"

"Yes," Li Jianhong said. "I like you all grown up like this."

Duan Ling laughed. Though his father always said as much, he knew Li Jianhong hid his true feelings in his heart. Things had changed between them ever since Li Jianhong had begun teaching him the sword. They no longer shared the same bed when Duan Ling came home from Biyong Academy—Duan Ling still slept in the bed, but Li Jianhong had moved to a spot on the floor in the outer room.

That night, however, Duan Ling felt hot and sleepless after the wine he'd drunk. Li Jianhong padded over and lay on the bed beside him, and Duan Ling shifted toward the wall to make space.

"Son," Li Jianhong said. "I'll be leaving tomorrow."

Duan Ling didn't know what to say. He turned over and stared silently at the wall.

Li Jianhong reached out and rolled Duan Ling back to face him. As expected, Duan Ling's eyes were red-rimmed.

"What, are you embarrassed?" his father teased with a smile.

Duan Ling didn't speak. Over the year he'd trained in martial arts, he'd developed and grown into his own sturdy physique. But now, held in Li Jianhong's arms, he felt like he'd gone back to being the same small boy he was when they first met. Li Jianhong gazed into his eyes and hooked two fingers around the red string at his neck, tugging the jade arc out of his sleeping robes.

"I failed you and your mother."

Duan Ling looked up into Li Jianhong's eyes—eyes like the starry sky on a pitch-black night.

"The biggest regret of my life is not searching for the two of you earlier," Li Jianhong said.

"That's all in the past—"

"No," Li Jianhong interrupted, shaking his head. "If I don't say this now, I'll never be at ease. I was young and hotheaded. I thought Xiaowan didn't know what was good for her, leaving like that. I assumed she'd come back someday. Almost ten years went by, and I never once thought she had passed on."

"Why did she leave?" Duan Ling asked.

"Your grandfather wouldn't agree to our marriage," Li Jianhong said. "She was a commoner, while I was a prince defending the borders of the empire. She waited and waited for me to marry her, but I never did. The ministers wanted me to marry Mu Kuangda's younger sister; now she's the fourth prince's consort."

"Then…what happened?"

"Lang Junxia committed a crime. I intended to execute him according to military law," Li Jianhong continued, "but she pleaded for mercy on his behalf. She thought the crime shouldn't cost him his life. We fought over it all night, and she left at dawn. I ordered Lang Junxia to stop her, and he chased after her with a sword. Later, he told me she threatened him right back. She said if I wanted her to return, I'd have to settle for her dead body. How stubborn she was…" He clicked his tongue and shook his head, defeated. "Your dad also had a fiery temper. I thought maybe if she went back to the south, she'd marry someone there, and so I let it go. For years I never looked for her—not until Zhao Kui used the court to strip me of my military command. After fleeing north all the way from Jiangjun Ridge, I finally ordered Lang Junxia to find her. I never imagined she'd already passed," Li Jianhong said. "Or that she'd left me you."

"Do you regret it?" Duan Ling asked.

"Of course I do," Li Jianhong said. "I think often that, one day, I'd like to confer her the proper title of princess consort—but what good is a title to the dead?"

Duan Ling fiddled with the matching jade arc around Li Jianhong's neck, head resting on his arm. Li Jianhong heaved a long sigh. "Forgive me, Ruo-er,"[19] he pleaded. "Say, 'I don't hate you, Dad.' I'll take your words as your mother's too."

"No."

Li Jianhong froze and looked down at his son in his arms.

"You owe us much more." Duan Ling smiled. "You have to stay alive and well until you're very, very old. Then ask us again."

---

19   An affectionate diminutive suffix added to names, literally "son" or "child."

The corners of Li Jianhong's lips lifted. "All right," he said. "I promise."

"Seal it with a clap."

Li Jianhong hugged him with one hand, and with the other, clapped his son's palm three times.

Overnight, the biggest snowstorm yet descended upon Shangjing. Snowflakes swirled like goose feathers through the sky.

When Duan Ling opened his eyes in the morning light the next day, Li Jianhong was gone.

"Dad!" He shot out of bed and searched every corner of the house. His school supplies were there and ready; only Li Jianhong was gone, having left Duan Ling's sword atop his pack.

Today was the first day they moved back to the school dorms, and Biyong Academy was a hive of activity. The buildings had been fully repaired from the fire damage, and they even received new wooden name plaques. Duan Ling found his way to the dormitory with ease, greeted his peers, and made his own bed.

"Where's your dad?" Cai Yan asked, also making his bed by himself.

"He left on a trip."

"When will he be back?"

"In a year or so," said Duan Ling.

He and Cai Yan sat on their respective beds and stared at each other in silence. When Cai Yan smiled, Duan Ling smiled back, as if they shared an unspoken understanding.

On the third day of the first month, Mu Kuangda, Changliu-jun, Wu Du, Lang Junxia, and Mu Kuangda's chief strategist gathered around the map hanging on the wall in Zhao Kui's study in Xichuan.

"Li Jianhong is marching south with an army of ten thousand Liao soldiers," Zhao Kui said. "He is setting out on the Shangjing road and traversing through Boshan, Qixue Spring, and Jiangjun Ridge; then he'll take the west road to Xichuan. It's a path full of natural defenses."

"What is his justification for this?" Mu Kuangda asked.

"To cleanse the court, he says," said Zhao Kui.

"His Highness the fourth prince will no doubt hear of this."

"Prime Minister, Grand General," said the strategist, a scholarly man named Chang Pin, with utmost courtesy. "We should accuse him of defecting to the enemy; the fourth prince will have to move against him."

Mu Kuangda nodded. "Indeed."

"A decree must be issued to deploy troops, as was done four years ago when Li Jianhong fled," Zhao Kui added. "Right now, all his old subordinates are stationed along the west road; they'll surrender to him without a fight."

"Then we shall proceed with the decree." Mu Kuangda stood. "This matter cannot be delayed. I will go to the imperial palace the instant I leave here to issue a letter of censure in the name of His Majesty, announcing Li Jianhong's crimes of defection and rebellion and listing the major charges against him. I shall then issue the decree to deploy troops—but if we hope to intercept him, it may already be too late."

"I have other methods of stopping him," Zhao Kui said with confidence. Mu Kuangda's eyes narrowed slightly, but Zhao Kui cut him off before he could inquire. "Prime Minister, please see to the decree."

Mu Kuangda led his civil and military advisors from the general's manor and onto a horse-drawn carriage awaiting them at the gates.

Changliu-jun took the reins, while the prime minister and the scholar sat within.

"Chang Pin," Mu Kuangda said, leaning back in his seat.

"Yes, Your Excellency," Chang Pin said politely. "Wuluohou Mu must have found Li Jianhong's weakness."

"What weakness could he have?" Mu Kuangda mumbled.

Chang Pin paused in thought, then continued: "Six years ago, when Wu Du and the shadow squad rushed to Shangjing, the squad leader died there. We know Li Jianhong was elsewhere at the time, so what else could have motivated Wuluohou Mu to fight Wu Du out in the open? This humble subordinate thought then that the only possible reason was that Li Jianhong's wife and son were in Shangjing."

"Yes," Mu Kuangda agreed. "That makes sense. If we have his wife and child, we can slow him down—but not for long, I'm afraid."

"Unfortunately, Zhao Kui does not merely want to slow his progress. He wants him dead."

"Then he really is out of his mind," Mu Kuangda laughed.

"Zhao Kui approaches everything like a general. He would never make a move without the next one already planned. If Li Jianhong's wife and son are killed, he will be shaken; it will be easier to lure him into a trap and kill him. If Wuluohou Mu succeeds in this endeavor, Zhao Kui need not even meet Li Jianhong on the field. He can simply send Li Jianhong their heads, and victory will be within Zhao Kui's grasp."

"I gather their heads would be much more useful than His Highness the fourth prince's, in this respect." Mu Kuangda chuckled heartily, and Chang Pin laughed along. "It's a difficult task, however..." he reflected.

The carriage rolled to a stop. Changliu-jun stepped down, and Mu Kuangda entered the imperial palace.

Li Yanqiu, the fourth prince, was standing under the eaves of the veranda with his princess consort. As Mu Kuangda approached, the prime minister brought his hands together in a courteous bow.

Princess Consort Mu Jinzhi turned to her attendants. "You are dismissed."

Mu Kuangda smiled at her, waiting on the veranda with hands behind his back. Mu Jinzhi watched him for a moment, but when he stayed silent, she also turned and left. Li Yanqiu eyed him, and Mu Kuangda brought his hands together in another bow.

"Your Highness."

Li Yanqiu cast a glance at Changliu-jun behind him. "You have not entered the palace in some time, Prime Minister Mu."

"An urgent military situation has arisen, so I came in person to report to His Majesty."

"His Majesty has taken his medicine and retired for the evening," Li Yanqiu said. "But you may speak of the matter with me."

"The third prince has borrowed ten thousand of Yelü Dashi's Khitan soldiers to march south in the name of cleansing the court. He is taking the west road, and will reach Xichuan within three months."

"I knew my third brother was still alive," Li Yanqiu said evenly.

Mu Kuangda said nothing. He waited for Li Yanqiu to say the critical words. Yet, after a long silence, all Li Yanqiu offered was: "I miss him."

With that, he turned and left.

Only then did Mu Jinzhi show herself, stepping out from behind a pillar. She stared at her brother.

"I've always been a tactful person," Mu Kuangda said with a small smile. He took out a memorial to the throne and passed it to her, tacitly leaving the task in her hands.

Lamplight shone through the gaps of the latticed window and glittered on the falling winter raindrops. Within the fourth prince's study, Mu Jinzhi unrolled the golden imperial brocade of the memorial on the jade table, dipped a brush in ink, and placed it in Li Yanqiu's hand.

Mu Kuangda waited outside with his hands behind his back. A moment later, there was a loud clatter from within. Li Yanqiu had swept the brush holder and ink onto the floor.

Mu Jinzhi retrieved the imperial decree from the desk and handed it to Mu Kuangda.

Mu Kuangda strode out of the palace, smiling faintly.

On the fifteenth day of the first month, the imperial decree reached Yubi Pass, and Southern Chen's army began to march.

On the first day of the second month, Li Jianhong arrived at the Great Wall, whereupon he disappeared into the desert like a dust storm. On the tenth day of the second month, as Yulin, Yudai, and other cities near the Wall braced for battle, Li Jianhong suddenly emerged four hundred li to the east, at Juyong Pass. He deployed his vanguard for a nighttime ambush, then sent his main forces after them to successfully take the pass. But instead of forging ahead, Li Jianhong issued a Due Diligence Order—a formal call to rescue the emperor—in hopes of amassing more troops. Every soldier who joined his army before he took Xichuan, he announced, would be forgiven for their past transgressions.

On the first day of the third month, Southern Chen's Jiang, Yang, Jiao, and Jing Prefectures were thrown into upheaval. Simultaneously,

CHAPTER TWENTY-NINE

the court issued an imperial decree stamped with the imperial jade seal listing the major charges against Li Jianhong.

Li Jianhong set up camp at Juyong Pass and waited with immense patience for the first and hardest battle he would face: striking when his enemy's weary troops converged on the pass from the east and west roads.

Back in Shangjing, Duan Ling held fast to his routine even in Li Jianhong's absence. He went to school during the day and practiced his sword forms with Cai Yan in the evening.

An enormous sandstorm swept over the city in the early days of spring, darkening the sky. The time had once again come for the students to make their monthly trip home. Duan Ling gathered up his belongings alone. As he left Biyong Academy, he spotted a girl speaking with Cai Yan in the alleyway.

When she cast him a glance, he saw that it was Ding Zhi. It had been a while since Duan Ling had last seen her. He remembered she'd been involved with Cai Wen—it made sense that she would look after his younger brother, who now had no one to rely on. Duan Ling greeted her as he passed, and Ding Zhi slipped him a blank envelope. He knew at once that it must be a letter from Li Jianhong and rushed home to scrape off the wax.

The letter was written in neat, squared-off strokes like those of a woodblock print instead of Li Jianhong's usual fluid style—a precaution in case it fell into the wrong hands. It bore no greeting and no signature.

I turn restlessly in bed, kept from sleep by my thoughts. I am two-tenths of the way through my journey. Dust and sand stretch for miles in the northlands. All I can think of in this vast, mortal world is the vibrant, colorful garden in your little corner of it.

Nothing in this life would please me more than to guide you like a compass, charting your path hand in hand with the Guardian of the Realm.
Burn this letter.

But Duan Ling couldn't bear to burn it. He read the letter over and over, tucked it under his bed, then rose in the middle of the night just to read it again, eyes lingering on every word. When he finally resigned himself to burning it, he felt as if a knife twisted in his heart.

30

On the seventeenth day of the third month, Li Jianhong emerged from Juyong Pass, defeating Southern Chen's southwest army on the open plain. 3,300 soldiers fell under his army's blades, while the remaining 16,700 were absorbed into his own troops. He continued at a rapid march south to Hangu Pass, seizing six cities along the way.

"Li Jianhong has come to pay his respects," Li Jianhong announced from his saddle. "Is Zhao Kui here?"

The garrison immediately balked.

"What's there to be scared of?!" yelled a guard from Hangu Pass. "Do your duty and guard the pass! It's not like he can grow wings and fly over it!"

Li Jianhong waited for a response. When none came, he called out again, "Did he not come? Then I shall wait here for him to arrive!"

News of his 26,000 soldiers setting up camp outside the pass spread to every corner of the south, and unease coursed through each region in its wake. Everyone had their eyes on Jiang Prefecture, waiting to see which side it chose. However, Jiang Prefecture's governor, Shao De, refused to engage in any combat whatsoever.

For a month, the imperial court sent more and more troops. By the fifteenth day of the fourth month, the defensive forces arrayed at Hangu Pass numbered 215,000.

Li Jianhong appeared to be waiting for an opportunity.

Zhao Kui waited too, more patient still. Though few knew it, at that moment, he was already inside a tent at Hangu Pass.

"If we send 200,000 soldiers, we'll trample him flat," Wu Du said.

"The time is not right," replied Zhao Kui.

"I don't understand," Wu Du said, staring at the map hung up on the tent wall.

"There is much you don't understand. Sometimes, you have to approach a problem from a different angle."

Wu Du fell silent, thinking.

"You don't understand why Wuluohou Mu defected to us," Zhao Kui guessed.

"Yes, he—"

"This is far from the first time he's switched allegiances," Zhao Kui reminded him.

Wu Du quieted again.

"Hasn't it occurred to you that there must be a reason he betrayed Li Jianhong? That old lady can only be part of it. There must be more—because if Li Jianhong learned of this, he would cut off Wuluohou Mu's head."

Wu Du narrowed his eyes.

"Report! Report from Jiang Prefectural City!" A messenger burst into the tent. "General Xie You has defected!"

Leaving 10,000 Khitan soldiers at Hangu Pass as an impressive decoy, Li Jianhong had arrived at the Yangtze River that very night and led his troops silently along the river toward

Jiang Prefectural City. As Jiang Prefectural City hesitated, Li Jianhong had already marched his army right up to the foot of the walls.

Jiang Prefecture was renowned for its Black-Plated Army, which existed solely to uphold the authority of the imperial family. Brandishing the Guardian, Li Jianhong reined his horse to a halt before the Yangtze River and looked out at an enemy force 50,000 strong.

"I face you with this sword in my hand and my brothers-in-arms of the Chen Empire behind me," he announced. "There are those of you in this world who do not bow down to power or play petty games of politics, but fight only for the sake of the dynasty!" Li Jianhong swept his gaze over the army. "Zhao Kui is a traitor to the throne! If you are unwilling to add your forces to my cause, let me fall today and dye the river red with my blood. No need for any more words. We fight!"

As the armored soldiers before him raised their shields, a voice boomed from the rear, "Wait!"

"Your Highness," a mighty soldier said, emerging from the lines on a black horse. "Please come into the city and have a cup of tea from Mount Yuheng."

Li Jianhong pushed up his tiger helm to reveal his handsome face. "Xie You, have you been well?" he asked, locking eyes with the warrior. "My father is not long for this world, and his treacherous court ministers have forced my fourth brother to issue an imperial edict condemning me. So—will you join me?"

"Passion still burns in my breast," Xie You said. "'The Golden Age, the Beautiful Land'—whether that holds true, we will only see in time. Your Highness, let us speak within the city."

The Black-Plated Army drew apart, clearing a straight path into the city. That very day, Jiang Prefectural City announced its surrender to Li Jianhong.

On the fifth day of the fifth month, the day of the Duanwu Festival, the peach blossoms were beginning to put out their lush blooms in Shangjing, and Duan Ling returned home to a second letter.

> *Dark blue rivers rush through Jiang Prefecture. A sea of clouds rolls over Mount Yuheng; the north is a vast stretch seen from its summit. "We gaze at the moon for we cannot see each other. Would that I could follow the moonbeams to look upon your face."*[20] *I'm borrowing your future personal guards. Quite handy. Already captured.*
> *Burn this letter.*

News traveled quickly from the south: Li Jianhong had seized twelve cities in rapid succession. Jiang Prefectural City surrendered unconditionally along with the commander of its Black-Plated Army, Xie You, and Li Jianhong marched onward toward Jianmen Pass.

Duan Ling now understood the term "personal guards" in a new way: The Jiang Prefectural army existed solely to safeguard the heirs of the imperial family and remained loyal only to the dynastic line even after centuries of restructuring, splitting, and reforming again. Even if another member of the imperial family presented them with the tiger tally that represented imperial authorization to deploy troops, this alone could not move them. Only an heir in the

---

20 Lines from "The Moon over the River on a Spring Night" by Tang Poet Zhang Ruoxu.

direct line of succession could command them with the dynasty's sacred token.

Li Jianhong had successfully captured Jiang Prefectural City, and with 50,000 soldiers added to his host, he marched to face the last natural stronghold before Xichuan. The heads Zhao Kui had demanded never came—and at this point, even if they did, they would be of little use. Were Zhao Kui to stubbornly keep his troops at Hangu Pass, Li Jianhong would make off with everything to the south. Zhao Kui's only option was to direct his army southward and attempt to meet Li Jianhong head-on.

"Do you know why Zhao Kui has moved the capital again and again? Why he brought my father to Xichuan, instead of declaring Jiang Prefectural City the capital?" Li Jianhong asked Xie You as he reined his mount to a halt in front of Jianmen Pass, the final barrier between their army and Xichuan.

Xie You was silent. Zhao Kui had obviously moved the capital away from Jiang Prefectural City to avoid interference from the Black-Plated Army—how else could he stage a coup? Thus there was an unspoken accusation beneath Li Jianhong's question: *Why didn't you do something about him sooner?*

Li Jianhong stuck a foot out and kicked at him. "Hey, say something."

"I'm no good at speaking, only killing," Xie You said. "It's been too long since I killed a man."

"We can't fight them with direct force. We have to outsmart them," Li Jianhong muttered, looking out over the pass.

Zhao Kui's army had arrived before them and was using the natural fortification of the pass to mount a strong defense. The general himself, however, was nowhere to be seen.

"The longer we stall, the worse things will be for us," Xie You said. "And the more the situation may change."

"We can't cross here," Li Jianhong grumbled, shaking his head. "We'll have to think of another way. There are many, many days ahead of us. We can't throw the lives of the Black-Plated Army away here, now, for nothing, and I don't want a pointless massacre—if only to accumulate a bit of virtue for Southern Chen."

Xie You cast him a glance. "That isn't like you."

"I have a son now," Li Jianhong said.

"Understood. We'll retreat for the moment."

The Black-Plated Army and Li Jianhong's northwest army drew back northward, setting up a perimeter twenty li from Jianmen Pass.

With that, the south was in a deadlock, and the age-old saying—"Jianmen, the world's most impregnable pass"—proved to be true. Moving the imperial family to Xichuan had been a stellar play by Zhao Kui: Jianmen Pass was easy to defend and hard to attack. If one wished to reach Xichuan from the north, there were only two options: Hanzhong Road or Jianmen Pass. So long as Zhao Kui secured both, no army could touch the capital.

Beneath Jianmen Pass were rushing rapids, while the pass itself cut through steep and lofty mountains. Zhao Kui had set up no shortage of traps on both sides. If Li Jianhong were to throw his entire force at him with no regard for casualties, his chances of victory were less than a third. While Zhao Kui could comfortably continue lying in wait, Li Jianhong faced dangers on all sides.

The major powers all had their eyes on this battle—the outcome of which would determine the power dynamics of the Han, Khitan, Tangut, and Mongol peoples for the next few years. If Jianmen Pass held and Li Jianhong's army was successfully barred from Xichuan, the ensuing civil war would split the Chen Empire along an east-west line, with the west under Zhao Kui's control and the east under Li Jianhong's. Southern Chen, broken into pieces by internal strife, would be vulnerable to invasion from a greater power.

"What if Li Jianhong can't take Jianmen Pass?" one student wondered aloud.

"Then the Chen Empire is done for," another student from a foreign tribe sighed in sympathy. "How could the Liao Empire watch them splinter into two and not strike?"

"With the Mongols watching us from the north like tigers eyeing prey, there's no question that the Southern Court will march south and conquer Jiangnan," another student added. "Li Jianhong has lost the support of the court in Xichuan. The Black-Plated Army only exists to protect the imperial heirs; they never go north of Yubi Pass, much less march out on foreign campaigns or fight drawn-out wars. When the Liao Empire marches south again, it'll spell the end of the Chen Empire."

The boys were practicing archery on Biyong Academy's drill grounds. In the aftermath of the Mongol army's siege of Shangjing, the frequency of their martial arts lessons had increased significantly. No one wanted to be left helpless again, and thus the students began taking their riding and shooting lessons much more seriously.

Duan Ling listened to the boys debating next to him in silence.

"If the Chen Empire splits," another boy said, "Li Jianhong will surely become the scourge of the Han people."

The Liao Empire was wary of their Yuan neighbor to the north, who in recent years had fixed a hungry eye upon them. As a result, Liao in turn watched for opportunities to expand southward. If the south were to fall into true chaos, the Yelü imperial clan's first order of business would be to launch their own campaign: first to annex the southern half of the Central Plains, the easternmost lands around the Yangtze River, and then—once they achieved a solid foothold there—to slowly conquer Jing Prefecture and then Xichuan in the west, all the way up to the Great Wall in the north as a defense against Yuan.

Li Jianhong watched Xichuan, the Liao Empire watched the south, and Yuan watched the north—including Shangjing. The three powers were like the mantis stalking the cicada, unaware of the oriole lying in wait behind. A massive chain of events stood to be set off by a single trigger.

The debate over events in the south continued after archery class, but Duan Ling had grown tired of listening. Over the past few days, he'd first received heaps of good news, then heaps of bad news. If Li Jianhong couldn't cross Jianmen Pass and take Xichuan within the year, he would be risking an attack from behind.

"I bet Yelü Dashi foresaw this," Cai Yan said as he entered the dorms.

"Huh?" Duan Ling shook off his distraction. "Uh... Maybe... But there are also many things out of Yelü Dashi's control. I suspect Han Weiyong of the Southern Court will deploy troops and use this opportunity to conquer our land south of the Huai River."

"Our land?" Cai Yan repeated.

"The land of the Han..." Duan Ling suddenly realized that Cai Yan was, in fact, Khitan.

"When is your father coming back?" Cai Yan asked.

"I don't know. I haven't been getting news from the south. But he can protect himself."

Cai Yan nodded. The boys had just finished washing their faces when the bell in the courtyard tolled—three rings, three rings,

CHAPTER THIRTY

and one ring—calling the students to gather for an urgent matter. Cai Yan and Duan Ling rushed to line up in the front hall.

The Grand Prince of the Northern Court, Yelü Dashi, had come to Biyong Academy for an unannounced visit, and everyone was at a loss for what to do. Chancellor Tang led the students out to greet him and his retinue in the main hall. He and their former classmate, Han Jieli, trailed behind a young man dressed in garish robes.

The boy had handsome features and an aristocratic air. Duan Ling could tell at a glance that his station was even higher than Yelü Dashi's—and in the Liao Empire, only one person sat above the Great Prince: Yelü Zongzhen.

"Your Majesty."

Several members of Biyong Academy recognized him at once and hurriedly bowed in deference. Yelü Zongzhen smiled warmly back at them. "Please rise."

Yelü Zongzhen looked to be a few years older than Duan Ling, around Cai Yan's age. He walked along the front row with his hands behind his back, speaking to every student. Whatever questions he asked, the students answered dutifully.

Catching sight of prayer beads on one boy's wrist, he asked, "Does your family also practice Buddhism?"

Duan Ling immediately removed the red pouch from around his neck. There was no time to go and hide it in his room.

As he fretted, he felt Cai Yan tap the back of his hand with two fingers. Duan Ling loosened his grip, and Cai Yan slipped the pouch out of his grasp, then bent forward under the guise of fixing his robes. When he straightened back up, he slipped the red cloth pouch back into Duan Ling's hands. Duan Ling squeezed it to find that the jade arc inside had been replaced with a copper coin. He was astounded.

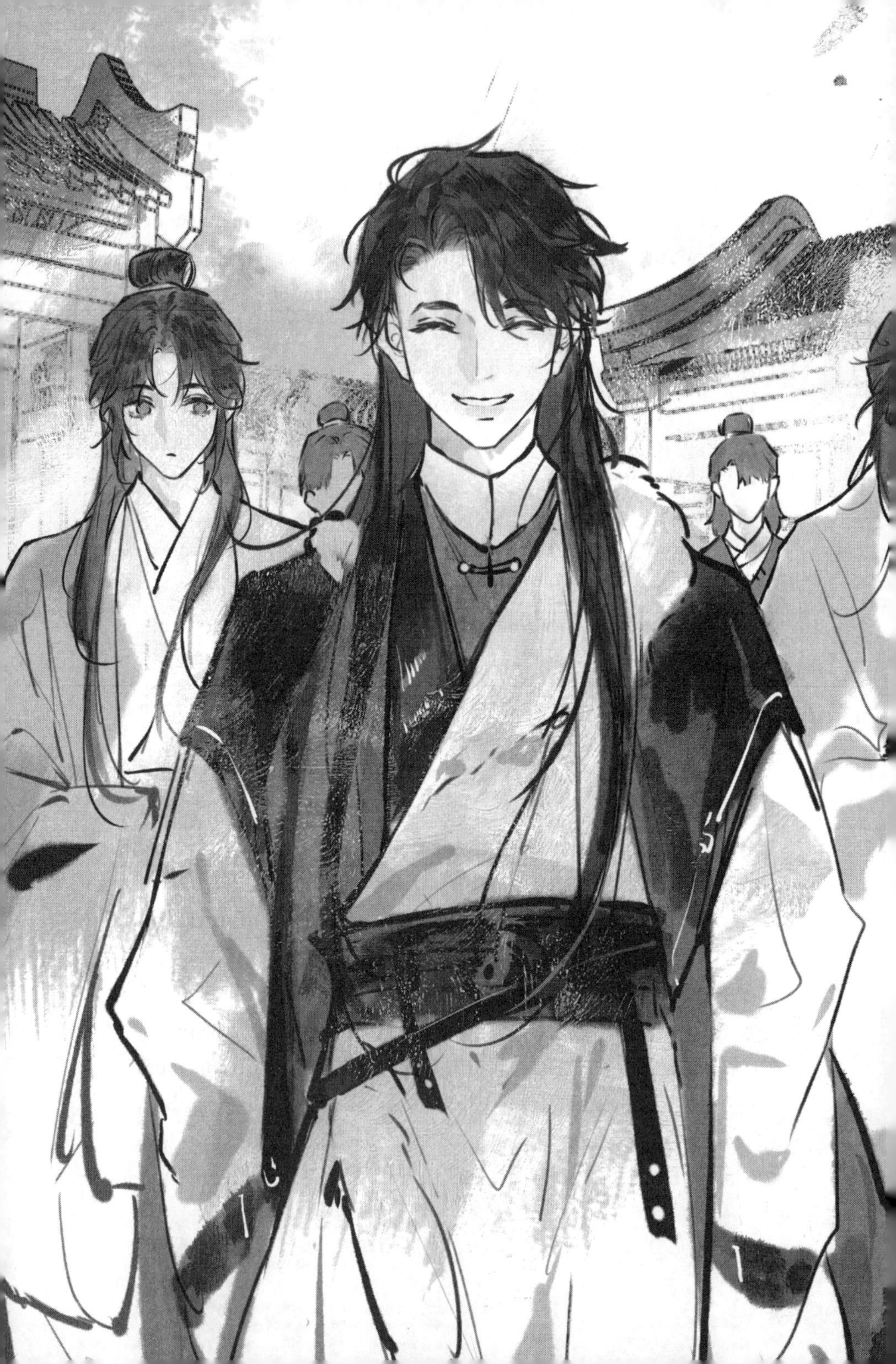

Cai Yan knew exactly what he was worried about, but he didn't reveal his secret.

On Duan Ling's turn, he took a step forward. Yelü Zongzhen studied his face, then smiled.

"I remember you. You're, uh…" Han Jieli scoured his memories for Duan Ling's name.

"Duan Ling," he supplied, also smiling.

"Yes, yes—the boy who beat up Borjigin."

"In that case, you have avenged us." Yelü Zongzhen laughed in merriment. He and Duan Ling scrutinized each other for a moment and he asked, "What does your family do?"

"We're merchants who trade between the north and the south."

Yelü Zongzhen nodded, about to ask more, when he spotted Cai Yan watching them from the back row.

"Cai Wen's younger brother," Yelü Dashi informed him.

At this, Yelü Zongzhen appeared to understand. He waved Cai Yan forward and offered him a few kind words for his brother's sacrifice on behalf of Shangjing. Duan Ling stepped aside and observed. At first he'd suspected Yelü Dashi had come looking for him, but that didn't seem to be the case. Yelü Zongzhen wasn't particularly interested in learning the family background of each student. Rather, he seemed to be searching for boys who caught his fancy. Those who were handsome were called forward to chat, and everyone else was dismissed with a nod.

Once Yelü Zongzhen had seen every student, Chancellor Tang dismissed them from the hall. They returned to their dormitories under a cloud of anxiety. As Duan Ling stepped out, he remembered the jade arc—but when he caught Cai Yan's eye, he suddenly felt like Cai Yan had read his mind.

"Swap back?" Cai Yan asked. "That's my emergency fund."

Duan Ling of course agreed, but before they could exchange items, Chancellor Tang called from the walkway: "Cai Yan, Duan Ling. You're required in the side wing."

31

Yelü Zongzhen considered a list of names while Han Jieli conversed with Yelü Dashi. A total of five students had been called to meet with them in the side wing: Helian Bo, Cai Yan, Duan Ling, a Xianbei boy from the Huyan family, and last, a boy whose family was part of the Northern Administration.

"Whatever His Majesty asks, you must answer," Chancellor Tang instructed, then gestured for Cai Yan and Duan Ling to walk with Yelü Zongzhen.

Duan Ling's heart pounded madly. He had no idea what Yelü Zongzhen intended. If he had come to choose students—what for?

Hands clasped behind his back, Yelü Zongzhen strolled along at the front, and the boys followed in his footsteps. Occasionally, he would toss out questions like, "How many years have you studied at Biyong Academy?" or "How are your grades?" He appeared to be primarily investigating their academic performance, and to Duan Ling's astonishment, the young emperor was no less learned than they. He must've also put in plenty of work studying in Zhongjing.

Aside from Helian Bo, all of the chosen students had written essays that ranked highly in Biyong Academy's entrance examinations.

"We read through your essays yesterday," Yelü Zongzhen said. "They were all outstanding. It seems you are all very learned, each with your own literary style. Very impressive."

The five boys hastily bowed and thanked him.

Yelü Zongzhen took a seat in the yard and spoke to Cai Yan and Duan Ling. "Both of you are Han. You've surely heard some of the news from the south. What are your thoughts?"

The chancellor carried over a tray with tea and pastries. Yelü Zongzhen sipped from his cup and said with a smile, "Don't concern yourselves with rules and decorum. Speak freely. We do not expect any of you to put forth groundbreaking ideas; this is simply a casual chat."

"Your Majesty," Cai Yan spoke up. "I am Khitan."

Yelü Zongzhen's hand holding the cup froze for a moment, but then his cheerful demeanor returned. "You are right, Cai-qing.[21] We were careless."

"Considering the current situation in Jiangnan," Cai Yan went on, "it would be foolish to hastily invade. Across the century that we in the Liao Empire have ruled in the Central Plains, there have been more favorable conditions for taking the south than those at present, yet we have never succeeded."

"Indeed." Yelü Zongzhen nodded.

"Right now, Li Jianhong and Zhao Kui are two tigers fighting for dominance. Considering Liao has already offered Li Jianhong our support, we could go a step further and help him restrain Zhao Kui—in exchange for the six commanderies along the west road."

Yelü Zongzhen lapsed into silence, and Cai Yan also concluded there, letting the emperor consider his words.

"Duan Ling, what say you?" Yelü Zongzhen asked. "In your essay, you introduced new ideas within the age-old saying 'a sage within and a king without' that were a delight to read."

---

21 *A term of familiar address from an emperor toward one of his ministers.*

By now, Duan Ling had an inkling as to why Yelü Zongzhen was suddenly visiting Biyong Academy. This wasn't about Duan Ling, and Yelü Zongzhen hadn't uncovered his identity. Instead, his reason for coming to Shangjing was simple: The young emperor wished to find some study companions with whom to pass his time.

"I think it's best to win people over the kingly way," Duan Ling answered. "Your Majesty, what your heart points to is the kingly way—that is, the act of working in the open and putting the upright cause first in all endeavors and staying true to, among others, the principles of trust and righteousness. With Yuan at our borders eyeing the territory of the Liao Empire, we must not lose the trust of the people, for mistrust leads to loss of ground."

"Indeed." Yelü Zongzhen nodded and smiled again. "Coming from a merchant family, you must value trust and righteousness above all. Only by keeping one's word can one win over others. Very good."

Yelü Zongzhen glanced at Duan Ling, still thinking. From just this brief look, he could tell from Duan Ling's inquisitive eyes that he had more to say on the matter. Duan Ling, however, simply shook his head with a smile.

Choosing not to press him, Yelü Zongzhen smiled back.

When he had finished questioning them, Yelü Zongzhen asked, "Are you all willing to accompany us to Zhongjing?"

Who would dare refuse a direct request from the emperor? Duan Ling's heart plummeted, but he had no choice but to nod his agreement.

"Very good. Go back and reunite with your families for now. When the time comes, a messenger will find you."

Han Jieli appeared again to guide Yelü Zongzhen out. All of Biyong Academy, including the chancellor and the directors, gathered to send him off. Yelü Zongzhen climbed into his carriage and was soon out of sight.

Only after he was gone did Duan Ling realize his back was drenched in cold sweat. Everyone stared at each other. The boys who hadn't been chosen looked at the others with envy, yet the ones who had been each carried their own concerns.

"Those who were chosen, you may either return home or stay at Biyong Academy, as you please," Chancellor Tang announced. "But you must not leave the city."

Given a choice, Duan Ling would have absolutely refused to go. He didn't believe Yelü Zongzhen was aware of his identity; Yelü Dashi may not have even informed him that Li Jianhong had a son. Judging by the prince's solemn expression, he'd likely been embroiled in power struggles with Han Weiyong for the past several months. He would have had no time to spare for wondering about Duan Ling.

The crux of the matter was whether or not his father could win the war in the south. As long as he won, everything could be resolved in a breeze. Whether Duan Ling stayed in Shangjing or went with Yelü Zongzhen to Zhongjing wouldn't matter. Li Jianhong was powerful enough to whisk him out of any city at any time. But if the Liao Empire took advantage of Li Jianhong and Zhao Kui's stalemate to invade the Central Plains... At that point, things would become much more complicated.

Back in his room, Duan Ling lay on his bed and let his mind drift. Golden rays of sunlight streamed through the latticed window.

Cai Yan had come back as well. He drew out the jade arc and placed it on the table with the lightest tap.

"A fine piece," he said. "Don't lose it."

"Thanks," Duan Ling replied, returning his coin. Cai Yan seemed ready to say more, but stopped. Duan Ling sensed that he must know, with some certainty, who Duan Ling really was—but if Duan Ling wasn't going to bring it up, then Cai Yan wasn't going to ask.

"Are you going to go home for now?" Cai Yan said finally, sitting on the bed with a beleaguered sigh.

Of course Duan Ling wanted to stay at Biyong Academy, where he could more easily catch news from the south. After thinking for a moment, he said, "My dad hasn't come back yet, and it's more lively here."

"You should go home. Now that we've been chosen, the other boys are seething with jealousy. They might say bad things about you or come looking for trouble."

Cai Yan had a point. Duan Ling gathered up his things and left the academy with him.

"I'll come to your place tonight, and we'll talk," Cai Yan said.

"Let me go to yours," Duan Ling countered.

"I'll come to yours," Cai Yan insisted.

Ultimately, Duan Ling nodded. They made plans to meet on the bridge at sunset, eat dinner together at a restaurant, wash at the bathhouse, and then spend the night at Duan Ling's residence.

The sixth month had arrived, and Shangjing was covered in lush greenery. Whenever Duan Ling went home for his monthly break, he always found his flowerbeds thriving. Someone must've been watering them often—perhaps his father had instructed the girls from Qionghua House to stop by from time to time to take care of their residence.

The peach tree in the garden had produced many green fruits that never fully ripened. Duan Ling lay down for an afternoon nap and dreamed of Li Jianhong in the south, but the details slipped from his mind when he woke. The whole affair of being selected to go to Zhongjing was something he needed to tell Li Jianhong, and so Duan Ling wrote him a letter—quoting a line from a poem,

"I walk down the farewell pavilion in the wind and misty mountain rain,"[22] as a hint that he would be on the move. He would give the letter to Xunchun, who could surely find a messenger to deliver it to Li Jianhong.

In that case, he needed to make it to Qionghua House before sunset. Duan Ling slipped the letter into his robes and was about to leave when a knock sounded on the gates.

"Duan residence?" a guard asked as he walked in, looking around.

"Yes," Duan Ling said.

On the street in front of his residence was a horse-drawn carriage from the Northern Court. The guard gestured toward it—*if you please*. Duan Ling, letter still tucked in his robes, said, "Let me quickly tidy up before I go."

The guard gestured sharply. "We're leaving now."

Duan Ling began to panic, but he had no choice but to step up to the carriage. A hand brushed aside the curtain, and Yelü Zongzhen's face came into view.

"Your Majesty!" Duan Ling exclaimed in shock.

"Shh," Yelü Zongzhen said, flashing a smile. "Come in."

Slightly calmer, Duan Ling climbed into the carriage with Yelü Zongzhen, and they set out on the road toward the east district with a host of guards in tow.

"Batu wrote me a letter once. He mentioned you in it," Yelü Zongzhen said.

Duan Ling noticed that Yelü Zongzhen had shifted the way he referred to himself, switching from the royal *we* to the casual *I*, and felt the atmosphere shift along with it.

"Is he well?" he asked. "He never writes to me."

---

22 Excerpt from "Waking from drinking at dusk to a person long gone, I walk down the farewell pavilion in the wind and misty mountain rain," from the poem "Farewell at the Xie Pavilion" in which Xu Hun, a Tang dynasty poet, describes his melancholy after seeing a dear friend off on a journey.

"He's fine. We crossed paths a few times, years ago. He told me you're his anda."

"I'm not actually," Duan Ling corrected. "I haven't given him a token."

A smile curved Yelü Zongzhen's lips. Duan Ling smiled back sheepishly.

Yelü Zongzhen had inherited his eyes from Empress Dowager Xiao. Many years ago, rumors that he was the illegitimate child of the empress dowager and Han Weiyong had abounded in Zhongjing. As he grew into his features, however, the ruggedness of the late Taizu Emperor began showing in his thick eyebrows, and the wild speculations were finally laid to rest.

He had the brows, nose, and mouth of a warrior. His face, when he wasn't speaking, contained the faint threat of death. But the instant he smiled, the threat dissipated. He was like a sugar-coated knife: He loved to smile, and his smile was always amiable—but then his eyes would flit aside, and for a split second, his deeper concerns would flash to the surface.

"What else did you mean to say, earlier?" Yelü Zongzhen asked as he leaned on the carriage window looking outside, his fingers knocking lightly on the frame.

Duan Ling was struck by a daring thought. Given that Batu had already unintentionally closed the distance between them, there were certain things he felt he could say. "I..." Duan Ling began, then hesitated.

"Speak freely, Duan Ling," Yelü Zongzhen told him. "We often rue that there is no one in this world with whom we can have a genuine conversation. Do not disappoint us."

Now Duan Ling understood, and thus he spoke his mind freely: "The Han clan wants to go forward with an invasion," he said.

"'To attack an enemy fording a river, wait until they have crossed halfway.'"[23]

"Indeed."

"However, the Great Prince of the Northern Court wishes to repair relations with Southern Chen and reestablish the Huai River Alliance to fend off Yuan together."

"That's right."

There was no doubt in Duan Ling's mind that the Northern and Southern Courts had already debated the matter on countless occasions. The true ruler of the Liao Empire was Empress Dowager Xiao; Yelü Zongzhen might have held the title, but in truth, he had no power. His reason for coming to Shangjing now wasn't for something as trivial as finding study companions—more importantly, he wished to convene personally with Yelü Dashi.

"The Han clan...and um... The Great Prince of the Northern Court..."

Yelü Zongzhen cast him a glance. In his eyes lay the same conflict Duan Ling had once seen in another young man's.

Cai Yan's.

For a fleeting second, Yelü Zongzhen's gaze resembled that of his friend's—helpless, enraged, and resentful. Yelü Zongzhen could no longer stand Empress Dowager Xiao's improper relationship with Han Weiyong, and seeing power continually kept from his grasp had filled him to the brim with hate.

"Now is not a good time to launch a campaign," Duan Ling said firmly. "Once it's begun, it'll be impossible to pull back on the reins. In the best case, the Liao Empire will take Jiang Prefecture and the surrounding area, while Xichuan remains in the hands of Southern Chen and the north is ceded to Great Yuan. Inevitably,

---

23 From The Art of War by Eastern Zhou dynasty strategist Sun Tzu.

Yuan will ally with Chen to attack our territory. In the worst case... The Liao Empire will fail to gain a foothold in Jiangnan while also being pushed out of the Central Plains, and Yuan launches a grand-scale invasion."

"Mm," Yelü Zongzhen hummed his agreement.

Duan Ling fell silent.

"Tonight, let's be patrons of Shangjing's renowned Qionghua House," Yelü Zongzhen said.

"Okay," Duan Ling said, smiling.

32

As the hour grew late, Duan Ling remembered his plans with Cai Yan. Yelü Zongzhen sent a messenger to invite him to drink with them as well, but the streets around Qionghua House had been sealed off. The instant Duan Ling stepped out of the carriage, he felt like it was a mistake to come here.

After their last visit, when Xunchun had introduced Li Jianhong to Yelü Dashi, the Great Prince had begun to regard Qionghua House more warily. To bring the young emperor there, now, seemed an utterly brainless idea. Trailing behind Yelü Zongzhen through the corridor, lost in thought, Duan Ling happened upon the madam herself.

"Gongzi." Xunchun greeted Yelü Zongzhen with a demure nod.

Although the two had surely never crossed paths, and Yelü Zongzhen kept his identity hidden, Duan Ling knew it must be crystal clear to Xunchun who this young man was. Qionghua House settled Han Jieli and their assorted company in their own building. Yelü Zongzhen went into its main hall and took a seat, as did Yelü Dashi. Duan Ling sat in the outer hall and waited for a summons. He passed the hand towels and plates of food inside, but otherwise shut his ears to their conversation. Yelü Zongzhen, rather than calling him in, made small talk with Han Jieli.

Ding Zhi stopped in front of Duan Ling, carrying a tray with plates of food and wine.

"Let me try a bite," Duan Ling said.

She gave him a penetrating look, then smiled. Her slender, delicate fingers plucked up a small plate and handed it to him. By way of his request, Duan Ling was warning them against reckless action. Although he didn't believe Qionghua House would do anything so bold as lacing the food with arsenic, who was to say whether they might use a slow-acting poison? If they were truly set on it, there wasn't anything he could do to stop them.

The guard outside the building tasted the dishes first, and Duan Ling tasted them again in the outer hall. Only then did he personally bring the refreshments inside. After all the food and wine was delivered, Yelü Dashi and his company continued speaking to one another in quiet voices Duan Ling couldn't make out. Before he stepped back through the door, he saw that Han Jieli hovered at Yelü Zongzhen's shoulder at all times, giving him no chance to talk business with Yelü Dashi—a troublesome character indeed. Duan Ling now realized why Yelü Zongzhen had invited him: He was to think of a way to distract Han Jieli.

Before long, the group ordered another pot of wine. Duan Ling again took the tray from the serving girl and carried it in. Yelü Zongzhen didn't fall silent when Duan Ling entered but continued speaking: "If the war drags on, Zhao Kui may march his troops down through Yubi Pass as well to catch Li Jianhong in a pincer attack."

With his next step, Duan Ling tripped on his own hem and stumbled forward, spilling half the wine on Han Jieli.

Han Jieli was stunned. Immediately, Duan Ling sat the tray down and began wiping at Han Jieli's robes. But Han Jieli had a good hold of his temper, and his anger dissipated as soon as it came. "Duan Ling," he said, frowning, "you must drink three cups of wine as your punishment."

"Curse my clumsiness." Duan Ling smiled apologetically.

Yelü Zongzhen, immersed in his conversation with Yelü Dashi, said without looking over, "See if Qionghua House can provide a change of clothes for you to borrow."

"I always keep one on hand," Han Jieli said. "It's in the carriage—call my servant to fetch it."

Duan Ling sent the servant to gather the spare robes and gestured politely for Han Jieli to step out of the main hall and followed after him. Standing in the brightly lit side hall, he held Han Jieli's clothes and waited on his former schoolmate.

The hall was eerily silent as Han Jieli changed, the only sound the rustling of cloth as he arranged his robes. It wasn't until he was finished and about to return to the inner hall that he said his first and final words to Duan Ling: "At first, I didn't think you seemed like someone from a merchant family. But after today, I see you have the mind of a merchant after all."

Duan Ling broke out in a cold sweat. Han Jieli had seen right through him. He was mocking him for shamelessly seeking profit: Only a merchant would have the gall to bet everything on a card like Yelü Zongzhen the moment he was placed on the table.

"Han-gongzi must be joking," Duan Ling laughed. "Normally I'm closest with Cai Yan."

It hadn't escaped his notice that Cai Yan remained absent. Yelü Zongzhen had likely only said he sent a messenger to him, when in truth he hadn't. Cai Yan and Han Jieli were close, and Yelü Zongzhen didn't want another eavesdropper. Yet with Duan Ling's comment, Han Jieli began to see connections that weren't there. Duan Ling had obviously drawn him away to create an opportunity for Yelü Zongzhen and Yelü Dashi to speak privately. But then he had hinted that he stood with the Han clan through his connection to Cai Yan. What did it all mean? Han Jieli was confused, unable to read Duan Ling's intentions.

No such thing as too much deception in war, Duan Ling thought. *A little bit of confusion will do you good. I have no future in your Liao Empire, so think whatever you want.*

"This way, please," Duan Ling said, letting his voice carry into the main hall to forewarn Yelü Zongzhen and Yelü Dashi. When they stepped back inside, Yelü Zongzhen announced, "Duan Ling, you agreed: three cups of wine as punishment."

He drank his three cups while Yelü Zongzhen looked on cheerily, the promise of additional reward in his eyes.

"When I first saw Duan Ling," he told Han Jieli, "I thought we had a natural affinity. I took a great liking to him."

"Hurry up and thank His Majesty," Han Jieli said to Duan Ling.

Duan Ling took a step forward, ready to sink to his knees in a bow, but Yelü Zongzhen dismissed the formality with a wave. "We Khitan don't follow such customs. Go and have some food outside; you needn't attend us right now."

The young emperor must've already said all he needed. Duan Ling stepped backward out of the main hall and closed the doors behind him, leaving the other three inside, and followed the corridor to the side hall. Faint, melodious flute-song drifted through the air. Once again, he recognized the notes of "Joyful Reunion." Duan Ling couldn't help but remember the day he'd come visiting with his father.

He followed the sound of the flute to a two-story building nestled amid a bamboo grove—the very same he'd stayed in on the day Lang Junxia first brought him to Shangjing.

Xunchun sat on a stone bench, her red robes fanned out across the ground as she drew forth the melody. Duan Ling stood to her side, watching. She'd played it to call him there—only he knew the song. Moments later, the notes faded, and the flute fell silent.

The moon overhead shone brightly, illuminating the world below.

Feeling for the letter, Duan Ling removed it from his robes and held it out. A serving girl came and took it. He'd wanted to add a few more words about the situation in Shangjing. But considering his father's cleverness, even if he said nothing, Li Jianhong would be able to guess.

"When I first saw you that winter night, you were asleep," Xunchun said. "It must be six years ago now. I had some idea of who you were then, but I couldn't be certain. The second time I saw you was in my carriage. When you entered, you called me 'Madam.'"

Duan Ling watched her quietly.

"You carry yourself more and more like His Highness the third prince," Xunchun sighed.

Duan Ling's voice had settled at last into a man's deeper timbre, and within the past year, he'd shot up in height. Eyeing Xunchun, he said, "If you act recklessly and frame Yelü Dashi, the Han clan will seize control of the Northern Court. Han Weiyong wants a war, and the moment the Liao army marches, the south will be placed in imminent danger. Madam, please remember: You cannot act rashly. Think, and think again."

Duan Ling punctuated his warning with a bow of respect. Xunchun scrambled up to return the bow, and Duan Ling left without another word.

Back in the great hall, they drank and made merry and drank some more. It was late in the night when the men stepped out and split off, each into their own carriages. Yelü Dashi was first to depart, leaving Han Jieli and Yelü Zongzhen behind.

"We will accompany you home," Yelü Zongzhen said to Duan Ling. He instructed Han Jieli, "Han-qing, you go on ahead."

The carriage sped through the streets in the dead of night. Yelü Zongzhen, slightly tipsy, remained silent until they arrived at the Duan residence gates. As Duan Ling exited the carriage, Yelü Zongzhen happened to catch sight of a branch reaching over the wall.

"What is that tree?"

"To answer Your Majesty: It is a peach tree," Duan Ling said.

"In the eyes of you Han people, everything is beautiful," Yelü Zongzhen said. His lips quirked up as he recited, "'Bountiful peach blossoms, with the brilliance of a flame.'"[24]

When Duan Ling smiled, Yelü Zongzhen urged him, "Go on."

Duan Ling bowed and left the carriage. Yelü Zongzhen hadn't said a word the whole way, but it was the kind of silence that held in it a tacit understanding. Having finally arrived home, Duan Ling heaved a long sigh. The only thought in his mind was: *I'm so tired.*

All the information he had and hadn't said seemed to spin up into a whirlpool, thoughts swirling too fast to ponder. He suspected Yelü Zongzhen hadn't staked much hope on the night until Duan Ling had removed Han Jieli from the main hall. It was then that the emperor had decided the future of the Chen and Liao Empires.

Lost in his thoughts, Duan Ling wandered through the gates and entered the courtyard—when he suddenly heard an almost imperceptible tapping noise.

On any other day, Duan Ling might have assumed he was hearing the footsteps of a wandering cat. But now, the sound put him on alert:

---

24 From "Tao Yao," an ancient poem preceding the Qin dynasty, recorded in the section "Airs of the States: Odes of Zhou and the South" from The Book of Songs.

It was the sound of an assassin summoning their inner force to bound off roof tiles. When Li Jianhong had taken him leaping along the roof ridges and walls, Duan Ling had occasionally heard the same noise.

"Who goes there?" Duan Ling demanded in a dark tone.

The sound vanished, and Duan Ling's instincts screamed a warning. He snatched his sword from the courtyard, sprinted back into the street, and pelted after Yelü Zongzhen's carriage.

He caught the flicker of a shadow out of the corner of his eye—*assassin!* Then came more muffled sounds: An arrow struck the carriage driver in the neck, and the slash of a sword finished the job. The assassin stabbed their blade into the carriage, but Yelü Zongzhen had already fled through the window, sword in hand. The assassin followed close on his heels; with a flick of their wrist, they twisted Yelü Zongzhen's blade out of his grip.

Without hesitation, Duan Ling vaulted off a nearby stone guardian lion, clearing the wall beside him and landing in a courtyard bordering the street. Disarmed, Yelü Zongzhen turned and fled, and the assassin followed, stabbing toward the emperor's back.

Suddenly the gates of the bordering household burst open. Duan Ling's sword shot out, its tip striking the flat of the assassin's blade and deflecting their strike. The assassin missed their target, merely grazing Yelü Zongzhen's neck. Duan Ling held his sword steady and yanked Yelü Zongzhen behind him, meeting their attacker head-on.

In the blink of an eye, Duan Ling and the masked assassin were embroiled in a deadly battle.

Duan Ling stabbed for the assassin's throat, and the assassin instantly sheathed their sword, switching to fists. Duan Ling thrust out his palm to meet the blow, putting his whole body into it—but he'd barely made contact when the assassin stepped back, tugging him along with the full force he'd poured into the strike. Duan Ling stumbled and crashed to the ground.

"Who's there?" someone shouted, and a handful of guards rushed into the street, forming a shield around Duan Ling and Yelü Zongzhen.

At the sight of the crowd, the masked assassin leapt onto the wall and vanished into the night.

"Duan Ling!" Yelü Zongzhen cried, pulling him to his feet. Staggering, Duan Ling looked all around them.

"Who was that?" he asked. "I heard a noise outside, so I chased after you."

Yelü Zongzhen shook his head—now wasn't the time to talk; there could be more hidden assassins nearby. He turned to the four guards who had come to their rescue, all wearing dark robes. "Who do you work for?"

The guards fanned out in a semicircle and knelt before him. One said, "The Northern Court, Your Majesty. After Your Majesty left Qionghua House, the Han clan sent a spy to follow Your Majesty's movements. This humble subordinate, in order to stop the spy, was held back and came a step too late. This subordinate deserves ten thousand deaths."

"Go back and tell your prince to clean up the mess here," Yelü Zongzhen ordered. He turned to Duan Ling and said, quietly, "You mustn't tell anyone what happened tonight."

Duan Ling nodded, and Yelü Zongzhen nodded back. From the look in his eyes, Duan Ling surmised he could leave the rest in the emperor's hands.

33

WAS THE ASSASSIN a man or a woman? Back at home, Duan Ling thought back on the assassin's movements. They'd cloaked themselves well—he couldn't guess their gender—but they couldn't have come from anywhere but Qionghua House. Only an assassin from there wouldn't dare harm Duan Ling. If their assailant had been sent by the Han clan, they would've killed him with their first strike.

"You're back?" Cai Yan's voice came out of the dark and nearly scared Duan Ling to death.

"I'm back," he replied, heart racing. "What are you doing here?"

"Didn't we agree I'd be staying over?"

Seated in the courtyard, Cai Yan was drinking by himself with a jar of wine he'd obtained somewhere at his elbow. Duan Ling cast aside his sword, walked over, and splayed out across the seat opposite. He lifted the jar, pouring himself a cup of his own.

Although Cai Yan was one of the boys chosen to accompany the emperor, Yelü Zongzhen likely wouldn't make use of him unless Cai Yan defected to his side. Otherwise, being on close terms with the Han clan did him no favors. But Duan Ling wasn't overly worried about Cai Yan's future: Sooner or later, Duan Ling would be leaving, and Cai Yan was more than capable of looking after himself.

"I don't know why, but I thought of my dad today," Cai Yan said. "If he was still alive, he'd be happy for me."

"My dad would be happy for us, too, if he knew," Duan Ling assured him. "Once we arrive in Zhongjing, I'm going to write to him to come get me."

Cai Yan drank one cup after another. Duan Ling didn't dare drink too much for fear he'd let something slip, but he needn't have worried. Cai Yan dissolved into a drunken mess, first laughing then crying. In the end, he sprawled across the table and became a wailing mess.

After carrying him into the main house, Duan Ling tucked Cai Yan into bed while he lay down in Li Jianhong's old spot. Cai Yan continued mumbling nonsense. "The golden…age…age…this age…" Cai Yan continued.

Duan Ling's heart jumped into his throat, but Cai Yan said no more beyond a few slurred, drunken words before falling into a deep sleep.

When Duan Ling woke the next morning, Cai Yan was gone. Not long after, a soldier knocked on the gates.

"My lord is asking if you are willing to leave for Zhongjing today," the soldier said.

"Huh?" Duan Ling had a mild headache from drinking the night before, but suddenly, he snapped into clarity. "Who is your lord?"

"I was told you would know when I gave you the message," said the soldier, perplexed. "Do you not? My lord asked if you are willing to move to Zhongjing today. He set out yesterday to travel ahead and attend to some affairs. No one else knows; you are the only one he's told. If you say yes, the Northern Court will assign soldiers to escort you. This must all be kept secret. But if you wish to wait for him in Shangjing, that's also fine.'"

Duan Ling mulled this over for a moment before it hit him. Had Yelü Zongzhen already left the previous night? But Duan Ling couldn't leave right away; it would upset all his plans.

"I still have business here," he said. "I can't leave just yet."

"These are gifts from my lord," the soldier said. "There's something here you must take extra care with; you mustn't lose it. And you must also give me proof of our meeting to bring back to Zhongjing."

The guard from the Northern Court handed him a food box and a small wooden case. The box was filled with pastries shaped like various types of flowers. Yelü Zongzhen had also bestowed upon him a brush, ink, paper, inkstone—and a sword. Lastly, when Duan Ling opened the case, he saw a heavy tablet of pure gold. He nodded, then went back inside, wracking his brain for what to gift Yelü Zongzhen in return. In the end, he broke off a branch of green peaches, placed the whole branch in the case, sealed it with a strip of paper, and gave that to the guard.

The branch was a reference to an ancient poem: "Throw me a peach, I'll throw you back a plum; a token, not a return gift, of our dear and lasting friendship."[25] The poem originally mentioned a wood peach, which was a papaya, but as Duan Ling had no papaya on hand, a regular peach would have to do. Yelü Zongzhen would surely understand.

For the next several days, Duan Ling didn't leave his house except to buy food from the street stalls. Each time he passed a teahouse, he loitered, listening for news from the south. He heard all sorts of tales: Zhao Kui had staged a coup, Mu Kuangda had defected to Li Jianhong's side, the emperor and the fourth prince of Chen had both passed. Duan Ling didn't know what to believe.

Cai Yan came to visit him again during this time. "His Majesty went back to Zhongjing a fortnight ago," he said.

---

25 From "Mu Gua," a pre-Qin-dynasty poem celebrating friendship, recorded in The Book of Songs.

Duan Ling, scrubbing his robes by the well, asked with false surprise, "Already?"

"Zhongjing's army is ready to march at a word," Cai Yan informed him. "Yelü Dashi wrote a secret letter, which His Majesty took back with him. Once back in Zhongjing, His Majesty convened all the ministers of the court to stop the deployment despite Grand Preceptor Han's dissent."

Thank the heavens, Duan Ling thought. Finally, he could rest easy.

"Is your dad still not back?"

"No."

"Did he write to you?" Cai Yan asked. "The letter on the table in the main hall is from him, isn't it?"

Duan Ling rushed inside to find an unopened letter, seemingly having appeared out of nowhere, sitting squarely in the center of the table. Cai Yan tactfully stepped out so Duan Ling could open it in private.

> *You ask when I will return, but I do not know. The nightly rain swells Mount Ba's autumn pools. When can we trim candles by the window once more, side by side, and speak of these rainy days on Mount Ba?*[26]
> *Wait for me.*

Seven days ago, Jianmen Pass had fallen to Li Jianhong.

On the evening three days before his victory, rain poured over the pass in a sky-swallowing torrent. Lightning forked across the mountains and flashed at the edges of the horizon. The roaring deluge ate away the mud and stone on both riverbanks and carried them downstream through the pitch-black mountains.

---

26 "A Letter Sent North on a Rainy Night" by Tang-dynasty poet Li Shangyin.

CHAPTER THIRTY-THREE

A visitor arrived at the camp of the Black-Plated Army with a boy and a masked guard in tow.

Within, Li Jianhong sipped a cup of wine, one foot propped on a weapons case. The light cast his shadowed profile onto the tent wall behind him.

"This rain is too heavy," sighed the visitor as he removed his bamboo hat and straw raincoat. "Had Changliu-jun not carried me on his back across the mountains and rivers, I would never have made it to Your Highness."

"It's been many years, Prime Minister Mu," Li Jianhong said, gesturing toward a chair. "Have a seat."

Xie You, sitting cross-legged at Li Jianhong's side, observed Mu Kuangda in silence.

"Bring Prime Minister Mu a cup of ginger tea to warm him," Li Jianhong ordered his guards.

"This is my son, Mu Qing. Qing-er, bow to His Highness the prince."

Mu Kuangda's son came forward, sank to his knees, and kowtowed to Li Jianhong. Li Jianhong lifted his hand slightly, inviting him to rise—there was no need for such formalities.

"You are my guests who've come all this way," Li Jianhong said. "No matter why you came today, out of consideration for your courage, I promise you shall leave safely. No one shall stop you."

"When I said I intended to come in person, Changliu-jun worried over every detail," Mu Kuangda laughed. "'Don't worry,' I said. 'As long as we make it there in one piece, His Highness will let us leave in one piece.'"

"Well, state your business," Xie You said seriously. "His Highness is waiting."

"His Majesty has passed away."

"When?" Li Jianhong asked, unruffled.

"Five days ago, at midnight."

"Why was I not notified?" His voice remained light.

"Zhao Kui has sealed the imperial palace, withheld the funeral announcement, and kept His Majesty's passing a secret. Your Highness, you must know that the imperial order six years ago was not my idea; it was Zhao Kui who overstepped his bounds."

"Oh, I know," Li Jianhong drawled.

"Neither could I stop him from dispatching the shadow squad."

"I know," Li Jianhong repeated.

"If you don't bring this war to an end soon, Your Highness, we will no longer be able to ward off Han Weiyong and Empress Dowager Xiao. And if Liao invades again, our empire may very well see the end of its days. We cannot afford to divide ourselves in two. You and His Highness the fourth prince are both sons of the same imperial family; there is no reason to do so."

"Mm-hmm."

"Today, Zhao Kui issued a military order to deploy more than half the troops stationed at Yubi Pass into the Central Plains. He is planning an encirclement. Xichuan is already under his thumb; Your Highness, if you are defeated here, Zhao Kui will most certainly march back to Xichuan and stage a coup at the imperial palace itself."

Li Jianhong's brows drew together, but he held his silence.

"My proposition is this: I will work together with Your Highness from the inside. I will issue a decree for Zhao Kui's arrest and deploy the shadow squad to provide backup. In three days, a whistle will signal the opening of Jianmen Pass."

"Prime Minister Mu, what do you want from me in return?" asked Li Jianhong.

"No tax increases or conscription in Xichuan for the next ten years," Mu Kuangda said. "And...it is time to move the capital to Jiang Prefectural City."

Li Jianhong burst into laughter. "Prime Minister Mu, you've planned out every little detail, haven't you?"

"I have always striven to be a tactful person." Mu Kuangda chuckled in return.

Li Jianhong shifted his gaze to Mu Kuangda's son. Mu Qing, intimidated, shrank back.

"This is my dearest son, Qing-er. Your Highness, from now on, Qing-er will stay by your side and learn from you. Please..."

"There's no need," Li Jianhong cut him off. "I trust you. Go, and I shall await your signal three days from now."

Mu Kuangda thus left the camp with both Changliu-jun and his son.

Three days later, in the depths of night, birds cried from the rugged mountains. Jianmen Pass's guards were slaughtered, and Li Jianhong captured the fortress in a single night. Zhao Kui's army of two hundred thousand fell to pieces and fled on the road toward Xichuan with Li Jianhong's army in hot pursuit. At daybreak, the two forces met in battle at the foot of Mount Wenzhong. Though Zhao Kui hastily tried to pull his army back together, he was routed by Xie You, then ambushed by Li Jianhong as he tried to retreat.

Corpses strewed the official road and deserters filled the mountains. Li Jianhong assembled a squadron to chase down Zhao Kui, but Wu Du spirited the general away, and the pair fled toward Xichuan.

JOYFUL REUNION

Nine tolls of the mountain bell: A new rule has begun.
The maple trees and rivers thaw; winter departs, spring has come.

As Zhao Kui was fleeing at the foot of Mount Wenzhong, children far away in Xichuan sang this rhyme. Awaiting him on the official road was the shadow squad, who had turned against him. Wu Du alone held them off, a force of one, allowing Zhao Kui to escape further west.

In the vast wilderness, a giant maple tree towered over the land. It was there that Zhao Kui and his last dozen personal guards reached the end of their journey, with the lofty Mount Wenzhong towering in the distance.

"I should have died a proper death rather than meet a pathetic end like this!" he cried ruefully.

The autumn sky was boundless and blue, and golden fields of wheat whispered below. A tall assassin cut through the stalks against the wind.

"Who goes there?!" Zhao Kui's guards shouted in alarm.

Light flashed; before they could react, their bodies littered the ground.

"Hello," the assassin said. "My name is Changliu-jun."

"I finally get to hear these words," Zhao Kui said.

"I've come to kill you," Changliu-jun said, cordial as he removed his mask. The last thing Zhao Kui saw was the White Tiger tattooed on the side of Changliu-jun's face.

Dusk dyed the horizon with wisps of blood. That lone, grand tree in the rugged wilderness rustled in the wind. Wu Du, wounded from head to toe, followed the official road until he reached the gorge where the maple grew. There he was met with the sight of Changliu-jun bent over Zhao Kui's body, wiping blood from his sword with the general's tattered cloak. Zhao Kui's entire host of guards lay dead all around them.

Wu Du's pupils dilated, yet Changliu-jun didn't spare him a glance. He said, "You have two paths. One: Choose to die here, and I'll afford you the dignity of an intact corpse. Two: Flee. I will count to ten. When I've finished, I will chase you down and kill you."

Tremors seized Wu Du, but he didn't flee. Neither did he kill himself. Instead, shaking, he drew the sword strapped to his side.

"Do I look like someone who would run?" Wu Du sneered.

Changliu-jun hefted his blade—yet in the next instant, both their expressions abruptly changed. Sheathing his sword, Changliu-jun spun and disappeared into the wheat fields, while the badly wounded Wu Du stumbled to Zhao Kui's side and howled in grief.

The steed galloping down the official road carried Li Jianhong in his full suit of armor, cloak fluttering in the autumn wind. Wu Du whipped around to face him.

"Sheathe your sword," Li Jianhong commanded.

As Wu Du hesitated, Li Jianhong tossed a letter to him. Wu Du opened it with trembling fingers. After he finished reading, Li Jianhong repeated, "Sheathe your sword."

Wu Du slammed his sword back into the sheath, the clang as loud and earth-shaking as a dragon's roar as it joined the other age-old echoes in the gorge.

The city of Xichuan surrendered to Li Jianhong without the loss of a single soldier, and Mu Kuangda led a procession of officials out of the city to welcome him. Li Yanqiu came out of the palace to greet him personally.

"Third Brother, you've returned."

Before Li Jianhong could reply, Mount Wenzhong's large bell began tolling in the distance, again and again, the sound bounding across the sunset-red horizon.

34

IN SHANGJING, Duan Ling jerked awake.

The bell was ringing. Panicked voices came from outside. As he reached for the sword at his bedside, from within the din, he managed to make out: "The Mongols are attacking!"

The Mongol army was at Shangjing's walls for the second time in two years. The last siege had also been on the cusp of autumn, almost exactly a year before. Duan Ling strapped his sword to his back and grabbed a bow from the wall in the main hall. As he ran into the courtyard, he saw boulders and flaming jars of oil raining down on the city; the fire had already begun to spread.

Outside, people were running amok, calling for help putting out the fires. Duan Ling joined the crowd in the streets to hand down buckets of water, but before long, more boulders crashed down into the city.

"It's no use," Duan Ling yelled. "Head to the north district!"

Chaos had broken out in Shangjing's west district as well. Somehow, the Mongol army had crept up to the city walls without anyone noticing. Flames rose on all sides, and siege ladders were already on the walls of the west gate. The Mongols hacked a path into the city, their weapons raised high.

But Shangjing still stood—they were merely caught off guard. Leaping onto the roof, Duan Ling drew his bow and shot a solitary

Mongol soldier dead. Another galloped by on a stolen horse, setting fires to the buildings as he traversed the back streets, and Duan Ling shot him off his horse too.

By the third shot, the enemy discovered him. A Mongol soldier cursed and greeted him with a bolt from his own crossbow. Duan Ling ducked behind the eaves and jumped down, drawing his sword. He circled through the inner courtyard and stabbed the soldier from behind.

The city guard swarmed through the streets. They cut a broad swath through the invading enemies, finally taking control of the situation. The thunderous beats of war drums began to sound beyond the city walls—Yelü Dashi had raced out with his troops, and the portcullis lowered behind him, cutting off all paths in.

At daybreak, Duan Ling ran toward Cai Yan's residence, only to discover the gates firmly shut and not a soul within. He turned back, speeding toward Helian Bo's home, yet found it similarly empty. With the streets in utter disarray—people praying, people fleeing—Duan Ling had no choice but to return home, where a girl was waiting for him at the gates. He placed her as one of the serving girls of Qionghua House, though he couldn't recall her name.

"Madam invites Duan-gongzi to take refuge at Qionghua House," she told him, dipping low in a bow.

Duan Ling slung his bow over his shoulder and followed her through the streets. Shangjing slowly settled into quietude, with only the occasional sound of weeping in the distance. The afternoon sun had grown harsh and piercing. When they arrived at Qionghua House, the girl said, "Gongzi, please rest here. When the madam is done with her business, she'll request an audience."

"You may go," Duan Ling said.

Ding Zhi arrived as the other girl left, exchanging nods with her. "Gongzi, would you like anything to eat?" she asked Duan Ling. "I'll have it made for you."

"No need to go through the trouble," Duan Ling replied.

Ding Zhi bowed and stepped out again. Duan Ling drank water and filled his belly with pastries. Then he set down his sword and bow, scaled the courtyard wall, and looked into the distance. Dark smoke was rising all over Shangjing. He leapt onto the roof, seated himself on the tiles, and gazed out over the city.

"The madam is ready to see you," said a crisp voice from below.

Duan Ling glanced down. Xunchun had come, and after dismissing the serving girls at her side, she greeted Duan Ling with a bow.

"What's happening?" asked Duan Ling.

"The south has been stabilized. His Highness the third prince confronted Zhao Kui at Jianmen Pass. Zhao Kui transferred thirty thousand troops from the Yubi Pass Garrison down the east road, marching them south toward Jiang Prefecture to catch His Highness in a pincer attack. Despite this, he lost—before Zhao Kui's reinforcements could arrive, Mu Kuangda struck a deal with His Highness, and Jianmen Pass fell. Within two days, the length of the Xichuan road was recaptured. The bell on Mount Wenzhong tolled nine times, and His Highness the third prince took the city."

Xunchun gazed out into the courtyard before she continued: "However, with the redeployment of the garrison, Yubi Pass was left unguarded. The Mongols were able to traverse the stronghold of Jiangjun Ridge into the Liao Empire, circling around the city of Huchang and riding directly for Shangjing. Three days ago, they dispatched men into the city disguised as a group of merchants from the northlands, and last night they launched an ambush, killing the gatekeepers and opening the gate from within. Fortunately they were discovered early, and the west gate held. A hundred thousand Mongol soldiers are currently waiting outside the city with no one to oppose them. Shangjing only has two thousand in the city guard; ten thousand soldiers in total. Before we were completely surrounded, the Great Prince of the Northern Court sent messengers along the north and west roads seeking reinforcements."

"What about my grandfather?" asked Duan Ling.

"He has passed," Xunchun said. "Before leaving, His Highness the third prince said that as long as the south is stabilized, whether he or His Highness the fourth prince should succeed their father, you will be named crown prince and must be treated as such."

Duan Ling nodded.

"Therefore, Your Highness," Xunchun continued, "you must stay safe at all costs. If there is anything that must be done, we are at your service."

"Thanks," Duan Ling said, jumping down from the upturned eaves.

Xunchun turned and drifted away.

With no idea where Cai Yan had gone off to, Duan Ling stayed the night at Qionghua House, where they passed the time as if nothing was amiss. Outside their walls the city was noisy, but the girls within made pastries for the approaching Qixi Festival, held on the seventh day of the seventh month, in the garden. Duan Ling discovered that no matter where he went, the men and women of Qionghua House stopped and lowered themselves into a bow as he passed.

Yet he couldn't stop worrying about Cai Yan. Afraid he might seek revenge for his brother's death at all costs, Duan Ling sent servants to search for him.

In Xichuan, Li Jianhong sat on the imperial throne. The throne itself had been brought over from the capital, but the place it had once occupied now belonged to the Liao Empire.

"Father was in poor health even in those days," Li Jianhong said.

Standing in the corner, Li Yanqiu gazed out the window. Golden sunset light shone in. "I still remember chasing each other in front of that chair when we were young," Li Yanqiu said. "The years have passed in the blink of an eye."

"You be the emperor," said Li Jianhong.

"You."

"You," said Li Jianhong. "No more arguing, that's that."

Li Yanqiu shook his head helplessly, while Li Jianhong began to chuckle.

"I have a son," Li Jianhong said. "You'll love him when you meet him."

"Where have you been hiding him?"

"In Shangjing. After you ascend the throne in a few days, I'll take you there to retrieve him."

"I swear to treat him as my own."

Li Jianhong nodded, and the two brothers fell into a long silence.

"Is it time to move the capital?" Li Yanqiu finally asked.

"Xichuan is the territory of the Mu clan, after all. Let us leave the city to them," Li Jianhong replied, solemn. "Even back then, when Xichuan was established as the capital, I was against it."

"You must watch out for that man," Li Yanqiu said.

"Right now, he cannot be touched," Li Jianhong said. "Our new court is still unstable, and the Xichuan gentry have already been illegally seizing land. We can't do anything about him yet."

Li Yanqiu let out a long sigh, and Li Jianhong whistled piercingly through the imperial hall. A guard pushed open the doors and entered.

"Bring him in," Li Jianhong said. "It's about time."

"You should've let Changliu-jun kill him. Why go to all this trouble?" Li Yanqiu asked.

"I'm tired of killing," Li Jianhong said with an air of exhaustion. "I've killed enough. Besides, the Mu clan won't risk making an enemy of me over him; he's not important enough."

Moments later, the guards dragged in Wu Du, his face swollen with bruises. The wounds on his body had already been dressed, and his arm, too, was wrapped in bandages.

"Speak," Li Jianhong commanded, leaning back on the throne.

Li Yanqiu sat beside him, and they both stared at Wu Du.

"Your words will decide who lives and who dies—including you," Li Jianhong said, closing his eyes. "Now speak."

Wu Du gazed silently down at the glazed white bricks of the floor. The White Tiger tattoo on his neck looked incredibly lifelike.

"I didn't spare your life so I could stare at a mute," Li Jianhong said. "How deeply was Mu Kuangda involved in Zhao Kui's plans?"

"Not at all," Wu Du replied. "Master Wangbei has his own disciple, also an assassin."

"Did Mu Kuangda say as much?" Li Jianhong asked.

"The general said it himself," Wu Du replied. "He wanted to hire this person to send after Your Majesty."

"And did Prime Minister Mu agree?"

"No."

"Did he refuse?"

"No."

Li Yanqiu chuckled. "A crafty old fox indeed."

"What else?" Li Jianhong demanded. "If one of my own subordinates answered me question by question, his head would be rolling by now."

"The prime minister only spoke and never acted. There's no proof he did anything, but he certainly had treasonous intent."

"If one could be convicted just for having treasonous intent, how many would already be dead?" Li Jianhong said. "Fine," and then, to the guards, "Let him live."

Wu Du looked up at Li Jianhong.

"Go," Li Jianhong told him. "Wherever you want."

The assassin took a hesitant step back.

Before he got any further, the hall doors burst open. A messenger ran in panting, dropped to his knees, and held up a military report with both hands.

"The Mongol army is marching south. Shangjing is surrounded by a hundred thousand cavalrymen. Yelü Dashi seeks reinforcements, and requests Your Majesty break the siege on Shangjing!"

Li Jianhong had just returned to Xichuan, and already his own backyard had gone up in flames. He was temporarily at a loss for what to do.

The Mongol army truly moved fast. The moment Zhao Kui pulled away the defensive line, they marched straight in to attack the Liao Empire. More troublesome still, Liao seemed to have no power to fight back; much of the territory north of Huchang had immediately fallen into the enemy's hands. Zhongjing had deployed reinforcements, but Yelü Dashi was also urgently recalling the soldiers Li Jianhong had borrowed, hoping Li Jianhong could save them before it was too late.

Mu Kuangda was the first to speak when Li Jianhong reconvened his court. "Your Majesty, it is this humble servant's opinion that we must not deploy the troops."

After ten years, the golden imperial palace of Xichuan had finally found a master before whom all the ministers had to kneel. But Li Jianhong hadn't yet donned the emperor's robes, and his bearing was different from those of emperors past. The ministers, having escaped being purged by Zhao Kui, now expressed their unwavering loyalty by urging him to take this chance to let Great Yuan and the Liao Empire consume each other—as it was said, when the snipe and oyster fought, the fisherman would come out on top.

Now that Yuan and Liao were embroiled in battle, this was the first major opportunity for Chen to take action since the Battle of Huai River. The humiliation of Shangzi and the sack of the former capital had yet to be repaid. How could they recklessly dispatch troops now?

At most, perhaps he could simply return the soldiers he'd borrowed from Liao. Chen could break their promise to Yelü Dashi and therefore be ridiculed by all, but—perhaps—they could take their time getting there.

His ministers entreated him to recall that he already protected Shangjing at Yelü Dashi's behest once—the Khitan were only repaying him for kindness.

Li Jianhong simply listened, impatient, his brows tightly knit.

"Your Majesty?" Mu Kuangda prompted him.

"Are you done?"

All the ministers in the hall looked toward Li Jianhong. They'd heard of the Prince of Beiliang's stubborn nature, and now they saw it for themselves.

"Your Majesty," Mu Kuangda said. "The emperor has passed, and the empire cannot be without a ruler for even a day. You must ascend at once to put the people at ease. As for deploying troops, this must be thoroughly planned out; no empire in history has deployed troops in aid of another without a ruler on the throne. It is inappropriate on the grounds of both sentiment and principle."

"Don't *Your Majesty* me just yet. Did I agree to become emperor?" Li Jianhong asked. "Make preparations for the fourth prince's coronation tomorrow. Have the Ministry of War take an inventory of the army's supplies and set aside the excess. We march at noon tomorrow."

"But we must choose a suitable date for the coronation ceremony," protested the imperial astronomer. At a glare from Li Jianhong, the man dropped to his knees, crying, "This goes against all custom!"

"Your Majesty," Mu Kuangda insisted. "We must respect the principles of seniority, which ought to be followed even by the imperial family."

"When I was being chased across the northern frontier by Zhao Kui's men, why didn't I ever hear you mention the principles of seniority?" Li Jianhong shot back.

Silence fell over the hall. A threat laced Li Jianhong's words: *Stop me from marching, and I'll investigate you for all your past crimes.*

"Then perhaps Your Majesty can ascend the throne first," Mu Kuangda conceded. "We shall expedite the ceremony in consideration of these extraordinary circumstances. Then, with Your Majesty overseeing the court here, we will send Yan Prefecture's forces and the Huben Imperial Army, assisted by the Falcon Squad, to meet the Mongols' front line at Yubi Pass. Ögedei will be forced to come to their aid, and the Liao Empire will be freed from their predicament."

"The Liao Empire will be freed from their predicament," Li Jianhong said coldly. "But by that time, there will be little left of Shangjing."

"Indeed, the Mongols slaughter the cities they defeat," Mu Kuangda said. "This karma will one day be repaid to their descendants. When the Khitan army trampled the territory of our Great Chen under their iron hooves, they too razed the cities they took, and they too are having karma repaid to them. Your Majesty, Shangjing will most likely fall."

Li Jianhong said no more on the matter. "Let us adjourn for today. We shall hold the coronation ceremony tomorrow and proceed as before. Have the Ministry of War give orders to ready the military rations tonight. Come noon tomorrow, if they've still not been issued, those responsible can present me with their heads. The court is dismissed."

Despite listening for so long, Li Jianhong had budged not a single inch. If any ministers dared agree now and defy him later in secret, he might become the first emperor in their history to personally take up a sword and execute them one by one. The ministers all looked at each other with an unspoken understanding—a new era had come. They shook their heads and sighed, but had no choice but to file out of the hall in defeat.

35

"I'M TRULY NOT SUITED to be emperor," Li Jianhong said to Li Yanqiu, who was teasing his pet bird on the veranda.

"Mu Kuangda may flex his power in the court," Li Yanqiu replied, coughing. "But he doesn't let it go to his head—not to mention he has become resolute in his old age on the issues of the court. He does not always speak without basis."

"Speak without basis? Far from it," Li Jianhong said. "He's right about everything. But I still can't do as he says."

"When will you take the throne?"

"Tomorrow."

"When will you set off?"

"Tomorrow."

"Let me go," said Li Yanqiu. "I haven't met my nephew yet."

Li Jianhong shook his head. "Stay and rest."

"My condition has improved recently," Li Yanqiu said. "Thanks to Third Brother, I can finally stop bickering with the princess consort."

Li Jianhong smiled, shaking his head helplessly. With a sweep of his robes, he strode off.

The next day, Li Jianhong ascended the altar in military attire and made offerings to the heavens. He succeeded the throne in the ceremonial style reserved for times of crisis instead of the grand ceremony, indicating that he did not dare claim those rites with their ancestral lands to the north yet to be recovered. Afterward, he led his troops along the northwest road through Hulao Pass to meet the Mongol army.

Far to the north, Shangjing entered its fifth day of resistance with crumbling walls. The Mongol army was burning the plains outside the city. Thick smoke billowed from raging flames, blotting out the sun and shrouding the city in darkness.

The previous year's siege had left a deep impression on Shangjing's populace, and they had learned the requisite lessons: They'd stored enough provisions to avoid starvation. But this Mongol army had come with far greater numbers than the expeditionary force the year before. The initial attack a few days ago had only consisted of their vanguard; since then, reinforcements had arrived in a steady stream until the enemy numbered nearly a hundred thousand.

Xianbei slaves dragging battering rams arrived at the scorched outskirts of the city, and boulders flew at the south gate one after another. Yelü Dashi's forces had already dwindled below ten thousand. The city walls were smashed, shored up, and smashed again. The city guard put their lives on the line, fighting with only their flesh and blood bodies for six whole hours to force the Mongol invaders back out of Shangjing.

If no reinforcements came, Shangjing would fall before the tenth day.

The city was shrouded in a fog of terror. Duan Ling finally managed to locate Helian Bo and Cai Yan, but when he brought them both back to Qionghua House, Helian Bo said only one word to him: "Go."

"Go where?" Duan Ling asked, rolling open a map. "Mongol troops are everywhere around us."

The map was covered with circles.

"You won't even make it out the gate," Cai Yan said.

The night before, some men had snuck from the city, leaving behind their wives, children, and all their worldly possessions. The Mongols had captured them, beheaded them, and hung their heads on their siege engines. Morale in Shangjing had instantly plummeted.

"Why haven't reinforcements come?" Duan Ling asked.

The three boys looked at each other in silence. Someone passed by, walking through Qionghua House.

"If we don't go…die!" Helian Bo told Duan Ling angrily.

"We'll die if we go too!" Duan Ling said. "Unless there's a battle outside—then we might have a chance to escape."

"Wait!" Helian Bo said.

Cai Yan and Duan Ling exchanged a glance.

"Where will we go after we leave?" Duan Ling asked.

"My home," Helian Bo said.

Duan Ling understood: Helian Bo wanted to bring them back with him to Western Liang.

"I'm not leaving," Cai Yan declared. "I have nowhere else to go. My father and brother both died for the Liao Empire. No matter where I flee, I'll always be a stray dog."

Helian Bo stared at Cai Yan for a long time before nodding his understanding. "You. Come," he said to Duan Ling.

"I can't go with you either," Duan Ling said. "I'm sorry, Helian."

Helian Bo looked a question at him, and Duan Ling said, "I'm waiting for someone."

Helian Bo nodded, not pressing any further. He got up and left alone.

Duan Ling chased after him. "When are you leaving? I'll help you escape."

His offer was dismissed with a wave, but in the next moment, Helian Bo turned back and swept him into a fierce hug. He cast one more glance over at Cai Yan, then fled Qionghua House in all haste.

Cai Yan sighed as they watched him leave.

"Stay here for now," Duan Ling suggested. "We can look out for each other."

"No. I have to go home and keep my brother company."

Duan Ling had no choice but to let him go. With his friends gone and the furtive sounds of the city under siege in the background, he became numb to the endless stream of news. Over the past few days, he'd often heard that the city had fallen or that the Mongol army had invaded; everyone was inured to it and carried on with their daily lives unaffected.

"The madam wishes to speak with you," Ding Zhi whispered to Duan Ling as she walked by.

The next night would be the seventh day of the seventh month, and a colorful variety of pastries were on display in the main hall. When Duan Ling entered, Xunchun was in the middle of polishing a blade. Ding Zhi left them, closing the doors behind her.

"This is my sword," Xunchun explained.

"The Cleaver of the Land." Duan Ling stated its name.

Taken a little by surprise, Xunchun fixed her eyes on him and nodded. "I haven't used it in many years. Before my shiniang's[27] passing, I promised her I would never kill again."

"Will the city fall?" Duan Ling asked.

---

27 *The wife of one's master.*

"It very well may." Xunchun sighed lightly. "News came from the road to Zhongjing that the reinforcements Yelü Zongzhen sent have been cut off by the Tangut, and will not arrive for some time."

Duan Ling's eyes widened in shock.

"The Mongols must've come to some agreement with the Tangut. After this battle, Western Liang will surely break free of the Liao Empire's control and reestablish itself as its own kingdom."

"What about my dad?" Duan Ling asked, urgent.

"His Majesty has already ascended the throne. On the same day, he deployed troops up the west road toward Shangjing. We can expect him within three days," Xunchun informed him. "As of now, Southern Chen's calvary has become Yelü Dashi's only hope."

She ran her cloth over the dragon engraved on the sharp tip of her blade. "Four hundred years ago, the imperial family of Chen bestowed this sword onto my sect—naturally, I will use it to ensure Your Highness's safety. The Mongol army has caught wind of the reinforcements coming up from the south; their attacks over the past two days have been their fiercest yet. I've made two plans: If Yelü Dashi can hold the city, we do nothing. But if he can't," Xunchun continued, "then Qionghua House will see Your Highness safely out of the city at any cost. We will protect Your Highness until Your Highness is reunited with His Majesty."

"That won't happen," Duan Ling said with total certainty. "My dad will come and get me."

"Just so," Xunchun said. "Your Highness must not trust anyone else. The messenger Yelü Zongzhen sent asked the Great Prince of the Northern Court to send you to Zhongjing. But considering our present circumstances, the idea is far too dangerous."

Xunchun had made her point: He should not leave with the Helian family, nor allow himself to be taken away by Yelü Zongzhen.

So long as he remained in the city, no matter what happened, he still had some room to maneuver.

"I understand."

Li Jianhong was still within Hulao Pass on his way north when his scouts detected troops Western Liang had hidden there to stall him. He split the rearmost ranks of his urgently marching army into thirds and sent them to ambush the Western Liang troops' flank. Almost at once, the ambushed soldiers fell into disarray.

In Shangjing, Duan Ling knew that, right then, his father was likely less than six hundred li from the city. Yet that night, Shangjing was the closest it had ever been to falling.

A few minutes past midnight, a loud rumble sounded in the distance, followed by the thunder of marching troops and panicked chaos among the people. They'd gotten used to being jolted awake in the night, but this time, the danger seemed more present than before.

Dong, dong, dong—the gong called Shangjing's soldiers to retreat.

For the past few days, Duan Ling had gone to sleep fully dressed. The instant he heard the gong, he snatched his sword and bow, leapt from his bed, and ran into the courtyard to find that flames in the southern district had already dyed half the sky red.

His first thought was: *The Mongol army has breached the city walls!*

On the sixth night of the seventh month, another wave of reinforcements arrived for the Mongols, and they launched a full-force attack. Seeing Shangjing on its last leg, Yelü Dashi met them beyond the city walls and fought until blood flowed like rivers across the plain.

Together with the despairing rings of the gong, countless flaming jars of oil rained down on the city like shooting stars from the Mongols' catapults. Those infernal meteors exploded upon landing, and a wall of fire swallowed more than half the southern district. Carried by the wind, the flames swept toward the east and west districts, turning Shangjing into a sea of fiery light. Agonized shrieks and howls of anguish broke through the billowing smoke—a hell on earth.

A group of Liao soldiers rushed into Qionghua House. Duan Ling, sword in his hand, stopped them in the courtyard. "What are you doing here? Get out!"

They were obviously deserters, their faces streaked with blood, panting as they stared at Duan Ling. From within Qionghua House, Duan Ling's ears caught a series of soft clicks. The girls emerged, each holding a crossbow leveled at the deserters.

The soldiers slowly backed out of the gates, only to be shot down by a passing cavalryman galloping for Qionghua House at full speed. Moments later, a guard from the Northern Court rode in smelling of smoke. "Where is Madam Xunchun?" he asked, quickly dismounting his horse.

Lowering her crossbow, Ding Zhi beckoned him inside, where the guard waited as Xunchun rushed into the courtyard and found Duan Ling washing his face. "Your Highness, Yelü Dashi's old wounds have reopened, and he has gained new ones leading the soldiers out of the city today. He asked to see you upon his return, but I turned his messenger away."

"How is the city gate?" Duan Ling asked.

"Holding for now," Xunchun said with a small shake of her head. "The Helian family have successfully fled. To save their lives, Yelü Dashi didn't hesitate to leave the city and fight the Mongol army head-on, but he's been in bad condition since he was shot off his horse last year. Do you wish to go to him? If so, I will have a carriage prepared."

Why did Yelü Dashi want to see him now? Perhaps he'd discovered Duan Ling's identity, or perhaps it was by Yelü Zongzhen's request. Judging by Xunchun's expression, his condition was dire. If the prince died from his wounds, Shangjing would fall.

Duan Ling had to go and see him. If Yelü Dashi succumbed to his injuries, he would return, notify Qionghua House, and escape.

Finally he nodded, and Xunchun made the preparations.

"Don't stay too long," she reminded him as the carriage rolled away.

Shangjing welcomed the seventh day of the seventh month under the pale light of dawn. Inside the city, the heat was smothering, as if they were trapped within a giant steamer basket. The southern district still burned in the distance as the carriage hurtled down several streets at a gallop before stopping in front of the manor of the Great Prince of the Northern Court.

The manor was filled with people anxiously waiting for news of the prince's condition. The guard rushed Duan Ling inside to the sound of severe coughing. The princess consort and several serving girls were clustered at Yelü Dashi's bedside, and his confidants loitered in the hall.

Duan Ling's heart sank. This was a scene of someone passing on their final wishes from their deathbed.

"Your Excellency," the guard said, "the young man you asked for is here."

"Leave us," Yelü Dashi ordered weakly.

Everyone stepped out, leaving Duan Ling and the prince alone in the room.

"Come here...let me see you," Yelü Dashi gasped.

Duan Ling stepped closer, meeting Yelü Dashi's gaze. A gory hole had been punched into the prince's shoulder, which was bound in cloth bandages.

"Your Excellency?" Duan Ling ventured.

Yelü Dashi lifted his hand a fraction, and Duan Ling hurriedly said, "Your Excellency, please don't try to speak."

Duan Ling quickly pressed his fingers over Yelü Dashi's pulse to examine his condition. Seeing the bloody foam at his mouth and nose, Duan Ling fetched a wet cloth to wipe it away. Yelü Dashi's internal organs had been injured—perhaps he had been rammed on the battlefield or trampled by a horse. Though he had no visible wounds aside from the one on his shoulder, his spleen, lung, liver, and other internal organs were bleeding. There was no recovering from this kind of wound.

"It's you," Yelü Dashi said. "Isn't…it?"

Duan Ling didn't answer.

"The night I left after drinking…with His Majesty…at Qionghua House," Yelü Dashi said, pausing for breath. "I saw your shadow on the screen… The more I thought…the more I thought you…"

A complicated feeling welled up within Duan Ling's chest. "It's me, Your Excellency."

"So your father…didn't deceive me. You are…still here. I know… your father will come… Tell him…be careful. There's a—a…traitor…"

Duan Ling's breath quickened, his heart pounding madly.

Pinning Duan Ling with his eyes, Yelü Dashi slowly parted his lips again. His expression was expectant, as if he wished to ask how close Li Jianhong was, or tell Duan Ling something more. Duan Ling, aware that Yelü Dashi was on the verge of death, leaned closer. "Your Excellency?"

But blood had blocked Yelü Dashi's airways. He coughed wetly, choking before he could say another word.

The princess consort flung open the door in alarm, doctor in tow. "Out! All of you out!"

The guards hurriedly dragged Duan Ling out of the hall. Before he could ask anything, loud wailing spilled from the room.

The Great Prince was dead.

The manor descended into mayhem. No one had any attention to spare for Duan Ling. Unease washed over him. He rushed from the manor, leapt into the carriage, and ordered the driver, "Quick, back to Qionghua House!"

The carriage turned and galloped into the streets. Slumped back in the seat, Duan Ling closed his eyes in reflection, his brows knit tightly. He was certain Yelü Dashi had wanted to say something more—he'd looked as if he wanted to tell Duan Ling to beware of some unknown foe.

The clash of battle roared from outside the walls: The Mongol army had regrouped to attack the west gate. The carriage made another sharp turn, and Duan Ling snapped back to his senses. When he lifted the curtain and peered outside, he saw that he was headed not toward Qionghua House, but the north gate. Alarm crackled through him, but he didn't dare say anything in case the driver noticed. He suddenly realized that, since leaving the prince's manor, the driver hadn't made a single sound—not even a cry to spur on the horse.

When he'd left Qionghua House, the driver had spoken clearly. The man must've been replaced while waiting for him outside the manor.

Duan Ling stayed quiet until he saw his opportunity, then swiftly jumped out the back. The carriage screeched to a stop as the driver leapt off as well, chasing after him. Duan Ling ducked into a nearby alley; when he emerged, he took a shortcut, covering his nose with his robes as he plunged into the thick smoke and raging fire.

Having lost sight of his target, the driver came to a halt and slowly took off his bamboo hat. After a moment of thought, he turned around and sped toward Qionghua House.

36

Thunder rolled through the sky, and lightning split the dark clouds. In the next breath, countless thunderbolts plunged like dragons shooting from the sea to strike at Shangjing. A colossal storm raged above the city: Rain pelted from the sky, putting out the raging fires consuming the city. The Mongols' gong rang in the distance, signaling a temporary retreat.

Coughing, Duan Ling crawled from the smoking wreckage and wound through several small alleys. When he arrived back at Qionghua House, all was quiet inside.

"Xunchun!" he called. "Someone killed the driver!"

As he sped through the corridors, his shouts died in his throat. Amid the torrential downpour, two figures faced one another in the outer courtyard.

Xunchun held the Cleaver of the Land. Her gorgeous, flowing robes were soaked with blood, the hair at her temples plastered to her cheeks.

Lang Junxia held Chilling Edge. He stood at the center of the courtyard wearing a bamboo hat.

Neither moved.

Duan Ling's footsteps slowed. He stared at Lang Junxia in a daze.

"It's me," Lang Junxia said. "I've come to take you away. It's too dangerous here."

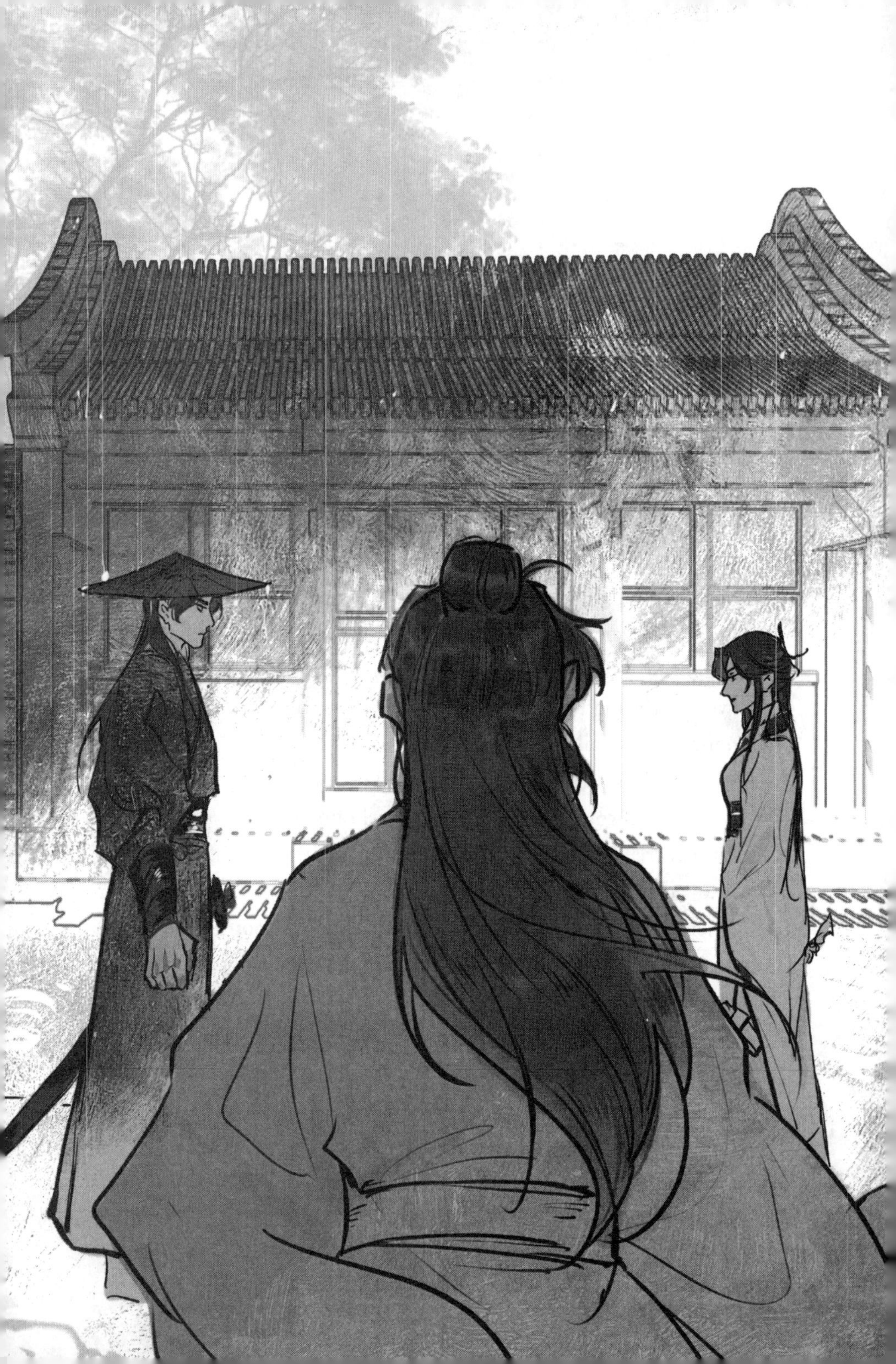

"Don't go with him, Your Highness!" Xunchun cried.

Duan Ling looked back at them, lost.

"Shangjing will fall today. You can't stay here any longer," Lang Junxia said.

"His Majesty has left instructions that unless he comes in person, no one else may take His Highness away," Xunchun said.

The deluge blocked out the sky and drenched the earth, drowning out all further conversation. Thunder crashed overhead.

"Stop!" Duan Ling cried.

But already Xunchun had struck. Lang Junxia angled his sword slightly, and the white flash of the lightning pierced Xunchun's eyes; she flinched, missing her opportunity. Lang Junxia stabbed for her throat. Xunchun whirled away, landing in the small stream running through the courtyard, her spinning red robe dripping with glistening raindrops.

With the next streak of lightning, it was as if those thousands of crystalline raindrops had frozen. They filled up with the scene before them, every droplet locked within this split second: Duan Ling, drawing his sword; Xunchun, taking a defensive stance; Lang Junxia, lunging forward.

Xunchun yanked her hairpin loose and threw it in the moment the blade sank into her stomach. The hairpin sliced through the air, piercing the raindrops into tiny splashes as it lodged in Lang Junxia's ribs.

Lang Junxia pulled Chilling Edge free, and Xunchun risked another stab to rush at him again, striking his chest with both palms. The strike sent a pulse of inner force through Lang Junxia's body, which was immediately blocked at the acupoint she'd sealed with her hairpin; the resultant shockwave tore at his viscera.

Spinning, Lang Junxia pushed off a wooden pillar and dove for Duan Ling, who whipped out his sword and pointed it straight at him. Lang Junxia, already heavily injured, stumbled. He hurtled toward Duan Ling's blade, and Duan Ling instinctively backed away for fear of hurting him.

Lang Junxia spat a mouthful of blood all over Duan Ling's sword. Then he turned and fled Qionghua House, disappearing into the night. The look he cast Duan Ling as he left seared itself into Duan Ling's mind, giving him a feeling he couldn't name. Rain hammered down on the courtyard. Duan Ling took a few steps after him, then slowly came to a stop. He turned.

"Xunchun!" he cried, panicked.

The madam's lower stomach, where she had been stabbed, was seeping fresh blood over her robes. Duan Ling quickly helped her into the main building, where Ding Zhi rushed over with a cry to examine her injuries.

Two hundred li away, the Southern Chen army was approaching the West Mountains near Shangjing when they were caught in a sudden rainstorm. The rain grew heavier and heavier, turning the foot of the mountain into mud. The army of forty thousand men forded the river under the deluge, pressing ever closer to the rear of the Mongol army.

"Report!" A scout ran over. "The Mongol reinforcements have arrived outside Shangjing, bringing their numbers to a hundred thousand."

Li Jianhong was drenched from head to toe. The freezing rain cascaded down his armor and soaked him to the skin.

"The city has fallen?" His voice sounded faint in his ears, as if it was no longer his own.

"They're fighting in the streets now," the scout said, gasping for breath. "Our vanguard rescued a group of fleeing students from Biyong Academy in the Benma Plains. They say Yelü Dashi is dead."

"Bring them here," Li Jianhong ordered.

Several students stumbled over, wet and muddy. Shaking off rainwater, they knelt before Li Jianhong. "General!" they wailed. "General, save us!"

"How many of you escaped?" Li Jianhong asked, breathing heavily.

"Only us," the students said. "The chancellor made everyone leave first; he was shot by Mongol soldiers..."

Li Jianhong felt the world tip on its axis. After he'd sped here at a forced march for days, his mental capacity was at its limit—and now, hearing this news, he had a burst of dizziness.

Without warning, one of the students jerked his head up and flicked his tongue. A cluster of hidden needles sliced through the air, piercing the raindrops, and lodged in Li Jianhong's right hand. He staggered back, drawing his sword with his left. As he turned, the assassin disguised as a student lunged, and Li Jianhong's sword ran through his throat.

"Your Majesty!"

His subordinates, pale with fright, swarmed the false students and shot them full of arrows. Li Jianhong took quick breaths. Numbness was creeping up his right arm. Without hesitation, he pressed his fourth finger that had been pricked to the edge of his blade and sliced it clean off. The wound dripped at first with black blood, then flowed dark red. He could feel the poison spreading through his arm.

"Find the medic!" someone shouted.

"No need," said Li Jianhong. "Give the orders to march. Tell our Khitan soldiers Shangjing's walls yet stand—that there is still a chance. Give them a burst of morale!"

Li Jianhong carried on, leading ten thousand Liao soldiers and forty thousand Southern Chen cavalry through the ridges of the West Mountains, cutting through sharp gorges and broken cliffs in their rush to reach Shangjing.

"Report!"

The vanguard rotated. A man spurred his horse through the rain to Li Jianhong.

"There's an ambush ahead." Wu Du took off his helmet, revealing a face smeared with mud. "Almost ten thousand soldiers are guarding the main road through the next gorge. Your Majesty, we should go around. It's too much of a risk."

"Trample them," Li Jianhong declared instead. He raised his voice and shouted resolutely, "Liao soldiers, follow my lead! Take the van and we Chen soldiers will follow. We shall cross the West Mountains within two hours. Archers, keep pace!"

Wu Du was stunned, but Li Jianhong merely tossed him two sabers before shooting to the front on Skychaser, leading the army into the gorge.

The Liao soldiers rushed after him with a mighty roar, the thought of Shangjing spurring them onward. They held up their shields, covering the central battalions as the hooves of their mounts kicked up mud. Li Jianhong ruthlessly slammed into the Yuan ambush with his host of nearly fifty thousand.

The Yuan forces had been waiting for Li Jianhong to make a detour, and had planned various traps like unleashing floodwater or rolling logs down onto the path. Who could have guessed Li Jianhong would charge them head-on? The two armies slammed into each other, and the Guardian sang from its sheath; a Mongol soldier was sliced in half along with his shield. Blood spattered;

Li Jianhong's crimson cloak flared. Everywhere he turned became a scene of carnage, the afterimage of his blade flashing as he cut a path through the perilous gorge.

The Liao troops rushed through first, forty thousand Chen soldiers close on their heels. The charging forces converged into a flood that smashed through the Yuan defensive line. Li Jianhong cut down soldiers until his arms grew tired. He could barely see in front of him; the heavy rain blurred his vision. Amid the wanton fighting, the poison was spreading, pumping from his arm up into his heart.

His lips drained of color, but he used all his strength to bring his enemies down. There were fewer than a thousand steps to the terminus of the gorge; the end was in sight.

Wind whistled over the top of the cliffs, and a man dropped down toward the army with apelike agility.

Li Jianhong had crossed paths with death countless times; he had a keen intuition for danger. Jerking his head up, he flung himself off Skychaser's back into the air. Skychaser whinnied, shying aside as the assassin flew down with a massive sword in hand, easily cleaving the Liao soldier who had rushed to take Li Jianhong's place in two.

The assassin smirked.

The earth shook, and the rain drummed down. Lightning flashed; thunder cracked. The two armies could no longer hear one another over the din. Despite having landed in the center of a large battle, the assassin moved nimbly. He fixed his eyes on Li Jianhong and dodged past the horses and soldiers with his broadsword in hand. As Li Jianhong leapt up onto the cliff face, the assassin caught up with him.

Li Jianhong brandished the Guardian, and the assassin hefted his own great sword. They met with a clang of metal that echoed through the gorge before war cries drowned it out.

Wu Du was racing toward the end of the gorge with the army when he heard the sound through the heavy rain. He whipped his head back toward Li Jianhong.

Li Jianhong had fallen silent. He and the assassin exchanged a dozen blows with the speed of a whirlwind before the cliff face, their strikes growing faster and faster. The assassin's sword moved like raging wind and rain, while Li Jianhong's style resembled the angry pounding of waves. A fight like this would come down to strikes made on instinct, split-second calls that could only be made by those at the peak of their martial power. Lightning forked over the vast, mortal world, and in that split second, his opponent's sword gleamed in Li Jianhong's eyes.

The Ender of the Profane.

Life is short, life is pain; end the ties to the profane.

Li Jianhong let out a furious roar and brought up the Guardian—yet at that precise moment, it was as if a knife twisted in his heart, sending tremors down his left arm that held the blade. Li Jianhong's blade screeched along the edge of the Ender of the Profane. The assassin took a great leap back, leaving four of his fingers behind, severed at the knuckle. In turn, his blade had skidded across Li Jianhong's vambrace and bloodied his left hand. Li Jianhong lunged again, ready to strike the killing blow, when the assassin opened his mouth and spat a handful of needles as fine as a cow's hairs.

It was then that Wu Du arrived on the scene. He thrust out his palms, and black magnetic discs appeared in his hands, pulling the flying needles into his palms with a series of bright clinks. Li Jianhong rushed forward again, but the assassin had already jumped from the cliff and disappeared into the army below.

Li Jianhong propped himself up with his sword, his vision flickering.

"Your Majesty?!" Wu Du cried.

"Letting you atone for your sins," Li Jianhong huffed out, "is one of the few good decisions I've made in my life."

"Your Majesty, I've got the needles—they're likely coated with snake venom. I'll concoct an antidote."

Li Jianhong gasped for air, numb from the poison that had spread through his body during the battle. He summoned all the vital qi in his body, attempting to push the poison back into his right arm.

"Let me rest a bit," he said in a low voice, chest heaving as he watched his soldiers march through the gorge below.

Wu Du waited at his side, not daring to speak. Once Li Jianhong had gathered his strength, he sheathed the Guardian. "Let's go!"

At last the army poured out of the gorge. Shangjing was in sight now, a distant smudge through the rain. Chunks of the walls were collapsed or destroyed, and smoke billowed into the sky even through the downpour.

"Report!" The army messenger ran up to Li Jianhong. "Yelü Dashi has cleared the road to Western Liang, and Princess Consort Helian has returned to her nation. The troops traveling from Zhongjing have passed Western Liang and are rushing here as fast as they can."

"Where are they?" Li Jianhong gazed at Shangjing, blurry on the horizon. Amid the pouring rain, the Yuan army had caught sight of the arriving reinforcements and made their rearguard their van, deploying a force of nearly fifty thousand to counter their new adversary.

"Two days away!" the messenger said.

"Where did Wu Du go?" Li Jianhong's voice was hoarse and low.

"He went into the Xianbei Mountains to make an antidote for Your Majesty," said his subordinate. "He'll be back within half a day."

"Good. Onward!" Li Jianhong said. "We cut a path to Shangjing!"

At his words, the decisive battle began. Under Li Jianhong's command, forty thousand Chen reinforcements and ten thousand Liao soldiers charged into the Yuan's hastily assembled formation, the earth shuddering beneath their feet.

37

LIGHTNING LIT UP THE SKY and the rumble of thunder followed. Rain poured down like the dark sky had collapsed in on itself. After twelve days of continuous siege, Shangjing's gate came crashing down with a boom that shook the heavens. The northern capital of the Liao Empire, having stood tall for nearly a century, fell at last.

Yuan soldiers streamed in unopposed, the ground rumbling in their wake.

"The city has fallen!"

For the first time in his life, Duan Ling faced down enemy troops surging toward him like a flood of ravenous beasts. His father had once told him that even a peerless warrior would find it hard to hold his own against the onslaught of thousands, which would hit like a landslide. If it came down to that, the only path left was to kill or be killed.

Duan Ling was prepared to kill.

"The city has fallen!"

Arrows rained from the sky, pinning the trapped civilians to the ground and cutting off their cries.

"Reinforcements are here!" someone else hollered before letting out a shriek.

Duan Ling leapt onto the rain-slick roof, firing four arrows in quick succession that knocked the Yuan soldiers off their horses.

Wanton fighting soon broke out in the streets. The city guard officers gathered what few remaining soldiers they had, prepared to defend the city to the death. Now that the gate had been breached, the Mongols would rape, pillage, kill, and set fire to the people of Shangjing in a three-day massacre—no one would be left alive. Every citizen, whether they knew how to fight or not, picked up a weapon and threw their lives behind taking down the Mongols.

A girl fled into Qionghua House, only to be run down and trampled to death by the Yuan cavalryman chasing her. The man shouted in a foreign language, leading more ferocious soldiers into the courtyard.

"Retreat to the inner courtyard! Protect the madam!" Ding Zhi cried.

Duan Ling was in the middle of stitching up Xunchun's stomach wound, his hands covered in blood as he tugged on the string, when he heard the main gates kicked open behind him. He grabbed his sword, and without a word, threw all his strength into a charge, lowering his head and ramming into the Mongol soldier's chest. He swiftly spun and, with an angled slash of his sword, opened the soldier's guts. Duan Ling leapt out from behind the dying man, and with a few more flashes of his blade, three more soldiers were dispatched in rapid succession.

"Fire!" Duan Ling yelled, diving to the ground.

The girls behind him pulled their crossbow triggers, unleashing a storm of bolts that felled the Mongol soldiers. One lucky survivor, panicked, ran through the corridor and hacked at Duan Ling with his saber. Duan Ling met the blade with his own, his eyes flinching shut on reflex. There was a *clang*; when he opened his eyes, he found his opponent's saber shattered.

Duan Ling's legendary sword had once belonged to Kublai Khan; it had been cast by the Rouran from steel refined a hundred times. Though the sword couldn't compare to Li Jianhong's Guardian of the Realm, it was still made from meteoric iron. How could any common weapon hold up against it? Duan Ling's keen blade cut down the Yuan soldiers before they could realize they'd underestimated him, until finally, they no longer dared fight on. Only then did he retreat to the main hall.

"Attack!"

Flying arrows and racing horses were everywhere outside the crumbling city walls. In order to protect their own troops who'd invaded the city, the Mongols raised their shields to fend off Li Jianhong's armored cavalry; when the front ranks broke under Li Jianhong's onslaught, the Mongol flanks quickly closed in from the sides.

Li Jianhong felt another painful twist in his chest. He opened his mouth, but his voice had left him. Amid the storm of arrows, he used his faltering strength to raise the Guardian high, point it forward, and squeeze his horse with his legs as hard as he could.

Neighing, Skychaser galloped onto the plain. Li Jianhong took the lead as forty thousand soldiers charged in unison.

The thunder of hooves shook the earth. The Liao soldiers struck the Yuan front line like a tidal wave, and the Chen cavalry charged in behind. The armies were like great, stormy waves swallowing each other up. Slowly but surely, the Chen army pushed the Mongol army into a steady retreat toward the city gate.

War drums pounded. Ögedei rallied his troops, turned back from Shangjing, and faced Li Jianhong.

Li Jianhong's vision blurred. Wherever the broadsword in his hand went, blood flew. He was like a god of death descending from the heavens onto the battlefield, cleaving through the enemy forces. With much difficulty, he managed to keep his seat on his horse as he channeled his inner force to help him cut a bloody path.

"Your Majesty!"

"Your Majesty!"

An arrow punched into Li Jianhong's back, and he tumbled off his horse, instantly submerged within a sea of enemy soldiers.

Both armies' formations had fallen into chaos. The Mongol army once again tried to outflank them, but there was no way to tell where the Chen formation was, where the Liao formation was, or even where the rest of the Yuan formation was. Everyone hacked indiscriminately with their weapons, churning the plain into mud. Levering himself to his feet with his sword, Li Jianhong staggered across the sodden ground, yanked the arrow out of his back, turned, and looked up.

Atop the destroyed city wall stood an assassin with a crossbow aimed right at him.

The crossbow's bolt winged toward him on a burst of wind. Risking taking the shot in the arm, Li Jianhong stabbed a Mongol soldier rushing toward him, stole the man's bow, and fired back at the top of the city walls. The arrow whistled through the air, and the assassin fell, his body promptly trampled to a pulp by the galloping horses.

Li Jianhong swung himself onto a horse and, with a crack of the reins, charged the city gate. The Guardian left a wake of flying blood and rent flesh behind him. The Chen and Liao armies, witnessing Li Jianhong opening a path from the battlefield through the gate like a god of death, charged fearlessly after him. The Mongol soldiers who had gained the city fortress loosed a volley of arrows, but Li Jianhong didn't balk as he charged through the city gate, taking arrows in his arms, legs, and shoulders.

As he entered Shangjing, his war steed whined and collapsed under him. Li Jianhong was tossed to the side, slamming into the ground.

The reinforcements had finally made it into the city. The rain worsened until only a vast curtain of water spanned heaven and earth. Li Jianhong slowly found his feet and staggered into an alley.

Shangjing was on the brink of collapse, shattered beyond repair; corpses littered the streets and alleyways. Li Jianhong left a trail of blood as he dragged himself through the alley with the support of his sword. He saw the west district burning—the entire street, including his and Duan Ling's home, was ablaze. Not even the deluge could quench the fire.

More and more Mongol soldiers appeared, converging on Qionghua House from every direction.

Xunchun, clutching her wounded stomach, ran over with her sword in hand. "Escort His Highness safely out of the city!" she yelled.

"I can't leave!" Duan Ling hollered back, then, "Fire!"

A storm of crossbow bolts shot through the window frame, beating back the Mongol soldiers and horses that had charged into Qionghua House's courtyard. Duan Ling threw open the building doors and slashed through the formation of archers, hacking them down. Xunchun provided support at his side, killing a dozen men, until the Yuan soldiers finally retreated again. Swapping his sword for his bow, Duan Ling nocked an arrow and shot down another fleeing soldier.

"Your Highness!" Ding Zhi called with alarm.

Duan Ling had slain so many he had no more strength. His sword was slicked with the blood of countless men. As he sagged against a pillar, catching his breath, Ding Zhi rushed over. She touched his back, and he cried out in pain. He hadn't even realized he'd been shot.

"Pull it out." Duan Ling squeezed his eyes shut.

As Ding Zhi extracted the arrow, he felt his insides twist; his vision blacked out as if he was about to faint. Another girl hurried to his side and helped him into the courtyard to rest.

The rain had finally lessened a bit. A servant hurried forward to close the gates, but the moment the latch fell, there was a *boom* from the other side—someone was already trying to knock them down.

"Your Highness, we must leave!" Xunchun said, her voice cold.

"Reinforcements are here!" Duan Ling yelled. "Stand your ground!"

"The reinforcements aren't coming!" Xunchun shouted back. "We must leave through the secret passage in the back."

"No!" Duan Ling insisted. "My dad is here! I know it!"

Li Jianhong tugged off his helmet, his hair in disarray. He raced toward Qionghua House, which held his last hope. All along his way were bodies scattered over the ground and Mongol soldiers killing, slaying, raping, and looting. One saw him and charged with a pike. When Li Jianhong cut him down in a single slash, more soldiers got in formation and charged him with their pikes raised.

"Move aside!" Li Jianhong roared. *"Move aside!"*

Li Jianhong used all his might to shear a bloody path through the enemy troops. Ignoring the Mongols' arrows, he ran toward Qionghua House until, at last, he had no more strength to lift the

Guardian. As he cut down the last remaining soldier, he finally reached his limit and collapsed in the street.

After a day and a night, the rain finally stopped.

The poison had spread to Li Jianhong's neck. The right half of his body was paralyzed and could no longer move. Still, his left hand clutched the Guardian tightly. Rainwater streamed down the gutters of the street, washing over the side of his face.

In the distance, a roar cut through the night.

"He'll be here any minute! I'm not leaving!"

It was Duan Ling's voice.

"My son... My son..." Li Jianhong's lips trembled.

It was as if that voice had breathed life back into him, pouring strength into his failing body. The dark, rolling clouds split apart to reveal a brilliant starry, clear night sky.

The shining Milky Way streaked across the heavens. Across the scarred city of Shangjing, billions of puddles reflected this splendid, starry vision. Li Jianhong dragged himself along with the sword, lurching toward the gates of Qionghua House.

A crossbow quietly clicked.

From almost forty paces away a bolt flew, gleaming with cold light. Li Jianhong whipped around, the Guardian flying from his hands. The spiraling sword brushed past the bolt and whipped toward the assassin lying in ambush on the eaves.

The assassin's expression was one of shock as the Guardian plunged through his chest, knocking him from his perch. But that cold arrow, as if shot with the brutal force of ten thousand pounds, brazenly pierced Li Jianhong's chest armor and lodged in his beating heart.

Li Jianhong's mighty body tipped backward, trailing blood, and he fell to the ground with a thudding splash.

"We must leave now, while we still can, or it will be too late, Your Highness," Xunchun urged. "We still have days ahead of us."

Suddenly the world went quiet. In Qionghua House, as Duan Ling leaned against the wall, he heard the phantom sound of crying from afar, like the song of an elegy for a dying hero. For some reason, Duan Ling's heart went very, very still. He sank down in a corner of the courtyard, separated from the flooded road beyond by a single wall pressed against his back.

On the street, Li Jianhong's blood pooled around his body, flowing in rivulets and soaking into the stone of the street. His eyes were open, and the jut of his throat bobbed gently. "My son..."

He wanted to call out to him—but he could no longer make a sound, only taking weak gasps of air. The eyes that shone with the splendid, starry sky slowly lost focus.

Duan Ling looked up at the Milky Way, his eyes full of tears. "He'll come," he choked out. "My dad said to wait for him; don't go anywhere..."

When he turned to the survivors of Qionghua House, they held the same grief in their eyes.

Duan Ling finally swallowed his tears, his eyes red-rimmed. "Okay. Let's go."

A wall away, Li Jianhong closed his eyes, the last bit of starlight snuffed out. He lay, peaceful, on the Milky Way reflected in the puddles, as if lying on the resplendent silver river itself, lips curved in the same gentle smile he smiled whenever he saw the son he truly, deeply loved.

On the seventh day of the seventh month, the maiden of heaven wove the sky brocade, draping the infinite Milky Way over his mighty body:

On the seventh day of the seventh month, the wispy clouds take wonderous form, and the falling stars trail so; I silently cross the silver river and meet you in the morning dew of a golden autumn. Thousands of meetings in the mortal world compare not to one of ours.[28]

On the seventh day of the seventh month, Emperor Wu of Chen, Li Jianhong, passed from the world.

---

[28] Adapted from lines from "Immortals at the Magpie Bridge," by Northern Song dynasty poet Qin Guan.

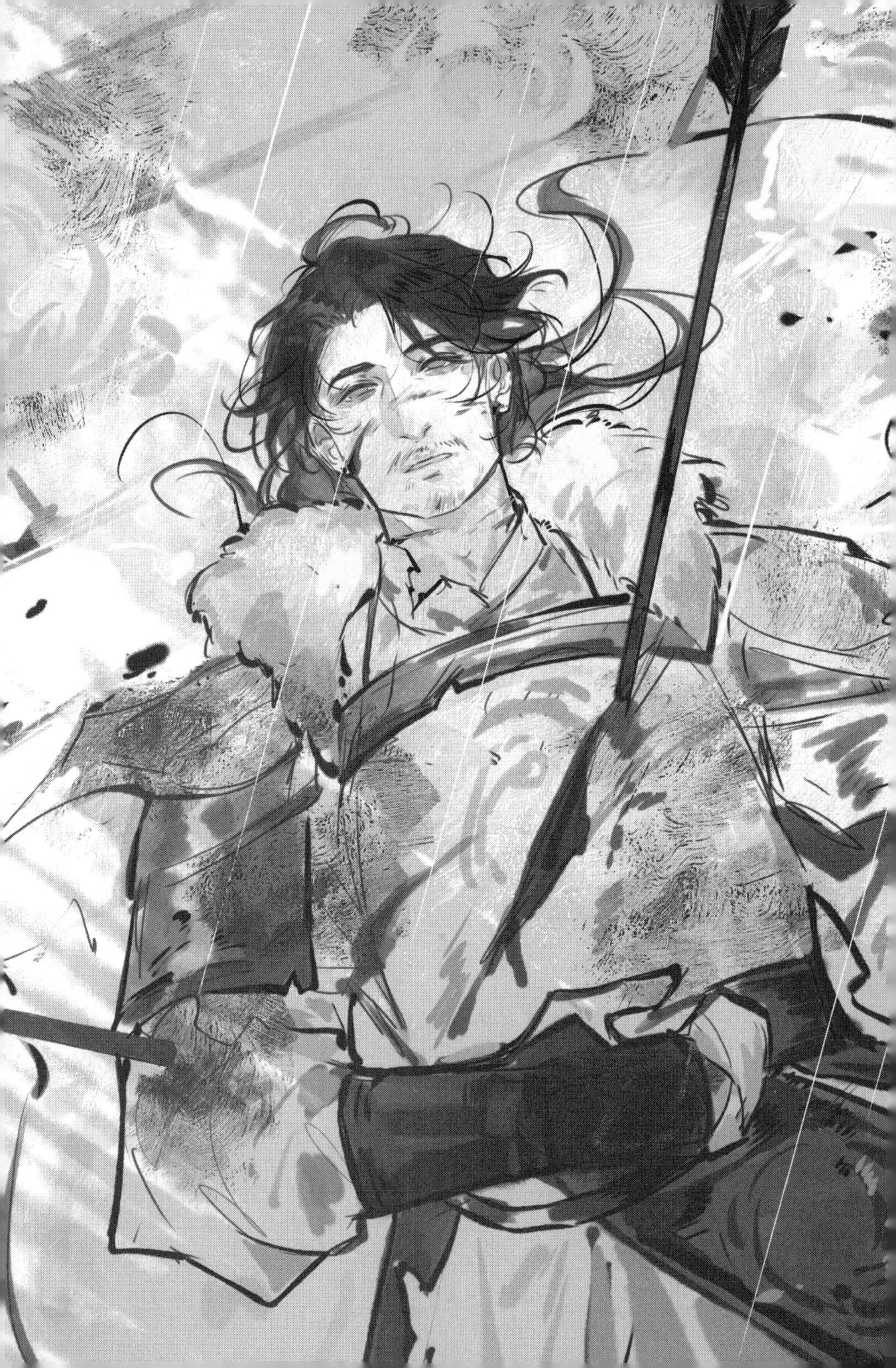

THE STORY CONTINUES IN
Joyful Reunion
VOLUME 2

Character Guide and Glossary

CHARACTER AND NAME GUIDE

HISTORICAL PERIOD

Joyful Reunion takes place in a fictional historical setting. It takes inspiration from empires such as the Liao dynasty (916-1125 AD), the Mongol horde prior to the establishment of the Yuan dynasty (1271-1368 AD), and the Chen dynasty (557-589 AD); and from peoples such as the Xianbei and the Tangut, who existed throughout Chinese history.

As such, many of the characters in Joyful Reunion are fictionalized versions of historical figures, including the Yelü imperial family of Liao, Kublai Khan, Ögedei, and Borjigin Batu. Other characters, such as the four great assassins and the Li imperial family of Southern Chen, are created for the sake of the story.

CHARACTERS

MAIN CHARACTERS

DUAN LING 段岭: Royal courtesy name Li Ruo (李若). Li Jianhong's only son and the future emperor of Southern Chen.

LANG JUNXIA 郎俊侠: One of the Four Great Assassins. Also known as the Nameless Assassin and Wuluohou Mu (乌洛侯穆). He took Duan Ling from his abusive relatives and brought him to Shangjing.

LI JIANHONG 李渐鸿: The third prince of the Southern Chen dynasty and a military genius. He was cast out and hunted by the former administration, but ultimately ascended the throne.

SUPPORTING CHARACTERS

BORJIGIN BATU 布儿赤金拔都: A Mongolian boy, and one of Duan Ling's schoolmates.

BORJIGIN KUCHI 布儿赤金奇赤: Batu's father.

CAI YE 蔡邺: Cai Wen and Cai Yan's father, who was once a great scholar of the Central Plains.

CAI WEN 蔡闻: The captain of the Shangjing city guard and Cai Yan's older common-born brother.

CAI YAN 蔡闫: A boy of mixed Khitan and Han descent, and one of Duan Ling's schoolmates.

CHANGLIU-JUN 昌流君: One of the Four Great Assassins. He works for Mu Kuangda.

CHANG PIN 长聘: Mu Kuangda's strategist.

DING ZHI 丁芝 ("ANGELICA"): One of the courtesans of Qionghua House.

MADAM DUAN 段夫人: Duan Ling's maternal aunt in Runan.

DUAN XIAOWAN 段小婉: Duan Ling's mother, a commoner.

HAN JIELI 韩捷礼: A chubby, cheery child who is also Duan Ling's schoolmate. Han Weiyong's son.

HAN WEIYONG 韩唯庸: The chief of the Liao Empire's Southern Court, and the sole Han minister. The Southern Court's capital of Zhongjing is under his jurisdiction.

HELIAN BO 赫连博: A Tangut boy with a stutter. One of Duan Ling's schoolmates.

LI YANQIU 李衍秋: The fourth prince of Southern Chen and Duan Ling's uncle.

MASTER KONGMING 空明法师: A bad-tempered old monk. His sect once possessed the sword Ender of the Profane before it was stolen by his traitorous shidi.

MU JINZHI 牧锦之: Mu Kuangda's younger sister and the fourth prince's consort.

MU KUANGDA 牧旷达: The prime minister of Southern Chen.

MU QING 牧磬: Mu Kuangda's son.

NAYANTUO 那延陀: The number one swordsman of the Western Regions. He was killed by Li Jianhong.

ÖGEDEI 窝阔台: A Mongol general.

CHANCELLOR TANG 唐祭事: The head of Biyong Academy.

EMPRESS DOWAGER XIAO 萧太后: Acting regent for the Liao Empire.

XIE YOU 谢宥: The commander of the Black-Plated Army of Jiang Prefecture.

XUNCHUN 寻春: The madam and owner of Qionghua House in Shangjing.

LAO-WANG 老王: An old wonton seller in Runan.

MASTER WANGBEI 忘悲大师: Master Kongming's master.

WU DU 武独: One of the Four Great Assassins. He works for Zhao Kui.

YELÜ DASHI 耶律大石: Also known as the Great Prince of the Northern Court, he is the chief of the Liao Empire's Northern Court. The capital of Shangjing is under his jurisdiction.

YELÜ LONGXU 耶律隆绪: The former emperor of the Liao Empire, and Yelü Zongzhen's father.

YELÜ ZONGZHEN 耶律宗真: The current child emperor of the Liao Empire. Empress Dowager Xiao rules in his stead.

ZHAO KUI 赵奎: The Grand General of Southern Chen.

ZHENG YAN 郑彦: One of the Four Great Assassins.

ZHU 祝: An assassin from the shadow squad of the Southern Chen Empire.

NAME GUIDE

NAMES, HONORIFICS, AND TITLES

Diminutives, Nicknames, and Name Tags

A-: Friendly diminutive. Always a prefix. Usually for monosyllabic names, or one syllable out of a disyllabic name.

DA-: A prefix meaning "big" or "elder," which can be added before titles for elders, like "dage" or "dajie," or before a name.

LAO-: A prefix meaning "old." Usually added to a surname and used in informal contexts.

XIAO-: A prefix meaning "little" or "younger," which can be added before names or titles for juniors like "xiaodi." Often used in an affectionate and familiar context.

-ER: Affectionate diminutive. A suffix meaning "son" or "child." Usually for monosyllabic names, or one syllable out of a disyllabic name.

Family

DI/DIDI: A word meaning "younger brother." It can also be used to address an unrelated (usually younger) male peer, and optionally used as a suffix.

GE/GEGE: A word meaning "elder brother." It can also be used to address an unrelated male peer, and optionally used as a suffix.

JIE/JIEJIE: A word meaning "elder sister." It can also be used to address an unrelated female peer, and optionally used as a suffix.

XIONG: A word meaning "elder brother." It can be attached as a suffix to address an unrelated male peer.

XIONGDI: A word meaning "brother." It can be attached as a suffix to address an unrelated male peer.

Martial Arts and Tutelage

SHIXIONG: Older martial brother, used for older disciples or classmates.

SHIDI: Younger martial brother, used for younger disciples or classmates.

Other

GONGZI: Young man from an affluent household.

-QING: A term of familiar address from an emperor toward one of his ministers.

SHAOYE: Young master.

PRONUNCIATION GUIDE

Mandarin Chinese is the official state language of mainland China, and pinyin is the official system of romanization in which it is written. As Mandarin is a tonal language, pinyin uses diacritical marks (e.g., ā, á, ǎ, à) to indicate these tonal inflections. Most words use one of four tones, though some are a neutral tone. Furthermore, regional variance can change the way native Chinese speakers pronounce the same word. For those reasons and more, please consider the guide below a simplified introduction to pronunciation of select character names and sounds from the world of *Joyful Reunion*.

More resources are available at sevenseasdanmei.com

NOTE ON SPELLING

Romanized Mandarin Chinese words with identical spelling in pinyin—and even pronunciation—may well have different meanings. These words are more easily differentiated in written Chinese, which uses logographic characters.

Duàn Líng
    Du as in **do**, àn as in **Anne**
    Líng as in smi**ling**

Lǎng Jùnxía
    L as in **l**ive, ǎng as in t**ong**ue
    J as in **j**eep, ún as in **b**in, but with lips rounded as for **boon**
    xí as in **she**, a as in **ah**

Lǐ Jiànhóng
    Lǐ as in fami**l**y
    Ji as in **j**ean, à**n** as in e**n**d
    h as in **h**ad, **ó**ng as in pr**o**ne, but as a nasal vowel

GENERAL CONSONANTS

Some Mandarin Chinese consonants sound very similar, such as z/c/s and zh/ch/sh. Audio samples will provide the best opportunity to learn the difference between them.

    X: somewhere between the **sh** in **sh**eep and **s** in **s**ilk
    Q: a very aspirated **ch** as in **ch**arm
    C: **ts** as in pan**ts**
    Z: **z** as in **z**oom
    S: **s** as in **s**ilk
    CH: **ch** as in **ch**arm
    ZH: **dg** as in do**dg**e
    SH: **sh** as in **sh**ave
    G: hard **g** as in **g**raphic

GENERAL VOWELS

The pronunciation of a vowel may depend on its preceding consonant. For example, the "i" in "shi" is distinct from the "i" in "di." Vowel pronunciation may also change depending on where the vowel appears in a word, for example the "i" in "shi" versus the "i" in "ting." Finally, compound vowels are often—though not always—pronounced as conjoined but separate vowels. You'll find a few of the trickier compounds below.

IU: as in **ewe**
IE: **ye** as in **ye**s
UO: **war** as in **war**m

GLOSSARY

DUE DILIGENCE ORDER: A military order to rescue the emperor in times of crisis. Over time, however, it also became an excuse used by usurpers to seize the imperial palace under the guise of ridding the court of treacherous ministers.

FOUR BOOKS AND FIVE CLASSICS: The canon of Confucian texts that became central to both primary education and the imperial examinations. The Four Books are: *The Analects*, *The Doctrine of the Mean*, *Great Learning*, and *Mengzi*. The Five Classics are: *The Book of Songs*, *The Book of Documents*, *The Book of Rites*, *The Book of Changes (I-Ching)*, and *The Spring and Autumn Annals*.

IMPERIAL STATE EXAM: The system of examinations in ancient China that qualified candidates to serve as officials in state bureaucracy. Achievements in civil service and scholarship brought the highest prestige for any citizen, regardless of background.

LAWFUL AND COMMON-BORN RELATIONSHIPS: Upper-class men in ancient China often took multiple wives. Only one would be the official wife, and her lawful sons would take precedence over the common sons of the concubines. Sons of lawful birth were prioritized in matters of inheritance. They also had higher social status and often received better treatment compared to the common sons born to concubines or mistresses.

LUNAR CALENDAR AND ASSOCIATED HOLIDAYS: For most of Chinese history, years were divided into twelve lunar months of twenty-nine to thirty days, and certain festivals were held when the number of the day and the month matched. Examples include:

FIRST DAY OF THE FIRST MONTH: New Year's Day.

THIRD DAY OF THE THIRD MONTH: Double Third, or the Shangsi Festival, is Maiden's Day, a day to celebrate a girl's coming of age.

FIFTH DAY OF THE FIFTH MONTH: Duanwu, commonly known as the Dragon Boat Festival, is a folk festival to ward off the evil that causes sickness and plagues. It also commemorates Qu Yuan, a patriotic poet who drowned himself in grief over the state of his nation.

SEVENTH DAY OF THE SEVENTH MONTH: Qixi is known as the Crafter's Festival, a celebration of deft hands. Legend has it that a celestial maiden, the weaver girl, came to earth and married a cowherd. Despite wanting to stay on earth with him and their children, she was forced to return to heaven by her father, the Jade Emperor. The cowherd tried to follow her on an oxcart but was stopped at the Milky Way, a silver river cutting through the sky that separated the two lovers. On a single day of the year, Qixi, magpies swarm together and create a bridge that allows the cowherd and the weaver to reunite. Thus, Qixi is also known as a celebration of romantic love.

MANDATE OF HEAVEN: The Mandate of Heaven is the approval of heaven that justifies and legitimizes the rule of the emperor, also known as the Son of Heaven, over the people. If the emperor is not a virtuous ruler and fails to fulfill his obligations, then he would lose the mandate and the right to govern. Signs of a loss of mandate include societal unrest and uprisings, foreign invasions, natural disasters, and similar calamities.

MEMORIAL TO THE THRONE: A carefully crafted essay presenting an issue to communicate to the emperor. Depending on the circumstances, it was sometimes directed toward certain officials as well.

QI AND ACUPOINTS IN MARTIAL ARTS: Qi is a vital force that courses through the body in channels known as meridians. Acupoints are specific spots on these meridians that are said to stimulate the central nervous system in characteristic ways. A martial artist cultivates the qi in their body and manipulates it as a form of energy, either to boost themselves internally or expel it as a form of attack.

TIGER TALLY: A token used as proof of imperial authorization to deploy and command troops.

TRADITIONAL CHINESE MEDICINE: A holistic system of medicine used throughout most of Chinese history. Herbal remedies were boiled into decoctions or ground and applied as a poultice to treat injuries.

Fei Tian Ye Xiang (Arise Zhang) is a Chinese novelist who has been active since 2008. A romantic who crafts fantasy worlds suffused with eastern mythology, he has published a number of books in places such as Mainland China, Taiwan, Hong Kong, Southeast Asia, and Germany. Many of his works, including *Legend of Exorcism* and *Dinghai Fusheng Records*, have received manhua and popular animated adaptations. He considers writing to be the act of bringing boundless adventure to the mundane life of the real world, allowing his readers to follow his characters in exploring the endless possibilities of time and space. He hopes every world will leave his readers with everlasting memories.